midlife crisis

L.B. DUNBAR

www.lbdunbar.com

Midlife Crisis
Copyright © 2018 Laura Dunbar
L.B. Dunbar Writes Ltd.
www.lbdunbar.com

Special Edition cover (2024)
Content Edits: Melissa Shank
Editing: Editing4Indies – Jenny Simms
Proofread: Karen Fischer
2021 Proofread: Gemma Brocato

other books by L.B. Dunbar

L.B. DUNBAR

Sexy Silver Fox Collection
After Care
Midlife Crisis
Restored Dreams
Second Chance
Wine&Dine

Collision novellas
Collide
Caught

The Sex Education of M.E.

The Heart Collection
Speak from the Heart
Read with your Heart
Look with your Heart
Fight from the Heart
View with your Heart

A Heart Collection Spin-off
The Heart Remembers

BOOKS IN OTHER AUTHOR WORLDS
Smartypants Romance (an imprint of Penny Reid)
Love in Due Time
Love in Deed
Love in a Pickle

The World of True North (an imprint of Sarina Bowen)
Cowboy
Studfinder

dedication

God, Grant me the serenity to accept the things I cannot change.
Courage to change the things I can.
And wisdom to know the difference.

For those who battle and overcome addictions,
And the people who stand by them.

L.B. DUNBAR

chapter 1

Reflections In the Mirror

[Midge]

How do I get myself into these things?

Oh, right, I can't seem to say no.

I'd gotten roped into coordinating the fundraising service project for my son's high school band. Ronin, my middle child, is a freshman, and he's struggling. Since his older brother is a stud athlete, Ronin suffers from second child syndrome. Add in the fact he's a band geek and theater nerd—his words, not mine—and guilty mother disorder kicks in for all the times I've hosted team dinners, contributed to the booster club, or attended a million football games. This event needed a parent representative, and the Miss-Never-Say-No in me volunteered to make Ronin happy.

One minute, I am standing at the Mystic Music Therapy School, introducing myself to the director, Ivy Everly, and her manager, Edie Carrigan, and a few weeks later, I'm attending a party.

Edie is a pixie blonde beauty, showing only a hint of her age, and we hit it off instantly. Both of us are transplants from the Midwest to California. She's only been here six months while I've been here six years. My ex-husband, Paul, was transferred, and we took the move as a fresh start to our marriage. The Golden State would be an opportunity, and San Gabriel would be the perfect area for us. How wrong I'd been to believe him.

Anyway, Edie and I are both in our forties, which is depressing to think about. I thought I'd be so much more accomplished by forty. Forty-one makes *un*-accomplishment seem so much more unnerving.

7

Edie is somehow related to Ivy. I can't remember the connection. I can hardly remember my own family's names, let alone the relations of others. Either way, they seem close despite their age difference. Although she looks barely nineteen, I'd place Ivy at mid to late twenties. It must suck to be beautiful, I think, chuckling to myself, envisioning the California blonde who eagerly greeted me at her therapy school and walked me through all I needed for the fundraiser. I can't help admiring her hair. As I've grown older, my brunette color has dulled, turning mousy brown with streaks of gray woven through it.

"This is so exciting," she exclaims after we run through the list of things I need to do with the high school students in preparation for the day. Rhythm Walk is the name of the walkathon to raise money for the therapy school. The high school band volunteered their support to show music is important to people of any ability and age. An event like this reinforces the private high school's mission of service for others. I also volunteered because band sponsorship reduces the exorbitant tuition my ex and I agree to pay per the joint custody stipulations in our divorce decree. I sigh at the thought, reminding myself band keeps my kid out of trouble.

Prior to the party invitation, most of our interaction has been via email. In our first face-to-face meeting, I find I've made a new friend in Ivy and found a kindred one in Edie.

"I'm a bit lonely here," Edie whispers, not wanting her younger counterpart to hear. "I mean, I love my new family, but I don't know many other women my age." It wasn't an insult. It was a show of solidarity. Sisterhood of the Over Forty. Hurray! Cue dying noisemakers.

"You know," Ivy interjects. "You should come to a party we're hosting. We're introducing Edie to some family friends."

Edie rolls her eyes at me. "Get this. The party is called Meet the Wife." A soft chuckle follows the title. "My new husband thought it would be a good way to show everyone he got married."

I'm certain there's a story there, but I don't inquire. The knowledge that someone in her forties has found love again makes me smile, and Edie beams like a teenager at the mention of her man.

"Anyway, the party is tomorrow night. You should come. Bring a date."

"Oh, I don't date," I blurt, exposing myself before I think. I look up in horror at the admission. A knowing smile curls on Edie's face, and Ivy's eyes widen.

"You should definitely come then. This isn't a party for the young'uns," Edie teases. "You never know who you might meet."

Ivy giggles, shaking her sunshine-colored hair, and again, I'm certain there's a story between them.

"I'll think about it," I lie, accepting there's no way in hell I'm going to a party where I don't know anyone other than the two women I just met.

"I know that look," Edie says, narrowing her eyes and waving in a circular manner at my face. "If I have to drive to your house, and chauffeur you to mine, you're coming."

I laugh at her persistence.

"It will be fun," she adds, reaching out to pat my arm. "I think." Her brows pinch, but then she smiles. "On second thought, come for me. I might need the support."

"You'll be fine," Ivy interjects. It's a good thing she runs a music school. Her hearing seems impeccable. I didn't even think she was listening as she sat at her desk, shuffling papers, and typing on her computer. "And Edie's right. It will be fun. Come join us. We're going to spend a lot of time together over the next month. Let's hang out."

The invitation seems strange to me, but why not. I haven't gone out in a million years unless you count band concerts, high school football games, and travel baseball. On second thought, I don't count those things as valid *getting out*.

"Okay."

+ + +

So here I stand, nursing a glass of wine and watching people mingle. Wait, let me correct myself. Rich, famous, and beautiful people mingle.

The big hair, big watches, and big boobs give away that I am out of my league.

"Is that. . .?" My voice trails off as I observe a young man and the petite brunette beside him, uncertain of the identity of the musical power couple standing before me.

"I think so," Edie answers. "My music knowledge is pretty pathetic. Just ask my husband."

"But it's one of the things I love about her." A gruff, Southern sounding drawl filters from behind us, and as I turn, Edie is enveloped in thick arms, wrapping around her waist and tugging her back against one of the most handsome men I've ever seen. A true silver fox. Inky hair with streaks of silver and a scruffy beard with more salt than pepper. He's delicious in a *he's-another-woman's-husband* sort of way.

Edie giggles, and her husband kisses her neck before looking up at me. "I'm Tommy," he offers. With one arm still around his wife, he extends his other hand forward with the introduction. "Tommy Carrigan, and I belong to this woman."

I chuckle at his unabashed announcement. "I thought this was a Meet-the-Wife party."

"Just clarifying I'm the husband. Oh, I like the sound of that so much, darlin'." He kisses his wife again and then steps back from her. "Holy shit! Hank?"

Edie and I both look up at a larger man. I'm typically not attracted to tattoos, but I can't seem to stop staring at his forearms. My eyes roam up to his jaw. Roughly covered with more silver than black, it's the opposite of his ink-colored hair, which is cropped close to his head with here-and-there gray. He's the perfect mix of salt-and-pepper. A silver fox, actually, and suddenly I'm thinking of silver glitter for some reason and wanting him to paint my skin with his scruffy chin. The thought makes me tingle in places I thought forgot how to tingle. My face heats at getting caught staring and his responding expression gives away the possibility of a hard life. Crinkles around his squint announce the lines of age, but his hazel eyes sparkle with mischief. *Oh, he's dangerous.*

"Hank. Hank Paige, is it really fuckin' you, man?" Tommy's voice carries. He reaches out to man-hug this bear of a man. Watching them clap each other on the back, I turn to Edie, hoping for some clarification.

"I have no idea who he is," she murmurs, sipping her wine and pasting on a smile to prepare for an introduction.

"Edie, darlin', this is Hank Paige. The best dru—"

"Just Hank," he interrupts, holding out a hand for Edie but shifting his eyes back to me. "Hank," he offers once he releases Edie and reaches toward me.

"Midge. Midge Everette." I hold my breath a second, waiting for a man of his stature to make a snarky comment. His appearance is one of a former football player. Definitely someone who was a bully. He'd be the first to make fun of my name if we were still kids. Midge. Mudge. Sludge. Midge. Fidge. Fudge. I've heard it all.

"Midge? That's an unusual name. One I don't think I'll quickly forget." *Oh, he's smooth*, I think as the warmth of his hand still lingers over mine. His fingers are thick, and thoughts race to things I shouldn't be thinking like how they would feel rubbing up my thighs. I could get lost in...*Sweet cheese*, what's wrong with me? My mind went straight to the gutter within thirty seconds of meeting a totally tall, strong, and all wrong for me stranger.

"How unfair is that? Not a strand of gray hair on your head," Tommy teases his friend. Hank rubs a hand over the cropped hair, and it stands up as he scrubs back to front. His eyes don't leave mine.

"It's there, but it seems to like my jaw more."

Oh, I like your jaw more, I decide as my eyes return to his chin and the scruff covering it. My thoughts flitter to how it might feel if he tickled my skin with his stubble. Heat spreads on my cheeks a second time. Something is definitely wrong with me. Maybe it's the wine?

His gaze finally leaves me, and I turn to Edie. "Where's the bathroom?" I just need a minute. I don't know what I'm doing among this collection of born-beautiful and potentially talented people. I'm out of my element and suffocating from the uncomfortable feeling.

"Down the hall. First door on the right," Edie explains. She twists and waves her arm.

"Last door on the right," Tommy corrects. Edie laughs.

"We've only lived here a month or so. I'm lucky we even got unpacked for this party," she adds.

"It's been more than a month, darlin'. We've been married for forty-three days."

What the heck? I chuckle at his declaration.

"Already counting the days. You have a long-ass future if you start there." Hank scoffs. He has a nice voice—smoky and smooth.

"A long-ass future is all I plan on having with this woman," Tommy retorts. "I'm counting the days to make up for the years it took me to find her."

For some reason, I just want to cry at the sweetness of this man. On that note, I need a break before I make a fool of myself.

+ + +

Suddenly, I really have to pee, and I can't find the light switch. Thankfully, a candle illuminates the small powder room, and since I know where all my body parts should go, I sit in the dark. After I finish my business, I wash my hands and catch my reflection in the mirror. The candlelight produces an angelic effect highlighting my face, and my hair disappears in the darkness behind me. My hands shake as I smooth down my neck and tug at my cheeks. I turn my head side to side. I'm not awful but compared to the people on the other side of this door, I'm nothing special.

In the midst of my self-examination, the door opens outward, and Hank's large body fills the space.

"Just give me a minute," he breathes, holding out a hand to someone in the hall, and then slams the door. I step back as he's blocking the doorway, and he spins. Leaning against the closed door, he breathes deeply, exhaling slowly as he scrubs his hands over his face. He roughs his hair, rubbing back and forth, before looking up.

"Umm...I was just..." It couldn't be more obvious. I've used the bathroom, but he's obstructing my exit.

"I just need a minute," he says, making no motion to move out of the way. Should I be frightened I'm in a small, enclosed space with a large man I don't know? It's dark. There's candlelight. It could be romantic. I sigh. It's a freaking powder room, for heaven's sake.

"I can just leave if you'll let me—" He straightens from the door, and my words falter.

"Don't be frightened."

"I'm not," I say, and I mean it. I realize in the space of the two minutes we've been in this room that I feel completely at ease with his presence despite his hulky size. He presses forward, but when I move to step around him, the sink wedges us together. He's behind me, and I press into the counter, my backside brushing the front of his jeans. We stop. Our eyes meet in the ripple of candlelight reflected by the mirror.

"Are you drunk?"

"Don't drink." His voice is husky like his size.

"Never?" I blink.

"Not in a long time." He watches me a moment as if gauging my reaction. When it seems he's decided on something, he says, "You have beautiful eyes."

His compliment startles me, and I blush, thankful the dimness of the room hides my heated cheeks. My eyes tend to shift color. In this low light, they glow with flecks of gold among the deeper brown tone. I don't have a chance to thank him before his hands grasp my shoulders, massaging them. Thick thumbs press into the back of my neck. Shit, his fingers feel good.

"Take a breath," he suggests. "Breathe. I'm not going to hurt you."

I do as he says and inhale. He continues to stroke the side of my neck, then whispers, "Close your eyes." A smoky sound resonates from his voice, gravelly and gruff, and I like the robustness of it. Something sounding strangely like a purr rumbles from me. And then I do the unthinkable.

I lean.

"Feel good, little lady?" A tender kiss greets my neck. My eyelids flip open, and I stand straighter, embarrassed for swaying. He still crowds my space. He isn't fat. He's broad—solid—and the feel of his chest against my back has me relaxing into him. I nod in response because, honestly, words escape me. He's touching me as if he cares about me, as if he wants to take away my stress. Uncontrollably, I melt into the sensation.

"I could make you feel good in other ways." The suggestion causes me to stiffen, and he chuckles. "Relax, lady." His raspy voice right at my ear sends shivers skittering over my skin.

With a boldness I've never felt before, I speak. "How?"

"How to relax or how to feel good?" His eyes meet mine in the mirror. There's a mischief to the color I know is gray but sparkles like steel in the reflection.

"Wouldn't they be one and the same?" His lip crooks in the corner at my question. His eyes twinkle with mirth, and he chuckles, lazy and low, causing my skin to goose bump. With his hands stroking my shoulders, the white peasant blouse I wear stretches, slipping off over the curves.

"Hmm . . ." He moans as his thick fingertips rub my cool skin. "I think I'd start with a nip to this neck." I watch the roll of his Adam's apple, and my throat clogs. My mouth waters. "I'd suck right here." He presses into the apex of my shoulder and neck with the tip of a callused finger. I imagine the deep suction on my sweet spot, and my knees buckle. My lids flutter closed a moment. Another gravelly chuckle sounds by my ear, and I open my eyes to find him watching me in the mirror.

"I think next I'd go for a breast. Lick around your nipple before tugging at the tip."

Holy. Shit. I'm instantly wet, and my thighs clench. He's observant, so he doesn't miss the squeeze of my legs. His hands drift from my shoulders to my hips, and ever so gently, he tugs me back against him. With one slow pump, the unmistakably firm length of him hits my lower back.

"You're a tiny thing," he huffs, spreading his fingers and then tightening them on my hips. "But I'd still fit." The thought brings up my head, my eyes searching for his again in the reflective glass; only he's looking down, over my shoulder, focusing on the swell of my breasts peeking out of my bra. I didn't realize my shirt had slid down so far.

"I'd definitely need a taste between those thighs." A rush of liquid leaves me as a flock of seagulls ripple up my abdomen. If words could cause an orgasm, I'm certain he could give me one. The smoky tone. The brash intention. The silver stare reflected in the mirror. "You like the thought."

It isn't a question. He's reading me, and he's right. If he put his scruffy jaw between my thighs, I'd come in an instant. The image makes me rub my legs together once more, and I reach for the countertop, needing stability before I purposely lean into him again.

"I've never done this before," I whisper, uncertain what I'm admitting, and what I'm suggesting. He's a stranger to me, but do I want him to take me against the counter? *Hell yes, I do.* Do I think I could follow through on the actual act? Actually no, I don't.

"I'm here for you," he groans, pressing into me again. Our heights don't lend to aligning body parts, but I'm well aware of what he packs in those jeans, and he can't miss the subtle squirm of my thighs.

"Mmm, Hank," I purr. "Yes." The word escapes, the hiss lingering as my sex pulses. My hips roll back. My backside hits him. "I think I'm—"

"About to come, baby? Let me get you there." *Can* you orgasm from the sound of a voice? Who am I kidding? Just listen to Jamie Dornan or Sam Heughan—an accent does it all the time. I won't admit I am close, but the tenor of his tone...

A sharp pounding on the door startles me, and I stiffen.

"Hanky, you in there still?" The singsong squeal of a female spins my head back to focus on his face in the mirror. For some reason, tears instantly prickle my eyes.

"Oh, God," I whimper, horrified at what I was doing, at what I'd almost done, with a perfect stranger. Pushing back from the counter, I press into him, forcing him away from me. His touch lingers as I reach for the doorknob, shoving open the door and rushing past a woman I hardly see. Riled up and embarrassed, I race for an exit and an end to my evening.

chapter 2

Eyes In the Mirror

[Hank]

"What the fuck did you do?" The sharp Southern drawl of my old friend catches me as I stumble from the bathroom and into the hallway. "Did you just get it on in my bathroom?"

Almost nearly escapes my mouth, but instead, I say, "I didn't do anything." Watching a woman exit the hallway behind me, Tommy Carrigan's brows raise. He doesn't seem to recognize the lady.

"Man, I see some things never change," he mutters. I sense a chuckle in his tease, but there's also a sadness. He doesn't know I've changed. Old memories haunt us both, and he's correct. It would be sad if I had taken a girl in a bathroom at a party, only I didn't take *that* girl. The one I wanted ran away from me.

"Some things completely change," I defend, not offering any further information. I search the room but don't find her. *Midge.* There was something in her eyes. I can't place what it is, but I want to know more about her.

"Oh, man." He pauses, scanning the room after me. "I recognize the expression on your face. You're a goner," Tommy snorts.

"Nope, she is," I mutter. I don't see Midge anywhere, and I sigh in defeat. Coming to this party was a mistake. When the invitation found me, I couldn't believe it because I hadn't seen Tommy in years—almost nine to be more exact. The death of his sister was the end of everything. An even greater shock was finding out Tommy got married.

"So, you're hitched?" I muse, hoping to deflect the conversation.

"Proudly," he states, standing taller, his barrel chest rising.

17

"She's a pretty thing," I admit. His wife is our age, in her forties, and she's adorable with short-styled hair and bright blue eyes.

"She's all mine," Tommy clarifies, and I huff at the hint.

"I don't doubt it."

Tommy's not really a domineering man, but he's loyal and protective of those closest to him. No one understands this better than I do. Friends for nearly fifteen years, I was around the Carrigan siblings for a long time before everything fell apart. The thought brings a hint of memories long since told to disappear.

"Want to explain why my wife's new friend just rushed out of here?"

"Nope." I can't because I don't understand what happened. One minute, I was trying to get away from the old groupie, and the next, I'm outlining the curves of a little body in the darkness of the bathroom. Her eyes pinned me in place the second she looked up at me. Mesmerized by the swirling combination of gold and chocolate with a hint of sorrow mixed in, I couldn't let her leave. Thank goodness my bulk accidentally trapped her against the sink. The space was compact but not so tight she couldn't escape, had I let her. Then the way she responded to me, to just my voice. I never had the power to sing, but I would have sung songs for her just to watch those eyes flutter with pleasure, and she was almost there. *Damn groupie.* "How'd Stephie get in here?"

"Stephie's here?" Tommy whistles, looking around me as if he hadn't seen her. The woman hadn't given up after all these years, still hoping to latch onto a rock star although most of us are has-beens at this point. Tommy smiles tightly, and then his face drops at the reality. "Fuck, Stephie's here. I gotta get her out of here."

"You doing something you shouldn't be?" I bark. I instantly liked Tommy's wife, so the fact Tommy might be stepping out on her has me all kinds of bristly.

"Are you fucking kidding me? Did you see my wife? My *wife*," he emphasizes. "I wouldn't let her go for anything." For a man who avoided marriage most of his life, I'm shocked at the instant loyalty he has to this one lady. Then I remember his sister. They had a rare closeness. Best of friends. He knew how to protect a woman.

"Good to hear," I confirm, thankful he has priorities. On that note, his wife enters the hallway.

"What happened?" she asks her husband.

"Whatcha mean, darlin'?"

"One minute, Midge is drinking wine and enjoying herself, and the next, she can't wait to leave. I don't understand." Edie looks crushed at the disappearance of her friend, and a touch of guilt pinches me.

"Your friend? What was her name?" I snap my fingers like I'm trying to remember.

"Midge Everette. I just met her, but we were insta-friends. I don't know what upset her." Her brows pinch with concern and I nod in agreement as if I understand what she means by insta-friends. *Women, huh?* "And you know her how?"

I'm hoping she throws me a bone because I'm thinking I need to see Midge again. If nothing else, I need to apologize, and I *never* say I'm sorry. At one time, all I did was apologize, but it never got me anywhere.

"She's working the 5K fundraiser for the music school." I have no idea what this means, and I'm tapping my chin, working up to another question when Tommy's eyes narrow on me.

"Some things never change," he repeats, muttering as he rubs a hand up his wife's back. Little does he know, everything has changed for me.

chapter 3
It Always Starts with Burnt Toast

[Hank]

"I burned the toast." The hysterical female voice drowns the line with her sobs after this statement.

"Ma'am, this is the Central Valley Crisis Hotline." I pause. "What seems to be your issue?"

Through hiccups, I hear her blow out her breath. "I burned the toast." A sniffling snuffle ripples through the phone, and I hold the device away from my ear for a second. She's a hot mess of tears and heaving gasps of air.

"Want to tell me what happened?" I've worked at Central Crisis for more than four years. After completing my time in a mandatory service program, I volunteered to stay on to help people, thinking I could make a difference for someone. The thought saddens me for the briefest moment before I return to the woman at hand. Crying over burnt toast stems from something deeper, and my job on the hotline involves getting to the root of such things.

"I'm at the end of my rope."

"You don't sound like you're at the end." She doesn't actually. Something about her voice sounds familiar and a touch more confident than a woman frazzled by life. Typical callers to the center include punk kids wanting out of school. Sometimes a veteran who needs more than the crisis hotline offers. An occasional druggie who is beyond help. Those calls leave me feeling hopeless. It's easier to connect with people when I can see them, place a hand on their knee, and assure them there are other avenues in life. Manning the phone lines is the worst part of volunteering for me, but I made a promise to myself—help those in need—because I was once one of them. Volunteers each take a night or two a month, and tonight is mine.

"You don't know me. How can you say that?" She's right—I don't know her—but between the familiarity of her voice and a knowledge of what the end of a rope feels like, I have a good idea of how she's feeling. Despair. Desperation. Downtrodden.

"Why don't you tell me a little about yourself? Tell me about your day." It helps to be pleasant, encouraging, and for some reason, I want this voice to keep talking to me. It's the hint of recognition. I need more.

"My d-day?" she stutters. "No one asks about my day."

Ah. Piece number one.

"Well, I'm asking. Tell me. How was your day?" My lips curl as I realize I kind of do want to know about her day.

"My children forgot."

"Forgot what?"

"One son needs a suit for the spring dance." She deflects as if she didn't hear my question. "Another needs some last-minute Hawaiian t-shirt for a concert. And my youngest. He's just lost, not certain who he wants to be, even though I keep telling him to be himself. Being eleven is difficult."

I sigh, nodding my head. Picking up a pen, I start to doodle on the desk pad calendar. My designs add to those already scribbled there. I wish I was a sketch artist. I'd be able to capture her eyes. Not the woman on the phone—I can't see this lady—but the eyes that stared back at me a few weeks ago. The ones in the mirror, dancing in the candlelight as I stood behind her.

"And I don't know how I got talked into hosting this event. Although, actually, I do because I can never say no. *No.* How hard can it be?"

She takes a deep breath, pausing. I imagine the tears have dried, and she's working up the steam for annoyance before the anger strikes. I've seen this in many women. Especially the ones who expect something of me after I've given *it* to them. Given them *me*. They want to fuck the

21

infamous Hank Paige. *I'm not one to complain but don't expect anything from me afterward.* I gave my heart once, and it was the biggest mistake of my life.

"Honestly, how hard?" Yep, annoyance to anger in sixty seconds. I don't have to see this lady to envision her shifting expression. Her question snaps me back to the conversation, but she plows on in her growing irritation.

"I said no a few weeks ago. It was the only time I wanted to say yes." Her voice lowers on the second statement, a dip in the octave as it grows huskier.

This stops my scribbles on the pad.

Piece number two, possibly.

"What did you say no to when you wanted to say yes?"

"Him." She sighs—breathy, deep, wanting—and something stirs in me that shouldn't on these types of calls. "I'm divorced, and there was this man," she clarifies. "It's been a long time since someone looked at me like that, you know. But then again, I don't suppose he was really looking at *me.*"

This has me sitting upright, stretching my back with a twist as I sit in this too-small rolling seat. I'm a large man, and this donated piece of shit chair can hardly hold me. I should do something about it, but I promised myself I wouldn't throw money at this place. It needs my time, not the green stuff.

"Tell me about the man," I prompt. It's part of our training. *Keep 'em talking.* Though, I admit, I'm curious.

She sighs again, and for a moment, I imagine a dreamy gleam in her eye. Maybe a sparkle of desire. A hint of unbridled passion. A need for someone to take the lead. The thought circles around to the eyes haunting my dreams every night; the ones from the mirror, reflecting back at me as I tell her what I'd like to do to her and the ways I want to pleasure her.

"He was so different." It's as if she's stolen the words from my mouth. The woman was different. I felt it in the way she leaned against me. The way she said my name—as if it was an ordinary name and not a symbol of who I once was. The way she looked at me. She wanted *me.*

"He touched me." A nervous huff fills the phone. "Not in an inappropriate way, but in a way. . .his touch still lingers on me." She giggles. "It's hard to explain."

"Try." My throat clogs, and a croak mixes with the typical smoky sound of my voice. I swallow, wondering when her tone softened and took on a purring lilt. When did this call to a crisis line turn into phone sex for me?

"I've never done this before." A sultry dip in her tone has my brows pinching. Déjà vu knocks at me, hinting I've heard this statement before. The familiarity of her voice ratchets up a notch or two, and recognition seems just a whisper away.

"Done what?" Something in my chest pinches.

"Called into a crisis center. You must think I'm crazy." Her voice returns to a more even tone, and I've lost the connection.

I blink, aware I was searching for something, *hoping*, at least. "No, I don't." I mean what I said. I honestly don't think people who call in are mentally imbalanced. It's a cry for help, and it's what I want to do— help. "Tell me more about the man."

"He didn't do anything. But it's what he said he wanted to do. And then I told him no."

I swallow. "Why?"

"Because I'm stupid."

"Don't say such things about yourself."

She exhales sharply. "What woman, who hasn't been touched in ages, denies a man who wants to touch her? I mean, maybe it wouldn't have meant anything to him, but it doesn't have to, right? It could have just been sex. It could have been for one night, right?" She sighs. "Why can't I have a one-night stand? Just let loose. What's wrong with me? Why couldn't I say yes to something I wanted instead of telling him no?"

I don't really have an answer here, and my job isn't to dispense advice. I just listen. We've come a long way from the burnt toast, so maybe we are getting somewhere.

"Why did you tell him no?"

"Because I'm old."

I bite my lip, trying not to chuckle. Her voice doesn't resonate anywhere near an advanced age, but voices can be deceiving. My lip slides free of my teeth, and I ask, "How old are you?" It's not really proper to ask these things. No identifiers of any type are allowed. Pure anonymity.

"I'm forty-one. Today."

Ahhhh. Here we have it.

"Happy Birthday."

"I wish I was happy. I mean, I should be, right? I have a decent job. I have a roof over my head. I have three amazing boys." I hear her pride in the last remark. She's a good mother.

"But you want a little *more*," I offer, sitting back in the swivel chair. I don't know where the words come from, and I shouldn't be prompting her like this. Yet somehow, I know the feeling. I'm still waiting for something more myself.

"Yes." She sighs. I bounce back and then sweep forward, sensing I'm about to tumble from the seat at the purr in the word. The hint of recognition rings again.

"Excuse me." I'm a musician at heart. Sound is my trade. I remember rhythms and beats, and the linger in her *S* reminds me of something, someone.

"Excuse me?" she repeats as if she misunderstood me.

"I'm sorry. Could you repeat—" I swallow. *This is so unethical.* "Could you say yes like you just did?" I pause another beat. "I mean, didn't it feel good to say yes?" There. Nothing wrong with prompting her in a positive way. Nothing suspicious here.

"Yes." *Huh?* I fall back in the seat. The answer is too sharp, too direct. I must have misheard her, and I shake my head, telling myself I'm an idiot. I'm imagining the lingering lilt to be what I want it to be—the desperate plea in *her* voice, my pretty eyed lady—but it isn't her.

"Are you still there?" she asks. We've remained silent too long.

"I'm here for you," I assure her, reaching for the pen again. I think of those sparkling, gold-speckled eyes one more time when her voice hitches. Another sound. Another trigger.

"Um . . ." I begin.

"Oh, God." She draws out with a breath.

Shit. "Midge?" I question.

And the line goes dead.

chapter 4

Lingering Silence

[Hank]

The quiet on the other end of the phone lingers in my ear. Her birthday. Thoughts of entertaining her fill my mind, but I shake my head. My gut twists with the knowledge I crossed so many lines by calling out her name. I want to call her back, but the anonymous phone line provides no callback number. *Dammit.* How can I help her if I can't reach her? I could always call Tommy, but do I want to breach the silence of our long-lost friendship? I still can't believe I received an invitation to his wife's party.

I don't know why I went.

Curiosity, maybe. I've often wondered what Tommy has been up to. Hell, I've been thinking more and more about all of them lately, for some reason. Denton Chance. Tucker Ashe. Friends from a lifetime ago. A history I don't wish to repeat or reenter.

Maybe self-inflicted torture made me do it. An unfulfilled hope remains that Tommy might offer some answers about Kit. I chuckle at the false anticipation. His sister had been special to me. She was a star in the music industry when girl rock bands were all the rage. Vibrant. Larger than life. A wild child. She grew into a woman with passion and a dream. *But life was cruel, and I was a fool.* The lyrics scroll through my head like a classic song, one of many I try to forget in her voice. My personal demons are told to get back in their cage where they belong.

More likely, I went to prove I could handle a party. The drinking. The atmosphere. The memories. But I quickly realized I wasn't ready, and I left shortly after the disappearance of Midge. Sweet, innocent, wanting to play Midge. It was in her eyes. She hadn't done anything like this before, she said. A stranger. An encounter. It would have been a new experience. One I gladly wanted to give her. I'm ready for the next steps in my recovery, but with the party invitation, old hurts resurface.

Damn Tommy Carrigan.

It's best for me if we don't reconnect. So, no, I won't be contacting Tommy for Midge's number.

+ + +

It's been a month since I met Midge, two weeks since I heard her frazzled voice on the phone, and three seconds since I last thought of her. The intake of her breath. The way she looked at me. The ripeness of her breasts. The curve of her hips. The wrench slips from my hand, and I curse again.

"What's gotten into you, boss?" My nephew, Chopper, is a good kid, wanting to do the right thing and showing me respect by calling me boss, but today, I'm out of sorts. I stand and nearly knock my head on the hood of the 1969 Boss 429 Mustang I'm working on. She'll be a black beauty of machinery once I get her restored, and she's all mine. I've been rebuilding her for six years. The same amount of time I've worked on rebuilding my life. Not trusting myself to handle one of the other projects in our shop, she's my focus today. The faded red Stingray Corvette needs my attention, but I passed the baton to my nephew. He and Brut can handle her.

Scrubbing at my hair, I swing my head to my older brother, Brut, and find him watching me. I owe him—I owe him too much—and today, I'm reflective of the fact. At forty-five, he hardly looks a day over thirty while, at forty-three, I look aged from the wear and tear of a lost lifestyle. My skin is wrinkled. My hair feels thinner. My jaw wears a shadow of salt-and-pepper. Brut got the good genes in the pool with his early white hair and clean face. He also got this shop—Restored Dreams. The name isn't lost on us. Our momma picked it, along with our literary names, before she decided we weren't for her. Who names their kid Bronte Austen? Poor Brut. On the other hand, I'm Henry James. My mother left the life she never wanted. Eventually, Brut inherited this life, this garage, although he secretly didn't want it either, just like me. Yet here we both stand.

He nods in my direction. "What's your problem today?"

I shake my head. How can I tell him I can't get a woman off my mind? Not the distant memory of one, but a new one. There was something about her. She didn't seem to recognize me. No judgment in those eyes—gold flecks streaming among a dark forest. She looked at me like she wanted me to take her worries, take *her* even. Always playing the damn knight in shining armor, I live for that shit. But living that way nearly wrecked me once upon a time, and my armor remains rusty.

I bend for the engine of the only solid girl for me when Brut's voice interrupts. "You've got other things to concentrate on today. That Stingray needs the transmission replaced. It's due for paint on Thursday." I whistle low. Not an easy task. "And that Charger needs an inspection. Owner says something's happening with the brakes." Brut rolls his eyes at the ignorance of some classic car owners. "And this one just arrived for an overhaul."

I spin to see the baby blue 1969 Mustang convertible I'd recognize anywhere. *Kit?* I vigorously give my head a shake. It would be impossible. I remind myself there's more than one car out in the world like this, but what are the chances of one being here today.

"Someone you might recognize brought this one in." Brut spins his tablet to show me the name on the docket. His tone hints at his displeasure. "He says he knows you'll take care of her." Tommy Carrigan. Goddamn him. What's he playing at? I don't need these ghosts haunting me. Something in my expression must frighten Brut, and he exhales.

"I can take it," he offers.

"No, I got it." My eyes haven't moved from the car. A gift. My heart and soul poured into the vehicle, into the girl who once owned it. I lost her, I remember, but like a tiny hammer knocking on my head, I'm reminded I couldn't lose what I didn't have. Kit Carrigan was never exclusively mine. She belonged to the rock 'n' roll industry.

"You feeling okay?" Brut asks, concern in his voice. He worries about me even though it has been six years. Six years sober. It wasn't an easy feat. I tip my chin to assure him I'm good. I don't need a drink. I need to get working.

"Give it to me," I demand, barking harsher than I intended. I tug the tablet from him and peruse the ticket. My head shakes as I'm certain the car needs nothing but a routine checkup. Again, I wonder what Tommy's playing at. He's never brought it here before, so why now?

+ + +

"Your car's ready," I snap into the phone, frustrated by my day spent working on Kit's old vehicle.

"That was fast." Tommy chuckles. Hearing his easy voice again brings back wave after wave of memories—late nights drinking, days singing, too many bad things in between.

"There wasn't anything special needed." I exhale. "You know, there were probably other places to go." Tommy lives in Los Angeles while our location is a good twenty minutes outside of the city *if* you subtract traffic.

"I'm happy to support." The words aren't lost on me, nor is the implication I need the financial assistance. Tommy has long since given up on me in other ways. He knows my history better than anyone, and while he tried to help me financially at one time, I was beyond saving mentally. I had to dig myself out of both holes on my own. The heavy silence between us forces him to clear his throat. "I didn't mean anything..."

"Forget it, man." The awkwardness lingers. I feel like a fucking teenager, and I'm ready to end the call when Tommy speaks again.

"Look, Hank, I've got a favor to ask." His hesitation gives me pause. Tommy hardly asks for anything, other than when he asked me to walk away from all of them. "Ivy owns a music therapy school. You remember Ivy?"

How could I forget Ivy Carrigan—now Everly? She was her mother in a younger form—just as beautiful—but thankfully untainted by the music industry. I loved that little girl when she was little. Now, she's a woman in her own right and runs a school?

"What do you need from me?" Tommy knows I don't have money for a grand donation, but I'll give what I can.

"Ivy's hosting a fundraiser for her school. Some kind of walk-a-thon." He clicks his tongue. "A 5K. We're trying to support her. The band and me. Show of solidarity and all." Sounds like there's a backstory here, but I don't want to pry. Collision, the band he manages, isn't my business. "Anyway, we'd love for you to come."

"Why?" It's been years since I've seen Tommy, even longer since everything fell apart, so I don't understand.

"I want to have as many people who love Ivy around her for this big day. She had a grand opening back in August, but this is her first real event, so getting the name of the therapy school out there and trying to promote it are important to her."

"Yeah, but why me?"

"I'm trying to get the old band there—the older set, so to speak—to show her we're proud of her." There's more he isn't saying. I hear it in his voice.

"Is Denton coming?" The last of Kit's posse stopped speaking to either of us long before we officially separated. When Tommy doesn't reply, I have my answer. "Does this have to do with Kit?" When Ivy's mother passed, Tommy tried to rally the others around her, but she was lost. At first, Ivy even found herself on a path similar to her mother.

"No," he snaps, then takes a deep breath. "I don't know. I just thought it would be nice if people who were once important to her were around." *Once* important. The word is not lost on me. The problem is, I wish I was still important to somebody. Thoughts of Midge creep back into my mind. Dragging a hand over my head, I sigh.

"Yeah, sure. I'll be there. When is it?"

chapter 5

Because Cupcakes

[Midge]

The event day finally arrives. I've been a basket case for the past week—worried the band kids won't show, worried it would rain, worried, worried, *worried.*

The day after my crisis center phone call, I didn't think I'd be able to face Ivy and Edie, as if they could read my guilt. I'd never done something like that before—called a crisis hotline—like my forgotten birthday was a catastrophe instead of just a bad day. I only wanted someone to talk to, someone anonymous, but it was just my luck the person on the other end of the line knew me. What are the odds the volunteer would recognize my voice? And as soon as he said my name, I realized it was him.

Hank.

I hadn't been able to stop thinking of him. He haunted my daydreams. He filled my nightly fantasies. I sigh, rubbing my temples. I don't need my thoughts straying to him today. I need to focus, but I'm on edge. My mind races back to meeting Hank and the way he caressed my neck. How he massaged my shoulders in the dim candlelight. How he looked at me in the mirror. I relax for a minute until I hear my name.

"Mom!" I turn to find a sweaty Ronin running toward me. He used to look like me—brown hair, brown eyes—but now, his jet-black hair has streaks of purple. "We forgot the cake."

Oh my God. I knew I'd forget something. A bakery donated a gorgeous cake decorated with the high school colors and shaped like a musical note, but it was still in my refrigerator.

31

"Okay, don't worry." Easier said than done, knowing my house is thirty minutes away in good traffic, which is never a possibility in LA. Ronin nods when I squeeze his shoulders. He's grown taller than me. When did that happen? He wants everything perfect as do I since all the kids know his mom's in charge.

"Be cool," he warned me prior to the event. I noticed my boys never said these things to their father. When I decided to highlight my hair after hanging out with Ivy and Edie, adding streaks of purple to complement the school colors, Ronin said I went too far. "You're kind of old to color your hair like that. Plus, it looks like you copied me."

The comment stung, especially coming from the artsy son.

"Mom's not old," Elston defended. The spitting image of his father—bulky, blond, blue eyes—he stands before me as a constant reminder of the man I once loved. "I think it looks...ballin'." Is this a compliment? I don't understand kid lingo most days, and just when I figure it out, it changes.

"Mom looks like the hip moms," Liam added, always my little protector. He still looks like me with his matching eyes and smaller frame, though he sports his light brown hair in a crew cut. He could pass for Ronin Junior if Ronin wasn't always changing his image.

An afterthought occurred. I wasn't hip before? The possibility hurt. Regardless, my longer locks held new highlights to disguise the gray and some violet streaks to add some fun.

"I'll just run to the closest bakery and find something else." I'm explaining my dilemma to Ivy, but she's dismissing the thought. "We don't need cake."

We're walking as we talk, my legs racing to keep up with hers as she wants to do a final check on her own students marching in the 5K. With varying mental and physical abilities, Ivy's protective of her crew. She wants people to trust her school, not just her name. I've learned her mother was a famous singer, a dozen years back. I remember the name— Kit Carrigan. Something about breast cancer and dying too young also crosses my memory, but I don't remember exactly, and I don't wish to pry. A large black and white image of Kit standing next to a child in a wheelchair graces the front entryway of the school. The boy in the chair holds rhythm sticks in his hand and wears a sweet expression on his face. The former female rock star looks lovingly down at him. It's a touching picture in a sad way.

"Anyway, I can get to a bakery and back before the race finishes. I'm so sorry about the donated cake. I'll bring it back tomorrow for your students, but if—"

Without watching where I'm walking, I smack into another person, the body hard and firm as my cheek hits a chest. Ivy stopped short, but I continued forward, and the impact with another human propels me backward.

"Whoa, little lady." A scratchy, gravelly chuckle stops my heart, and my eyes close. *Sweet cheese, no, this can't be happening.* Warm hands cup my upper arms to prevent me from falling—or fainting—whichever might happen first. I want to melt into the pavement and disappear. *That* voice haunts me and when I think of what it almost did to me a few weeks ago...*sigh*...

"Uncle Hank?" Ivy questions, and I pry my eyes open. Standing in a dark gray t-shirt which hugs his upper body and black track pants with white striping down the side, he's a vision of athleticism. I'm wearing a purple shirt with the high school band logo and a light gray skort. I'm a mess with my hair piled on my head, and my makeup is minimal, just some mascara and purple lipstick to complement my highlights.

"Uncle Hank, is it really you?"

Hank releases me just as Ivy flings her arms open and steps up to the burly man. He cups her head and wraps an arm around her back.

"It's me, baby girl." The moment is sweet, intimate, and something riddles me as I witness the reunion of two people familiar with one another.

"What are you doing here?" Ivy asks, leaning back but still holding him.

"Tommy told me about your party, and I didn't want to miss it." The corner of his mouth quirks up. He's holding back some truth. I see it in the dull spark of his steely eyes, but his smile spreads, and Ivy's lips respond. She's happy he's here.

"Hank, have you met the woman in charge of everything today? Midge, this is Hank. Hank, Midge." I wrap my arms around myself deliberately avoiding the social nicety of extending a hand. I don't dare touch him without thinking about those thick hands massaging my shoulders, then slipping to my hips and tugging me back against him.

"We've met," I mutter, lowering my eyes from his gaze. Ivy's head spins toward me, her mouth opening in question, but I interject. "The cake."

"Forget it." She waves.

"But I feel awful. I'll just find a bakery around here and—"

"I know of one." The smoky gargle brings my attention back to Hank.

"Excuse me?"

"There's a bakery about five blocks from here although this isn't the best neighborhood to wander around alone." His brows raise, and he peers at Ivy.

"Don't start," she snaps, lifting a hand. I've heard all about how her husband didn't approve of the location, but Ivy was adamant the place remained where it was originally founded. Speaking of her husband, Gage Everly walks toward us, and I blush. He's incredibly good looking in an *I-shouldn't-stare-but-can't-help-myself* sort of way, especially since I'm definitely ten-plus years older than him. His chocolate-colored hair hangs to his chin, blending with thicker scruff on his jaw. His deep eyes suck you in, but he's not even looking at me. Focused on his wife, he's about to lay one on her, and I'm holding my breath because I know what's coming. I've only seen kisses like theirs in the movies. It's like a train wreck. I know I shouldn't look, but I can't look away.

The kiss happens, but within seconds, a sharp cough to my left reminds us there is more than me as an audience.

"Gage," Hank gruffly speaks.

"Hank?" Gage looks from the larger man to his wife and back. "Hank Paige." There's respect in his voice along with disbelief. "Man, you look good. Really good."

The comment implies at one time he didn't appear so healthy, which strikes me as odd while the two men clap hands and lean in for a bro-hug. If I thought Gage was attractive, Hank redefines attraction for me. He's not only my age, but there's a playfulness about him. He seems rough but sort of reckless, and I'm drawn to him. Typically, I'm not into tattooed men with silver scruff, but on Hank—I want to trace those designs and gently scratch his chin. The thought I had upon first meeting him returns. *I want to rub up against him.*

As the two men shake hands, I admire the flex of Hank's forearm and the strength under his inked skin. I want to feel those hands on me again, and my eyes travel up the intricate pattern to find him looking back at me.

"Midge?" I blink. *Shit.* Did he say something to me? Should I know what he said? "The cake, little lady."

"Right," I squeak. "Cake." *I want to eat him.* I shake my head. I'm a mess.

"Come with me, so you can pick what you want. I'll drive."

I nod, a needy moth to a bright flame. "Wait!" I turn to Ivy as my practical side slams on the brakes. "The boys."

"Liam's fine. He's found Petty who can watch him." Gage chuckles, and I know why. Jon Petty is the drummer for Collision, Gage's band, and he's the least likely to be responsible for a rock let alone a child. Liam's only eleven and has more sense.

"Maybe I should just—"

"Midge. He's fine. I'll find him. Just go." Ivy's smile assures me. She's met my boys on a few occasions over the past six weeks, and my Liam has a serious crush on her. If I didn't know better, I'd say she encourages it. I grin at the thought.

"Okay. I'll just get my purse."

"You don't need it. I've got this," Hank interjects. "Consider it my contribution to the day." He places a hand on the small of my back and guides me toward a large SUV. We walk without a word as all I can concentrate on is the warmth of his hand on me. Like a true gentleman, he opens the door and helps me into the vehicle.

As we ride in uncomfortable silence, my mind races through a checklist, confirming I haven't forgotten anything else. I'm mentally scrolling the list, so I don't think about how turned on I am to be in a confined space again with Hank or how awkward I feel because of it. I'm also hoping he's forgotten about my call into the crisis center.

"So, you have boys?" he asks, rolling his free hand over his wrist, moving a collection of bands. His arm rests lazily over the edge of the steering wheel as he maneuvers us down the side streets.

"Yes. Three." His head swings toward me.

"You have three kids?" Serious gray eyes roam my body.

I'm uncertain what that look means, so I continue. "Elston is seventeen. Ronin, my son in the high school band, is fifteen, and Liam is eleven." I pause, recalling I'd spewed this information to him when I thought he was a crisis center operator. *Cripes.* My fingers twitch to cover my face. Please don't let him remember anything.

"Not married," he confirms, eyes shifting to my naked left hand. I used to wear the ring. It brought me a strange comfort even when the marriage was over, but about a year ago, the weight of the ring was heavy. Maybe it was the impending marriage of my ex to his younger girlfriend.

"Nope." My eyes drift to his hand, dangling over the steering wheel. As if he senses my perusal, he flexes his fingers. The fingers nervously stroking the beads on his wrist reach over and lift my left hand. Drawing it to his lips, he sucks at the empty space on my ring finger.

"Me neither," he mutters against my skin. "Never been."

I shiver with the touch, the tone of his voice, and the overall gesture of his lips on me. I'm pathetic.

"What about children?" I ask.

"I would have liked to have them. But have none I've been told of." Although I catch the hint of humor, there's something underlying his comment. *None that he knows of.* What a strange way to phrase things.

"Is there the possibility you have children out there somewhere?" I try to jest in return, but I'm curious. He simply shakes his head, absentmindedly stroking a thumb over my ring finger.

"You're Ivy's uncle?" I'd only heard of Tommy Carrigan as her family.

"Just in name. We aren't family like that." His silence after his answer lingers in the air. He isn't going to offer more, and I'm not in the mindset to pry.

"Where are we going?" I'm hoping to deflect my overactive imagination, which conjures up a scene where he pulls this SUV over and takes me in the back seat.

"Because Cupcakes. It's a bakery near here." I don't question how he knows these things. We've crossed through some questionable parts at the outer edge of the city. If I didn't know the reasoning behind Ivy's desire to stay in the area, I'd have pushed her to relocate as well.

Suddenly, we stop in front of a shop with a frilly pink awning and the words Because Cupcakes in a feminine scrawl. Gauzy curtains dress the window, framing shelves of cupcakes which look like designer confections instead of edible treats. They're beautiful with piles of icing in silver, white, pink, and light chocolate. My mouth waters.

Hank surprises me again when he opens my door and assists me out of the SUV. He holds my fingers for a moment longer than necessary before leading me to the bakery entrance and holding the door open for me. It's been a long time since a man's been a gentleman toward me.

"Hank?" The woman behind the counter seems both surprised and pleased to see him as we enter. I recall the woman in the hallway the night we met, and I wonder if he goes anywhere where some woman doesn't know him. This can mean only one thing—player.

"Lily." His direct address to the blonde behind the counter startles me. My guess is she's in her forties. She's pretty with caramel colored hair, cut to her chin and bright blue eyes.

"Is Brut with you?" The fold to her shoulders alerts me this woman hates that she asked at the same time she wants an answer.

"Nope." Again, Hank's directness shocks me. More surprising is when his hand returns to my lower back, caressing lightly before he urges me forward. Lily's eyes shift to me.

"How can I help you?" She's gone into business mode, ignoring the fact Brut isn't here, whoever he is. I delve into the explanation of the high school fundraiser for the music therapy school, clarifying my connection, and my error with the cake.

"Why didn't you come to me?" This question goes to Hank, who shrugs, looking away like an errant child. I don't understand what's happening, but there is some kind of history here. "Did you say Ivy Everly owns the school?"

Hank nods, and the woman's face brightens. "How is she?"

"Married with children." Hank replies.

"Children?" Lily's eyes widen.

"She has three," Hank clarifies.

"Three kids. Whoa." They laugh for a second although I'm not certain why having three children is funny. Without further explanation, Lily continues. "This might take a few minutes. Let me step in the back, and I'll gather up what I think you'll need." She winks. "But while you wait, what would you like to sample?"

Hank coughs once next to me, but my eyes fixate on a mini round cake with a dollop of white icing and a raspberry on top. "Oh, I'm good." I dismiss with a wave, but a graveled voice in my ear encourages me.

"Try a sample, little lady." I close my eyes to the innuendo as a shiver ripples over my skin. I try to refocus my thoughts and order the white chocolate with raspberry treat. Lily adds two other cupcakes to a pink plate and hands it to Hank, instructing him to, "Take a seat."

We walk to the counter spanning the length of her second window and sit on high stools. Hank adjusts his stool to bring it closer to me. We face each other, and his knee slips between my thighs.

"Take a bite." The words roll over me, and I shiver again, wanting nothing more than to open my mouth and nibble on him. He's holding out the cupcake, and I'm wondering how my mouth will fit around the tower of icing. For some reason, my eyes lower to the seam of his jeans, but then I look away quickly. A man his size has to be large in other areas, and my mouth reacts in the same way it does toward this cupcake. Would it fit? How would it taste? I lift a trembling hand to my forehead as I reprimand myself to get a grip.

"Wait." He drags the white covered mini cake from my open mouth, and I sit up, a little embarrassed and a lot frustrated as my mouth hangs open in anticipation. Setting the delicacy on the plate, he slips off his stool, disappears behind the display counter to the back room, and then returns. He stands at my side, sticking a candle in the icing next to the raspberry. My eyes widen, and my stomach flips—uncertain of his gesture and equally apprehensive of his memory. He flicks a lighter, and a single flame tops the candle.

"Happy birthday," he singsongs beside me, raspy and rumbling. His eyes find mine, pinning me to my seat when all I want to do is melt under it.

"You remember?" I lower my head, picking at the hem of my athletic skirt. My cheeks heat with humiliation. A thick fingertip props up my chin as he takes his seat across from me.

"I'm so embarrassed," I add, closing my eyes, unable to face him.

"Open those beautiful eyes, Middy."

"Middy?" I chuckle nervously, snapping my attention up to him.

"Midge seems too old-fashioned for someone like you."

"Someone like me," I quietly parrot him. What do I look like to him? Who does he see? What must he think of me for calling into the hotline? He doesn't explain and I chew my lip. His thumb reaches up and tugs the tender skin from my teeth.

"Don't be embarrassed about calling in to the crisis center. We all need someone to talk to sometimes."

I wish I could believe him, but I am a bit ashamed. My call seems so frivolous, not a real issue. I'm typically stronger at handling things. In hindsight, I don't remember what I said.

"How old are you, Middy?"

"Forty-one."

A twinkle sparks in his steely eyes, making them silver. I like how he's looking at me. "Time to walk on the wild side. Make a wish, little lady, and take a bite."

Why does the nickname make my belly flutter? Moreover, what wish should I make?

I wish I may. I wish I might. I blow out the candle, blushing from the warm sunshine steaming through the window and the sweetness of this man.

He holds the cupcake up to me again, minus the candle, and I open wide, dragging my teeth over the whipped sugar. My lids lower, and I may have purred at the pure heaven exploding in my mouth. White chocolate and raspberry. Yum.

"Better than an orgasm." I sigh.

Then realize what I've said. My eyelids snap open to find his widened and flickering with something I haven't ever seen directed at me. Like a big, bad wolf, he looks like he wants to eat me, and somehow, I'm certain the pleasure will be all mine.

"You've got . . ." His voice trails off as he swipes at my nose. *Cripes.* Here I thought he wanted to devour me, and he's only staring because I have frosting on my face.

"Oh dear." I reach for my nose, but he grips my wrist. His knee slips between my thighs again.

When did he scoot so close? He sets the cupcake down, pokes a finger into the creamy frosting, and looks up at me.

"You have more here." Before I can speak, he coats my lower lip with the icing. A gasp parts my lips, and he leans forward. "Let me get that."

Instantly, soft lips cover mine, sucking the sugary treat and spreading the delicacy before his tongue sneaks out and licks along the line. I open without thinking, and it's all the invitation he needs. His hand cups the back of my head, and his mouth takes mine deeper, rougher, stronger. Savoring my lips, he cleans off the frosting and adds a new layer of sweetness. I might have purred again, and his lips curl. He's smiling while he kisses me, and I'm so turned on.

My hands lower to his knee between my legs, feeling the thin, slippery material of his track pants. My fingers outline the muscular bulge of his leg, and my thighs clench around the bulk. The curve of his knee hovers an inch away from where I need some friction. I'm already damp. If he presses any closer, I'm sure to leave a stain on him. His fingers comb into my hair, holding me in place to continue our kissing. Icing lingers on our lips while other areas grow stickier. I'm ready to hump his knee like a dog in heat when a strong cough comes from my left. Breaking apart, I turn away from the business owner, covering my lips with shaky fingers. I need a moment to regain myself.

"Thanks, Lily." Sarcasm drips from Hank's voice, but it isn't really her fault. We are in a public place, in broad daylight, kissing like two teenagers on an afternoon date. *Sweet cheese*, if only.

Hank stands, blocking me from Lily's view. I can't look at the other woman yet, embarrassment hitting me hard. "How much do I owe?" he says.

This pulls me back to reality.

"No. I've got this. It was my mistake." I fumble around me to remember I don't even have my purse. This man has me so mixed up I walked away from everything: the fundraiser, my boys, and my belongings.

"It's okay, Middy. This one's on me." I'm not certain if he means the cupcakes or the potential mistake of kissing me. I'm firing up to protest to the first option when Lily interjects. "Count it as my donation to Ivy."

Ivy. She must be someone special. Everywhere I drop her name or others use it, people are giving her things. Twelve large boxes rest on the display counter, which means Lily allowed our kiss to progress for as long as she could before she interrupted us. I flush again with the thought while Hank takes a stack of boxes out to his SUV.

"Sorry about that," I mutter, pointing toward the window.

Lily pffts me. "I'm so happy Hank has a girlfriend. How long have you two been together?"

"Oh, I'm not—"

"Not long enough," Hank interjects. I hadn't noticed he returned inside the bakery. "And I've been waiting too long for her."

The words sound like the lyrics from a song, but I can't place the tune. My heart sings its own melody at the moment. A dangerous ballad which will lead to nothing.

chapter 6

Icing On the Cake

[Hank]

"You want to tap that, don't you?" I turn to Tommy as I unload a tower of cupcake boxes from the back of Brut's SUV. Thankfully, Midge stands a few feet away and doesn't hear him.

"Dude," I groan. "Lower your voice. We aren't fifteen. Show some respect."

Tommy's brows raise as his lips twitch. "Oh, I recognize that look." The intensity of his dark eyes holds mine.

"I don't know what you mean."

"I wore the same look about a year ago, and lucky me, look where it got me." His head swivels toward his wife.

"You're out of your mind." I'm not getting married. There was only one woman for me, and she didn't want my proposal. Besides, I only kissed Midge. I didn't ask her to marry me.

The thought makes me stop because I did kiss her, and she was sweet in an untapped kind of way. In a—*she could be wild, might want to be wild—if she only knew how* sort of way. I remember seeing it in her eyes in Tommy's bathroom. She would have given herself to me had Stephie not interrupted us.

My gaze drifts to Midge as she stands deep in discussion with Edie. I twist back to pick up the second pile of boxes.

"Whatever you do, stay away from that thing." I look up and follow Tommy's line of direction. His eyes seem focused on Midge's short, stretchy skirt. I narrow my glare at him, not liking his implication.

"What are you talking about?"

"That *thing*. It's a chick thing, and it's complicated as fuck to get into." My brows pinch, and I turn back to Midge.

"Are you talking about her skirt?"

"Skort, man. Whoever invented it was not a guy. It's like shorts attached to a skirt. Sexy as fuck but hard to get into. Just get her out of it first."

Holy shit. "Tommy, man." I groan followed by a deep laugh. He's still the same guy he always was even if he's attached to one woman.

"Why aren't you participating?" I ask, hoping to shift the subject far away from getting into Midge's pants, or skort, or whatever the fuck. Since the moment her mouth touched mine, it's all I can think about anyway. I need more than a sample of icing. I want the entire cake.

"I don't partake in structured athletics," he jests. He's an avid runner, and by the size of his body, I know he purposely keeps in shape.

"You like yoga," Edie adds as we near the women.

"Only with you, darlin'."

Her face brightens, and I don't even want to know what Tommy's referencing.

+ + +

Hours pass. The 5K ends. Kids celebrate the victory of money raised for a good cause. Ivy cries with the attention given to her school and her students, and I search for Midge every chance I get, feeling shaky whenever she's out of my sight. She didn't say a thing about kissing me on our ride back in the SUV. She chattered about the cupcakes, learned Brut was my brother, and rattled on about the fundraiser, but she didn't mention our kiss. She's deflecting, and while I thought I was fine with her ignoring what happened, as the time ticks by, I find I want her to address it. I want her to own it.

I want her to give me another taste.

When I see her heading toward the school entrance, which is actually an old, renovated church, I follow. I lose sight of her inside the building, but then notice the swing of a bathroom door. Stepping inside the ladies' room, I turn the lock. Midge stands before a singular porcelain sink, her hands balanced on the edges.

"We've got to stop meeting like this," I tease, but she closes her eyes.

"I just needed a minute."

I don't know if it's a hint to leave, but I have no desire to separate from her. Not liking our distance, I step forward to stand behind her. It's similar to our first meeting, though the space isn't quite as intimate. Daylight streams through the etched windows, and the fluorescent light isn't the same as the glow of a candle.

"Talk to me," I murmur, similar to what I say on the crisis hotline.

"I can't believe I pulled this off. I've been so stressed out about it. I just wanted it to be right for Ronin." Ronin? One of her boys, right? I nod, meeting her eyes in the reflective glass. "He's...he's so complicated. Sweet Jesus, forgive me, but he's the one I just can't connect with sometimes."

I knew what she meant. Once upon a time, it was the same for me. I'd been the one my father couldn't understand. A rock band hadn't been his dream for his youngest son.

Midge continued, "But I'm trying. I want to be there for him."

Therein lay the difference. I recognize Midge is a good mother. I'd watched her—in a non-creepy way—interact with her sons throughout the afternoon. A tender touch. A sweet smile. They are her pride and joy.

"The day went great, Middy. You did good." I grin at her reflection in the mirror, and her eyes glisten back at me.

"What I'd say?" Tears border her eyes. *Shit.* I can't handle when women cry.

"You're very sweet." She sniffles, as if to will the tears away.

"You're very pretty. I like the purple in your hair." She watches me as she shakes her head, said hair tumbling in loose tendrils here and there from the bundle on her head. Her eyes reflect the sunlight bouncing in the mirror. "Your eyes are fucking gorgeous."

The sharp tone of my voice catches her. She inhales, and my hands slip over her arms, stroking down to her wrists, and covering her hands at the edge of the sink, pinning her against the porcelain.

"Did I mention earlier how glad I am to see you again?"

"No." Her voice is hardly more than a whisper.

"What happened, little lady?"

"I don't know what you mean," she lies, looking at my reflection.

"I kissed you." I pause, waiting for her to interject, to add something, or say anything, but the silence lingers.

"I kissed you back." Her words are soft spoken and low.

"Did you like it?" The question forces her eyes closed.

It's the only answer I need. I skate an arm around her waist, tugging her back against me. There's no denying I want her, and she can feel my desire on her lower back. My mouth moves to her neck, peppering her exposed skin with open-mouth kisses. "We didn't get to finish what we started, and I'll be damned if you leave another bathroom unsatisfied by me."

My thumb teases into the waistband of her skirt, stretching the fabric as my hand dips lower. Her breath hitches.

"I shouldn't be doing this." Yet she isn't fighting me off. Instead, she's gripping my wrist, guiding my hand inside her skirt. Instantly, my fingertips touch dampness.

"Is it crazy how I want you?" I mutter.

"Not as crazy as what I want you to do to me." The challenge spurs me forward.

"Oh, yeah. What would that be, cupcake?" I lick her neck, tasting her sweet skin. She shakes her head, refusing to answer me. I'd give her everything against this sink if I thought she could handle me, but it might be a bit soon to take her.

"You ready for me, little lady?" I tease, noting the moisture deepens as I slip my fingers under elastic and brush against wet heat. "Holy shit, baby." She's slick and needy, pressing back against me. Her ass nudges my dick, though she's too short to meet me. I spread my legs, evening us out a bit, but I'm not worried. I only want to make her feel good. As my finger invades her, she shoots her ass back, stretching for friction.

"I can't believe I'm doing this," she mutters between sharp inhales. Her hands grip the sink as her body rocks over my fingers and her ass finds a teasing rhythm of bumping into me. I'm desperate for her, despite the bathroom scene.

"What did you wish for, Middy?" Her eyes jump back to me. Shaking her head, she's refusing to speak as her back arches. She's a cat in heat, and I love the stretch of her around my fingers. "What's your birthday wish, little lady?"

"Hank, I—" Her voice drops husky as she bites her rosy lip. I watch with full attention as she throws her head back to my shoulder and squeezes her thighs. She wants to scream, but she clamps her lips tight.

"I want to hear you, baby." Rolling her head on my shoulder, she refuses, and her screams become my next mission. "Give it to me." Her thighs clench. Her head falls forward. She presses back on me and detonates. Her mouth falls open, but she sucks in silence. Her sparkling eyes roll closed, and her body relaxes. Fucking gorgeous.

"Mom?"

Her head shoots up to the locked door. A young male voice hesitates on the other side.

"Sweet cheese." Midge presses at my wrist, willing me to release her.

Sweet what?

"Tell him just a second," I mutter.

"I'll be right out," she squeaks, her voice a little too high. I release her and lift my fingers to my lips. Licking them, I watch her straighten her skirt. She looks up at me in the mirror, observing me savor my forefinger.

"Better than frosting," I murmur, holding her gaze. Her mouth gapes open but no sound escapes. I want to hear her. Why won't she make a sound? She steps left, as if to go around me, but I twist to block her exit.

"Midge," I demand.

"Mom," her son calls again.

"I'll be right there." Frustration fills her eyes when she glances up at me, but I can't have her walk away. My back presses against the door. She shakes her head. "I've got to go."

"Not like this." I hold my ground, counting the seconds to keep her with me. She stares at me. Strength builds in those maddening eyes.

"Midge." I point at her. "Kiss me."

To my surprise, she leaps for me. Her arms circle my neck as she drags herself up my body and kisses the crap out of me. Her lips move with mine, sipping at me like she can taste me. Her tongue laps at me as if she wants to memorize mine. She's saying goodbye in this kiss, and I won't allow it. Too quickly, she pulls back. Stunned from the eagerness of her mouth, I step to the side so she can slip out the door.

Tommy was wrong. Her skort was easy enough to get into, only I want Midge completely out of it. I want into *her* instead.

chapter 7

Not A Quitter

[Hank]

"I quit my job."

Instantly, I recognize her voice. Finally hearing from her, after her silence in the bathroom and no communication over the past few days, my heart taps an extra beat. Then I realize what she said.

"Wait, what?"

"Sweet cheese. What did I do?" She pauses. "I quit my job." The hysteria in her voice warns me she's on the verge of tears. I do *not* want her to go to pieces on the phone. I want to be there to pick them up for her, and I can't do it from the crisis center. She called in again. Going against every oath I made, the code of conduct, and patient privacy, I do something I shouldn't do.

"Hang up," I snap.

"What?" Her voice cracks. This woman has haunted me for weeks, and I can't subject our conversation to the recording of a hotline. Morally and ethically, it's undeniably not right to say this to someone in need, but I repeat myself.

"Hang up."

A sharp gasp occurs before the line goes dead.

Instantly, I dial another number from my personal cell phone, cursing as the line rings. "Come on, come on, come on," I mutter.

"Hello?"

"Tommy, I'm calling in a favor." A snort follows my request. Lord knows I owe him more than he owes me, but then again, this isn't exactly true. I don't have time for those thoughts, though. I need to get to someone. "I need Midge Everette's number."

"Why?" The sharp question startles me. Has she said something about me? Did she tell Edie what we did? What *I* did, and how she walked away? But then again, why did she finally call me?

The truth hits me like a sucker punch. She didn't call me; she called the hotline. For a moment, I'm reminded of Kit—never calling me directly but sending someone to fetch me. I shake the memory and try again with Tommy.

"Look, something happened, and I need to speak to her."

"Is she in danger?"

"No, nothing that extreme. Just...she needs me, and I don't have her number." I would have gotten her number had she not disappeared again after her son interrupted us. I lost her in the crowd of kids, parents, and the ongoing party.

"How do you know she needs you?" I didn't. In fact, it might be *me* who needs *her*. There's just something drawing me to her, and I don't want to look away. Maybe, I just want to make myself feel better about taking advantage of her. I overstepped boundaries, and I've tortured myself all week with what we'd done. I remind myself she isn't a groupie. She's a lady.

"Tommy, I know you and I have history. And I know you have every reason to distrust me. But I have reason to distrust you. Can we just call it a draw for a second and you give me the number of a woman who needs my help?" Silence follows a beat.

"Darlin', can you get me Midge's number?" There's a shuffle, and I'm assuming he covers the phone to give a brief relay to his wife before he comes back to me. "If you fuck her, I mean really fuck her, you better not fuck her over. Don't make me regret this." Seconds later, he gives me the digits.

"I owe you." I hang up without further explanation.

It's Hank. Answer this number. I text and then hit send. Then I dial her number. It goes to voicemail.

Fuck.

I try again.

And again.

Finally, she picks up.

A quiet sniffle crosses the line.

"Don't cry, Middy baby. Talk to me." Her silent tears kill me. I project back to the days of Kit, but I don't want to go there. This isn't her. Midge is nothing like my former lover. "Tell me what happened."

"I work for Bigle Marketing. We design graphics, event displays, and campaigns for clients. I like my job, I really do, but my boss . . ." She exhales. "I can't stand her. How can women be so insensitive to other women? A mother to another mother?"

I don't actually know what she means about motherhood, but I know how cruel women can be to each other. I saw it often enough with Kit and how the other female artists were jealous of her success.

"She just pushed me too far today. I mean, I work hard. I give everything to my job when I'm there, and too often work over weekends and holidays. I have something for Liam this weekend and she asked me to work on a campaign she refused to give me in the first place. *Mark Vanderburg needs a vacation*," Midge mocks. "I snapped. I'm just...I'm over it. I'm over everything."

"What do you mean 'everything'?" I sit back in the rickety swivel chair. I have got to replace this thing. Swiping a hand over my hair, I hold my breath, waiting for her reply.

"My ex-husband is getting married this summer."

There's always something deeper. I sigh, remembering my training and my own desperate measures. I drank because Kit didn't love me, but it was deeper than her rejection. I didn't love who I was.

"You still in love with him?"

"Hell, no," she snorts. "I don't really care that he's getting married. It's the principle of it. He moved out, he moved on, and I'm still...stuck. I took this job when we moved here, because he wanted to move here."

"How long you been divorced, little lady?" The endearment falls easily from my mouth, but her breath hitches through the line, and I fear

I've overstepped again. I've already leaped a triple, bold-typed line in the volunteer handbook.

"Three years." She sighs. "He just didn't love me anymore."

I can relate. Then again, I'm not convinced Kit Carrigan *ever* loved me. Time after time, she proved she didn't. Lying to me was the biggest telltale sign.

"I'm sorry to hear this, Middy. But you know, I'm secretly delighted."

"Why?" She chuckles without humor, and I realize the statement might sting.

"I'm hoping his loss is my gain." Silence ticks between us, and I want to see her face. I want to hear the thoughts running through her brain. I clear my throat when she doesn't say anything. "Anyway, I really wish I could see you, make sure you're okay, but I'm working."

"You work for the center, right?"

"Actually, I volunteer here." She waits, and I take a deep breath. "I ran into some trouble a while ago. I hit rock bottom, as they say. I wasn't in a good place, and I crashed. Detonated. Burned." A heavy exhale escapes. "I went to rehab, got my head straight, and decided to give back a little." Without realizing it, I'm scrubbing at my hair so hard, I'm giving myself a headache. The nervous habit soothes me, but I'm working up a lather of remorse at the moment.

"Is that why you don't drink?" The question reminds me of what I said as we watched each other in the mirror at Tommy's.

"Yeah."

"How long have you been dry?" Hearing her use the correct terminology surprises me, and I smile slowly, proudly.

"Six years."

"That's a good thing." I hear the pleasure in her voice, a hint of pride, and my chest swells. For some reason, I want this woman to be pleased with me.

"Yeah, it's a real good thing, baby." She quietly laughs in response, and I feel lighter, relieved. Somehow, this conversation turned around to me, and as much as I don't like talking about myself, I don't mind sharing with her. "Look, I'm working the hotline, which means I'm on call until midnight. Where are you?"

"I'm still sitting in the parking lot at work. Maybe I overreacted." She guffaws, a threat of hysteria returning as she rethinks her decision.

"Can you do something for me? I want you to get the hell out of that parking lot. Go home. Eat if you can. Get a glass of wine and fill your tub. Then call me on this number. It's my cell. I'll be here for a while, okay?"

She must be nodding because I hear the sound of clothing rustling, like the phone's perched on her shoulder. "And drive safely." I laugh after the demand.

"Okay," she replies weakly.

"Okay, you'll call me, or okay, you'll drive safely?"

"I'll do both," she says, her voice a touch more confident. We hang up, and suddenly, I'm holding my breath again.

+ + +

The call center is slow, and Reggie lets me leave just before midnight. I race home, hoping not to miss the one call I want to answer. When my phone rings, I'm already holding it with anticipation.

"Middy?"

"Hey Hank." Her breathy voice tells me she's been drinking. The subtle slosh of water lets me know she's in the tub. Suddenly, I realize I didn't think my request through. She's naked on the other end of this conversation, and the thought instantly makes me hard.

"You relaxing, little lady?" This is dangerous territory, but I want her to feel good. I want her to release her worries. She hums through the line. I'm on her speakerphone. "You home alone?" Damn, I want to be there.

"Elston's working. Ronin's at a friend's house. Liam's asleep in his room." I imagine her mind is like a calendar; cataloging places, dates, and events.

"Little lady." I nearly choke as I stretch back, my dick straining in my pants. I'm sprawled out on my bed. "Circle your breast, baby. Cup the weight of it."

"What?!" Her voice cracks as it rises.

"Do as I say," I command, finding control in my voice. I need her to listen to me. *She* needs to listen to me, so I repeat myself. "Touch your breast."

Water sloshes, and I close my eyes, imagining the heaviness. She's tiny, but she has serious tits for a little body.

"Pinch your nipple. Squeeze it, baby." *Ah, fuck.* Unsnapping the catch at the top of my work pants, the crown of my dick busts through the opening with relief. I lower the zipper, moaning into the phone when I hear her breath catch. "Like that, little lady. Do it to the other side, too."

I imagine the massage, the pressure, the tug. Hmm...I bet she feels good. The heel of my palm rubs along the stiff length edging out of my pants.

"Hank." She gulps on my name, and I know she's feeling it, the weightlessness of giving into herself.

"Tickle those fingers down your stomach. Comb through the hair at the top of your legs." I didn't see her, but I know she has a strip down there. I remember the prickly feel of it against my palm as I dipped my fingers into her. Fuck, she was so wet for me. "Go lower, baby."

"Hank, I—"

"Do it," I encourage. My hand slips into my boxers, encircling the engorged mass and tugging fiercely. What would she feel like all wet and slippery over me? The thought curls my hips, forcing more pressure from my fist. "Can I tell you what I'm doing, lady? I'm thinking of you. Wet. Slippery. Sliding down on me."

A gasp escapes and water slaps in her tub. I want to be there. I keep my eyes shut, my head in the vision. I'd fill her little body as she straddles me.

"You touching yourself, baby? Touching where you want me?"

A lingering, breathy, "Yes," reminds me of when we first met, and I'm growing close to exploding. Moisture leaks from my tip, and I use it to lubricate the shaft. I bet she's fucking tight, being so tiny, and I squeeze my dick harder, imagining her riding me.

"Rub, baby. Feel how good it feels. I'm touching you, little lady. I'm slipping into you. Feel me."

"Oh, Hank." She chokes. "My finger—"

"No, *my* finger, little lady. Slip it inside. Feels so good, baby. So good." Fuck, I'm almost there. Just another stroke. Another squeeze. My balls tighten.

"Hank, I'm gonna—"

"Come, baby. Come all over me." She moans through the phone, and I release, making a mess on myself. I throw my head back and let the relief cover my fist. My eyes remain closed. In my head, I imagine her clenching, milking, drawing all my seed into her. I groan. "Ahh, Middy."

She sighs. "I've never done anything like this before."

My eyes fling open focusing on the ceiling instead of the sticky mess on my fingers.

"Never?" I choke, unable to believe she hasn't touched herself before.

"Not like this." Something fierce fills me. My chest swells as I reach for a t-shirt on the floor by my bed. Damn, she makes me feel good.

"Feel better, then?" I tease, knowing there's no way an orgasm didn't distract her for at least a few minutes.

"Good enough I might try it again." Her sultry voice hints at the wine and the satisfaction of an orgasm. What kind of man would I be if I didn't support her suggestion to perform again?

"I just got off myself, listening to you."

"You did?" Her surprised tone makes me chuckle.

"Absolutely, so let's start there." And I talk her through touching herself one more time.

chapter 8

Monday Morning Blues

[Midge]

I fidget as I wait inside the auto restoration office. Even with all the interactions Hank and I have had, I find we still don't know much about each other. I'm assuming he got my number from the hotline. I've learned his work address from Lily at Because Cupcakes. It's Monday morning, and I didn't know what to do with myself, so I came here.

I cleared out my desk on Thursday evening, said a few goodbyes to startled faces, and walked out of the building I'd been going to for the past six years. The job had been a fresh start, like my marriage was supposed to be when we moved to California. But just like my ex-husband's upcoming marriage, I find it's time for me to move on, which brings me to thoughts of Hank.

God, what he did to me. Or rather, what I did to myself with the guidance of his voice. I'm the self-proclaimed poster child of *Yes, indeed, you can get off from the smoky tone of a man.* I giggle with the thought, but nerves hit me as I can see a young man speaking with someone who looks strangely similar to Hank with sharp white hair. His face is peppered with light scruff, contrasting with the starkness of his head as tufts of black fall among the silver on his jaw. He looks in my direction, and I turn my head. Maybe I've made a mistake.

"Hank," I hear shouted through the glass panes and over the sound of machinery. I peer down at myself. I'm dressed for work—heels, skirt, casual shirt—but I had nowhere to go and something I wanted to say in person. Fiddling with the cellophane topped box in my hands, I look down at the confection.

"What the hell?" a voice barks just outside the door, and my heart drops to my stomach. The office door is thrown open, and a big body fills the space.

"Midge?"

"I'm sorry." I don't know why those are the first words out of my mouth. Suddenly, I'm so sorry I'm here, tears prick my eyes. I turn to set the single cupcake box on the desk, determined to leave it, and go.

"Midge, I...what are you doing here?" I spin back to face him, but his eyes avoid mine. He's scrubbing his hair, making the short pieces stand upright as he looks through the office window into the working garage. Two heads turn away the second I follow his glance.

Hank steps over to the blinds and roughly drags a hand down the vinyl slats of the blinds. "Shit."

"I'm sorry," I apologize again. "I'll just go." I step forward, but he steps toward me, holding two grease-covered hands up in my direction.

"No, just...I'm a little surprised."

"Not a good surprise." I shrug, swallowing hard. There would be nothing worse than bursting into waterworks in front of him, so I have to get out of here.

"No, little lady, an amazing surprise." My head shoots up, and his curling lips reward me. I smile slowly in return, memories of the other night seeping into my head. He holds my gaze. "You just caught me off guard." He steps for the desk, reaching around me for a cloth, and begins rubbing his fingers with it. His motions slow as he sees the pink box on the flat surface.

"Did you bring me a cupcake?" His eyes jump to mine.

"I wanted to thank you. For listening to me the other night." He blinks, the removal of grease from his fingers stalled. He stares at me.

"You went to Because Cupcakes?" He peeks to my right. "And got me the double chocolate, chocolate chip with light chocolate, colored purple, frosting cupcake. My favorite."

"Well, Lily said—" I stop short when his eyes hit mine again. The steel-color shimmers with something I can't read.

"Is that how you found me?"

"Are you hiding?" I snap, uncertain where the directness came from.

Shaking his head, he laughs, a deep rumble of a chuckle that jostles his whole body. "Fuck no, I'm not hiding. I just . . . Why didn't you call me to ask me where I am?"

Good question and one I can't exactly answer. One reason being because I wanted to surprise him. Two, because I wasn't sure he'd want to see me. I mean, I did sort of use his voice to get off the other night. When I nearly collapsed after the second time, he talked me into stepping out of the tub and slipping into bed. Too tired to argue, I followed his directions. He wished me a good night, and I fell asleep with his voice echoing in my head. Maybe there's a number three. I'm uncertain if I could use his number. Dating, or whatever we are doing, is new to me.

"I don't know." It's the only honest answer I have.

"You look pretty," he says, and I look down at myself again.

"Old habits die hard. I didn't know what to do with myself today. I guess I need a new job."

"Know anything about cars?" he chuckles.

"Nothing. If my car didn't ding to remind me to fill the gas tank, I'd be at a loss."

"Modern cars." He scoffs, continuing to rub his fingers. I watch the pattern he forms, stroking up one and around the tip, dipping between two, and then curling around another. Strangely sensual, I've focused on his fingers for too long before my eyes lift to find him smiling at me. I swallow from the intensity.

"What do you do here?" I nod toward the closed window. The office is dim with no outside light.

"We restore and maintain classic cars. It was my father's dream, his business. Now Brut, my older brother, owns it, and I work for him." His tone saddens.

"Is this what you've always done?" Something tells me it's not *his* dream.

"No." The abruptness of his answer startles me, and he looks away again. Although I'm curious, his hesitation tells me not to pry. But I want to know things about this man. He finishes rubbing his hands and tosses the rag on the desk behind me. Stepping closer, I back up and bump into the desk at my back.

"You wanted to thank me, huh?" His voice returns to a playful tone. "What did I do to deserve your gratitude?" His lips curl, and those eyes sparkle. He's teasing me. He takes a step forward and my hands brace on the edge of the surface. Another step and I'm gripping the desk, desperate for an anchor or I'm going to launch myself at this man. He smells of oil and man and something spicy, and I want his fragrance on me.

"The other night, you . . ." I can't spell this out. The words jumble in my head. I want to tell him he distracted me in the most pleasant way and thank him for being so kind and supportive.

"The other night I wasn't nearly close enough." His hands cup my cheeks, overwhelming me with the smell of oil until his head dips and he kisses me. I like him kissing me. He takes his time, his mouth savoring the corners and the curves of mine. His tongue follows quickly, and I groan.

With his still lips pressed against mine, he mutters, "I don't want to get your pretty clothes all dirty. Hop up on the desk for me." He leans around me and brushes at the stacks of papers. "Damn, Brut. He's such a slob."

I press up on the desk, his nearness forcing me back. Suddenly, Hank drops to his knees, placing his thick hands on my kneecaps.

"You wearing undies?" His question should shock me, but instead, dampness pools and my thighs tingle. Before I can answer, he demands, "Take them off."

I don't know why I jump when this man says jump, but I'm instantly turned on and so needy for where I hope this goes that I'm ready to ask *how high?* the next time he commands I leap.

I scrunch up my skirt and wiggle down my underwear. Hank takes it from me and brings the scrap of fabric to his nose. The contrast of his dirty fingers around my white panties is a direct shot up my middle. Fireworks explode inside me, and my legs spread of their own volition.

I want him. Solid palms drag up my thighs, separating my legs farther. My hands fall back on the desk. I've never been taken on a desk before, and the possibility thrills me.

His hands tug me forward to balance precariously on the edge of the flat surface.

"I can't put my dirty hands on you."

I whimper at the thought. He's being conscious of the chemicals on his skin and not mixing them with my sensitive parts, but dammit, I almost don't care.

"Other parts could touch me." The boldness I find around this man startles me, but I don't back down. He brings it out in me somehow. Softly, he chuckles.

"The first time I take you isn't gonna be on some damn dirty desk, little lady. That's not the type of woman you are."

While the words are sweet, I'm slightly cross. Why am I not worthy of a desk fuck? The snap of the cupcake package draws my attention away from this thought. I watch as Hank gingerly picks up the delicacy, touching only the wrapping. I'm expecting him to leave me hanging here with my legs spread, my privates pointed at him, and my ego dying a slow, mortifying death. Instead, he dips his head, kissing the inside of my thigh while he balances the cupcake off to my right. His mouth is heaven, sucking at my inner leg and nipping on my skin. The stubble on his jaw tickles like I imagined it might, and the excitement spurs me to spread my legs farther.

"You brought me a cupcake."

He blows on my sex, and I squirm on the desk. Pulling back, he tips the cupcake between my legs. I'm too shocked to wiggle away when the cool icing suddenly coats already slick folds. "So sweet," he says, setting the dessert back on the desk, then gripping my knees and diving back between my thighs.

His mouth hits me with a force which buckles my elbows, and I fall back on the desk. His big tongue flattens, spreading icing over me, but at the same time, he laps and licks, swirling the creamy treat and moaning while he devours me. My eyes roll back at the sight of his head bobbing between my legs. Prickles of light flash before me. I've never experienced anything like this before.

My knees quiver, and his heavy palms steady me. The orgasm races from my toes, rippling up my legs and crashing into me. My knees clench around his ears as my body jackknifes forward. My hand covers the back of his head, holding him to me a second while I fall into the strongest release I've ever had. Seconds later, I collapse back onto the desk. My hands catch me as my legs dangle, limp and languid. I don't trust myself to stand.

Hank pulls back, and I have to laugh. A trace of light purple frosting remains on his chin, mixed with the silver and ink of his scruff.

"You've got something . . ." My voice trails as I reach forward, and he covers my finger with his lips, sucking on it, causing tingles to return. I don't want to be selfish like the other night, though. I came here to thank him.

Hank stands slowly, his knees cracking as he rises from the hard surface beneath them.

"Let me get something to clean you up." He's holding my knees while he speaks, and I curl my fingers into his waistband, tugging him toward me. He questions me as I work his belt. "Midge?"

"Let me return the favor."

"Not here, baby," he mutters. I'm not prone to pouting, but my lower lip protrudes. I don't give up. My fingers quickly unbuckle him and unclasp the hook of his work pants. His fingers dig into my knees, and I know he wants me to continue even though he said otherwise. I have the zipper down and my hand inside his pants, massaging him over his boxers, when my breath hitches.

"Hank. You're huge." I'm not kidding. He's thick, rock solid, and long. Really long. He chuckles at my enthusiasm.

"Well, those are words every man longs to hear." Who would tell him otherwise? A Greek god would have nothing on what I'm cupping. I tug gently before sneaking my fingers over the waistband of his forest green boxer briefs. He's hot, throbbing, and stiff, and my mind flashes to visions of him filling me. His mouth distracts me as he kisses me aggressively, capturing my lips and tugging at them. I'm almost falling backward, but I'm not giving in to the pleasure of his mouth. I push back at his shoulders until he's upright and then I slither to the floor before him.

"Middy?" He chokes, hesitant but eager.

"Where's that cupcake?" I twist for the damaged delicacy, swipe a finger through the icing, and coat his warm dick with the cool treat.

"Fuck," Hank growls, but my focus covers his large crown, sucking at the mushroom shape while sampling the icing running down the length. I release him with a pop and lick along the rigid length, lapping up the sticky sweetness before returning to the tip. There's no way he'll fit, but I'm giving it my best shot to bring him to his knees. I want him to want me like I want him. *So much wanting…*

My jaw tightens as his hand slips into my hair, gentle but firm. One of my hands circles the base of him, squeezing as my other fingers tickle the trail of hair leading to this prize. I'm practically slurping when his hips rock forward.

"Little lady…baby…" He rocks again, hitting the back of my throat. I'm determined not to give up. He's warning me, but I want this from him. "Lady, fuck it." He's pulsing against my tongue, liquid slipping down my throat, and I smile around him. Slowing, I hold him inside my mouth until he mutters, "Enough."

I pull back, releasing him as a dribble falls from my lips. It isn't pretty. However, he's spent, bending over me to hold the desk behind me, and I'm so pleased.

"I don't think I can move," he teases. His soft chuckle thrills me, and I press a kiss to his tip. He hisses. "No more, baby."

Holding out his hand, he helps me stand, and I tug at my skirt that's still riding up my thighs.

Suddenly, Hank releases my hand like I'm scorching him. His demeanor shifts and he won't look at me, despite the faltering smile on my face. I brush my knees to avoid the awkwardness.

"I'll be right back." He's straightening his pants but heads for a door behind the desk.

Hearing water run, I assume it's a bathroom. I realize I can't find my underwear, and instantly, I'm embarrassed by my behavior. *What was I thinking?* I hate how I feel almost ashamed. My heart races, and I mentally say fuck the panties. I'm reaching for my purse when Hank exits the bathroom with a damp cloth in his hands. His eyes shift from my purse to my eyes.

"I thought you might like to wipe off." I'm too humiliated to accept his offering, knowing there's no way I can lift my skirt again in front of this man. I don't even want to go into the bathroom. I just want to walk off my shame and get out of here. I shake my head to ward off his offer.

His shoulders fall, and he tosses the cloth toward the bathroom.

"What happened here?" His voice hardens, and while I'm not afraid of his size, this tone frightens me.

"I came here to thank you. I wasn't expecting anything else. I guess I...I guess I went too far."

With two powerful steps, Hank is before me. He grips my shoulders, forcing me to look up at him. "Why would you say that?"

I shrug. I don't know how to answer him. Something changed. I can't put my finger on it, but he seems displeased. Maybe I sucked, no pun intended.

"I..." I almost apologize, but I'm tired of saying sorry for no reason. I'm not sorry. I just experienced the best oral sex of my life, and I put everything into giving him head. I'm just going to take my memory and leave.

"Cupcake, I don't know where your thoughts are going, but that..."—he points at the desk, disheveled with scattered papers—"was fucking hot as hell. I thought we were good, so why are you about to run off?"

"You don't seem pleased. I didn't mean to take advantage of anything." He laughs, full-on belly rumbling if his rock-hard abs could move. I snap at him, "Don't laugh at me."

Hands cup my cheeks and I'm tugged upward as his head lowers. His mouth crashes against mine again, smothering me with his lips. He's kissing the life out of me, literally. His lips work mine—nipping, sucking, dragging—until I relax under this attention. He pulls back but holds my face, keeping his close.

"I'm not laughing at you. I just told you how fucking hot I thought that was. You, little lady, you're something." He kisses the tip of my nose as he stands to his full height, and I feel only slightly better. "Go out with me."

"On a date?" I choke. Of course, he means a date. What am I saying?

"Yes, a date." He bites the corner of his lip, holding back more laughter. "A real date. Let's get to know one another."

A slow smile cracks my face. "I think we're doing okay."

His silver eyes lose some of their glimmer and I don't know what I've said. "That all you want from me?" His head tips toward the desk, implying what we just did.

My cheeks fall. He looks hurt and my heart pinches. "No," I assure him. "No, absolutely not."

"Okay." He nods, but a bit of playfulness disappears. "How about Friday? I'll pick you up at six thirty?"

chapter 9

Date Night

[Hank]

Midge's house is in the San Gabriel area, which is a far cry from our Pasadena shop even though the burbs are near one another. The two-story, yellow-sided home with a bay window looks like something out of a movie. Its petite size fits Midge, but the sunny color doesn't fool me. Midge is a complicated woman on the verge of a sexual rebirth yet struggling with her confidence. I recognize this because she's exactly like me.

After what we did in Brut's office, we sort of fell apart. My mind caught up with me. Thoughts of Kit clouded my judgment and dulled my immediate reaction to the powerful orgasm this little lady gave me. Images of Kit flipped through my mind—her pleasure in bringing me to my knees, knowing I'd give her whatever she wanted once she got what she wanted from me. The memory momentarily steamrolled the moment with Midge. I needed a minute to get my head straight, and I lost Midge in the meantime.

To make it up to her, I asked her out on a date that's over the top, taking the advice of my twenty-one-year-old nephew. Watershed Rice is one of the fanciest Thai restaurants in the city, and I dress in my old suit, hoping to impress Midge. She isn't some rocker chick; she's a lady. Standing in my office with her fuck-me pumps, a tight red skirt, and an innocent white shirt, she looked like a piece of candy, and I wanted to lick her all over. However, the grease on my hands is a reminder that I'm well *beneath* her league. At one point in my life, I might not have given someone like Midge a thought, but now, she's all I think about. I'm not being a snob; I just mean Midge is too clean for who I once was.

Nerves rattle me as I cross the sidewalk. We talked during the week, and she told me how her boys would be spending spring break with their father in Santa Barbara. She's stressed about finding a new job, and I want to distract her for one night. After knocking on the front door, I swipe my forehead, rolling my shoulders to loosen the tension.

When Midge opens the door, my breath catches. She's another delicacy, draped in black lace, and I want to skip dinner, rip off the dress, and get straight to dessert.

"Hey," she says sweetly, leaning against the door.

"You're fucking beautiful." I blurt the compliment without thought, and she pinks. I want that blush. I want the sweet color all over her body where I can chase the outline. My dick rocks to life. Fuck, I need to calm down. I already whacked off before coming here, hoping it would relieve the pressure, but just the sight of her looking at me like she does, has me wound and ready again.

"Are those for me?" I forgot about the flowers in my hand, another suggestion from my nephew. I never buy flowers. Kit thought they were weak compensation. Her father sent flowers, and she threw them away. Her ex-husband sent them as an apology when he fucked up *again*. Managers, lawyers, and other industry members all sent flowers to congratulate her, but she didn't like the message they lacked. She wanted words.

Standing before me, glowing like night fauna, Midge reaches for the flowers I brought her, draws them to her nose to inhale, and looks up at me under lowered lids. It's sexy as fuck, and I plan to trace her body later with those petals.

"I love wildflowers." Her tone expresses how much she means every word. She gestures for me to enter her house, and I follow her to her kitchen.

"This is a nice place," I say for something to say. I'm not noting any one thing, other than the layout is open, simple, and bright like Midge. The kitchen has a huge island and a large table with seating for six. She fills a vase with water and arranges the flowers in the container before setting it in the center of the table.

"Thank you," she says. Her teeth peek out as she bites the corner of her lip and I'm ready to ask her if we can skip dinner when she suggests, "Should we go?"

+ + +

When we arrive at Watershed Rice, we find there are no seats. Literally. You sit cross-legged on the floor to enjoy your meal. I'm a big guy. I can't sit on the floor like that. I've already unbuttoned my suit, swiped my forehead a thousand times, and shifted in the stiff fabric of my shirt which clings to my skin.

"Are you all right?" Midge asks me as we wait to be seated. A waitress nears the lobby with a tray of unidentifiable, bite-size food.

"I'm good." I pause, redirecting my attention to the hostess. "What was that?" It looks like it still had eyes, antennas, and legs. I don't even listen to her answer as I wipe a hand over my hair.

"Hank?" Midge glances up at me, shifting her gaze worriedly from one eye to the other. Her shoulders fall. "Let's go someplace else."

"No, this is fine. This is good. It's the best place in LA." I sigh. I had to pull strings I didn't like to pull to get my name on the list with only a week's notice.

"Hank," she admonishes. "Please. Let's leave." Her fingers tighten on my suit coat, and I curse myself for ruining the evening before it even starts. Her gaze roams my face. "You're sweating like crazy. Either you're sick or you don't want to be here."

She's right. I don't want to be here, but I want to be with her. Embarrassed, I slip my hand on her lower back and guide her out the door. I don't even know what to say. Apologizing wouldn't be enough. I help her into Brut's SUV and take a deep breath as I round the back of the vehicle.

"Dammit." I slap at the back door in my frustration. Trying to tame my temper, I slowly shut the driver's door, so I don't slam it. We sit in silence as I push the ignition button. I'm not ready to move. "Look, I'm—"

"Tell me something about you. Anything." The gentle command startles me, and I twist toward Midge to find her body turned in my direction. She toys with the hem of her pretty lace dress, and I'm crushed because she didn't get to show it off in the restaurant.

"I never wanted to fix cars." Her eyes shoot up to mine, and she waits for more. "My pop owned Restored Dreams. He thought all those rich dicks...sorry"—I swipe over my hair—"rich and famous types wouldn't know how to care for the expensive toys they owned. He counted on it, and in many ways, he was right."

"What did you want to be?"

"A musician." I don't really want to have this conversation, and I nervously tap the steering wheel. "A drummer, actually."

"That's my Ronin." She smiles with pride. Her kid isn't actually anything like me. He plays percussion in the high school marching band, but that wasn't me. I was the kid with a kit in the back of the garage, banging away to piss off my dad.

"What about you? Did you always work in graphic designs?"

"I did. Back in Chicago, I worked for a large advertising agency until I had the boys. Then I stayed home for a few years. When we moved here, I went back to work. California is expensive."

"Do you miss Chicago?" I ask, recalling how much I loved visiting the Windy City once upon a time.

"Not as much as I first did."

"Why did you move here?"

"Paul, my ex-husband, got a transfer. He thought it would be good for our family. Our marriage." Her eyes drift toward the windshield, and she chews her lip. "Obviously, the marriage didn't survive the move."

"But you did," I say, raising a brow at her. "You've been successful in your own right, with your job and your boys."

"The job I used to have." She scoffs.

"You're just moving on again, that's all. Change is difficult but sometimes necessary."

She stares at me a moment. "Is that why you don't drink?"

"Definitely a necessary change." She pauses, again waiting, but this is not something I want to discuss when I've already ruined our date. "But I don't want you to worry about me. I'm in a better place now. Much better." My eyes scan her body and I shift my shoulders. The suitcoat constricts me.

"Take that off." The sharpness of her tone surprises me, and my head swivels back in her direction.

"Excuse me?"

"You look incredibly uncomfortable. Why are you dressed like this if you aren't happy wearing a suit?" She nods at my attire.

"I'm fine wearing this."

"You are not." She chuckles sarcastically. "You're miserable. You've been sweating all night, which leads me to think you're either too warm or terribly nervous." She stops and blinks in confusion. "Are you nervous?"

I swipe a hand down my face. "I'm not nervous. I'm just—" I don't know what I am. *Fuck it*, I am nervous and overheated. I don't date. I don't know how to do these things, and I twist as I struggle to remove my suitcoat.

"Much better," Midge teases, her brown eyes shimmering lighter.

"Your eyes are so pretty."

"You're pretty," she mutters, her focus on my chest. She leans over the console and loosens my tie enough to slip it from the collar.

"Midge?"

"Getting closer." She unbuttons the top button of my shirt. Then the second button. Her fingers slip into the opening she's created. Her fingertips tickle the coarse hair just under my collarbone. "I like this hint of hair."

I reach for her hand and lift it to my lips, kissing her fingertips. I need a breath. My dick hardens with her touch, and I don't want to wreck what we have going in the front seat. I like her talking to me.

She kicks off her heels, kneels in her seat, and reaches for my wrist. After unbuttoning the cuff, she then rolls back the white material, continuing to fold until the sleeve is short enough to press over my elbow. Stretching over my lap, she does the same thing to my other sleeve.

"You undressing me?" I exhale with a smile. She's so close to me, nearly sitting on my lap. My fingers itch to outline her, and I reach for the neckline of her dress. Dipping my finger inside the lace, I trace over her collarbone. Her eyes flit up to mine, then she leans forward and kisses me. Sweet, gentle, sugary. Even without icing, she's delicious, and I like how she takes her time to savor me. She outlines my lips, drawing them into hers as she sucks on the lower one and nips at the corners.

"I like how you kiss me," I murmur against her lips, taking over, diving in with my tongue. My arms wrap around her, pulling her awkwardly to me in an effort to bring her closer. The console still separates us too much, but our mouths continue to meld together until I'm overheating for a new reason. "Keep this up and we won't be leaving this car."

She purrs in response against my lips, not letting up on the kisses. I like how desperate she is for me, but my dick strains, and my leg twitches. I'm on the verge of breaking, ready to drag her into the back seat and turn this into a teenage thing. I want to do tonight right, though, which involves dinner first. Slowing the pressure to gentle kisses, she whimpers when I retreat.

"I promised you a date." I pull back. "I don't want to imply any other expectations." Her head hangs, but I tip up her chin. Her brows pinch, but I don't want strain there and I kiss the crease.

"I don't need fancy dinners, Hank. I appreciate the gesture, I really do, but not if you're uncomfortable with it." She's misunderstanding me, yet I can't explain. I don't know how to date someone like her.

"I want to be with you." The words tumble forth before I can catch them. It's true, but it sounds desperate. Maybe I am desperate. I want her to like me *for me*; although I can admit, I'm not much of a package. "How about a hamburger?"

A small smile graces her face with the invitation. She slowly sits back, righting her dress. My hand covers her knee, wanting to keep contact with her. Her skin is cool, smooth, and tempting, and my fingers spread, disappearing under the lacy edge.

"You keep that up, and we're headed for the back seat." Her head tilts to the side, and I break into laughter.

"God, little lady. You're something." She softly grunts, twisting in the seat to face the windshield again. I'm not certain she likes the compliment. "Don't you want to be something?"

"One day, I'd like to be somebody's someone." Her voice softens, sadness filling her tone, but wide eyes reveal her surprise at the personal honesty. "Forget I said that out loud. Yes, let's go for a burger. There's a diner near my house that's pretty good."

"A diner." I swallow, my mouth already watering as I ignore the twist in my gut. *Somebody's someone.* I like the sound of that, but I'll admit I don't want her to be someone else's somebody. I want her for me. I'm hungry to know everything about her, but I think we need to eat first.

chapter 10

Diner Dinners

[Midge]

"Tell me about the crisis center. Besides the fact crazy women call in and you try to calm them," I joke although I don't know why I'm laughing. We sit on swivel stools at the counter of the diner, waiting on our hamburgers and fries. The 1950s rock 'n' roll décor of white subway tiles and red Formica countertops projects us back in time.

Hank gulps his water. I ordered a cola. He told me I could have whatever I wanted—the place serves beer—but I declined. I don't want him any more uncomfortable than he already seems.

The signals are so mixed from this man. He's sexual energy in one breath and nerves in another. I want to swing for a home run when I might need to bunt instead, and I need to rein in the growing desire to throw myself at him.

"Not crazy women," he interjects, snapping my thoughts away from how freaking sexy he looks, more relaxed in the rolled-up sleeves. His forearms redefine arm porn, especially with the tattoos. He's so different from me, yet I feel like with him I've met a kindred spirit. Impossible, considering he looks like an aged rock star while I'm wearing lace and carrying a faux leather clutch.

"Desperate women?" I tease although there's no humor in my chuckle.

"Look, we all need help sometimes. Someone to talk to about things. I don't know what made you call, but some things, like birthdays, can be a trigger." The answer is very textbook, but he's not wrong. My birthday triggered a whole slew of disappointments in myself at forty-one. I thought I'd have my body back. I thought I'd be more advanced in my career. I thought I'd still be married.

"I've never done that before," I mutter, crumpling the paper straw wrapper next to my glass.

"So you said. And it's okay. Whether it was one time or two," he teases, and I look up to find a playful gleam in those steel-colored eyes.

"The second time was more selfish." One brow rises as he waits out my answer. "I wanted to talk to you."

His eyes narrow as his smile grows. "I'm honored." For some reason, I think he means it. He's pleased to be a support for someone.

"You like helping people." It's more a question but comes out as a statement. A keen observation.

"I like feeling needed, I guess." He shrugs it off, but I can sense it's not that simple for him.

"Tell me more."

"There was a time I was too selfish. Drinking is a good example, though I had my reasons. I did things for me and only me until I hit the bottom. The only person I had left was me, and I missed...people. Once I turned myself around, I decided I'd try to be there for others even if they were random strangers."

I nod as if I understand. And I think I do. He's had a rough life. The lines by his eyes prove it, but his smile remains young. He's full of spirit even if his heart weighs heavy with guilt.

"Well, I, for one, am thankful you were there for me." I tap my cola glass against his water and drink.

"Really? What did I do for you?"

"You listened. And the second time, you spoke." Heat rushes my cheeks as I remember him talking me into touching myself—*twice*.

"I'll talk to you anytime you need." He winks. "Or listen, if you want that, too."

I appreciate the offer.

"May I ask about the drinking? Was it about a girl?" For some reason, I want to know if he loved someone even though he said he was never married.

73

"It's always about a girl." He exhales, raising his water to his lips. His eyes shift to me, knowing I'm waiting. "The long and short of it is I loved a woman who never loved me. She had big dreams which didn't involve me directly." His voice turns bitter.

"But you weren't married?"

"Fuck no." He snorts. "She wouldn't have me." His voice lowers, sadness and heartbreak filling the normally smoky sound.

"I'm sorry, Hank." I want to touch him, lay my fingers on those solid, colorful forearms and give him some strength, some reassurance. I know what it's like not to have love reciprocated. I thought Paul was the love of my life, but after years of therapy, I realized love isn't one sided. It's not selfish. And it isn't always given back if received.

I gave. Paul took.

Hank shrugs, dragging his finger through the condensation on his water glass. My question has ruined our playful mood. He stares at the ice in the bottom, but then he surprises me. He sets down his glass, places his hand on my knee, and leans in to kiss me. Short, direct, but sweet. He pulls back without saying anything.

Thankfully, our burgers arrive.

"You gonna eat all that?" His lips curl, but the smile doesn't reach his eyes. "You're a little thing." He's trying to get back to where we were, but I'm guessing my questions have caused lingering memories.

"Gotta keep up my girlish figure," I tease, running a hand over the pooch of my belly. My dress isn't snug. I bought it one size larger so it purposely wouldn't pinch me in the wrong places. I also bought it in anticipation of this date—the first new dress I've had in a year. Dating has been difficult since the divorce, and after my first few attempts, I decided I'd just do it later. The boys grieved my separation from Paul, and they needed me. My job demanded more work hours out of me. I didn't have time…for me. Dating became a someday thing on my to-do list.

"I like your girlish figure." Again, he winks before biting into his burger. Hank's sweet. I wish I felt secure enough to think he liked me-

liked me, but I'm just not there yet. Hamburgers feel more like he's placating me, but I'll bite. He's nice to spend time with.

+ + +

Two hours later, we arrive at the awkward how-to-end-the-night moment. I've enjoyed Hank's company, and I appreciate his dry sense of humor. Not to mention, he's nice to look at when he smiles. He told me stories about his brother and the restoration shop. He mentioned Lily, the cupcake bakery owner, who has the hots for Brut, and he explained how Chopper makes Brut a single father.

"One day, he wakes up to a baby and a note on his doorstep. Happy Father's Day, it read. No lie."

I could never imagine giving up my children. Elston, Ronin, and Liam have been my rocks, and I tell Hank more about them. How Elston is obsessed with girls, and I fear he's gone too far too young. How I'm concerned with Ronin's struggles to fit in and find his place. And how Liam, my baby, needs to learn to be his own person, not one of other two because he's in their shadows.

"My boys are a handful, but they are my everything."

Hank nods. He doesn't offer thoughts on children. He already told me he doesn't have any.

Like a gentleman, he walks me to the door. Only I'm not sure what to do here. Do we kiss on the front porch? Do I invite him in?

"Mind if I come in for a bit? You said the boys are at their dad's, right?" I appreciate his remembering and smile with relief that he asked first.

"Please come in." My voice shakes, a bit breathy. I sound anxious, and my eyes close for a second as I will myself to calm down.

"Don't be afraid of me." His tone drops, and my eyes open.

"I'm not frightened." But it's a lie. Hank Paige could break my heart, and I'm scared to death of anything like that happening again.

I lead Hank to the kitchen. This is my comfort spot in the house, a gathering place with a large island and open eating area.

"Got any coffee?"

"I'm embarrassed to admit I don't. I have a coffeemaker, but I don't think I have any beans." I cannot stand the smell, and with Paul gone, I moved the maker to the pantry.

"Never mind. It would just keep me up all night." Hank steps closer to me. "And I can think of other things I'd rather have keep me awake."

"Yeah," I whisper. He stands so close to me, my breasts brush against his dress shirt. With my arousal rising, I'm on the verge of ripping off his clothes. He cups my cheeks with his hands and his lips meet mine. Hank's kisses are meant to get lost in. He kisses slowly but with purpose, not missing any part of my lips before seeking my tongue. There, he takes equal time—spinning, swirling, twirling—and I melt into him.

His hands fall from my face to my hips. He lifts me to perch on the island, and my knees spread, allowing him closer. His fingers touch the lace over my thighs, working it up my legs while his mouth continues to undress me of every anxiety. I like him too much, too quickly, but I'm savoring this moment.

I reach for his shirt with eager fingers, untucking it with haste. He breaks our kiss to reach behind his neck and yanks the shirt off with one pull over his head. It sticks on his arms, but after a quick tug from me, he's shirt free. I moan, and my palms cover the landscape of his body. Firm pecs, a smattering of salt-and-pepper chest hair, and solid abs. A trail leads to the treasure bulging in his pants. He cups my cheeks again and kisses me with more pressure, his mouth growing wilder as my hands rove his body—over the flat of his belly, up the hills of his chest, and around his shoulders, until I squeeze his shoulder blades.

"Fuck, I like your hands." He groans against my mouth. His hands palm my lower back.

"I like your body." I exhale, my voice low as I struggle to speak.

"I'm gonna love your body, little lady," he says, lifting me. "Bedroom."

"Upstairs." Carrying me to the stairway, he sets me down at the base. "This is where we stop. Lead the way if you want to continue."

Taking his hand in mine, I walk backward up a step or two before turning to lead him the rest of the way.

"Thank fuck," he mutters. If my smile grew any bigger, it would crack my face.

My room is average with a queen-size bed. I got rid of the king once Paul left. After repainting the room to a light yellow, I added more throw pillows than necessary to the new bedding. Feminine and delicate, this space is meant for the female head of this household.

"Like pillows?" He chuckles, reaching for one and tossing it to the opposite side of the bed. He sits on the edge, then reaches for my hips, tugging me back to him. With him sitting, we're closer in height, especially with my heels off. I lost them downstairs when I sat on the counter.

"Where was I? Oh, right, this dress." His thick fingers find the zipper at my neck. Spinning me, he unzips the lace material to my waist. He peppers soft kisses up my back, and I shiver, catching the loose material against my front. My body hums with anticipation.

"Time to be wild. Let go," he murmurs between my shoulder blades, and I realize he means for me to remove the dress. My arms slip to my sides, and his hands slide the delicate material from my body. I'm suddenly self-conscious standing in my room with only waist high underwear and a regular bra.

"I don't own anything sexy," I say by way of apology. "It seems impractical when you aren't having sex."

He spins me to face him. "You'd be sexy in a dishrag," he mutters. "Besides, you think I give a fuck about your underwear? I don't plan on you wearing any for what I have in mind." His mouth returns to my skin, traveling just above my breasts. The ache between my thighs increases as a hand cups one heavy globe. I groan when he pinches me over the silk.

"Holy tits, lady." He tugs the cup down and envelopes me with an open mouth, sucking on me like a ripe peach. His tongue circles the sharp peak of my nipple, and I cry out when he nips me. "You're big for a little thing," he says, before trussing up my other breast and working it in the same manner. My hips rock forward, seeking friction despite the attention up top. Nimble fingers skate around my back and unclasp my bra with one snap. Tugging it forward, he teases me as he watches my breasts fall free. "You're so pretty, lady."

I'm clutching his shoulders, my knees weak. Melting before he touches my needy area is a strong possibility. Dragging my palms from his shoulders to his neck, I lower to kiss him again, needing his mouth to assure me we are really doing this. My underwear drifts down my hips, and he taps an ankle for me to step out of them. Our lips don't unlock, and I nearly split in two from sexual overdrive.

"I don't want to disappoint you," I mutter as he pulls back, eyes roving my body. He tilts his head, uncertain of my meaning. "You know, hot dog in a hallway and all that." I snort. Literally. *Could I be any more awkward with poor movie quotes and a nasal noise?*

"What the fuck are you talking about?" His steel eyes blink.

"I don't think I'll be all tight and neat down there." My awkwardness grows with each flap of my lips. I mean, every romance novel has the girls all fit and trim, but that's hardly me. I've had babies.

"What the fuck?" Suddenly, he grips my hips and tips me toward the bed until I land on my back. Perching on his side beside me, he trails his fingers between my breasts and down to the hair at the apex of my legs. *So close*, I think, as he drags back up my middle. "What the hell you talkin' about, little lady?"

"I'm just not young. I'm probably stretched out, and—"

"Stop talking," he interrupts, and I clamp my lips shut. Reaching for my hand, he yanks it to cover the bulge in his pants. "Feel this?"

I nod.

"He'll fill you just fine, baby. Relax." I take a deep breath, and tears prickle my eyes. He's still partially dressed, and the hand on his excitement lifts for his belt.

"You first," he says, trailing tickling fingertips down my skin.

"I want to feel you." The boldness surprises me, but I want to touch him while he pleases me.

"Oh, you're gonna feel me." He stands, strips, and returns to his side next to me. Deft fingers find their way and gently impale me. I arch off the bed, relishing the intrusion.

"So wet, baby. Your body wants me."

"So badly," I whimper.

"Soon, lady." He chuckles against my neck, sucking my skin while his fingers work their magic—dipping, digging, dragging out an orgasm so fierce I drown in the length of it. Awash in sensation, my knees come together, drifting in a weightless haze. I'm gripping the sheets as Hank climbs over me.

"Condoms?" His asking almost brings another snort. Another unnecessary supply when not engaging in sexual promiscuity. I shake my head, and he slips back, finds his pants on the floor, and returns fully sheathed.

Lining up his solid length at my entrance, he watches as he slowly disappears inside me, taking his time to fill me as I stretch around him, welcoming him into me. Tears escape the corners of my eyes. I'm not sure I've ever felt anything like this. So full. So free. Hank pulls back, almost exiting me before thrusting forward again. My eyes roll back and more tears leak.

"You okay, baby?" I can't respond, so I nod. He pauses, peering down at me as he balances most of his weight on his strong elbows. A thumb swipes at the corner of one eye.

"You must think I'm so inexperienced." Now isn't the time to share our sexual histories, but it's evident by the dance his body plays over mine that he knows more than I do.

"Not going there right now," he commands. "I think you weren't loved properly, and I'm gonna love this body." He rests on one elbow as his other hand hooks under my leg, stretching me, opening me to him.

"Let go of the bed sheets, little lady," he demands. "Touch me."

I'm still white knuckling the sheets at my sides as he slides forward again, the penetration reaching deep. "I'm afraid to let go. I might float away." I'm not certain all the words leave my mouth as I'm having an out-of-body experience, like I'm watching him fill me. The euphoric feeling makes me light-headed.

He chuckles, jostling us both, his dick pulsing inside me. "Hold on to me, baby. I'll keep you grounded."

I release the bedclothes and clap a hand to his shoulder blade. The other finds his ass, one firm globe of perfection, and I squeeze.

"Baby," he encourages my touch, rocking harder as I smooth over the fineness of his backside.

The bed begins to squeak as he thrusts faster, penetrating deeper, teasing another orgasm out of me. As my head comes off the bed, I scream into his shoulder, tears spilling, and hold him like I might fall off a cliff if I let go.

"Fuck, yeah, little lady," he quips through strained breaths as he rocks harder. His pumps quickening before he stills. His neck muscles bulge as he pulses inside me, and his strain pleases me. An aftershock sends ripples vibrating through my body. Hank collapses, rolling us to our sides but still buried inside me.

"My sausage do okay in your hallway?" he jests. "Got the reference now. *We're the Millers*." He winks.

I gasp before I chuckle. "Did you just make a joke?" My giggling jiggles him inside me, and he pulses once again.

"I just want you to stop crying," he whispers. He's so close to my face, still hard inside me.

"I'm not sad. I'm not hurt," I reassure him. "Just...I can't describe it. I'm overwhelmed fits the best."

"No, I fit the best," he teases, pressing a kiss to my shoulder before pulling out completely.

Yes, you do, I think. *You fit the best.*

chapter 11

Night Sweats

[Hank]

We go at it again after a brief reprieve. This woman needs some taking care of. Rest. Repeat. Finally, we only rest, tangling with one another. I'm a sound sleeper especially on my back, and she sprawls over me. I want to tuck her into a ball and hold her to my chest, but I also like the feel of her blanketing me, draped over my heartbeat.

Suddenly, she stirs, shaking me.

"Hank, someone's here." When I come to full consciousness, it takes me a second to remember where I am and how we got here. I warn my brain not to think of Kit, but it can't stop itself. Kit and I never had sex at her place. All her secrets were hidden there, and she never planned to share them with me just as she never shared her heart.

"Hank, I think someone's here," she repeats.

"Breaking in?" I'm groggy, but I'm slowly detecting the whispered panic in her voice.

"No, as in one of my boys." It takes me a second to register she means one of her kids and not a collection of men waiting for a turn with her. I bristle at the thought of others touching this sweetness. Pressing over me, Midge pushes off the bed and grabs a robe from her bathroom.

I hear her patter down the stairs and wonder what I'm supposed to do. I'm sprawled out, naked as the day I was born, on her bed, so I decide to dress. The only problem is my shirt is still downstairs. Her kid meeting me like this would be super awkward, but seeing as I plan to meet her kids, I slowly tiptoe down the steps.

"Elston, what are you doing here?" Midge asks her oldest son.

"Dad and I had a fight. I don't want to stay on the boat with him." Midge told me earlier how her husband decided he didn't want to be a husband one day and went to live on a friend's boat for a bit. The bit turned permanent, and the boys visit him there.

"Does Dad know you're here?" I don't hear a response from her son, but she adds, "I'm not getting involved. You need to call him. Let him know where you are and that you're safe." I didn't have a mother I remember, so the sound of Midge's concerned tone pinches my chest. I don't have a child to worry about like she does, and that wrenches the pressure tighter.

"I'm not talking to him," Midge stresses, but suddenly, she speaks cheerfully. "Yes, Paul, he came home." *Pause.* "No, I'm not getting into this with you. I'll talk to him and talk to you tomorrow." *Pause.*

Her son snorts, and it sounds strangely like the noise she made earlier tonight. I shake my head at her thought process. *Where did she come up with the hot dog in a hallway thing?*

"Good night, Paul. I'm hanging up now," she says, and I suddenly have an idea of where her insecurities come from.

"What happened?" she redirects, her voice lowering, and I feel guilty for eavesdropping.

"He thinks I'm seven instead of seventeen. Everything is football even though the season is over. USC this and USC that. He hates how I want to go to Illinois."

Silence follows, and a stool scrapes the wood floor. I picture the layout of her kitchen in my head.

"Honey, you need to talk to him. Work this out *with him.*"

"Why? You didn't."

"Elston!" His name mixed with a sharp intake of breath makes me not care for this kid, and he's about to meet me, like it or not. I creep down to the bottom step when he continues.

"That's not what I mean. I just mean, you eventually let him go, so why can't I?"

"Sweetheart, it's different. He's your dad. He was beyond loving me, but he'll never give up on loving you."

Silence follows. A stool scrapes again. "Head to bed, honey. Get some sleep."

This is my cue to crawl back up the stairs like a dirty little secret, especially if the kid comes upstairs first.

"Hey, who's shirt is this?"

Shit.

"Oh, that's where that went," Midge says, her voice too high. "I was trying it on and set it on the stool. It must have slipped to the floor."

"This is a guy's shirt." Silence.

"New fashion statement. Get some sleep, babe."

"Mom?" her son questions. "You're turning pink." I want to smile until I hear her response.

"It's nothing, honey. Now, get to bed."

And that's exactly where I return, feeling like what she said—nothing.

Sitting on the edge of her bed with my elbows on my knees, I wait for her. Old feelings, having nothing to do with her, return like a blow to the head. She turns the corner, enters her room, and closes the door.

"You're dressed," she whispers.

"You have my shirt." The observation is snappy and sharp. She dangles my dress shirt from her finger by the collar, like it's trash, like I am. I reach forward and rip it from her, hastily shrugging it over my head as it remains buttoned.

"Hank?"

"Time for me to go, right, cupcake?"

"Hank, this is so awkward." She steps toward me, but I stand, towering over her. "I'm sorry about Elston. He isn't supposed to be here."

"Did he go to his room?"

"Yes."

"Then I'll let myself out." My tone chills the air between us. I don't reach for her. My fists curl into balls at my side.

"Why are you being like this? What did I do?" Her shrill voice cracks with strain, but the sound remains quiet enough not to give away that a man is in her house. However, Brut's SUV is parked outside. There's no way the kid isn't putting two and two together. And I'm suddenly not feeling considerate.

"Can't do something to *nothing*." Fuck being somebody's someone. It never works that way. She blinks, her eyes going wide and glowing like they did in the candlelight long ago. I'll add it to the memories of women I need to forget.

"Hank?" She still doesn't get it, but she doesn't need to. I'm lost in my head because getting kicked to the curb is all too familiar for me. Sweat dots my brow. A distant need for a drink creeps through my bloodstream. Clutching the robe closed over her chest, she steps forward. She's too close. "I don't want you to go. Not like this."

"This is the way it rolls." I lie, my chest clenching. I step around her and leave while making as much noise as possible.

+ + +

We work Sundays. The garage is our church. Plus, it works best for our customers. I'm elbow deep in grease with my arms shoved under an engine when Chopper calls my name.

"Hank! Yo, a woman's here to see ya."

What the fuck?

My first hope is Midge, but I can't see her. I'm still too raw after the other night. I mean, I came like I've never come before, that I remember. I saw stars. My toes curled. But the sad thought is I can't remember most orgasms I've had with a woman. Were they all as incredible as I thought with Kit? Or did I just build her up to be something, someone?

Midge's voice filters through my brain. *I want to be somebody's someone.*

Me too, I think.

Midge made me feel this way for a few minutes. *She* had this effect on me. I don't fault her kid for coming home—I recognize she couldn't help it—but I am disappointed. However, being in her bed wouldn't have been the best way to meet her teen. Midge is a lady, not some hussy taking guys to her bed with her kid in the next room. She's good, and clean, and smells sweet—not smoky, and musty, and used like rock chicks can be. Like Kit could be. I realize leaving was all on me. I overthought, and I sigh as Chopper calls my name again.

"I'm coming," I bellow, the double entendre not lost on me. My head screamed it while I filled a condom. Midge did that to me. My heart races as I'm suddenly hoping Midge is here to see me.

I cross into the lobby and stop short.

"Stephie?"

"Hey Hanky. Haven't seen you around for a while. Then we crossed paths at the party. Thought I'd track you down. See if you were up for a hit."

Shit. I don't need this kind of thing here. Her here. Why can't history leave me alone lately? "I don't do that anymore." I scrub at my scalp, forgetting about the oil on my fingers. Stephie's nose scrunches as she takes in my dirty hands.

"Just one little hit. I'm good for it." She steps closer, and my life flashes before me. Kit. Her needs. Her way of getting me to do things.

"I'm not on that path anymore." My hands shake.

Her face pinches again, but she reaches for my belt, curling her fingers inside the waist.

"Hanky, please," she purrs. Her pouty lips are too red. Her eyelids layered in bright blue powder. I can't even describe what she's wearing because it hardly covers anything. Did I fall for this before? Did I fuck Stephie when she wanted drugs from me? When I had drugs in me? I tremble with the thought or, rather, lack of memory. *Maybe?*

"Look, I'm sorry. I'm not into that anymore. I can't even tell you who is." This goes against my training. I should be helping her like I'd help some kid at the center, but Stephie is too close to me, to my history. Some people I can't help. It took me a long time to realize that—in both others and myself.

"Not you, too?" she whines. "Look at Tommy. Now, you. Denton will be next. What happened to all of you?"

Mentioning our old bandmate, who refuses to speak to either of us, stabs my gut.

"Life," Brut says from behind me. "Get your own." He scowls at the washed-up, needy groupie, desperate for old times. Brut's eerie eyes linger. He's stronger than I am in so many ways, and his voice projects his strength at the moment.

"Get out of my garage," he demands, and I relax a little. My big brother. Always fighting battles for me.

"And who are you, handsome?" she trills, turning her wasted seductive sound on Brut.

"No one you need to know. Now leave."

The bell to the front door pings. Stephie turns to see who the next witness to this dog and pony show will be, and then swivels back to me. Her expression hardens as if a thought occurs to her, and she spins for the woman behind her.

"I know you," she meows, swaying her hips as she sashays toward Midge, who holds a Styrofoam cup. "You did him in the bathroom. How'd you get to him to score? Blow job?"

Fucking bitch. Midge's eyes open so wide, I'm positive they'll pop out. Brut hustles around me and grips Stephie's arm then drags her to the door.

"All right, that's enough. I see you again, and you're leaving in cuffs." He pushes the door with one hand while he yanks Stephie toward the lot. Midge silently stands to the side and stares after them through the front glass.

"Midge?" I choke, afraid to look at her, yet knowing I'll crumple if she doesn't look away from the scene outside.

Her voice shakes as she speaks. "I thought I'd bring you the coffee I owed you the other night. But I see that you're busy."

Forget Stephie.

Forget Kit.

Midge is the one who will break me.

chapter 12
Sunday Morning Lessons

[Midge]

I stare at the woman wearing a cheetah print top and a leather miniskirt hiding nothing of her thin body. She can pull off the look, but her makeup hardly covers the years on her face. Her hair is an overheated example of too much product and evidence of her age—dry with brittle split ends. I'm not into body shaming. If she thinks she looks good, who am I to speak, but it's sad to me. Then again, who am I? I'm standing here in a red cardigan with matching flats and ripped jeans. My hair is twisted in a messy blob at the back of my head. I was hoping for the not trying too hard look. My white tank billows instead of hugs my body, covering the slight bulge of bearing children that will never disappear. My ensemble reminds me of the arguments I had with myself after Hank left. He doesn't want me. I scream mom bod compared to the woman outside, and my heart sinks.

"Previous fan of yours," I tease with more heartbreak than humor. How could she not admire Hank? I do, or I thought I did. I step back as his brother re-enters the office.

"Do you know who I am?" Hank interjects, interrupting my observation of the woman, and the sick sensation she might have carnal knowledge of him. Why would she not? He's a striking man. I have no idea what he refers to with his question, but his shaky tone shifts my eyes quickly to him and then away.

"I thought so, but now, I'm not so sure." My eyes remain on the woman outside, dust kicking up as she stomps her feet to a rusty old vehicle.

"Big mystery man." Brut coughs, mockingly.

"Why are you here?" Hank snaps at him, and I turn at the rough sound. Negative energy brews between them.

"Hey, I just saved your ass," Brut barks, stepping into his brother's space. They're equal in height, though Hank has some pounds on his brother. Solid pounds, I recall, remembering Hank moving over me. My stomach flips at my stupidity.

"Shut up," Hank quips, and I flinch at the sharpness of his voice. While the two quarrel like I've seen brothers do, I zone out a moment. I stare down at the hot coffee I hold in my hands, thinking it would be a sweet gesture of apology for Elston's interruption the other night. I cried after Hank left, not certain what happened but knowing Elston's return ruined it. Maybe his appearance reminded Hank I have kids, and he doesn't want that baggage. I argued with myself over this concept a million times through the night, coming to the realization that a man who can't handle my kids can't handle me. We are a package deal. A gift, actually. I thought Hank would be accepting of it. At least, I hoped he would.

The phone starts ringing as I awkwardly stand in the waiting room of sorts. I'm a little surprised it's still a landline. It's excessively loud, adding to the noise of the drills in the background and the temper of Hank and his brother. It's trilling on and on and on while these two sling accusations at each other that I don't understand.

"Maybe...um...hello...the phone?" I try to interrupt. The organizer in me itches for someone to answer the damn thing.

Finally, I step around the generic, high counter cubicle desk and grab the handset.

"Restored Dreams, may I help you?"

"Who the hell are you?" snaps a surly older male voice.

"This is Midge. How can I help you?" I have no idea how I'll help, but at least the phone stopped ringing, and the argument seems to quiet.

"Your voice is certainly more pleasant than the last girl," the customer retorts, coughing after the comment.

"Thank you, sir. Your voice is pleasant, too," I lie. "Now, what can we do for you?" My eyes flick up to find Hank still clenching his fists, glaring at me, but his brother has stepped toward the counter, resting his arms on the surface as he watches me.

"Where's that worthless Brut?"

"He's busy at the moment, but I can take a message. Tell me what you need." I hold Brut's blue-gray eyes for a moment before looking for a pen and some paper on the mess of a desk.

"He's holding my baby hostage."

"Excuse me?" My head shoots back up, and I stare at Brut. He's really good looking with his snow-white hair, soft blue eyes, and the same matching edge to his face as Hank.

"My maroon 1960 Bentley S2. Lucy."

"You named your car?" I squeak as I swivel in the chair I took, searching through a window into the garage to see a large dusty red vehicle in the back of the shop. "Looks like you rode her a little too hard, sir."

The older gentleman chuckles. "That I did, girl. She back together yet?"

"Doesn't look like it, sir. When were you expecting her?" I turn back to Brut, ignoring the negative vibe humming from Hank.

"Yesterday."

"Now, Mister..." I'm sorry, I didn't catch your name."

"Mr. Pendelton."

"Mr. Pendelton." My brows shoot up as I hold Brut's gaze. I swallow, recognizing the name of the account I was scheduled to work on—one of the biggest accounts Bigle Marketing hoped to obtain. "As yesterday is no longer an option, when's the next best time?" I'm searching the desk for an invoice or a system of bookings.

"Today."

I stop searching. "Now, sir. I sense you want her perfect. That doesn't happen in one day."

He chuckles. "I like you."

"Thank you." My cheeks flush.

"What did that fucker say?" Hank hisses, stepping toward the counter, but I shake my head, finding two wide-eyed men staring at me. "Mr. Pendelton, can I ask you something not related to your car?" He hesitates, but I plow forward. A determination fills me as I need sudden purpose. "I recently worked for Bigle Marketing, and I'm just curious what you thought of your last campaign."

"I don't see how that would be any of your business." His tone tightens, and Brut waves two hands at me. "I noticed you said *worked*. Did they fire you?" He coughs again.

"I left. It was no longer an opportunity for me." The thought settles hard in my chest. I liked Bigle Marketing once upon a time, but I remember what Hank said. Time to move on.

"Sir, let me rephrase. If I can guarantee you your Bentley in . . ."— I look at Brut to confirm—"two weeks." I drag out the words, holding Brut's gaze for direction. He gives me a thumbs-up. "Then you give me a shot to pitch you a better marketing campaign than Bigle."

He chortles. "Not much of a deal, girl."

"You're right. It's a win-win for you. You get your car and a new branding campaign. And if you don't like the campaign, you still get your car in two weeks."

Brut smacks the top of the cubicle counter as he leans back, smiling broadly at me. Hank's lips twist, fighting the curl, but his eyes gleam steely gray.

"You drive a hard bargain, but it's a deal."

"Two weeks, sir?"

"Two weeks," he barks, and the line goes dead. I hang up and reach a hand up to Brut.

"Midge Everette. Sorry I answered your phone. You have two weeks to get Pendelton his Bentley so I can get a new job."

Brut laughs as he shakes my hand. He has a nice smile. I see why Lily might be attracted to him. His hand is warm and firm like Hank's, but it's not as thick—not the hand I want on me.

"Work here," Brut offers.

"What?" Hank huffs, and I have to agree.

"I know nothing about cars." I giggle to cover the hurt that Hank wouldn't want me here.

"You don't need to. We need organization and determination like yours." Brut points at the phone. Hank grunts again, and once again, I agree. Old scheduling books and piles of paper sporting coffee stains line the desk. There's a mug which looks like it's been here a while.

"I could use the money, but you can't afford me."

"In two weeks, you'll have another job with a sales pitch like that. Work here to tide you over," he encourages. Hank glares at his brother, boring a hole in his head.

"I don't think so but thank you." My voice lowers, and now Hank glares at me.

Brut continues. "Just take the job. Please. We could use you, and everyone could use a little extra money. Ask Hank, he knows all about that."

"Fuck off," Hank warns.

"Besides, you pretty up the place." Brut winks, and Hank shoves him, forcing Brut to slip from his balance against the counter.

"You're asking for it if you start sweet-talking my lady."

The growling voice surprises both Brut and me. My brows rise nearly to my hairline while Brut's forehead wrinkles. He turns to me and then back to Hank. A long whistle follows.

"If she's your lady, you better fix things, or I'm in line to take her from you."

Hank punches his brother's arm like I've seen my boys do, only I imagine it hurts a bit more than the sting my kids produce.

Brut rubs his upper arm, laughing at his younger sibling before turning to me. He winks. "I'll be waiting for you, sugar, when he messes this one up."

+ + +

Brut leaves the room, and the rough voice of Hank startles me.

"Could I speak with you?" He tips his head toward the office to the side of the waiting room we've been in, and I stand to follow him. Suddenly, I feel like last woman walking. I remind myself why I'm here—apology and answers—no matter what the result may be.

Hank enters the office and slumps onto the old leather couch, looking indifferent as he glances away from me. He sweeps a hand at the cushion next to him, and I assume it's an offer to sit beside him, but as he rests his large arm on the back of the couch, I decide against sitting. My escape will be easier, if I'm already on my feet. I don't know why I'm torturing myself, but I need answers.

"I think I misunderstood the other night. I mean, you asked me out on a date." I swallow, blinking rapidly. If I cry, I've sealed my fate. Paul hated when I cried. Most men do, right? But I'm emotional today. "But maybe I misinterpreted...everything. And I just need you to tell it to me straight." I'm unprepared to handle his rejection, but I'll take whatever he has to say.

"Was the other night a one-night stand? Because I've never had one, even when I was single some eighteen years ago. And I just thought...I guess I—" I don't finish because Hank suddenly crowds my space, cupping my cheeks. The overwhelming stench of gasoline coming off his fingers permeates the air around us.

"I just need to know if—" I'm swallowing back the lump in my throat when his mouth covers mine. Tender. Sweet. Taking his time. Hank kisses me as if I'm worth the wait. As if I'm an exploration and he's going to savor every step he takes, memorizing each detail. I'm backed into the desk, but there's no hint we'll go where we went before. This is just a kiss.

Drawing back, Hank strokes my cheeks with his thumbs. "I'm making you all dirty." The comment hints of innuendo.

"I seem to be back at this desk." I shakily pat the edge, which I've been gripping to hold myself steady. "Maybe I want to get dirty with you."

"Don't say things like that." He chuckles, eying the desk before peering down at me. "This desk is worse than my fingers, and I've got a Bentley to repair so my lady gets a job."

I smile, liking the reference to being his.

"I don't want to pressure you. This place is a hot mess, but if you need the money, take the job from Brut."

"I'm fine." I dismiss the offer with a wave. I don't want some kind of pity job, but I can already see myself getting antsy just sitting around my house. Some days, I dream of returning to my stay-at-home mom days. But then I realize there are no kids at home, only mom. I wallowed in a week of vacation-mode bliss, but slowly, panic creeps in at the thought of keeping up private school tuition and Elston's impending college. I'm too young to retire, especially since I don't have the means.

"Don't lie to me." Hank huffs. "I see the wheels spinning. You're a worrier by nature. We aren't hardcore. You can search for jobs here while answering a phone call or two. Besides, after the way you handled Pendelton, Brut may never let you leave."

I laugh, lowering my head to Hank's chest. "I'm sorry about that. It's just…you two were fighting, and the phone was so loud. I had to do something."

Hank kisses the top of my head, lingering for a moment against mine. "I can't work here if you don't want me. I mean, want me *to*. I've already made things so awkward."

Hank lifts my head, forcing me to look at him. "My fault, little lady. I got lost in my head after your kid came in."

"I'm sorry. He wasn't supposed to be there. No one is home but me all week." I sigh, biting my lip to keep from telling him I want him to come back and stay the night. I want a repeat.

"It's not his fault either. He just wanted his mom. Everything okay today?"

I appreciate Hank asking. It warms me to think Elston still needs me at seventeen. However, my son's fight with his father is more about his dad than me.

"Long story but thank you. He went back to Paul's today." Hank nods and silence slips between us. I can't hold back. "You said you got in your head. How? What happened?"

Hank's hands lower, but I reach for his wrists, holding him in place. I want him touching me when he tells me things. When I see his eyes hesitate and his forehead wrinkling, I sense any admission is going to be difficult.

"The woman I mentioned…she didn't always have time for me. She called me when she needed something, and the fool that I was, I jumped when she offered a high. She reeled me in, and I took the bait, only to be kicked to the curb when she was finished with me."

Hank looks away from me. I would touch his chin to force his gaze back to me, but I'm afraid to release his wrists. I hold my tongue and wait.

"She wasn't a bad person, just needy. Only she didn't need me. I didn't like how that made me feel, and the other night just—"

I gasp. "Hank, I'm so sorry. I never meant for you to feel that way."

His mouth presses mine with a quick kiss like the one from our date. "It wasn't you. It was me." He softens, lowering his eyes. "It was her."

My heart breaks. He loved this woman, and she never loved him. Or maybe, she loved him in her own way, but he couldn't see it. Either way, I'm sorry for him.

Love is so complicated.

"She was embarrassed of me."

"No, Hank. No," I stammer in shock. I don't believe a woman who calls him repeatedly is ashamed of him. But another thought occurs to me.

"Is she still around?" Oh, God. Does this mean if she called him tonight, he'd go to her? Was that woman—the one in the miniskirt and cheetah print—her?

"She's dead." Just when I thought I couldn't feel any sicker, my heart falls to my feet, leaving me empty inside.

"Hank, I'm so—"

"Don't say sorry. Please." He breaks my hold on his wrists, severing our connection. "I'm sorry she's dead, too. I am, but I'm not sorry we are over. It had to end. She . . ." He pauses.

He won't bring himself to share this with me, so I speak instead. "I wasn't embarrassed. Humiliated that my son caught me after having sex with a man not his father? Yes. But not ashamed." I bend to lower my head under his, forcing him to look at me. "Not ashamed, Hank. Please, don't ruin it for me. The other night meant too much to me." I take a deep breath, risking more of myself. "I'm upset, too. I know it wasn't Elston's fault directly, but I feel like he ruined something. But I have to say, Hank, if you can't handle my children, then you can't handle me. We come as one package."

His head shoots up, and I pull back, startled by his sudden movement. His hands grip my cheeks again.

"You are a gift, Middy. Wrapped up so pretty in these tight ass jeans where I can see your knees, and I just want to kiss you everywhere." My face heats. "I ruined the night. Me. Let me make it up to you."

Laying me out on this desk might be a start, but I don't say that. Hank tips his head.

"Does your son know anything about me?" Curiosity and hope line his face, but I don't want to tell him the lie I told Elston. After Hank left, making enough noise to wake the neighbors, Elston came to my room, inquiring about the slamming sound.

"I dropped something," I told him, but as long as he was in my room, a question left my lips. "Can I ask you something? What would you think of me dating?"

"Cool." He turned back for his room. Conversation over.

"I think I have his permission to date." I pause. *Do I need my kid's permission?* The answer comes quickly. In reality, I don't—I'm the adult. But I want his approval; I want all my boys' approval. Paul's already done enough damage, though Lord knows, they'll blame most things on me. "What should I tell my son about you?"

"You tell your son you're dating, little lady. Dating only me." The possessive command warms my insides. Looking down at the mechanic overalls covering his big body, my palms roam the length of his chest.

"I should have kept your shirt. I wanted to wear it."

"Want to see you wearing my things, Middy."

My gaze jumps back to his eyes. The cold steel color is restored to silvery heat as he looks at me.

"Then how about dinner tonight at my place?"

chapter 13

Spoiled Dinner

[Midge]

I'm nervous. I'm not a great cook, and it's been a long time since I've cooked to impress anyone, so this already spells disaster. My house specialty is spaghetti, but that's not a second date meal—slurping up pasta or splattering tomato sauce. With my luck, dinner would end up on my boobs.

With Hank being a bigger man, I settle on steak. The late March weather in California is pleasant enough for the Midwestern bones of my body to step outside and grill. I still laugh when people call sixty degrees cold. Zero is cold. Sixty is short's weather, but I acclimated to the West Coast pretty quickly as I love warmer temperatures. I miss the Midwest at the holidays, but we go back each Christmas. I wasn't aware Elston missed it so much.

Thoughts of him fill my mind as I fork the potatoes for baking. He'd been ten, almost eleven when we left Illinois. *He'll adapt; kids do*, my former mother-in-law told me. He did adapt, into what Paul wanted—a high school football star. The pressure on Elston from his father remains intense despite not living with him. Paul doesn't miss a practice, a game, a meeting. He hovers, and he's choking our son. We've talked about this, but Paul doesn't like to listen to me.

"Let him make his own mistakes."

"He's a kid. I want to help him," Paul argues.

"Love him then, don't smother him."

"I'm not smothering. I'm guiding."

The argument remains the same for Liam, our budding baseball athlete. However, for Ronin, Paul takes a passive seat. He attends what he can, claiming attendance at the football games counts for Ronin as he's in the band on the sidelines. Unfortunately, Paul often misses halftimes, trying to weasel his way into discussions with Elston. Thankfully, the varsity coach doesn't allow this as much as the junior varsity coach let it slide. This reminds me Ronin has a play in two weeks. He earned the role of Marius, one of the rebels in the French Revolution for *Les Misérables*. I wonder if Paul will attend. *Maybe I should ask Hank?*

I didn't realize I was stabbing the potato enough to almost make it a sifter. Wrapping it in tinfoil, I set it aside as I reach for my wine. I don't know if I can drink in front of Hank. He assured me he was fine the other night, but this is new for me. I don't want to cross a line or be insensitive, but I need this glass to calm my nerves. We still have things to discuss. What he told me about the other woman in his life rattled me, especially since she's dead. Seeing the woman outside his business worries me that his former lover was mixed up in drugs or something, and it's a heavy burden to carry. I want tonight to be easy, comfortable, and relaxed, even though I'm not feeling any of those things.

The doorbell rings, and I almost spill the wine as I set my glass back on the counter. Opening the door, I find another handful of flowers. The arrangement he brought me the other night was beautiful, and this one nearly matches it.

"These are lovely," I say, stepping back to let him in.

"So are you." He steps forward and kisses me. Pressed into my front door, I'm ready to forget dinner and eat him right here. His mouth moves over mine, and my knees shake. Without thinking, I reach for his belt, tugging him to me. Hank groans, the vibration rumbling over my lips, and I press against him. We don't physically align when we stand together, but like a magnet, my body is attracted to the right places on him. I'll get there with squirming and climbing if I need to.

He chuckles. "Eager?" The word whispers into my throat.

"Yes." The breathy response surprises me. More startling, Hank drops the flowers and hikes me up his body. My legs wrap around his waist, and we continue to make out against the open front door. A horn honks from a car racing down the street, and I break away. "Cripes. The neighbors." I laugh although the honking horn could have been for any number of reasons.

"Yes, what would the neighbors say?" Hank mocks with a touch of sarcasm. "And did you just say *cripes*?" I'm not embarrassed by him as he said this morning, but I also don't need my neighbors knowing my business. He settles me back on my feet, and my knees buckle. "Easy there, lady. You been drinkin'?"

Shit. I have, but it's not why I almost fell over. It's Hank. I'm drunk on him.

"Yes," I admit. "But I'm okay." He eyes me suspiciously. "One glass. Not even."

After gathering up my newest bouquet, he follows me into my kitchen where I find another vase for the new flowers and mention my menu.

"I'm warning you already. I'm not a cook. I don't know why I asked you over for dinner." Hank's eyes widen, his brow crinkling his forehead. Holding up my hands, I clarify, "No, I mean, I hope it's edible."

I pick up the plate with the steaks and foil wrapped potatoes while Hank grabs my wine glass and follows me to the back patio. A variety of white candles surround a small glass pitcher where I placed a few flowers from my first arrangement. The flames flicker in the early evening breeze. A multi-colored tablecloth covers the typically uncovered wrought iron table. I was going for an eclectic-seductive look, if that's even possible. I point at a seat for Hank and then reach for the grill to check the heat for the steaks. Setting the meat and potatoes on the grate, Hank asks me to explain who Pendelton is to me.

"Pendelton Wares is a boutique housewares company, and the account I wanted before I quit Bigle Marketing." I sense Hank's confusion in his stare, so I try again. "Think Burberry meets Magnolia Farms." He's still staring. "You have no idea what I'm talking about."

"Oh, were you speaking? I was too busy watching your mouth to listen."

Okay then. Turning the steaks, pleased with the grill marks, I smile to myself, and try again to explain the dishes and home décor Pendelton sells.

"Their problem is the old man. He needs to join the twenty-first century and move their collections online. Retail stores or catalogues alone won't sell his products. Not to mention, he could use a few updates to his offerings."

Hank motions to the seat across from him and pushes my wine glass toward me.

"Why is he so important to you?"

"I just think if I had had the chance to share my ideas with him, we would have landed the account. I would have proved myself to Katrina, my boss. And maybe proved something to myself."

Hank tilts his head in question but then his nose crinkles. "Umm..." He turns toward the grill, and I follow his gaze to see smoke steaming from the edges of the cover.

"Shit." I race for the grill to find flaming steaks and burnt foil around the potatoes. This reminds me I didn't start the vegetables. I turn everything and mention the medley I need to prepare inside. He chuckles, and I excuse myself, wondering how people do all the things. *It's all about timing*, my mother would tell me about cooking. With picky kids and most meals on the go, this dinner isn't the type of ensemble I typically make. Working the pan over the stove's flames, I hear the metal clink of the grill opening through the back door I left open, and Hank comments that he's going to remove everything. The plates are already outside on the side table, so I work fast at moving around the carrots, zucchini, and squash. The colors look pretty, but the presentation is lacking. Some look undercooked; others look overcooked. I like firm veggies, not mushy, but I'm making a mess.

"Can I help you?" Hank's voice behind me startles me, and the spatula slips from my hand. Wayward veggies flip through the air like food fireworks as the cooking utensil lands at my feet. Reaching down to pick it up, my backside bumps into him. "Damn, girl."

I stand quickly, face flushed as he grips my hips. "One day. This way. From behind." I shiver with the promise of more sex with him. I'm thinking I'd be willing to let him take me anyway he wants. I'm a hot mess, like the vegetables.

He reaches around me and lifts the pan. A flick of his wrist and the remaining combination flies, landing back in the pan, flipped and sizzling.

"How did you do that?" I mutter, his chest to my back.

"It's all in the wrist." His voice drops and so does a kiss to my neck. I tilt my head, allowing him access to more of me. I want his mouth all over my body. Forget the vegetables. He sucks the juncture of my neck and shoulder, and my knees quake once again. He laughs against my skin. "Having trouble staying on your feet, little lady?"

Yeah, well, that's what he does to me.

I scoop the veggies into a bowl and take them out to the table. Horrified, I stare at the burned steak and charred tinfoil potatoes.

"Sweet cheese, I've made a mess of this." I sigh. *Now what?*

"Sit. It will be fine." We do sit, but it's not fine. Hank jostles the entire table as he tries to cut his steak. I slice through the foil to find the potato still rock hard inside.

"This is awful," I whisper.

"It's good." Hank takes a bite, chewing slowly, then struggles before swallowing.

"You are such a good liar. Admit it, it's not edible." I clamp my lips shut, fighting a smile.

"It's just chewy."

I burst out laughing at his reply. "It's breaking your teeth."

"Nah, I broke one once. It's nothing like that."

"Ouch," I chuckle.

"Yeah." He grins. "Tommy and I were ..." His voice drifts, not filling in the words, but his smile grows. "He clocked me with—" He stops abruptly. There's a whole story here, but he's not sharing it. He chuckles to himself, but it's obviously a private moment I'm not going to be let in on. "Anyway, yeah, it hurts. Nothing whiskey didn't heal then, though." He scoffs, the humor escaping his mouth.

"Was it hard to give up?" I ask, curious about such an addiction. I'm becoming addicted to him, yet I know it's not the same thing. Giving him up might be difficult, though.

"It's hard to explain, but yes, it was. I mean, you tell yourself you don't need it; you just want it. But somehow, your body craves it. Your mind believes it's the only way through something. Sometimes, it was the only way I made it through certain patches of my life. Other times, I know it's what caused those rough spots. Then one day, hopefully, you decide you have to live without it or it's going to kill you."

"Is that what happened to you?"

"Maybe. Not really. For me, it was more like someone else died, and it took me a while to wake up."

The woman, I think but don't want to ask. I nod, acknowledging I know who he means.

"You really loved her." It makes me sad. Sad to know he loved someone who didn't love him. Sad to believe he loved so strongly, so powerfully, so all-consuming. Sad to accept that no one has ever loved me like that.

"I'm not certain I know what love is. When I look back on her, on us, and what we *didn't* have, that couldn't have been love, right? It was just sex, drugs, and rock 'n' roll." He tries to tease, but his words are steeped in sorrow. It would make sense. He seems like a wild child turned wilder man.

"Sounds like fun," I joke, but I'm not certain I mean it.

"Really?"

"I guess not." I sigh, running a finger around my wine glass, dinner forgotten. "I mean, who doesn't want to be so carefree sometimes, but I've never been that loose." My eyes leap up to his. I already admitted this morning I hadn't ever had a one-night stand. "I never did drugs, and I like music, but not rock 'n' roll."

He gasps, pressing a hand over his heart. "Lady, I could have guessed on one and two, but three? Not liking rock 'n' roll wounds me to my soul."

"Why?" I still from circling the rim of my glass. Leaning on the table, I feel like a big reveal is coming.

"Because rock 'n' roll is life." He goes quiet, willing me to absorb his revelation.

"That's it? I was expecting something more profound, earth shattering, and *rock 'n' roll is life* is all you got?" I laugh again.

"Oh, you're going to *get* something," he warns. Standing quickly, he scoops me out of my chair and carries me inside over his shoulder, fireman style. I squeak and squirm, but secretly I'm ecstatic with his teasing threat. He stomps through my house and drops me on my couch, then covers me, slipping his entire body between my open thighs. Brushing back my loose hair, he kisses me. I love his mouth. I love the feel of him over me; his weight covering my body. I feel safe under him. Fingers dip into my pulled-back hair, unsettling it from the messy bun. My hands cup the back of his head and scratch his short hair before slipping into the back of his t-shirt.

"I freaking love your hands on me," he mutters against my lips.

"I love touching you," I whisper. Caressing his skin comforts me. I've missed touching someone in this manner and I let my hands roam his body, tracing his tattoos, and absorbing the warmth of him. Moving my fingers over him ignites a deep desire in me, and I need to cool things down or I'll be stripping him on my couch. "But I owe you dinner."

"Yeah, about that."

"It sucked."

He shakes his head. "Don't use words like that with me, little lady." He peppers my neck and jaw with kisses.

"Why not?" I chuckle.

"Because sucking is something I'm hungry for."

Instant. Wetness.

My hips buck of their own accord, grinding against the hard length of him straining his jeans. He pulls back and then kneels between my knees and drags me upright. Reaching for the hem of my shirt, he tugs it over my head. Then he reaches for the back of his collar and removes his. Is there any move sexier on a man? I could watch him do it again and again, but I'm sidetracked when he sits back.

"Trade places with me, Middy." I swing my legs, and he repositions himself, then pats his lap. For the briefest of seconds, my eyes flip to the picture window behind him.

"Worried about the neighbors? Hit the lights, little lady." He's mocking me somehow, but I do as he says.

I flick off the table lamp, the only illumination coming from the dull streetlight outside. I want to pull the curtains, but he's watching me, daring me to leave them open. Can my neighbors really see me?

"Take off your jeans." The command stings like a tickling smack. My sex clenches, and I do as he tells me. His lids lower, narrowing as he takes me in. I'm awkward with the skinny jeans at my ankles, and I'm not certain I like this game. *Is he teasing me?* Finally free of my clothing, I stand, take a deep breath, and stare down at him.

"You are the most beautiful creature I've ever seen, lady." His voice rings serious, surprised, as if he hadn't noticed before and means every word. "Come here." He pats his lap again, and I straddle him.

Cupping his head like I did moments ago, I lean forward and kiss him. Only this isn't the tender kisses of our greeting, or the patience of discovery Hank usually gives me. This is a race, mouths galloping over one another, speeding forward, pushing, pressing, yearning to cross the line.

He's jostling his belt under me, but my mouth won't release his. He's moaning into my throat, spurring me onward until the soft cotton of his boxer briefs dampens under my panties. I release his lips on a moan of pure pleasure, feeling the hard length of him under me. My hips roll, and I grip his shoulders, anchoring myself to him as I ride the tide of growing friction.

"Gonna come, baby?" I can't answer him; the tension feels so good, the building wave catching my breath. He growls, "Fuck yeah, lady, take what you need."

I don't want to be selfish. I don't want to be like that woman he loved who didn't love him back. The thought stops me, and I slip from his lap.

"Middy, baby?" His voice drops as I lower to my knees between his legs.

"You said you wanted sucking." I tug at his briefs, freeing the head and slipping him into my hungry mouth before fully undressing him. He bucks up, filling me, moving his underwear over his hips so I have clear access to all of him.

"Fuck, lady, that feels so good. Your mouth is heaven." I've never heard that before, so I suck harder, circling the crown until I swerve to the tip. I lick over the seeping seam and engulf the full length again. "Fuck," he strains as his hands curl under my arms.

"Forget sucking, I want to—" He stops himself, his eyes meeting mine. The lingering word startles me but thrills me. The building tide races through my lower belly, growing like a storm. I've never been this wild or had someone speak to me this way. Silently shocked, I'm more than excited he almost used it on me. I stand to remove my underwear, sliding it slowly to my ankles as he watches me. I unclasp my bra and slip it down my arms, letting it drop to the floor.

"You want to fuck me?" I whisper, the question choppy and quiet, but I'm emboldened by his eyes roaming my naked body. Just asking makes me vulnerable, but his response restores my ego. Reaching forward, he grips my hips, lowering his face to the hair at the apex of my thighs. and inhales.

"So ready for this." He exhales warm air over me and reaches for his jeans. A foil square appears, and I internally knock my head, knowing I forgot once again. Condoms just aren't something I've had to think about. When Paul got a vasectomy to ensure no more pregnancies, protection was no longer a thought. I watch Hank cover himself, and it's the sexiest thing I've seen next to him removing his shirt. He is one sexy beast of a man.

I straddle him again. The aroma of sex surrounds us both. He holds himself upright, and I balance on the tip of him.

"Give it to me, little lady," he commands in a strained voice, and I lower myself, taking my time to swallow him into me. I'm holding the back of the couch behind him to steady myself.

I've hardly touched down, but he snaps, "Up." Hoisting my hips, he lifts me, teasing me as he halts me from falling over him again. My head lolls forward, and I see he's watching us, observing where I rest over him. With unexpected force, he tugs me downward, and I yelp. He's hit something deep inside me, and my eyes water with the pleasuring sting. "Okay, baby?"

"More," I whisper, taking freedom with him that I haven't taken before. He drags me to the tip and then slams me over him once again. I grunt, but he repeats the motion, picking up the pace. My body becomes his plaything, and I let him toy with me because it feels so *fucking* good.

"Squeeze your tits. Bring one to my mouth." Shocked by the request, I release the couch, worried I'll lose my balance but I'm too much under Hank's spell to care. I press my heavy breasts together, then lean forward and watch as he latches onto me, sucking one achy swell deep into the cavern of his mouth. His tongue tickles over my nipple which is so hard the nub hurts. Then his warm lapping soothes the pain.

I'm bouncing like a rag doll, sliding up and down his dick. Grunting, groaning, moaning, I feel the newly familiar wave cresting.

Hank releases my breast. "Now that's the sucking I meant, lady." He kisses my other breast, trying not to break the steady, rapid rhythm of me jiggling over him. "You're almost there, aren't you?"

"How can you ..." My thoughts scatter when he tugs me downward, forcing himself deep in this position. The depth shatters me, and I come hard. He pulses inside me, and I clench harder than I ever have, clamping around him as he pumps inside me. I scream his name as the orgasm continues. My nails dig into his shoulders, and my eyes close. I don't care if the whole neighborhood just gave us a standing ovation. That was the biggest orgasm I've ever had.

"Your body tightens up when you're ready," he says, answering the question I didn't finish asking. His head falls back to rest on the edge of my couch. Still gripping my hips, he holds me over him. An extra pump of aftershocks occurs from him, and I have an issue.

"Baby?" He tilts his head as he slowly slips out of me.

"I…um…" My sex clenches, thumping harder than my heart. His hand on my hip slips forward, his thumb finding the sensitive folds ripe for another round.

"You need to go again?" I do, but I'm biting my lip. He's turning me into a sex-craving-wanton. Without an answer, he reads me, and his thumb tenderly strokes over the hypersensitive skin, slick and slippery with what we just did.

"I can't go again so quickly, lady." He grumbles, but the pressure of his thumb increases. My knees tighten on the outsides of his thighs as I remain straddling his lap. My hips roll, heightening the pressure of his thumb. It should be embarrassing how quickly I'm ready to go again, but I feel so good, so turned on, so coming out of my skin with need for this man.

"Ride that thumb of mine, baby. You get there again while I watch. Holy fuck, are you hot."

I start grinding on him, doing as he says, until his thumb slips into me, and his forefinger taps my clit. I yelp with the pleasure.

"You like that, little lady?" He squeezes me again. "My sweet girl wants to be naughty." I cup my breasts in response to his statement. "Oh Lord, squeeze those beauties together again."

I follow his command, losing control, slipping into an abyss of pure pleasure. Suddenly, I'm flipped to my back, and he places one knee between my thighs. He tugs off the spent condom and tosses it to the floor.

"How do you feel about bareback, lady?" I don't know what he means, but I need his thumb again, or something, anything for relief from the churning inside me. My own fingers skate lower on my belly, stretching lower until heavy fingers press mine flat. "Oh no, baby. This is all me tonight. Say okay?"

"Okay," I murmur, drugged on him, the presence of his body over mine, the feel of his rock-solid tip, spreading me until . . .*Oof.* I'm filled again, and I sing a stream of unintelligible praises. The intrusion is so quick, the penetration so deep that I curl up from the couch and wrap my arms under his, reaching around him to cup his shoulder blades. My mouth opens, seeking his upper arm. I might have bit him.

"Damn, girl," he says hammering into me. I'm in that out of body space again, the euphoric state of unadulterated bliss as I slip one leg over his thigh, curling around him like a snake. My other foot falls to the floor, opening me up to the invasion of my body again, and again, and again until he strains forward, grunting. The pulsing fills me, warm heat collecting inside me. His naughty thumb finds my nub, and one flick sends me skyrocketing over the edge, streaming into ecstasy while I scream his name a second time.

Suddenly, Hank collapses over me. We are a sprawl of spent limbs and exaggerated breaths. He kisses my neck before pulling back. "Holy fuck, lady."

I lightly laugh, jostling him inside me, and hot liquid seeps between my legs. I roll my head to look up at him.

"We might be a bit late to have this discussion, but I'm clean. Get checked every six months because . . ." His voice drifts.

Sweet cheese, is he talking shared needles or just multiple partners or something extreme I should be concerned about? The questions crash through me in a millisecond, but then I let them go. Hank would not jeopardize me like that, but I've lost him in those seconds. He sits back, carefully removing himself and reaching for his tee.

"Hank?" The whisper of his name brings him back a little but not enough. He's going to bolt again, and my shoulders drop.

"Let me get something to clean you with." He stands and I reach for him but miss his thigh as he steps further away from me.

"Forget it," I mutter despite the mess, sensing him pulling away from me. "What about dinner?" I ask as if this was the more important issue. *We could order pizza,* I think. Watch a movie. Maybe cuddle. Thankfully, I don't suggest the last one because he speaks.

"It's late."

"Stay." I hate how needy I sound.

"I would, but you have work tomorrow." He attempts to tease me, but humor isn't present. The playfulness in his eyes is missing. He kisses my cheek instead of my lips, and I'm left naked on my couch as he gathers his things. He walks to my kitchen to deposit the spent condom in the trash, and I simply sit tight, holding my shirt to my chest. When he returns to the front room, I don't know what to say. His rejection cuts deep after the high of two orgasms. Leaning forward, he kisses me too briefly again, and says good night before leaving me.

chapter 14

Not Taking No

[Hank]

I'm a fucking asshole, and I admit it. I don't know why I left her. Caught between dragging her to her room and running, I ran. I should have at least checked on her later, but I didn't. Fear drove me away. I lost control with her. So willing. So receptive. Midge makes me lose my mind, and do stupid shit, like come inside of her. She could get pregnant.

I scrub a hand down my face, shivering with the thought.

Would it really be so bad?

Yes, I decide. Midge doesn't need this right now and neither do I.

Then, I remember the way she looked up at me, asking me to stay, eyes pained when I didn't. She crushes me, when I've done this to myself.

The next morning at the garage, I find coffee brewing in a clean coffeemaker, the windows washed, and piles of papers stacked neatly behind the waiting room desk when I enter work.

"What the hell?" I snap as I see Midge sitting at Brut's desk, him leaning over her, directing her attention to something on the computer screen. I don't handle any invoicing. I just do what I'm told to do and enter information in the main computer inside the garage. I have no understanding of running this business, mainly because I never wanted to know. I didn't want to work here—ever—and then when I no longer had a choice, I only wanted to rebuild cars, like I was rebuilding myself. But seeing Brut all business like, angling over Midge, sets my blood boiling.

"Good morning," Midge says quietly, and then returns her gaze to the computer. Brut nods in greeting and continues to direct our new office manager.

"Can I speak with you a moment?" I ask of Midge.

But Brut answers, peering up at me. "No," he says.

"Excuse me?" I growl at my older brother. I love him, but I'll think nothing of vaulting over his desk and taking him out.

"You're not doing this again." His eyes drift to Midge and back to me. "No."

"What the fuck?" I snap.

"Brut," Midge warns, her fingers paused on the keyboard.

"Midge. I'm sorry. I offered you this job. We have a deal with Pendelton's car, and I keep my promises." He looks up at me. "And he's not running off another office manager."

"I didn't run off the last one."

"Oh, right. You just slept with her, which fucked her over, and she quit."

God dammit.

Midge closes her eyes.

"Middy, please."

"Don't call me that." Her voice is hardly a whisper, and she stiffens. Her fingers return to typing, and she ignores me.

I deserve the cold shoulder, but I won't let Brut interfere. "Outside. Now," I bark at my brother.

He pushes off the desk and rounds the corner, leading the way out the front door. The second we are in the yard, he turns on me.

"You're a fucking idiot."

"I know." The response stuns my big brother into silence. I cross my arms and rub my chin. "I fucked up. How much does she hate me?"

"She didn't mention you, other than to say she wants to fulfill her commitment without it being awkward. She promised me a temporary office manager in exchange for Pendelton's car being complete in two weeks' time and I intend to keep her."

I'm not liking the innuendo in his voice. "Let her out of the deal. Cut her some slack."

"Actually, she's holding it over me. She says it's insurance. She needs the pitch. She wants to work for his company, and that car is her ticket in. I'm not screwing her out of an opportunity because you can't keep your dick in your pants. Or when your dick finds a good thing, and your head gets in the fucking way."

"You have no idea what you're talking about."

"The fuck I don't. I see the way she looks at you. You could shit yourself, and she'd think you hung the moon, but you're still hanging onto a ghost. A phantom who thought *you* were invisible even when she was alive."

"You think I don't know that?" My arms drop to my side, fists clenching at the reference. My stomach rolls with the reminder I drove to the cemetery after leaving Midge. The ritual has become a habit with no meaning. I have nothing left to say to Kit's grave, and I realized that after two minutes sitting in the truck staring into darkness. Two minutes I could have spent at Midge's house making things right between *us*.

"I don't know what you're thinking. Though you'd drool over Kit, wag your tail, and wait for her attention, she never looked at you like Midge does. Man, wouldn't it feel good to have someone look at *you* like you looked at Kit? It'd make me feel fucking alive, but what do I know?" Brut huffs. "We're both in love with women dead to us."

"Oh, are we talking about Lily now?" I mock. My brother has his own demons with women.

"No, we are *not* discussing Lily. We're talking about Midge. The beautiful, intelligent, successful woman in there." He swings an arm in the direction of our garage. "You know what, maybe I should ask her out? She needs a man who will treat her right."

"Like you treated Lily?" I step closer to him. His eyes burn with fire at the verbal slap I've given him about Lily. "You wouldn't dare ask my girl out."

"Your girl? That's not a fucking girl. She's a woman, Hank. A woman who needs attention, and you're wasting it on someone who could never give it to you." Brut swipes a hand over his white hair. "I'm tired of having this conversation with you. Just stay in the garage and let her do her thing in the office. I need some help getting organized, and she threw in some marketing tips as a bonus. I need to get a grip on this place." He brushes past me, purposely plowing into me like we are kids again. I stagger at the force and let him have his moment. My shoulders slump as he yanks open the front door. Watching it close behind him, I realize my brother might finally be done with me, and he was the last man in my corner.

+ + +

For three days, Midge and I circle one another, but her presence consumes me. The clean waiting room. The organized office. The fresh coffee. Everything has been scrubbed, covered, or removed. Brut drew the line at the old leather couch. He claims the crappy furniture has sentimental value, and the only thing I can imagine is him losing his virginity on it. Otherwise, the wasted DNA on those cushions could be a science experiment and a testament as to why certain people should not reproduce.

In the meantime, Midge works on sketches and graphics between fielding calls, placing orders, and filling our calendar. She's talented, though I don't understand all her drawings. I see dishes and home accessories as she described them to me, but I have no idea what it means. I don't own a home to decorate.

Eventually, I can't take the silence between us anymore. I know I need to be the one to say something, and as the third day draws to an end, I cross the waiting room to speak with her.

Fuck me, she's wearing glasses. The hot secretary look works on her. She's been wearing jeans each day. Once with a flannel shirt exposing a low-cut tank top underneath. Another day was a loose-flowing tee. Today, she wears a sweater over another tank, but who's keeping track? She looks at home here, and I both love it and hate it.

Midge is too good for this place, but damn if I don't like seeing her working at the front desk, especially with those sexy glasses.

"Can we speak?"

"Sure," she says, keeping her back to me as her fingers continue to fly over the computer keyboard.

"Let me take you out this weekend." Her hands freeze. "I need to explain some things."

"I can't. My kids are home now." There's more to her rejection. I wish she'd just turn and tell me she hates me. Then I could blame everything on her, instead of taking the fault as I should. I hate myself. "Ronin is in a play this weekend—Friday, Saturday, and Sunday—but on Sunday, Liam has a doubleheader, his first ball game of the season, and I'm going to that."

I nod, knocking a fist on the counter. "I could go with you." I don't know where the offer came from. I haven't even met her kids. She spins in her seat, peeking up at me over the rim of those fucking glasses. Damn, she looks hot with the whole naughty secretary thing going on and that sweater open over her tank top, hinting at luscious breasts that easily fill my mouth. *Fuck*, I fucked this up.

"Why?"

"What?"

"Why would you want to go with me?"

The question is a legitimate, and my answer is honest. "I want to spend time with you."

"But you didn't want to," she retorts as her eyes drop like her voice. She's wrong, so wrong.

"That's not true. I just—"

"Hank, I can't—"

"I know." It's my turn to cut her off. "I'm sorry. Just let me come to the play, come to the game." *Let me prove I'm better than I acted the other night.*

She pushes the glasses to the top of her head, and I want to lay her back, undress her, and ask her to wear only those glasses, but I'm promising myself I'll be good. I'll do better by her.

"I'm trying to be the bigger person here. These are my kids, Hank. I don't need you messing with them, too."

"I understand." And I do, more than she might think. I just want to know more about her. "No hands. Just time."

Her brow pinches, her face tilting away from me, considering me.

Finally, she shakes her head. "Fine. Tommy and Edie are coming to the play on Friday. Ivy plans to attend on Saturday with the kids, and Tommy, Edie, and Ivy are coming to the game which is at noon on Sunday."

What the...?

"How did they all get invited?" I sound like a jealous boyfriend, and I *am* jealous. She never asked me, though she might have if I hadn't been a dick.

"Edie and I spoke last week. I told her about the play. She wanted to see Ronin. She met most of the kids during the fundraiser." Midge shrugs. "Liam has a crush on Ivy, and he begged me to ask her to his game. To my surprise, she said she'd come see him."

My heart remembers a time when we did things like this. Tommy and the guys with little Ivy in tow. Kit and Tommy were always about family. Sometimes, I think that was her issue. She saw me as family but not more. I sigh, willing away thoughts of history.

"What time is the play on Friday? I can pick you up."

"I need to be there early. Crew dinner and all. I'm also hosting the after party on Saturday." She sighs, rubbing her forehead. Under her breath, she adds, "Why can't I ever say *no*?"

"To me?" I question, my tone falling an octave in concern.

"Oh, I doubt I'll have a problem saying no to you at this point," she mutters, and the comment hurts my chest. "But I meant in general. Like the party. Forty teens and me."

"I'll come supervise."

"Hank, don't—"

"I'll be there." Turning on my boot heels, I walk away before she can reject me. Before she keeps me out of her kids' life as one woman kept me from my own.

chapter 15

Why I Say Yes

[Midge]

The following day, I'm crabby. I don't know why I said yes to any of it—the pre-play dinner or the after-show party—and I'm still upset that Hank suggested he attend the hectic weekend activities. I'm also stumped on an idea for Pendelton, and this is when a marketing crew works best, bouncing ideas off one another. Pendelton wants a line of items for men. Masculine. Simple. The company wants to dispel the stereotype that only gay men like to decorate their homes. The single, successful man does as well.

In my frustration, I'm slapping papers on the front desk at Restored Dreams. I obviously don't understand men. I'm divorced. I can't escape a man who completely confounds me, aka Hank. Plus, I'm raising three boys, and that's an adventure in and of itself. Which reminds me, I have an appointment with Elston's academic counselor this afternoon. I wore a skirt and heels for the meeting today, instead of my typical jeans and cardigan sweater. The counselor will guide us through which universities we should visit this summer. I might break into tears thinking about my firstborn going off to college, so I push away the thought and pick up the pad with my drawing.

Walking toward Brut's office, clearly not paying attention, I slam into a male chest, dropping everything in my hands, including an empty coffee mug. The ceramic shatters on the floor, and I swear under my breath. Hank chuckles.

Where did he come from?

"You're sexy when you swear," he mutters, bending down to retrieve pieces of the cup. I bend as well, my knees kept together by the tight skirt. "And sexy as fuck in that skirt today, little lady."

My heart leaps every time he speaks to me this way. I'm more pearls than chrome, but when he talks naughty, I want to jump him. *Down heart*, I scold. No leaping allowed. I've already leapt too fast for this man and look where it's gotten me. Lonelier than before I knew him. His compliment adds to my irritation.

"I got it," I snap, but his hand covers mine.

"You'll cut yourself." He picks up the large pieces, holding them in his thick palm.

"I'm not that delicate," I mutter, and stand. His eyes follow the line of my legs and I stomp into the office after gathering up the dropped invoices. I'm working on making Brut paperless, but there are so many purchases outstanding.

Slapping the papers on the desk, I sense Hank right behind me.

"What's wrong today, beautiful?"

I spin toward him. "Just stop it. Stop flirting with me when I'm obviously not good enough."

"What the—"

"I get it. You made a mistake, and in another week, I'll be out of your hair. It's fine." I lie. "Just don't come to my kids' activities out of guilt or whatever you're trying to do."

"I'm not—"

"My kids don't need the confusion and neither do I. We've had enough."

I turn my back to him, but his presence is even closer, and his hands cover my shoulders. He begins massaging me like he did the first night we met.

"Why. . ." He exhales. "Why in hell would you ever say you weren't good enough for me?"

"I must not be. You ask me out but dismiss me afterward. I ask you out, and you ditch me. Which, I might add, was after I begged you to fuck me and—"

"Begged. Me." He inhales sharply, and I close my eyes. "To. Fuck. You." He exhales heavily, and goose bumps pebble over my skin. "Lady, you would never need to beg me."

"Really?" I bark. "You've already refused me on this desk. Twice, I might add. I mean, I know I'm not adventurous or all cheetah print, but—"

He entwines my hair in his fist and gently tugs back. "You don't need to be cheetah print, whatever the hell that means. I like you just how you are." He pauses, lowering his mouth to just under my ear. "Is this what you want? Do you need this for some reason? I'll give it to you because I definitely don't want Brut trying to find another excuse to get with you."

I smile at the thought of Brut. I'm not attracted to him, but it's nice to think he might be attracted to me. At least, someone is. I roll with the idea. "You think Brut wants me?"

With my back still to Hank, his hand remains fisted in my hair, holding me against his chest. He gives my hair another tug and my back arches. My backside hits the thick length in his coveralls. Despite the sleeves tied at his hips, the stiffness of his excitement is discernible.

Hank tugs my hair tighter and thrusts his hips forward. Then he presses between my shoulder blades, forcing me forward to the desk. He continues to hold my hair while leaning down and slipping his hand up my skirt. *Sweet cheese.* My heart races and I'm instantly wet when I want to stay irritated with him.

"Brut definitely wants you, but he can't have you. You were made for me. You're my cupcake, and only I get to sample you."

I scoff at the reference until thick fingers slip into my underwear and impale me. I sigh with relief I shouldn't feel. I should be mad at him. I *am* mad at him. He's been a total asshole, but his fingers feel so good inside me.

"You think I don't want you? Are you kidding me? You're all I think about, and this desk has nothing to do with anything. It's filthy, and you . . .you're so sweet, Middy. But if you want to be a dirty lady, I'm here for you." His fingers delve deeper, twirling in a way that makes me purr with pleasure.

"Don't move," he groans, removing his fingers. I might have whimpered at the release. My elbows collapse and I cover my face in my hands in humiliation. *What am I doing?*

A lock clicks on the door, the blinds rustle, and I turn my head to look at Hank over my shoulder.

"Don't move," he snaps again. He nearly rips the sleeves tied at his waist, loosening the material at his hips. He circles the desk, dragging open a drawer and slamming it shut. Within seconds, he's behind me, and I hear the rip of foil.

My head tells me I'm still mad at him and shouldn't want this. My body is screaming for him to take me and give me the sweet relief only he can give me.

"Not good enough?" He huffs, then tugs up my skirt, roughly pulls down my panties, and thrusts into me. The force pushes me forward, and I reach for anything to steady myself. Unfortunately, I've cleaned the desk, so I only slide over the flat surface.

"Lady, you're better than anyone I've ever known." His voice is a rough grunt in my ear as he continues to hammer into me. His hands grip my hips for several thrusts before one slips around my belly and lowers to find the sensitive nub he touched the other night. Flicking the spot in rhythm with his powerful surges, he continues to speak. "I'm not good enough for you, baby, but if you want me to take you on a desk, take you against a wall, or take you over that nasty couch, I'll fucking take you." His pace increases, and I grunt with each tap inside me. He's deep like this, deeper than anything I've ever felt before.

"No one else gets at you," he demands, working my clit until I'm almost drooling on the desk. I want this orgasm. I need this release. "Only me. Now come all over me. Make me yours."

I do as he commands, holding back a scream with the clamp of my lips. I press back, forcing him as deep as he can go within me. Then, I burst around him, the release washing me clean of all negative thoughts. He does this to me, and I both love it and don't understand it. Next, my favorite part happens. Hank pulses inside me, filling me as he strains from his own rapid explosion. He lets go of my hips and slides his hands down my arms, covering my fingers on the desk. I spread mine, and he curls his between mine, resting his chest on my back.

"You are so fucking incredible, naughty lady."

He presses a kiss to my shoulder, and I close my eyes, willing the moment to last. He's going to pull out at any second, break the connection, and then walk away. He's done it twice before, and I brace for his withdrawal again while struggling to catch my breath after the orgasm that just ripped through me.

Why did I say yes to this?

"You cleaned the desk," he mumbles at my ear. "Were you expecting something to happen here?"

"A girl can always dream," I snark.

"You dream of being taken over a desk?" He chuckles into my hair.

"Yes." I exhale on the admission.

"Why?"

"Because I never have been." The truth is too much. Admitting a fantasy to a man about to walk away adds to the deep wound he's about to inflict.

"Middy, let me make all your dreams come true." The comment stops my heart, and the breath I'm struggling to regain exhales on a gasp.

"What?"

"I'm an ass but let me try. I want to *try* with you, little lady. I think you're the girl to make all *my* dreams come true, too."

How can I say no to that?

chapter 16

Chrome Teardrops

[Hank]

Each time I look at the damn desk, I get hard. Picturing her creamy ass in the air, me entering her in such a way. I want her again, but I'm out to prove myself this time. I meant what I said—I want to make her dreams come true—because I'm starting to think she'll fulfill mine. The first promise to myself is no more sex. Not until I'm back in her good graces by showing her I want more than something purely physical from her. This starts tonight at her son's play. I'm nervous when I think about attending but remember Edie and Tommy will be present. Maybe that makes me even more anxious.

I've been thinking a lot since last Sunday night, realizing in my heart, I let Kit go a long time ago. Recalling the way she treated me always stirs up too much pain. She toyed with me. Late-night calls. Quickies on the bus. Stolen kisses before a concert. And we fought like crazy. I can't raise her from the dead for all the answers I seek. Some answers are just never meant to be had, I eventually accepted. I'm a slow learner. However, my former lover didn't get to me like Midge does. Kit was an addiction, an obsession. Midge is habit forming, and good habits take practice. I'm ready to learn.

She's sitting at the front desk talking to Chopper when I come in from the garage. I'm starting to think my nephew has a crush on this woman like his father. Hell, the whole garage likes her.

I've been spending every second working on Pendelton's Bentley. I want it done so the old man has no excuse not to see her. He's a piece of work, the ancient fart. He thinks the world revolves around him and

121

his shit don't stink, but I know men like him. Most of the world doesn't like him, and they can smell him a mile away. Why Midge wants to work for him, I don't understand, but I see her scribbling and making notes as she moves around our place. Her mind works in overdrive, and I'm waiting for a crash. I wish I could prevent it from happening, but if not, I want to be there to collect the pieces. She's tough, but underneath, I see the delicate side of her.

Not when her backside is in the air.

Not when she straddles me.

But in the little things, there's a fragility to her, and I want to be the glue holding her together.

I just need to get my head out of my ass.

"I'm taking classes at community college until I figure out what I want to do. Then I'd like to transfer to UCLA," Chopper says to Midge as I pass them and head to the office. My nephew is kind of a hell-raiser, like his uncle and his father, so him getting into UCLA is a long shot at best. Brut just wants him to have a college degree, which neither of us have.

"What are your main interests?" Midge asks. "You should always start there. I liked art, drawing specifically, and I knew I was a good planner. The two together became my graphic design and marketing degree." I sit at Brut's desk, imagining a lost look on Chopper's face. I purposely left the door open to listen to them. I'll kill him if he's lost to her words because he's staring at her lips, like I do, imagining what she can do with them, like I do. He's twenty-one, but he's not stupid. He recognizes a beautiful woman.

"I love music."

"That's a good start. What about it? Do you play something? Or just like listening?" As Brut raised Chopper in my father's house, playing an instrument wasn't a possibility. Hell, I wasn't allowed one either until I found an old drum kit thrown out in someone's trash. I brought it home and banged the daylights out of it, pissing off Pop until he threatened to throw it away. He thought I was only messing around. He didn't hear talent. When I left to join up with Tommy, Pop practically disowned me.

He wouldn't have encouraged Brut to let Chopper play music. He'd be too afraid Chopper might leave his old man like I left mine. Pop's only soft spot was his grandson.

"I'm more about mixing the sound," Chopper states.

"Like rap music?" Midge asks, and I close my eyes. Music is music, but some sounds I don't understand, and rap is one of them. The angry shit they screech about—I don't know how other kids hear it. Where's the meaning in those lyrics? Where's the soul? The beat is so fast kids miss the point. God, I sound like an old man.

"Nah, I like old-school music. Stuff from your age." I sit up, hoping Chopper's reference doesn't offend Midge. We aren't *that* old. "Ever hear of Chrome Teardrops?" My head shoots up, and I hold my breath. *Dammit.*

"I don't think so," Midge replies.

"They were led by a girl. Kit Carrigan." Silence follows only briefly.

"Kit Carrigan? Singer, right? Who didn't want to be her? Blonde. Beautiful. Wild." Midge sighs, like Kit was every girl's fantasy. She had definitely been many men's wet dream. "Didn't she die young? Heart attack or something?"

"Breast cancer," I interject from the office, unable to stop myself as the painful memories flip through my head.

"Right," Midge hollers back. "That's so sad. Wait, wasn't she Ivy's mother?" I don't have to see Midge, to know the wheels are spinning and I'm waiting for the puzzle pieces to click. I'm biting my lip when Chopper interjects.

"You know Ivy? She used to babysit me. God, I had a crush on her."

Midge laughs. "Doesn't everybody? My youngest son has one on her, too."

Chopper's laughter follows, and I recognize that the women I surround myself with are too often admired by several men at once.

"Chopper, don't you have work to do?"

"I'm on a break," he snaps back.

"Since when do we get breaks around here?" I scoff.

"Since my dad owns the place," he retorts.

Little shit. He's smart enough to know this is his inheritance and his destiny if he doesn't get his ass out of here. He works on cars because he can, but not because it's his passion. Brut wants a life for him. One Brut didn't have a chance at. I exhale, knowing part of Brut's position came from my decisions. The other part came from him not keeping his dick in his pants.

"Get to work," Chopper's dad snaps

I chuckle to myself when I hear Brut's rough voice.

"See ya, Midge," Chopper says, rapping on the counter like his father does.

"Bye, honey." Her sweet voice sends a ripple over me. I want her to use that endearment on me.

"You okay?" Brut's voice interrupts my thoughts as he stands in the doorway. His brow is pinched, and I'm wondering if he heard Chopper bring up Kit to Midge. It was innocent enough, but Brut doesn't like to hear about Kit. He blames her for many things, like me being unable to keep *my* dick in *my* pants, and my heart in my chest.

"I'm good." I tip my chin.

"Then get to work, too. The Bentley awaits." On second thought, Brut can *be* a dick.

chapter 17

Back To High School

[Midge]

Edie offering to come to Ronin's play completely flabbergasted me. She purchased the tickets, and I thought she considered it a donation to the high school, but when she walked in with Tommy on Friday night, I was equally surprised.

"I don't go to these things anymore," she says after taking a seat. "With Masie in college, I think I'm still in mourning over the high school years being over." Edie's daughter, Masie, attends Santa Clara University, a good five-hour drive from the Los Angeles area but certainly closer than her original home in Chicago. Edie's story of moving to California fascinates me, and truthfully, I'm a little jealous of her happily-ever-after tale.

"It is so generous of you to attend. Ronin is thrilled to have the support. He misses family most when these types of opportunities arise." My parents and Paul's used to attend as many of our children's activities as they could. With us living more than two thousand miles away, that's no longer a possibility.

"I'm so excited. *Les Misérables* is one of my favorite musicals."

"Darlin', you know nothing about music," Tommy teases beside her.

"I know about this," she huffs until his tattooed arm surrounds her. *Yep, happily-ever-after*.

"Got a seat for me?" All three of us look up at the same time to see Hank standing in a light gray crew neck sweater and dark jeans. Two bands of bracelets circle his wrist. He's a vision of masculinity, and I just want to lick him. I'd purposely left an empty seat next to me although, secretly, I was afraid to believe he'd show. I motion for him to sit as I don't trust myself to stand and greet him. I might tackle him in the aisle with my relief.

"Hank?" Edie states, a question in her voice as she looks over at me. Tommy leans over, and the two men shake hands.

"Surprised to see you here," Tommy adds, inquiry lingering in his tone, but Hank sits back the second they release hands and glances over at me.

"You seem surprised, too," he whispers.

"Not surprised, just…hesitant."

"I like it better when you're overwhelmed, lady." The statement reminds me of our first night together, the one when I cried during sex. The memory embarrasses me, and I blush.

In a classic Hank move, he leans forward and kisses me briefly. Sharp. Quick. Public.

"You look pretty," he says, staring me directly in the eyes.

"Oh my," Edie mutters beside me, and I hear the flapping of a program as a fan while a low whistle comes from Tommy. A tap on my shoulder opposite Hank turns my attention to Tommy. His firm finger presses on my shoulder.

"You've got some explaining to do." The words aren't too harsh, and I realize they aren't directed at me. Tommy's gaze goes past me to Hank. I spin to find Hank glaring back.

"So do you," he mutters, before sitting back and reaching for my thigh. He squeezes and then leaves his hand there, making a statement to his old friend. Fortunately, the orchestra starts, and the play begins.

I embarrass myself once again as I cry while Fantine sings "I Dreamed a Dream."

+ + +

Tommy and Edie stay long enough to congratulate Ronin. Hank lingers.

"Great job, man," he says to my son, shaking hands with him. Ronin met Hank at the fundraiser, and I'm reminded of almost being caught by him in the bathroom with Hank afterward.

"Thanks." It's the best Ronin can offer as he flits off to hug more crew members and receive congratulations from other families.

"I'll walk you out," I offer, nodding away from the chaos of after-show greetings. His hands slip into his pockets as I lead him toward the front entrance of the school.

"So tomorrow night," he says, and the holding breath feeling returns. I'm expecting him to say he's decided not to attend or has made other plans. "I'll see you then." He hesitates, his head lowering as if he's one of the teenagers from the play.

"I'll see you tomorrow." Relief washes over me, and I smile to reassure him when I feel like I'm the one craving reassurance. I've got to get this man out of my head and out of my heart, but when he leans forward for a brief kiss again, I melt.

+ + +

The next night, Hank carves out a permanent place for himself in my heart.

Ivy had to cancel at the last minute due to something with her husband, but she assured me she'd be at Liam's game on Sunday. I don't know why she'd come to watch him, but Liam is thrilled.

As we sit through the opening of the play a second time, Hank leans over and says, "Meet me in the hallway." His voice is alluring and demanding, so I give him a few seconds lead before I stand to sneak out of the theater. I feel like a naughty teenager breaking some unspoken rule.

My heels tap down the wide, empty hall, echoing behind me as I make my way toward the bathroom, though I have no idea if that's the general direction Hank went. Suddenly, two arms surround me, and I'm tugged into an alcove by a classroom door.

127

"Caught you sneaking out of class, Ms. Everette. There's punishment for that." He presses me into the corner and kisses me hard, taking his time to enforce his law by imprinting his mouth on mine. Too quickly, he pulls back, smiling to himself with his playful puns.

"In this school, they call them JUGs—Justice under God—if you get caught doing something, like sneaking out of class or kissing in the hallway."

Hank chuckles. "Oh, yeah. Tell me more about the school." He steps out of the alcove, still holding one of my hands and waves forward for a tour. At first, we walk silently through the emptiness.

"This place is large. Got a band room?" Hank asks.

"Of course." I laugh. We're here for the play we're skipping out on, so music and theater is obviously an important part of the opportunity the school offers. I lead him down the stairs and around a corner to the enormous band room. The space looks like a sound studio with golden wood paneling and rows of seats, music stands, and a kettle drum in the back. Hank releases my hand and walks right to the drum. His hand hovers over it as if he's afraid to touch it.

Tonight, he wears a deep-red sweater and black dress pants. The color reminds me of the giant car he's working on for Mr. Pendelton. Minus the mechanic clothing, and despite the dressy appearance, something about the way he stands next to the drum hints at him belonging here.

"Did you play in the band during high school?" His head shoots up as if he forgot I was with him.

Staring at me a moment, he draws back from his memory, then answers. "We didn't have band. My school cut the arts." He sits on the stool behind the drum, his eyes still drawn to it. He clasps his hands between his thick legs.

"That's sad." The comment seems weak. I glance around the surrounding room, recognizing my children are at an advantage. "It's expensive to go to school here. I mean, most kids who go here are rich but not everyone, like us. I just want things for my children. When we moved here, we didn't know which school districts were good, so we took our chances with the grade schools but decided private high school was best." I pause, hoping I'm explaining myself well enough not to sound like a snob. "When Paul and I divorced, Elston was about to enter high school, and we had it put in the decree that private education at this level remained a must. We share the cut. It's why I need to work for Pendelton. Besides, it could be the start of something for me."

Hank watches me, nodding for me to come to him. "Like what?"

"Just something I've been thinking about. Maybe trying to do this on my own. Be an independent contractor or something." I shrug, blowing off the idea since I've said it out loud to someone else. My head lowers, and I reach for the two bracelets at the edge of Hank's cuff. Rolling my fingers over them, I remain quiet.

"Hey." Hank palms my hips, jiggling me a little. "You can do anything you want, little lady. You're smart enough. Determined enough." I nod without taking my eyes off the woven leather band and the wooden beads around his wrist.

"What did you want to be when you were younger?" I ask, hoping to shift the conversation from my plans.

"I wanted to be in a band." My head shoots up and sad steely eyes meet mine. "Did you know that's how I met Tommy?" The question is cautious, hesitant as if he expects me to know something I don't.

"No. I mean, I know Tommy was in a band. Something about his sister, and they were famous, but I didn't want to pry. It wasn't my focus when I met Ivy and Edie. I was all about Rhythm Walk, the fundraiser." Hank's eyes lower to my chest, and he shakes his head. "Were you in a band?"

Swiping a hand over his hair, he turns his head. "Yeah, I was in a band with Tommy, but that was a long time ago, and a very distant me." He sighs. I sense this isn't something he wants to discuss, but he continues.

"His sister was the girl I told you about." He exhales, then takes a deep breath. "It's why I'm not married. I asked her several times, but she always said no." The sadness in his voice breaks my heart. I can't imagine someone not loving him. I reach for his cheek, drawing his

129

attention to me. As he peers up, I lean down and kiss him. Tender. Sweet. I want his thoughts restored to me, not some memory haunting him. He smiles when I pull back.

"Lady, those lips," he mutters. I'm standing between his spread legs, and his hands curve over my backside. "Can I ask you something? Why the fuck did Paul give you up?"

"He wanted a younger model and a different flavor. I caught them on the phone one night. He moved us here for her."

"Fucking hell," Hank mutters, and I realize now's the time to just get it all out.

"They eventually broke up, but by then, I wanted a divorce. He's found someone else, and they're getting married this summer. The boys don't really like her."

"He's a fool, but I'm glad he's stupid. He doesn't deserve you. Thank God he's an idiot."

"Why would you say that?" I chuckle, uncertain if he's teasing or serious.

"Because you wouldn't be standing between my legs if he was smart." With that, he stands abruptly, nearly knocking me over, giving me his signature quick kiss. "Show me more of the school."

Leading him up the stairwell and down a few hallways, we come to the gymnasium. The school actually has two, but the traditional wood floor one with the school insignia inlay is where we stop. Hank tugs the door handle, but it's locked. He peers through the windows. "There's a balcony."

This reminds me of another way into the gym, and we return to the stairs leading to the theater. Heading for the backstage of the performance, which is a hallway partitioned off by a large curtain, we turn just before the barrier. A door for the balcony remains open as a few of the props are stored here between sets. Walking to the railing, Hank takes in the dark gym. I'm about to speak when he climbs over the railing and reaches for me.

"What are you doing?" I laugh, feeling like we're about to do something we shouldn't.

"Hold my shoulders," he commands, barely giving me time to do so before hiking me over the railing as well. He balances me on the open bleacher before leading me down the steps. It's shaky walking in my heels, and as he hops off the last step, he turns for me, lifting me by my hips again. He spins me around and leads me to the center of the empty wooden floor.

"What are we doing?" I repeat, whispering with laughter in my voice. Hank holds my hand but walks me in a circle. Tugging me, I step into him, and his arms encircle my waist. My hands come to his shoulders, and he sways. *Oh my God, he's dancing with me.*

He hums for a moment, and I slip my hands around his neck. Definitely no longer teenagers, I can still picture us in my head as if we were—a pretty dress on me; a dark suit on him. The idea doesn't quite work. He's not the suit type.

"I never went to a high school dance."

I pull back at his admission and scratch lightly at the back of his neck.

"Stoner under the stands instead." He nods at the open bleachers. I can picture him—the cool kid with those hard eyes, a lost soul inside.

"I would have wanted to date you, but you wouldn't have noticed me. Quiet girl with a book and taking art class."

"Oh, I would have noticed you, but you would have been out of my league." He huffs, peering down at me. "But why would you want to date me?"

"Love a bad boy."

He chuckles lightly, shaking his head again. "There's a rebel girl inside you."

"Maybe." I shrug, knowing he's onto something. I'm not suggesting I want to be tied up or anything, but I like discovering sex can be a bit more than just the missionary position. I like sex with him, *a lot.*

"Paul ever see it?" The question seems strange, but even stranger is my answer.

"No."

"Then why me?" I can think of several reasons, all of which I fear Hank can't handle. I'm still uncertain of admitting those feelings to myself. Although his recent actions restore my faith in him, I'm still raw over his behavior the times we had sex at my house.

"Your sausage fits."

His mouth falls open, and he stops swaying. Laughing a deep belly laugh that echoes in the empty gym, he tugs me to him, holding the back of my head as he hugs me.

"You did not just say that." His chest rumbles against my cheek, and I can hear his heart beating through the soft cotton. Hank is security, and I want to curl into this man and have him hold me like this for the rest of my life. It's a dangerous thought.

"Pretty lady, will you go to the dance with me?" We are already turning in a slow, rhythmic circle again, but there's no way I can say no to this man.

"As your first? I'm honored," I tease.

"You're also my last, lady. And *I'm* honored."

My heart skips, and Hank returns to humming as he slowly spins me, unwinding the past.

chapter 18
After Party

[Hank]

The party is in full swing as I stand in Midge's kitchen, leaning against the sink, listening to her boys fight.

"Quit hitting on her," Ronin demands as he stands on the other side of the kitchen island. He's a tall, lanky kid, body like a boy in a band—only in this case, it's the marching band. His hair is long in the front and cut short up the back. I've been told it's brown like his mother, but it's more blue-black tonight.

"Why? You like her or something? She isn't your type." Elston is Midge's older boy with dirty blond hair like his father and blue eyes. He's large, appearing like a man, but still with a boy's attitude. He crosses his arms over his chest as he casually leans on the island, facing off with his younger brother.

"What type is that?"

"Band," Elston snaps. "Besides, I didn't think you liked her, or any girl, for that matter." The implication his brother might not like girls seems disrespectful, and I'm ready to intervene when Ronin stands up for himself.

"Just because I'm in band doesn't mean I'm gay."

"I didn't say that, but it doesn't mean you can get girls either, especially Athena."

"Oh, like you can? All you want is in her pants. Leave her alone." Ronin puffs out a chest he doesn't have.

"And what about you? What do you want from her?" The fight reminds me of Brut and myself at their ages, same distance in years apart. We'd argue over girls just as much, but we never liked the same one.

Ronin shrugs his shoulder and blushes with false bravado. "I've already had her."

"You're crazy. You have not."

"She likes a guy who can handle his stick."

"Band joke? Funny, I heard she likes a guy with balls."

"Football joke," Ronin snorts. "Original."

I'm not certain I should butt in, but the temperature between them rises, and if it were Brut and me, punches are coming next.

"You know talking about a girl like that isn't going to get either of you in her pants, not that you should be talking about her pants either." I scrub my chin, knowing I'm walking a fine line with these teenage boys. Brut has tried hard to instill respect for women in Chopper.

"Oh yeah, and what do you know?" Elston asks, glancing at me over his shoulder.

"I know girls don't like to be talked about, and they don't like boys talking about what's in their jeans either. If you can't treat her like a lady, neither of you deserve her."

Elston glares at me, but Ronin lowers his head. "I didn't have her. I said that so Elston would leave her alone. She's a nice girl."

Poor Ronin, his innocence might get him in trouble, but then again, protecting a girl's virtue might make him a hero.

"Don't worry about it, kid. I know for a fact that girls like a guy who can handle his stick more than a guy with balls."

Ronin's mouth falls open, and Elston's eyes narrow at me.

"Drummer," I add, patting my chest. "My stick knows what I'm talking about."

I shouldn't be talking like I'm a damn teenager, but I want to protect Ronin for some reason. Elston seems like an ass, and he needs to come down a peg or two. Ronin's lips twist, fighting a smile as he realizes my childish joke. Then he leans toward his brother.

"Just leave her be." He bumps his bigger brother's shoulder with a weak push and exits the kitchen.

"Is that what you're trying to do? Get in my mom's—"

"You better be very careful with your next choice of words, kid." I'm rubbing my chin again, holding back from standing to full height and letting him feel my presence. He disrespects his mother, and we'll have a big problem.

"You trying to date her?"

"And if I am?"

"You get me some beer, and I'm cool with that."

I should be stunned at the audacity, but he's testing me, so I'll play along. "Even if I did drink, I'd know better than to give it to someone underage."

"You don't drink? What's wrong with you?"

"I abused the privilege when I was your age."

"Yeah?" Elston smirks, but he must see something in my hardening expression.

I reply, "Yeah."

We're silent a second, and he's sizing me up. I want to hope it's because he's protective of his mother and not trying to be a punk.

"Getting drunk isn't going to win you the girl, either." Speaking from experience, I know firsthand.

"What girl?" Elston's brow pinches.

"The one you just teased your brother about."

"He's getting riled for nothing." Elston shrugs.

"Are you certain it's nothing? Maybe he does like her."

"He hasn't made a move." He lowers his voice.

"How do you know?"

"Because I'd know. I'd have heard something."

"You know, only dicks share stories, typically about something they haven't done, in order to compensate for something else." I lower my eyes, tipping my head, and Elston glares back at me again.

"You don't know what you're talking about, old man."

135

"Son, I ain't your old man, and if I were, you wouldn't be talking to me like that."

"He wouldn't be talking to his father like that either," Midge interjects, and I shift to find Midge standing in the doorway to her kitchen. I'm wondering how much she heard when she holds out her hand toward Elston. "Phone and go to your room."

"Mom. It's Saturday night. I have plans."

"Not anymore. Phone. Room. Now."

Elston huffs, lowering his head like a petulant child. I'm thinking he's about to sweet-talk her in the midst of the party chaos, so I intervene again.

"Kid, hand over your phone and do as she says, or you'll have more than overcompensation to worry about. It takes balls to be a man, so don't be a dick to your brother. Someday, he may be the only man standing beside you."

Elston doesn't respond, but bites his lip, like he's itching to talk back to me. Instead, he presses off the counter in irritation, hands his phone to his mom and stalks off to the stairs. I scrub a hand over my head.

"Shit, I'm sorry. I stepped into that. He's your son. I shouldn't have said anything." Reprimanding her kid doesn't play into my plans for making a good impression with her boys.

"Don't apologize. I don't know where any of that came from. He's never like that. Never. And I'm not just saying that because he's my son and typically a good kid. I really have no idea why he is acting this way. I'm embarrassed for him."

"How much did you hear?"

"Enough."

I tip my chin for her to come closer to me. "Hear him ask me if we were dating?"

Her lip twists as she stands close to my chest. Her hands come up and smooth down my sweater. "What did you say?"

Did I say we were? I only asked him how he'd feel, but he countered with the beer comment.

"I didn't get to answer."

"Too much conversation about getting into someone's pants?" She snickers, ignoring the answer as well. "I probably shouldn't have heard any of that."

"Probably not. That was guy talk."

"Oh, yeah?" She steps closer, rubbing up my chest to reach for my jaw. "Well, for the record, I'd like the feel of this scruff . . . in my pants." She kisses my jaw, too quickly, before stepping back. It's then that I feel eyes on us. *Shit.*

"Mom, Mr. Kraus is leaving. He wants to thank you for hosting the party." I don't know who this Mr. Kraus is, but Midge flits her arms. Mr. Kraus better not want in her pants.

"Oh, okay, good," she replies, pulling back from me without a glance and heads toward her front door.

Ronin steps forward, and I'm feeling trapped by this damn sink.

"You're Hank Paige," he says as if he's just heard my name although we've obviously met.

"Yep."

"*The* Hank Paige. The one from Chrome Teardrops."

I rub a hand over my face. *Oh fuck.* "What do you know about that?"

"Kit Carrigan rocked it. The band included her brother, you, and Denton Chance on guitar, but you had two solos within her first album." *Crap.* This kid is good. "I have a poster of you on my wall upstairs."

"What?" Do those even still exist? "Does your mother know about this?" My voice lowers. I haven't quite added it all up for her yet.

"My mom knows nothing about music. She pretends to understand because she loves me, but other than listening, she doesn't get it."

"Ronin, I don't believe in keeping secrets, but could we keep this between us for a little bit longer?"

"You trying to date my mom?"

Jesus, is this the question of the night? "Yes."

"Then she needs the truth. My dad lied too much."

He's right. I know this, but...

"You ever like a girl and want her to like you for you and not something she thinks you are, or something other than you are?"

Ronin ponders on this a second. "Like wanting Athena to see me as more than a band nerd?"

"Exactly."

"I'm proud of the band. I want her to like me because of it."

"Exactly again. I'm proud of who I am now, and I want your mom to know the *me* I am, not who I used to be. My past is over, Ronin. Does that make sense?"

"Yes, but I still want you to tell her." He fidgets with the hem of his old-school, classic rock t-shirt.

"I will, but I need a little more time."

Ronin seems to understand and nods, slipping his hands in his pockets. "I gotta go say goodbye to some other guys. The party's breaking up because we have another show tomorrow."

I nod, and Ronin leaves the room. I'm pushing off the sink when a younger version of Midge enters the kitchen. With the same brown hair and same speckled eyes, Liam is the male image of her. He's small for his ten years, but he'll grow. He's running to the fridge when he collides into me.

"Whoa, pal, where you headed?"

"Soda." He's breathing heavy, eyes wild, looking like he's already had a few too many.

"It's kind of late for that." I have no idea, but I know if I have caffeine too late, I get the jitters and can't sleep.

"Mom said I can."

"Really?" My tone must hold some warning because he stops tugging at the fridge handle.

"No." He sighs, shoulders falling. "You're Hank, right? Her date or something."

Oh Lord, here we go again. "Yes." I think it's okay to say that.

"Know how to play video games?"

"Umm, no self-respecting man doesn't."

He looks at me like he has no idea what I said. "Want to come play Minecraft?"

I wave a hand, gesturing for him to lead the way.

As I sit in a small den off the kitchen, I get whipped by a ten-year-old, but he cracks me up. Question after question escapes him between video game strategies. How tall am I? Have I ever been in a play? Do I like monster cookies? I can't keep up with his energy.

Thoughts of having children come to mind. What would it have been like? Would I have played video games with a son? Would he have asked me a million and one questions? Would he have loved me unconditionally? I know I'd allow any child of mine to be whatever he wanted to be, unlike my pop.

"What do those bracelets mean?"

I look down at my wrist, twisting them back and forth. I don't know what made me break them out of my drawer. It's been a long time since I've worn them, but for the past two nights, it felt right to wear them.

"The leather one has three straps woven together. It's for me and two old friends. A reminder we were a"—I almost say band but decide on something he'd understand—". . .a team."

"I'm on a team." His voice rises with excitement.

"I know." I pause, twisting the second band. "This one has beads. A reminder of how a team takes more than one player and lots of support."

"Like fans for a game?"

"Something like that." It's more than fans, though. A band is like a family—supporting one another, holding each other up—until one member brings them all down. I don't go into that explanation.

"That's so cool," he says, and then his attention bounces to other topics. Baseball. Summer camps. Failing science class.

After what seems like an hour, Elston stands in the entrance followed by his mom.

"Mr. Paige, I'm sorry for how I acted earlier. It was disrespectful." The language seems formal but his intention sincere.

I shrug. "Call me Hank and the apology is accepted."

"Deal." He nods, a boy on the verge of being a man suddenly.

"I'm sorry, Mom." He turns to Midge, who seems a little startled by his apology. "I didn't mean to act like that." He reaches for her, hugging her tight, and Midge holds him. She mutters something to him, and he responds, "Love you, too."

What would it be like to hold a child?

"Ugh." Liam sighs.

"Do they fight often?" I whisper, watching Midge embrace her son.

"Just lately. Since we came back from spring break. He's more mad at Dad, but he's taking it out on Mom. At least, that's what she says."

"What do you think?" I figure why not ask him. He seems full of information.

"I think she's right. Mom normally is." I chuckle at the response. "You coming to my game tomorrow?"

"I wouldn't miss it."

"Sweet."

Yeah, it is sweet. They are great as a family, and I dare to envision myself as part of one like them someday. Maybe this one, I hope.

chapter 19

Just A Game

[Midge]

As I sit on my camp chair, I watch Liam warming up while my mind flips through last night. Hank was a rock star with all those kids, keeping his eyes open for hidden alcohol or corner kisses as he put it. The night went off without a hitch. Except for Elston. I don't know what's gotten into him, other than this business with his father and attending college back in Illinois. Maybe it's Paul's impending wedding. The boys aren't exactly thrilled with Melanie, his future wife. She's young, in her twenties, and I wonder if Elston thinks she's too close to his age. I certainly do, but then again, I don't have a say.

I'm waiting for the game to begin when Tommy and Edie arrive with a cooler in tow.

"Whatcha got there?" I'm excited to spend more time with them, especially Edie. We've talked often lately. I explained to her what I did, how I quit my job, and how I'm working on securing another one. I shared some of my concerns, which include how I might be too old for such a dramatic switch. But she assured me I could do it.

"Plus, you already did, only six years ago when you moved here," she reminded me.

"We come bearing gifts," she teases. "I love Sunday doubleheaders, and Bloody Marys make them better." She laughs at her own rhyme. She's already told me about her son, Caleb, and his career as a minor league baseball player. He's hoping to be called up to a major club this year.

"I feel like a chump. I only brought chips."

"Good one." Edie claps.

"Darlin', you two already hit the bottle?" Tommy jokes, spreading out a blanket for him and his wife. He's wearing a baseball jersey for a team I don't recognize while Edie wears a shirt with her son's last name on the back and a large number twenty-five.

"Ivy still coming?" I ask. I didn't want to pry into her cancellation last night. I remember having three small children. Life can be chaotic.

"Talked to her this morning. She'll be here with the kids." Edie settles beside Tommy on the blanket he spread.

A few minutes later, Hank arrives. He looks delicious in a tight gray tee and faded jeans. He wears an open flannel over it, but he's already removing it as he walks. I wore shorts today with a long-sleeve shirt, thinking the day might be warm in the sun despite early April's mild temperature. Baseball season is always unpredictable.

He sits in the camp chair next to me, then leans over to give me his signature quick kiss.

"When you two getting married?" Tommy teases, and my face heats.

Married? *He won't even sleep with me.*

"We aren't getting married." I turn to Hank, expecting him to join the joke, but his eyes close, his fingers steepled against his lips. His pinched brow worries me, and I reach for his wrist, suddenly recalling what he said about his former lover never wanting to marry him.

"Actually," I exaggerate the word, and Hank's eyes flip open. I turn to Tommy. "After he asks me, you'll be the second to know."

"Why the second?" Tommy asks with a deep chuckle.

"Because I'll be the first." I haven't released Hank's wrist, and I give it a squeeze before turning back to face him. His crooked smile proves he's pleased with my answer. I'm still holding his wrist when I look up and find my ex making his way to us.

"Paul," I greet him.

I'm still upset about Elston's behavior and Paul's role in it, so I don't want to talk to him. He eyes the people around me, taking note of their tattoos. Paul is tallish, lanky, and lean. He wears an open denim shirt, a white t-shirt underneath, and a medallion necklace. He looks young, but he's not as young as he used to be and not as young as his future wife, who sits on a bleacher, ignoring me. We've met twice. She's almost half my age, blonde, tan, and very Californian. He has his work cut out to keep up with her, but that's her problem, not mine.

"Are you going to introduce me to your friends?" He looks me over and then eyes the men again.

"This is Tommy Carrigan, his wife, Edie, and Hank Paige." I release Hank's wrist, and he stands to shake hands with Paul.

"Nice to meet you," my ex offers, but a question remains in his tight-lipped smile. Why am I with him? Or rather, why is Hank with me?

"You look different," he says to me, taking in the light purple streak in my hair. I let it bleed out a bit and then had the hairstylist lighten it for my upcoming interview with Pendelton.

"Thanks," I say although I'm not certain it's a compliment. An awkward tension grows between us as I have no more to say to my ex-husband. I'm surprised he even walked over to our little party because he doesn't typically address me at events. It's better we act civil but not engage in conversation.

Paul looks over his shoulder toward the bleachers. "I guess I'll get back to Melanie."

I wave my fingers, dismissing him, and fall back in my seat the second he walks away.

"Tommy, how about that Bloody Mary?" I glance at Hank who waves at me to proceed.

A few innings into the first game, Ivy arrives with two little girls on either side of a stroller. She spreads a blanket for the girls to take a seat but the youngest immediately plants herself on Tommy's lap. Her blonde, wild curls tickle his stubbled chin, and he kisses her head. It's sweet. He's too young to be a grandpa, but he definitely fits the patriarch role of his family.

Within a few minutes, Paul makes his way back to us.

"Hank. Incoming," Tommy says, and instantly, Hank's hand is on the back of my neck. I'm not certain what's happening, but Paul walks with determination and a secret conversation seems had between Hank and Tommy. Hank squeezes my nape.

"I knew it. I knew I recognized you," Paul states, drawing closer to us. "Hank Paige, drummer of Chrome Teardrops, and Tommy Carrigan, you were Kit's brother. She was amazing."

"Thank you," Ivy interjects. "She was my mother."

"That's what Melanie said." Paul references his young fiancée.

I'm stunned at the revelation, slow to process what's been said. Hank Paige, drummer for Chrome Teardrops. He loved Tommy's sister, Ivy's mother. He loved the lead singer of his band because he was a flipping rock star, and the woman he loved was one, too. I'm ready to jump out of my chair, but Hank's hand holds firmly, massaging my nape, pinning me in place.

"Wow, Midge. How did you swing this?" Paul stares at me, and I want to slap him, then I want to slap Hank. My cheeks are flaming with shame at not recognizing him or the connection between them all, and I feel like a fool.

"We met in a bathroom," Hank interjects.

I want to dig a hole in the dirt and bury myself alive in it.

"A what?" Paul gasps.

"Never mind," I say, sliding forward in my seat, but Hank holds on to me. "I need to check in with Liam." I stand, releasing myself from Hank, and wait for my ex-husband to walk away. Fingers tickle up the back of my thigh and curl into the hem of my jean shorts. Hank tugs, but I can't look back at him.

Paul watches the movement, his eyes widening at Hank's touch. "Huh." He snorts.

My mouth opens, and then I clamp my lips. I have no retort for him. I owe him no explanation. In fact, I need a break from all of them. I brush past Paul and head for the chain link fence dugout where Liam rests on the bench, awaiting his turn in the batting order.

"You doing okay, buddy?"

"Yeah."

"What's wrong?"

"Can you keep Dad back? He keeps trying to coach me, and it's getting on my nerves."

This is a constant issue I have with Paul, running interference at his sideline coaching tactics. He's concerned for our sons, wanting them to be their best, but he rides the athletes the hardest. Liam's getting his first taste of things as baseball has become his passion.

"I'll talk to him."

I feel Paul's presence, but I don't want to address him in front of Liam. I hold my position, keeping my back to him, hoping he'll walk on by and give me a moment.

Instead, I find Edie walking up to me with baby Granger in her arms. I'm grateful for her company as it derails Paul.

"I know how you're feeling," she says, jiggling Granger on her hip. He's almost a year with shocking dark hair and big brown eyes. "I didn't exactly find out the truth from Tommy, and it stung."

"Hank has dropped hints, but I just didn't put the whole story together. He's a flipping rock star, and he loved one."

"I've heard something about that." Edie jostles Granger, cooing at him a moment as she nibbles his little fist. "Here's the thing. Everywhere they went, they were recognized. Women threw themselves at them because of what they were, not who they are. Tommy once explained to me how he wanted me to know *him* first, the rock star second. From my understanding, Hank's pretty far removed from the rock star in himself. Maybe he just wanted you to like him as Hank."

What she says makes sense, but still... "He loved Tommy's sister. She was...she was huge. Popular. Pretty." I wave a hand over myself. "Look at me."

"You're perfect for him." Edie winks.

"I don't know how I can compete."

"Is it a competition? I hate to state the obvious, but she's dead."

"She haunts him." I glance over at Hank, noting him watching me.

"She does?" Edie asks, turning in the same direction.

"He still hurts from her not loving him, and each time we get too close, he presses me back."

"But he's here today."

I stare at my new friend. What is she saying? "He came to the play, right? They don't get involved with the kids unless they want to be with you. I watched Tommy do it with my kids. He didn't have to. He could have been a one and done with me, which is embarrassing to admit, but he wasn't."

I note the huge rock on her finger, marking her as his wife. "I don't know what to say. I think I need to let this soak in a little bit."

"I understand, I really do, but realize that over there sits a man who just wants to be with you."

chapter 20

Take The Swing and Hope Not to Miss

[Hank]

Midge sits next to me but feels miles away. My hand covers hers, and she smiles weakly. I have some explaining to do, but now doesn't seem like the right time.

"Uncle Tommy, take me swinging." Ivy's youngest daughter, Emaline, looks like a porcelain doll. With blonde hair and blue eyes, she's precious as she plays with the medallion necklace around Tommy's neck.

Ava walks over and hugs him over the shoulders. "Yes, swings."

"All right, you two hooligans. Swing time." He stands as Ava latches onto his back, and Emaline curls around his neck. Carrying both seems like an unlikely feat, but he nods to me. "Follow me."

I peek at Midge, who's chewing her lip, thinking I shouldn't leave her when Tommy interjects.

"I need help, man. Come with me." The hint is there. *Give her space.* Squeezing her fingers, her responding squeeze is small comfort before I stand and follow my old friend.

We each push a girl on the swings, silent a moment while they squeal with delight and cry out *higher*. Standing here pushing them and watching Liam, I struggle with all the things I've missed out on. However, raising a child were never meant to be for me.

"We might as well get it over with. Just ask me so I can tell you for the thousandth time, no." I'm not surprised at Tommy's sharpness.

"I never believed her. I still don't."

"Maybe you don't. But she's gone. You can't help him."

Him. "I still want to see him."

"Why?"

"Because Lawson is my son." The words linger between us.

"You don't know that," Tommy grits his teeth, careful with his choice of words. Tommy's been conditioned to say Lawson isn't mine so often he can't shift his mindset to the truth.

"How do you know he's *not* mine?"

"Kit told me."

"Oh, and Kit was always truthful?" We both know Kit's honesty only fit her needs. She wanted me but she didn't love me. That's the only truth there was between us. And I gave into her each and every time despite the real lie. The lie that her boy wasn't mine.

"Look, what difference does it make? He doesn't know you're his father. He'll never understand the concept. Just let it die." Tommy pauses, lowering his voice. "No pun intended."

Kit's secrets went to the grave with her, but I still believe someone knows the truth.

"It matters to me. Let me take a paternity test."

"Are you fu— serious?" He pauses, hesitating to swear in front of his great-nieces.

"Yes. If he isn't my kid, I'll let it rest."

Tommy stares off into the distance a moment before speaking again. "See that woman over there?" I look, assuming he's implying Midge. "She wants to love you. Let her."

"I want to open up to her, and that means sharing *everything* with her."

"Like you did about being a rock star?"

The hit hurts, but he's right. I didn't tell her outright because it isn't who I am anymore. That life is in the past, as Kit should be.

"I had my reasons," I stammer.

"Let me guess. You wanted her to know you, not the fame, not the fortune." He stops, and I snort. We both know I have no fortune left. I blew it all. *Washed-up musician turns mechanic*, that's how the headlines read. The truth stings.

"Look, man. I loved you then. You were one of my best friends despite the drama with my sister. I tried to protect you both, but you were a train wreck together. In the end, I had to choose family first. My biological family. Kit was dying." There's a pleading note in his voice, almost begging me to understand, and I do. Brut holds the same loyalty to me as his younger sibling. That devotion is something I admired about Tommy and Kit, but when Tommy turned his back on me, it stung. It still does.

"I want to be friends again, if it's possible. I want our girls to be friends because Midge makes Edie happy. I want Edie happy. I love her." He exhales. "Dude, can you imagine it? Love. Real love where she loves you back unconditionally? It's why you didn't tell her, right? I get it." Tommy swipes a hand through his longer locks. "But this? This Lawson business isn't going to help. You need to move on."

Tommy knows I felt betrayed by Kit. If I only knew the truth, I could let old hurts rest. "I have moved on. I just don't want any secrets from Midge. Help me out and I'll let it go."

Tommy looks off in the distance a second. "And what if he is yours? What then? You gonna provide for him? Take him in? Take him from his home?"

"No." My adamant tone makes Ava flinch in the swing, and I push her gentler. "Sorry, honey," I mutter. Turning to Tommy, I continue. "I have no intention of taking away anything. I'll give what I can, if it's what he needs. If it's what you want. I just want to meet him."

Tommy stares off in the distance again before his shoulders fall and he sighs heavily. "It's Sunday."

Sunday. Kit's day to be home, sight unseen. My day to visit her grave. My routine to pass her house and watch the light in the house where my son lives.

"You can get old Doc to do the test, and you know it."

Tommy curses under his breath, forgetting the girls for a second and closing his eyes. "Let me think about this."

As far as I'm concerned, there's been too much thinking and not enough action in this matter.

149

+ + +

I return to our sideline set-up where Ivy jostles a crying Granger, and Edie looks up at me.

"Tommy asked if you could help him with the girls for a few minutes."

"Oh, yes. Of course." She stands, sensing more than what I've asked. Thank goodness. I need a few minutes alone with Midge.

"I think I'll go feed Granger in the car, turn on some air conditioning." Ivy follows Edie's hasty, awkward exit, and I sit behind Midge, spreading my legs around her while she sits outstretched on Edie's blanket. I want to drag her someplace private, but I don't want her to miss her son's game even though I sense she isn't following it.

"I'm gonna talk, baby," I say in her ear, not touching her though my fingers itch to rub her arms. "And I hope you'll just listen."

She nods slightly, keeping her eyes focused forward on the ball field. Our position reminds me of our first meeting, and I wish I had a mirror to see her reflection, but I won't pull her away from her child.

"I'm Hank Paige, drummer from Chrome Teardrops. We were the band who played with Kit Carrigan, Tommy's sister, and the woman I thought might be the love of my life."

Midge shivers, and I want to touch her, reassure her, but I can't make this a public display.

"But what do I know of love, Midge? I was constantly drunk, sometimes strung out. Kit was my drug. She called, and I went. We fucked. We fought. It was a recipe for disaster. She shared herself with others, and I did the same. We were reckless. *A train wreck*, Tommy called us, and he wasn't wrong." I exhale. "I can't change my past. I can't erase it. I can't erase her. She and the band were my life for almost two decades, and I loved her in my self-destructive way. And then, she got diagnosed with breast cancer. She dried up minus the pot for chemo. I spiraled down. I couldn't imagine life without her or the band, and I lost them both. I already told you, I asked her to marry me too many

150

times to count, and she always said no." Midge's head hangs lower, a hand rising to swipe at her cheek. Is she crying for me? I don't want her pity. I want her understanding.

"Midge, I understand now why she always said no. I wasn't responsible. I wasn't solid. Did you know her first husband overdosed and died? Ivy's father did that." Midge twists her head to look at me, and I wipe the tear at the corner of her eye. "It scared Kit. Any other man who got too close might do the same thing, and I was so much like him. Drinking. Drugs. And then…"

I don't know if I can finish, but I fear I'll lose her if I don't.

"And then she did something unthinkable. She lied. A major lie. A life-changing lie, and I just want the truth." I kiss her shoulder because I need to connect with her somehow. "A lie is unforgiveable sometimes. But please, forgive me for not telling you everything.

"I can admit I'm an alcoholic. I can say it easily enough, recognizing the truth about myself, but my history is a thick scab. Most of it I'm not proud of, and I don't want to peel it back off. I don't want you to see me in that light."

"I don't," she says quickly. I rest my head on her shoulder, as small relief creeps through me. She continues, "It's just a lot to take in."

"I know."

Midge continues. "She was a superstar, Hank. If you loved her, no matter what way, how could I possibly be enough for you? You're sitting here at my son's baseball game on a Sunday. You don't get any more mundane than that. And I wouldn't trade it *for me*." She pauses, swallowing. "But I'm not flashy, or fashionable, or famous. I can't . . ." She hesitates but doesn't add what she wishes to say.

"I don't want you to be famous. You're plenty flashy, lady, and I know nothing about fashion, so what do I care? Go naked." I stop. "Wait, not in front of others because I want you all for me. I want you, Midge."

She nods slowly, but her eyes remain concerned.

"Middy?" I question, but Edie's voice interrupts us.

"That's it, girls' night out."

"Darlin'?" Tommy questions, holding Emaline on his hip and Ava's hand as she stands beside him.

"We need some girl time—Ivy, Midge, and me. Call Gage and tell him tough shit, he's getting his kids. You can help him. Maybe Hank wants to hang as well."

"Darlin', it's pasta night." I'm sensing a ritual, and Tommy doesn't look too pleased.

"Not tonight, baby. Us girls need each other." Edie smiles weakly at Midge, and Midge nods in return.

"Want to come over for a bit?" Tommy addresses me as way of giving in. Maybe he does want to be friends again.

I cup Midge's face, turning her to look at me. She's trembling, and I reach for my shirt draped over the arm rest of a chair. Slipping it over her, I say, "Damn, I knew I'd like you in my clothing, but not when you look so sad."

She lifts the cuff and inhales while I watch her wrap her arms around herself.

"I think I need to go with them," she says, and my heart plops to my gut. She's going to walk away from me. And somehow, losing Midge seems worse than ever being rejected by Kit.

chapter 21

Girls Night Out and Hangover Sex

[Midge]

A break follows Liam's first game before the second game will start, and after the men leave, I help another mom distribute sports drinks and fruit slices for a snack. Returning to the blankets, I find Edie and Ivy in a serious conversation.

"I think Gage is having an affair."

I gasp at Ivy's revelation.

"How can you say such a thing?" Edie asks. I agree. I've seen Gage Everly kiss his wife. It's a porn scene. He couldn't possibly want someone else.

"It's bound to happen, right? I mean, he's a rock star," Ivy says sadly, blinking rapidly.

"That's not an excuse," Edie snips. Our eyes meet, and I see the sisterhood. We've both been cheated on. What is it with men? Can they not keep it contained? Committed?

"I don't believe it." I try to reassure her with a smile and a rub of her arm. She shrugs under my touch, not pulling away but resolved to a sad reality.

"He's been acting so strange. Late-night phone calls. The other night, he completely forgot he had to watch the kids, or so he says. He had Petty set to watch them after I left, only I was running late, and Petty arrived early."

"Not Petty," Edie shrieks with a sharp laugh. She covers her mouth in horror.

"Why? What's wrong with him?" I question.

"He redefines man-whore. He can't take care of himself, let alone three children," Edie clarifies.

"I don't know what to do. I don't know what to think. Gage pursued me so hard when we were younger, and he promised me so many things. Maybe he's had a change of heart."

"No," I say, holding her upper arm, hoping to comfort her. "I've seen him with you. The way he looks at you. The way he kisses you." I blush, but Ivy doesn't bat a lash. "He loves you."

"It has to be something else, honey," Edie adds. "Maybe he's planning a surprise for you."

Ivy adamantly shakes her head. "He isn't. He isn't good at those things. He'd tell me long before he could surprise me." She smiles weakly at the thought.

"This happens when men turn thirty, right? Some kind of midlife crisis or something." Her innocent eyes beg us to support her.

"Thirty-five," Edie and I say in unison and then laugh. She high-fives me.

Growing serious, Edie reaches for Ivy's hand. "Honey, you're both just busy. Three kids. The therapy school. Another album for the band. You have a lot going on."

Ivy swipes at the corner of her eye. "I guess so." Edie wraps her arm around Ivy, holding her husband's niece close to her chest.

This reminds me. I'm dating her mother's ex-lover, a man who professed his love repeatedly to Kit, and she rejected him. Why?

"I'm sorry I didn't know about Hank," I interject, not certain what exactly I'm apologizing for. "I didn't know he loved your mom."

Ivy's eyes widen, dismissing me with a wave. "They had a strange relationship. Love-hate. She hated how she loved him so much and couldn't admit it. He hated how he loved her so much because she never accepted him. She was scared after my dad, always telling me and my brother we didn't need men when we had her as our mama."

"You have a brother?" I blurt, not recalling having heard of him.

Edie and Ivy exchange a look before Ivy says under her breath, "I'm tired of hiding him."

Sitting up straighter, she looks at me. "Yes, I have a brother. His picture hangs in the entry to the therapy school." I recall the black and white of Kit Carrigan laughing with her arm around a young man in a wheelchair.

"Is that why you started the school?"

Ivy shakes her head. "I did it for me. I needed something, to be more than Gage Everly's wife, more than a mother. Lawson was the inspiration for my degree in music therapy. He's very important to me."

"Lawson? That's your brother's name?"

Ivy nods. "He's three years younger than me."

I have so many questions, but Ivy turns away from me to watch the game. Edie catches my eye, willing me to understand. Now isn't the time for answers.

Instead, I shift gears. "So girls' night out. I vote margaritas."

+ + +

I'm pushing my luck with margarita number four but being out with other women has been a treat. I didn't socialize with the girls at work often, always feeling a little bit too old for them. Besides, I had a husband and kids at home when some of them didn't. When it was only me and the boys, the pressure to get home as quickly as I could each night didn't afford me the opportunity to mingle with colleagues. Having new friends is refreshing, as are limes and tequila.

An hour later, the result equals slow recognition of being propped over my toilet with a thick hand on my back as my body convulses, expelling all four margaritas. My hair is pulled back to the nape of my neck as my stomach roils, and I throw up again.

"It's okay, baby." A smoky voice does nothing to calm me, and I realize I'm crying as well as vomiting. "Get it out."

Hank's soothing tone makes me whimper. I don't remember him arriving at the bar, and more importantly, what is he doing here?

"Sweet cheese, leave me to die."

"You're not dying, lady," he chuckles, smoothing his hand down my back. I have a strange sense of still wearing his too large shirt and my underwear. Nothing else. Lord, what have I done? Another bout of nausea rocks me, and I gag over the bowl, spitting in hopes something will happen.

Hank's lying; I'm dying.

"I'm sorry," I mutter, embarrassed I can't party like a rock star or like I'm still twenty-three. "Oh God, Hank, I'm so sorry," I say, remembering he's a recovering alcoholic, and I'm drunk. Tears still wash down my face, and I lower my head to the seat.

Hank folds his body to the floor, propping his back against the cabinet. He gently tugs me, so I curl between his legs and lay against his chest. A heavy hand plays with my hair, combing it back from my face and brushing it down my back.

"I'm sorry," I weakly repeat. "This is so embarrassing."

"Lady, this ain't nothing compared to what I've seen or done. Just relax. We'll stay right here as long as you need." My eyes close at his gentle touch, but that makes the world spin.

"What time is it?" I note the darkness, but my eyes drag closed again.

"After midnight."

"Cripes, the boys—"

"Know their mom isn't feeling well, and I'm staying to take care of her."

I sniffle, a choking sob exhaling with a heavy breath.

"You're kind of good to me." Tears begin to flow again with the thought.

"Want to be better than good," he mutters, his chest vibrating as he speaks. His heart beats a steady rhythm under my ear, and my lids grow heavy.

"You could be somebody's someone," I whisper, growing comfortable on his chest. He says something, but I don't hear him.

When I wake next, I'm in bed with my robe wrapped around me, wearing a tank top and my underwear. I'm on top of my duvet with three pillows under my head. I have a kink in my neck and a headache like Ronin's marching band struts through my brain.

"Holy God," I moan, holding my forehead and squeezing my eyes shut against the brightness of morning. My head rolls to face the clock, and I curse again. *Mother of all things holy*, my head. Noticing the time, I swing my legs off the bed and shakily press myself upward. Voices from downstairs alert me the boys are awake, and I need to explain myself. My legs tremble when I stand. Reaching for the wall, I think I can fake it, but I race to the bathroom. Expelling the last of anything left in my stomach, I stand to see a pallid face cleaned of makeup and my hair piled on my head. I don't recall washing my face or twisting up my hair. I look like death.

Making my way down the stairs, I stop when I hear one voice in particular.

"Don't you worry about your mom. She'll be fine. Just a little under the weather." His smoky, early morning voice warms my heart, and my knees collapse. I crumple to the stairs and sit.

"Is that what the kids are calling it nowadays?" Elston teases, and I hear Hank chuckle.

"Who gets ham? Want mustard?" Is he making them lunch? "Chips?" he questions.

"Only one crunchy, Mom says. We have to have a fruit."

"Good plan," Hank adds after Liam sets him straight on my lunch rules.

"Ronin, what do you want?" My head tips to the wall as I listen to Hank handle my boys and their morning routine. In fact, he might be handling it better than I do. I'm usually racing around, picking up clothing and barking out schedules. When I worked at Bigle, the morning chaos was even worse. It's one of the reasons I've been toying with going out on my own and working for myself. I could set my schedule to fit my needs, not the other way around.

When the kids leave for school, the kitchen grows quiet, and I close my eyes with the peace.

"You're alive," Hank teases as he stands at the bottom steps, holding a plate with two halves of toast and a small glass of something resembling a smoothie.

"I think I'll live." My voice cracks, hoarse from crying and throwing up. Brushing my teeth has done wonders for my spirits. "But I'm tired. I need to shower and get to work." I don't move, though.

"I called in for you. I think I might have some pull with the boss." He winks as he steps up the two stairs and sits next to me.

"I don't want to seem irresponsible. Last night proved I clearly can be."

"Lady, we all need to let our hair down at some point. Typically, it's not into a toilet, but—"

"Ugh. Gross. Did that happen?"

"Nope. I had it."

The comment makes me turn my head to him. He took care of me. My hair. My face. Even my robe. It was all him, there for me.

"Thank you," I whisper.

"Anytime." He leans forward for his quick kiss. "You brushed your teeth."

"I had to. Besides, how could you kiss me otherwise?"

"I'd kiss you any way I could, little lady." He makes me laugh, but it hurts my head, and I wince.

"Toast?" He holds out the plate.

"I think I'll pass for now." Setting the plate and the glass on the stair, he turns to me, scooping under my knees and around my back.

"Okay then. Back to bed for now."

I squeak as he struggles at first, tossing me gently to situate me so he can carry me up the staircase. Setting me on my bed, he heads for my bathroom as I fall over to my side. Returning, he holds my hairbrush in his hand. He crawls behind me, prompting me to sit up, then slips his legs on either side of mine. He removes my crazily wound hair and begins to brush it. The methodic movement soothes, and I close my eyes as he strokes over the long tresses. *Is there any greater pleasure than having your hair brushed by someone else?* We remain quiet for several minutes. Eventually, he separates my hair into three sections and braids it.

"Sweet cheese, Hank. Why aren't you married?" My eyes remain closed, languishing in the pleasure of him working with my hair.

He chuckles softly. "Guess it wasn't for me," he says, and I remember what he told me. *He asked several times, but she always said no.*

"She must have been crazy," I whisper.

"Why?" His fingers still. Curiosity fills his voice.

"I can't imagine why she would say no to you, Hank."

"I wasn't good." He exhales, rubbing his hands down my shoulders.

"You're perfect," I quietly murmur. A brief kiss lands on my neck before he scoops the single braid to the side.

"You need to lie down again." He's gentle in his direction, swinging his leg around me, and I tip to my side. He climbs up behind me, stifling a yawn, and I roll to face him.

"Why'd you quit drinking? Was it because of her?" He closes his eyes and rubs down his face, stroking at his stubbled chin. The beard has grown a bit thicker since yesterday.

"I almost killed a kid. I almost took a boy from some family. I'd never forgive myself." He pauses. "Not having a child of my own, I still knew the emptiness they'd feel, and that sensation just snapped me out of it. I went to rehab. Did the twelve steps, but sometimes, the meetings made me want to drink again. The sob stories. The heartbreak. I had to just make a clean break for myself, and that's how I lost touch with the band. I couldn't be around the lifestyle anymore." He rolled his head to look at me. "But the band was already done. Kit was dead, and we were over."

I stare at liquid silver filled with pain. I sit up and remove my robe. His gray eyes narrow at me.

"Middy, whatcha doing?"

"I want to curl into you." My voice is low, hesitant as I reach for his t-shirt, wondering where his flannel went, and tug it off him. The shirt hardly left much to the imagination, but in broad daylight, his naked chest is a masterpiece. Symbols and swirls, colors and calligraphy cover a good portion of his upper body and down each arm. I push at him to lie back and return to my side. He shifts, so I tuck into his chest, his arms wrapping over me.

+ + +

"Feels nice." I'm dreaming, and I purr as Hank laves my nipple. My tank top presses upward. My hips rock as he draws me deeper, lapping over the nipple before enveloping the achy globe into his warm mouth. "Like that."

My hand finds his head, scratching lightly at his short hair as I separate my knees. My other hand cups my neglected breast before skimming down my stomach, heading for the promise land. I'm almost there, wondering if an orgasm is a possibility in my dream, when I feel fingers engulf my wrist, and my eyes flutter open. My hand stills on Hank's head. *His head* which is literally in my hand.

I don't need to glance down to know where his face rests. And the noise coming from his mouth warns me he isn't stopping. He nips my taut peak before heading for the other breast.

"Hank." My voice squeaks. He still grips my wrist at my waist.

"You're all sprawled out, sexy and pliant, moaning in some dream. How could I resist you?" He looks up at me, his tongue dragging around my nipple before he blows on the warm wetness, pinching me more erect with the cool stream of his breath. My sex clenches, and my fingers twitch. He looks down at my hand and then back up at me. "Where were you going, little lady?" he teases, his voice low, smoky, gravelly.

"Let me see," he commands, rolling back to his side, propping up on one elbow. His drags a finger lazily around my breast, causing tingles to erupt from his touch. When I don't move my hand, he tugs at my wrist, dragging it to the waistband of my underwear. "Let me see, wild thing." The smooth tenor of his voice guides me like he did the night in the tub. I close my eyes and lower my fingers, finding the nub—hot, pulsing and ready.

"Fuck, that's hot, baby," he moans beside me before slipping his finger next to mine.

"I like it better when you do it," I admit. His mouth returns to my breast, sucking at the swell as his finger dives into me. I'm a bundle of sensory overload, and within minutes, I'm writhing under his eager fingers and holding his head to keep his mouth latched onto me.

"Hank," I warn. Arching off the bed, my knees coming together to hold his hand between my thighs. He pulls back from my breast to watch as I ride the wave, moaning and mewling with a long, languid release. My arms fall to my sides as I look up at him. He's such a beautiful man.

He scoots off the bed, quickly removing his jeans and boxers. Then, he tugs my ankles apart and crawls between my legs. Holding himself, he drags the head through wet folds, ripe and eager for him.

"I shouldn't have come inside you last week without protection. I'm clean, totally clean, but it was a bit irresponsible of me. You're still young enough to get pregnant."

Sweet cheese, I don't want to think about such things.

"But I liked watching me connect with you, little lady. It's quite the turn-on."

I take the risk to watch what he's doing to me, spreading me, seeping along my slit. He's intoxicating, and the freedom of touching like this in broad daylight causes me to clench. I want him inside me.

He pulls back and reaches for the back pocket of his jeans. I watch as he rolls on the condom, stretching it over his solid length. In the sunlight, I see for the first time how truly large he is. My mouth almost waters with the excitement that *that* is going to fill me. He's gentle as he presses inward, watching as his dick disappears within me. As he balances on two hands over me, he groans once he's as far as he can go. He slips a hand under my backside and pivots, rolling onto his back and forcing me to straddle him.

Staring up at my breasts, he begins to fondle them, massaging and squeezing, forcing them together.

"You have the best tits." The compliment seems brazen in the sunshine, yet the bit of exhibitionist in me doesn't care. I'm so lost in the movement of rocking over him, the angle somehow deeper with me above him. I set a steady rhythm, my breath catching as our pace quickens. My fingers slip down my belly, touching the pleasure point to add to the sensation. Something builds inside me, like a volcano rumbling, cresting, boiling.

"Hank," I scream as I clutch at his hips with my knees and hammer over him, milking him while I come a second time. I don't know how he does this to me. I've never come twice in my life, but with him, I just want to keep going, and the bliss drags on and on and on. I'm barely slowing down when Hank sits up, wraps an arm around my waist, and spins us again.

He's over me, sliding his hands up my stomach and over my breasts before skipping to my hands and raising them above my head. Entwining our fingers, he pins me to the bed, thrusting into me so quick, so hard, my breasts jiggle and the bed quakes.

"Goddamn, I . . ." His voice fades, but in my head, I complete the phrase. *I love you.* How difficult would the words be to say? How much meaning would they hold? A tear drips from my eye.

"You okay, baby?" His voice is strained as he pummels into me.

"More," I whisper without the breath to explain my meaning. He doesn't pause at my response, but stills, pulsing inside me with the tapping rhythm I like. Once drained, he collapses next to me, still buried within.

He kisses my shoulder, lingering, and I cup his head.

"What did *more* mean?" The question startles me, and I roll my head to look at him.

"More kisses, more than okay, more of everything."

He returns his mouth to my shoulder and smiles against my skin.

chapter 22

More

[Hank]

I'm insatiable for her, touching her in the shower until she gives in and gives me another orgasm. After a quick late afternoon meal of scrambled eggs and fresh toast, it's time to leave.

"Don't want your boys thinking I spent the whole day ravishing their mother." Her face pinches at the comment, and she looks away. Something fills her eyes, but she blinks too quickly for me to catch it.

Midge has a nice house, and it reminds me of all I had and lost. I don't want to leave, actually, but I don't want her boys to think I've been hanging out all day. Last night, Ronin thought we should take her to the hospital while Elston understood her blight. One too many margaritas in her small body backfired. Liam, on the other hand, had slept through the ruckus, but I worried he couldn't miss the loud sobs of his mom. While the boys remained protective, they were willing to let me deal with her. None of them questioned my staying the night.

Turning back to me, she asks, "Did I say anything or do anything I shouldn't have last night? Besides throwing up and ruining your shirt."

My lips twist. How can I tell her all the things she said? Sobbing into my t-shirt, she cried about never having passion like she sees in Gage and Ivy, never being loved like Tommy must love Edie, or how I loved Kit. It broke my heart, but it wasn't the time to explain how I'm questioning my relationship with my ex-lover more and more.

"What do you think you said?"

"If I was mean, I take it back."

163

My cheeks fall from the teasing grin. *Mean to me?* She's adorable, and everything she says sews my heart back together. "Don't take it back. Don't take any of it back." I reach for her shoulders. She's perched on a stool at the kitchen island, and I'm standing, ready to exit.

"What did I say?"

"Just don't take it back." My voice lowers, pleading with her. If she reneges on her words, I'll break.

"Hank," she whines.

"I don't want to tell you." I know enough to realize drunk Midge might have admitted too much. Isn't there some saying about alcohol setting you free? Wait, maybe that's the truth will set you free.

"How bad was it?" she asks, lowering her head and tucking her fingers into my waistband.

"You said if I asked, you'd marry me."

"Sweet cheese," she moans, her forehead hitting my chest. "I'm—
"

I cover her mouth with my hand, stopping any words which might ruin it for me. Instead, I lift her chin and force her to look up. Her eyes remain closed, so I kiss her quickly. A light brush.

"Why do you kiss me like that? So fast our lips barely touch?"

I stiffen, and she doesn't miss the tension. I hadn't realized I do it. It's a habit. Something I've done with someone else. Kit didn't allow me to kiss her in public, so I snuck in quick ones to get her attention. Sometimes, I did it to piss her off, knowing she didn't want anyone to see us.

"I—"

"Never mind." Midge cuts me off with a wave as I hesitated to answer. "Don't answer that."

I'd like to think I've gotten away with not explaining myself, but my stomach turns. Midge pats my chest like she's placating me, and I don't like the feeling it elicits after what we've done this afternoon.

"I'll see you tomorrow at work."

"I like the sound of that, Middy." I do. I like seeing her every day in the garage although I know she's smarter than our place and has more creativity than is required to be our office manager. Still, it's nice to see her daily.

I lean forward for the quick kiss and hesitate. Instead, I lay one on her cheek, but it doesn't feel right. A word whispers through my head. *More.* Does she mean she wants me to kiss her in front of her boys? Out in public? All the time? I'd gladly oblige, but right now, I need to go.

"I've got a car to work on." I wink.

She chuckles as she shakes her head. "I can't believe I've pulled this off. It won't be a reality until Friday, when I present to Pendelton."

I still don't understand why she wants to work for the man so much. In my opinion, she's got nothing to prove to him. He seems like such an ass, but what do I know.

"Friday. I'll bring champagne." Her eyes widen, and I chuckle. "For you, not for me. Don't worry." I don't want her to have any concern I'll break my promise to myself and drink.

"Tomorrow first," she says, and I smile at the thought.

As I'm driving home, I feel lighter, almost pleased with myself. It's strange feeling until it clicks that for the first time in years, I didn't visit the cemetery on Sunday. I didn't perform my ritual. I grow uneasy for a few seconds, wondering if I should head to Kit's grave, but then I realize skipping the habit might be half the reason I feel so much better.

When I arrive at Restored Dreams, Brut scowls at me.

"What the fuck happened?"

"She had a little too much ladies' night." I motion with my thumb and pinky, tipping my hand toward my lips.

"You got her drunk?" He eyes me suspiciously.

"No." I snort. "She went out with Edie, Tommy's new wife, and Ivy."

"Kit's daughter?"

I nod, and Brut lets out a low whistle. "You just can't get away from them."

I think about it for a moment. "You know, because of them I found Midge. If Tommy hadn't contacted the garage, looking for me, inviting me to his party, I would have missed out on…" I almost say *the woman of my dreams*. Is she? In many ways, yes, Midge is a dream come true.

"I'd say yes if you asked me." Drunken tears followed when she tried to backpedal, explaining she wasn't pressuring me, and she knew I wasn't ready for something so serious. Then she argued with herself that she wasn't ready either, claiming she was a hot mess with three boys and no job. God, can she ramble herself into a tizzy. I stroked her back and swept her hair from her face, letting her get all her emotions out.

"Missed out on what?" Brut interrupts my thoughts, muttering an additional comment. "Please don't say sex."

"No, it's not just sex. Midge is. . .different."

"That's like saying she has a good personality."

"She does. She's…special to me."

Brut inserts a finger in his mouth, fake gagging. *What are we, five?* "That sounds awful. Midge is different and special, but Jesus, she could be so much more if you let her."

More. "I am letting her."

"Yeah, and what are you doing for her?" I tap my palms on the counter. What am I to her? Kissing her like I kissed Kit isn't going to endear me to Midge. If Midge means more to me, I shouldn't be sneaking in kisses but kissing the fuck out of her. I stare at my brother a moment.

"I don't know."

A puff of air escapes him as he shakes his head. "You're a fucking idiot," Brut mutters, picking up his tablet and typing something on the screen. "After your day off, we need help on Carlson's Corvette, and Pendelton's Bentley is ready for paint." Discussion over, I'm dismissed. The shift reminds me of Kit, and I hate the restored feeling. Images of Midge's pretty brown eyes looking up at me make me think, maybe, just maybe, she'd never dismiss me.

+ + +

On Tuesday, I get the call I've been waiting for.

"Doc can see you at two." Tommy's gruff voice shouldn't sting, but it does. Drake Henderson was the band's physician. The one we went to when we needed a quick hangover solution or a remedy for bad drugs. He took care of an STD for Denton Chance, our guitarist, and referred Kit to an oncologist when he suspected her cancer. He also took care of her pregnancies—that is, he delivered both her babies. After her second child, she had her tubes tied to prevent any other mishaps. It hadn't been a condom thing the second time around. It had been unwrapped, too quick, too fast, without a thought to what could happen. Kit never wanted *that* to happen again.

My heart races with a million thoughts. What will this test mean? Will the truth really set me free? If it goes one way, I'll have lies confirmed. If it goes another direction, I'll have some honesty, but what will I do with it?

And what will I tell Midge? I want her to know everything—no secrets—but I also feel like I'm not ready to expose all until I have answers.

"I'll be there." It will be the first time I've visited Kit's house in almost a decade. Years of recovery after years of self-loathing after the years of her suffering and subsequent death. So many lost years, I sigh, leaning against the Corvette I should be working on, staring at the paint job on Pendelton's beast before glancing over at my own neglected baby, the black beauty of my Mustang. The half-finished car glares at me like a metaphor for my life. A dream waiting to be restored, only can something old be renewed? Even a classic isn't the same once it's been revamped.

I think about myself and my love for Kit in comparison. I don't want to revive a love like I knew. I want a newer model—one unused, untattered, untainted. My eyes drift to Midge. She's standing near the window that oversees the garage, laughing as she talks to Chopper. He's taken a real liking to her, and I wonder if he misses the mother he never had. Her smile lights up the place. The sound of her laughter like forgotten music in my ears.

I love her.

It hits me hard, right in the chest as I stare at her across a greasy garage and through a dirty window. I love that woman, and I want to make all her dreams come true because I know she's a dream come true for me.

First, I need to make this appointment. I have just enough time before my shift at the crisis center.

+ + +

The night is slow, and sometime around midnight, I decide to call Midge.

"You still up, baby?" I speak softly into the phone.

"Hey, yeah. You okay?" I love how she detects in my voice I might *not* be all right.

"Whatcha doing up so late, little lady?"

She yawns. "Working. I'm so close. I just want one more design for Pendelton." I hear the smile in her voice, and my shoulders relax. I hadn't realized how tense I'd been since the paternity test. Doc swabbed the inside of my cheek. Like an expectant parent, I'm nervous, anticipating the results. Within seventy-two hours, my entire life will change—one way or another. I could be a father.

"I like the sound of your voice," I admit. I close my eyes, imagining the curve of her lips and the hint of her grin.

"That's sweet, honey." My heart skips a beat. She hasn't called me names like this before. "Slow night tonight?"

"I think I'm the one who needs to talk." I doodle on the edge of the desk calendar, scrolling out the design of music notes. I haven't played in years, and my fingers twitch, shifting the pencil to a drumstick and tapping lightly on the pad of paper.

"What is it?" Her concern makes my eyes close again. The rapping beat of the pencil increases, the *tap-tap* growing louder.

"Can I ask you to go somewhere with me on Sunday, but not tell you where or why yet?"

"Sure." She doesn't hesitate, and I still the motion of the pattering pencil.

"Don't want you to worry, though, okay?" Taking her with me on Sunday will be a big step in our relationship. I'm asking a lot of her without telling, but I don't want her thinking about anything other than her interview in a few days.

"Okay." Now, she hesitates.

"Promise me?" I tease.

"Yes, I promise."

The breathy sound ripples over my skin, and I'm the one who smiles, blushing at the thought of things I want to do to this woman.

"You okay?" she asks again, and I pick up the pencil, twirling it around, a rhythm forming in my head.

"Much better now. How are the boys?" I listen as she talks about her kids. She's so proud of them, concerned for them, loving them. I let my mind drift, lulled into the comfort of her voice for several minutes. Hearing her stifle another yawn, I suggest I let her go, assuring her I'm much better since we spoke.

"I didn't say anything. I just rambled." She laughs.

"I could listen to you ramble for the rest of my life."

"Hank," she exhales lightly.

"Sweet dreams, cupcake."

"Of you," she says quietly before the phone goes dead, and another smile crosses my lips.

chapter 23

Getting Things Off Your chest . . . Or Just Getting Off

[Midge]

I stare at the image before me, wondering what I'm missing. I'm cutting this design too close, and it reminds me I miss a team of graphic artists.

"Midge?" My name draws my attention, and I blink up from the desk at Hank. "I've called your name like three times, lady." Concern fills his expression, eyes puzzled, and I laugh.

"Sorry. I need to finalize this design and then practice my pitch." I wave dismissively. "I need someone to bounce the last idea off of."

"Try me," Hank says, and I snicker. He's sweet, but he doesn't understand too much about what I say regarding my sketches. Then again, he's a rather attentive listener.

"I'm going for something masculine. Updated. Pendelton is a traditional housewares company, and they are looking to step up their reputation. I've been thinking of contrasts in materials, like chrome edges on china and leather straps on recycled products." Hank stares at me, and I sense he's watching my lips instead of listening to my words. "Maybe I should see your place. Might help me get some inspiration."

I'm thinking if I scope out a man's pad, I might get some ideas of what men need and the types of textures they like. Not to mention, it's a little curious Hank hasn't invited me to his place.

"I don't have a home." My head snaps upward at the brusque words. Something on my face must concern Hank, because he explains, "I'm not homeless. I just don't have my own home."

I blankly stare at him, waiting for an explanation.

"I used to. . ." He sighs. "I just don't anymore. I have a room at Brut's place." He swipes a hand back and forth over his head, his hair standing up as a result.

I don't really know how to respond. There's a story here that Hank isn't telling me. Saved by the ring of the phone, he steps away as I take the call.

Later in the evening, I'm still struggling when Hank's hands cover my shoulders.

"Why you still here, little lady? It's late."

He massages gently, and my eyes want to close, but my mind won't shut down. I've been thinking all day about him not having a home and the secretive date on Sunday. He's being so mysterious, but I don't have time to decode him. I need to finish this design.

"The boys are with Paul for dinner. I need to practice my pitch. Guess I didn't realize how late it was. It's been busy here today, and I don't want Brut to think I'm taking advantage of this opportunity."

I've had to call some suppliers, hound a few others for the parts Brut has been waiting on, and handle Mrs. Prescott, a woman my age who is hot for the garage owner. She's looking for a bad boy to rev her engine. Although, I'm sensing Brut isn't into someone who is already married. Her husband's latest gift is a Mercedes convertible. It doesn't exactly fit the classic repair and body shop's normal models, but what do I know about cars.

"Practice with me. I'll listen."

Without waiting for a response, he picks up my images and my laptop. I've been bringing it here, so I don't clutter up their system, which is permanently pulled up to their server. I follow Hank into Brut's office, a little leery of his rough handling of my design board. He sets the laptop on the desk and sets the board next to it. Sweeping out a hand, he steps back and takes a seat on the couch.

I begin.

Twenty minutes later, I end. Hank stares at me, an arm casually slung along the back of the couch.

"You are so fucking sexy," he says, and I gasp.

I'm wearing ripped jeans, another cardigan, and my glasses. "Hank, were you listening?"

"I'm sold. I have no idea what you said, but your voice is music to me, and watching your lips move...hmm...mmm...mmm." I break into laughter, and he waves me toward him.

He grips behind my knees, and I comb my fingers through his hair.

"You just need to relax," he says, tipping forward so I keep stroking over his head. "You look uptight but sexy when you're serious. You got this," he says, speaking to my lower belly.

"I don't know," I whisper, and his head shoots up. He gently presses on the back of my knees, and I collapse, falling forward to straddle him, awkwardly balancing on his thighs.

"What don't you know?"

I toy with the button on his shirt. He's changed from his work coveralls and wears a clean shirt, open to expose a white t-shirt underneath. The name etched into a patch reads *Hank,* and I trace over the design.

"What I'm doing. This is one of the craziest things I've ever done— quit my job and demand an interview from someone. Someone big like Pendelton. What if I bomb this?"

Hank kisses my neck before sliding me off his lap to the couch and shifting to kneel on the floor between my knees. He rests his elbows on the edge of the cushions, surrounding my legs with his forearms.

"Lady, listen to me. You are beautiful and intelligent, and you got this. Pendelton is going to eat up those designs because they're modern and masculine, like you said, and even a guy like me would want them in my house." He pauses, the idea of him not owning one lingers between us. "Hell, I'd buy the whole collection. He's going to love them." Taking my hands, he kisses each one. "You know what you need? You need to relax, and then you need a cupcake."

"Maybe I need a cupcake to relax." The suggestion isn't lost on him. In fact, I think the word *relax* was code for something else. Hank unzips my jeans and tugs them down my thighs, all while keeping his eyes pinned to mine. It's like he's speaking to me, willing me to understand him as he struggles with my skinny jeans. He remains between my spread knees, dragging me forward so my backside balances on the edge of the cushions.

"Cupcake it is," he says, lowering his head and exhaling over my underwear. I'm already wet, the aroma of sex swirling between us. He removes my panties next, taking his time as he gives open-mouth kisses from my thighs to my knees. Once the stretched cotton traps my ankles, his mouth finds my center, and with one forceful lap, I melt into the leather underneath me. Hank's tongue curls, and my fingers comb into his hair once again. I take calming breaths, releasing the tension of the presentation and falling into the presence of this man. His attention is similar to his mouth on my upper lips, languid and lazy and memorizing every bit of me. I drip with anticipation, slipping deeper and deeper into the euphoria of connecting with him.

"Better than icing," he mutters, and I recall the first time his mouth was on me in this very office.

"Feels so good," I purr, stroking his hair and holding his neck. Ripples of pleasure tingle up my inner thighs as the anticipation of release builds. I'm almost there when Hank pulls back.

"I was almost there," I whimper.

"Damn," he says, looking down at me. Hasty hands go to his buckle as he unzips his pants and shoves the material to his knees. "I know, little lady, but I want to feel you around me."

Hank is looking at me in a way I feel so exposed, while turned on. My knees press inward, but his body prevents them from closing. Thick fingers stroke through wet folds, spreading me and reviving the lost fluttering sensation. I'm building again at his touch, growing desperate for more.

"Dammit," he mutters, fumbling on his knees for something in his pocket. Foil rips. He sheaths himself. I whimper with need. With that, he surges into me, filling me in one swift thrust, causing me to grunt at the rapid intrusion. My back arches until he starts to pull out. I open my eyes to find him watching our connection. I'm more curious about him than what's happening—what is he thinking, what does he see between us—but he's totally enthralled with his body entering mine.

"Sure like the feel of being inside you, baby. This could be home to me." I don't miss the emphasis on a place he doesn't have, and the hint of something meaningful in what he said. I press his cheek with my hand, and he finally looks up at me.

"Thank you." I don't know why I say it. I'm grateful for so many reasons. His attention. His touch. His everything.

He retreats to the tip before slowly refilling me, fueling up the feeling of glitter floating inside me. I'm ready to explode, and after a few more slow-paced thrusts, I do. That's when the hammering begins. Slipping one foot out of the jeans trapping my ankles, he hitches my leg over his shoulder.

"I'm not quite that flexible." I gasp, struggling to breathe with the sudden release and my body jackknifed in half. The rapid-fire pummeling raises the possibility I could go again. The fast rhythm, deep taps, and hard crash of us together, feeling so full, feeling one with him, builds another orgasm.

"You there again?" he huffs with the exertion of holding off until I'm ready straining his voice.

"Hank." I breathe out his name like I need air, and he pummels me, pounding me into the cushions so quickly, I grunt as we rut like wild animals.

"More," Hank groans, and I'm ready to tell him I can't take anymore when I clench, and he flinches, and we're coming together.

"Hank, I . . ." My voice fades as he stills, and I milk him with spasms, sucking at him while he pulses inside me. If I didn't know better, I'd swear the position would ensure pregnancy. Thank goodness for his endless supply of condoms. The thought lasts only one second before he leans forward, going for my mouth next, and kisses me with a fierce tongue and greedy lips. It's nothing like we've done so far, and aftershocks of him twitch inside me. We remain connected for several minutes until he pulls back with prolonged, lingering tugs of my lower lip.

"You're a queen," he says before kissing me again. "You're a superstar." Another kiss. "You've got this."

The words empower me, and my mouth curls against his.

"Better, cupcake?"

"Better than icing," I tease, and he kisses me one more time. Slower, more Hank-like. I do feel better. As a matter of fact, I feel a little invincible.

chapter 24

Champagne Cupcakes

[Hank]

I've looked at my phone five million times waiting for her call. I told her to let me know what happens as soon as she's done. Pendelton's car was delivered around ten this morning, and her meeting was at nine. Brut wanted assurance Midge would make it through the door. He didn't trust the man who's been a thorn in our ass for years with his fancy cars and demanding schedule. This rich dick's toys are our livelihood. Brut's interest in Midge's future warms my chest but also makes me want to punch him. He has a crush on my girl—correction, *woman*—and that pisses me off.

"Well, aren't you all romantic?" Brut teases me as I sit at Midge's desk, staring at the wildflower arrangement and the champagne cupcake in a cellophane package. Lily outdid herself with this one. The frosting shimmers with silvery candy that looks like little bubbles from the foam at the top of a flute of champagne. Even the cupcake wrapper looks goldish like the celebratory bubbly, and I thought it would be a nice surprise for my cupcake instead of a glass of the real deal.

"Shut up," I whisper harshly, but a smile tugs at my lips. I want to celebrate with her. "She worked hard for this, and I'm happy for her success. She deserves it."

"You really like her, don't you?"

"Yeah." My face heats, then I admonish myself. *What am I, fifteen?* It reminds me of last night. . .

When she finished her designs, she was relieved at the final product and convinced it was the best she could offer Pendelton. I decided to take his Bentley for a final ride and invited Midge. We climbed through the hills north of Los Angeles as the sun set in the west. Pulling over at a lookout, we sat for a minute, quiet in the silence of a day ending. Midge needed to get home tonight. The boys were waiting, plus she needed to rest before tomorrow, but I was happy to have this stolen moment. The words I love you filled my thoughts. I wanted to tell her these things but worried it was too much too soon.

Midge's hand covered mine, stroking my wrist and thumbing over the bracelets I'd begun wearing again.

"Thank you for this. It's beautiful." She stared at the sunset, but I watched her.

"So are you."

She turned to me, and the need to kiss her took all my thoughts. I intended to give her a quick kiss, just a brush, just a touch, anything to connect with her, but I couldn't. I needed more. My mouth lingered, tasting, savoring. She leaned forward, and within seconds, we were a heated mess, making out like two teenagers parked on a hill in the growing dark.

"I need to get you home," I said, and she laughed. We both recognized the irony of a curfew—only in her case, it was because of her children.

"Have dinner with us." The invitation startled me, but I couldn't say no to her. I had nowhere to go, and I wanted to be with her. Before I could answer, she kissed me again, pressing into me as her body begged for more. More.

"I want to take you in this back seat," I muttered against her lips. She broke away and surprised me by climbing over the seats.

"Come join me," she said, patting the leather bench. There was no way I could hike my body over the front seat like she did, so I pushed open the driver's door and entered through the back, laying her out as I stretched into the rear of the vehicle. I was too big for the space and sensing our position wouldn't work, Midge pressed on my chest.

"Sit up," she said, her breaths rasping. We shifted, and she straddled me, but not before she loosened my pants, and freed my dick from them so my ass hit the cool leather. Her dress looked like a long t-shirt, and she wiggled to remove her underwear. I chuckled at her haste.

"In a hurry?" I questioned, holding my breath for some reason.

"Greedy," she said, throwing her legs over mine and positioning me at her entrance. She was slick and ripe, and I wanted inside. "Condom?"

Ah, the responsible thing. She picked on me for having an endless supply, but I assured her it was only so I was ready for when she wanted me. One day, I'd be bare inside her again. Struggling for my wallet, I balanced her on my lap. She distracted me as she nibbled my neck and licked the shell of my ear. Once covered, I was under her, forcing her hips downward, slipping into her.

I exhaled upon entering her. "Fuck, that feels so good." The sensation never ceased to amaze me. I loved how she wrapped around me. I loved her, and again, the words whispered over my tongue.

Within minutes, she rocked in a way I knew meant she was close; she'd found her rhythm.

"Hank," she cried softly. "Come with me."

I couldn't time it like that. It just happened the other night when we were wild on the couch in the office. I loved how pliable she was, willing to let me experiment with her and move her in the ways I liked.

"Right there, baby," I said, encouraging her to go for it. She let go, digging her short nails into my shoulders, her hips stilling as she clenched around me. Her head came to my shoulder as she pressed her lips against my neck. I followed her lead and released, filling her with my seed. The experience was better than watching fireworks. I saw color all the same, though, as this woman did that to me.

"I love you," she whispered, pressing light kisses over my neck.

She said it so softly, I took a second to decipher the words. The pause cost me. I wasn't quick enough, and she sat up. Looking down at my chest, avoiding my eyes, she didn't miss a beat in ignoring what she said.

"Dinner?" Her voice wasn't its typical strength.

"Midge, I . . ." She'd already pulled off me, squirmed to the seat and hustled on her underwear. She continued to avoid my gaze.

"My boys must be starving by now. Come have dinner with us. It will be fun." Still offering the invitation told me she hadn't changed her mind, but my grip on this situation slipped with each second. With her clothing straightened, she opened the back door.

"Midge, wait—" I was too late. She reentered through the front passenger door while I was still tucking myself back in my jeans. Facing forward, she watched the sliver of sunshine disappeared.

"It really was beautiful," she said quietly, and my heart dropped.

Returning to the present, my fingers spin the glass vase. Brut has wandered off, and my phone vibrates in my other hand.

"Hey baby, how'd it go?"

"It didn't." Sadness laces her voice.

Instantly, I'm on edge. "What happened?"

"He didn't show. His assistant took the presentation."

"What the fuck?" *That bastard.*

"Pendelton was detained, Julian said." Midge sighs.

"Who's Julian?" I lean back in her chair, swiping back and forth at the hair on my head.

"Julian Pendelton, his assistant and his son."

"Motherfucker."

"He liked the presentation well enough. Told me his dad would have the final say, though, and he'd pass on the information. Then he asked me to lunch. I thought he was being friendly. Trying to soothe my disappointment since his dad didn't show. When I declined, he asked me out for drinks. Said he thought there might be a way we could *ensure* I'd work with them."

"He was fucking hitting on you?"

"Maybe," she says, her voice lowering.

"No maybe. You are not fucking working for him." I don't know where the demand comes from, but I'm ready to punch someone and, sight unseen, Julian Pendelton is the man.

"Well, I appreciate the command," she snips. "But as I didn't get the job, I won't have to worry about it."

"You don't know the old man won't still hire you." I swallow the bitter thought of her working in close proximity to someone like Julian Pendelton. He's a sexual harassment case waiting to happen. Then again, I've been flirting and fucking her for almost two weeks now.

It's not the same thing. Midge means something to me even if I didn't say how I felt last night.

"That isn't how it works, Hank. If I don't get to show Pendelton myself, it's a firm pass on the project." Her voice shakes, and I worry she'll cry.

"What can I do?"

"Nothing." She exhales deeply again. "I don't know what I was thinking, quitting my job at forty-one when I have three kids still in school. I must have been crazy to think I could do this."

"Stop!" I bark. "I don't want you talking like this. We'll figure something out. Pendelton is an asshole." I'm huffing mad, body trembling with the need to crush something. This isn't fair. Midge Everette is one of the nicest people I've ever known. She worked damn hard on his campaign, and she doesn't deserve this kind of treatment.

"We," she whispers, the heartache slipping through the phone.

"Let me take you out tonight. Let's just hang." I'm brushing through my hair, fingers digging tunnels because I'm getting so worked up. I want to comfort her.

"My boys are home. It's pizza-movie night." She sniffs. "I'd like to just be home tonight." I recall how I didn't end up going to her house last night after my lost opportunity to tell her how I feel. "Let me come over." I'm practically begging. "My treat for pizzas." I need to do something.

"You don't have to do that. I'll be fine."

"I want to come over," I snap. I do, half thinking I might just show up even if she says no.

"Okay." Her voice quiet. "How about six?"

+ + +

When Midge opens the door, her frame looks even smaller although she smiles weakly. Her boys are fighting in the background.

"Deciding on a movie appropriate for all three of them is becoming more difficult."

I imagine the seventeen-year-old no longer wants to watch age-appropriate animation for a ten-year-old, but then again, the things I witnessed at ten were not cartoons. "Normally, blood and guts win." She chuckles lightly, leading me to her couch. Pizzas already cover her coffee table. Cans of soda line the edge of the surface.

"*Green Lantern* or *Hurt Locker*?" Liam asks me.

I look at Midge for support. She mouths *Green Lantern*, and I offer the suggestion. Elston groans, but Ronin high-fives Liam.

"Mom wants that one so she can drool over Ryan Reynolds," Elston mocks. "He's so cute, ew, ew, ew..."

The boys laugh, and Midge smirks. "I do not act like that, and I don't think he's cute." Her eyes shift to me, and my eyebrow rises.

"You can't say a girl thinks someone else is cute in front of her boyfriend," Liam states, serious and worldly at ten.

Midge's mouth falls open, and I chuckle.

Boyfriend? I mouth. She shakes her head, the weak smile returning. She sits near me on the couch but not close enough, so I reach out for the back of her neck, trying to make it appear as if I'm only resting my arm on the edge of the cushions. I massage lightly.

"How do you know this stuff?" Ronin asks.

"Carson says—"

"Ugh, not Carson," Ronin groans, covering his head with his hands.

"Who is Carson?" I whisper to Midge.

"Carson is Mick's little brother. Mick is Elston's best friend, and everything Carson knows about girls he learned from those two, which is nothing," Ronin explains, and Elston leans over the armrest and punches the arm of his younger brother who sits on the floor.

"Don't fight," Midge interjects, but the smile returns to her voice. Her shoulders are relaxing under my massage.

"It's true. Carson also says you shouldn't talk about other girls in front of the girl you like. This only makes her jealous," Liam continues spewing his limited wisdom about females. My head turns in his direction where he sits on the other side of his mother.

"You know what else you should do?" I offer and realize I have Elston's attention from across the room. "You should tell a girl how you feel about her. Be honest."

Midge closes her eyes while my fingers work to loosen the tension in her neck.

"You can't do that," Ronin interjects. "She might not like you back."

Elston snorts and returns his attention to his phone.

"Then again, she *might* like you back." I glance at Ronin a moment before turning to his mother. Her eyes remain shut.

"I don't even like any of the girls at my school," Liam interjects.

Ronin coughs, and Elston mutters something under his breath.

"Don't say that," Midge reprimands Elston, and then turns to Liam. "That's right, honey. No girls for you yet. You're too young."

"I kissed my first girl at eleven," Elston adds, portraying false bravado.

"Triple gold stars for you," Ronin snaps, rolling his eyes at his older brother.

"Who?" Midge asks, her attention on her firstborn.

"Maggie Schuster."

"What?" Midge laughs while Ronin asks, "Why?"

"Because she wanted me to," Elston says nonchalantly, but something in his tone hints he wanted to kiss whoever the girl is as well.

"Elston," Midge shrieks.

"It doesn't really matter who you kiss first, kid. It's who you kiss last." I tighten my squeeze on Midge's neck, but she doesn't glance over at me.

"Can we watch the movie already?" Liam groans. "I'm tired of talking about girls and kissing."

"That's right. You are only allowed to love me," Midge teases, curling her arm around her son's neck. He falls against his mom and remains there when she loosens her hold. My fingers toy with the collar of her shirt, and she turns her head to press her cheek against my arm. She rubs her face against my solid forearm for a moment and then rights her head.

I only want to love her as well.

The movie starts, and the boys interject throughout the show. Midge eventually leans against me while Liam stays tucked against her. The atmosphere warms my insides like hot coffee after a sleepless night. I'm comfortable here, enjoying her boys and their chatter. The feeling reminds me of all I once had. A nice place to live. A collection of people I considered friends. It also reminds me of all I long for. A family of my own. Whatever Sunday brings and my test results prove, I'll never have what Midge has here with her boys.

Unless I marry her.

My head swings in her direction, and I lower my lips to kiss her hair. My eyes shoot up to find Elston watching me.

Yeah, kid, the only woman who matters is the one you kiss last.

He looks away slowly, but Midge settles into me. I definitely want this. Every night.

L.B. DUNBAR

chapter 25

Secret Meetings

[Midge]

To my surprise, Hank doesn't try to kiss me when he leaves on Friday night, but he shows up on Saturday for Liam's second game of a doubleheader and then takes us out for burgers. Liam is falling for Hank like I have. Hank pays attention to details, and he asks Liam all kinds of questions about baseball. In true ten-year-old fashion, Liam sways the conversation through a plethora of topics before we finish eating.

"I'm sorry about that." I lightly laugh as we exit the diner.

"He's full of energy, but I enjoy him."

I like how Hank says this about my son. Unfortunately, he only hugs me before we part. I want to know what he's thinking. I totally messed up by blurting I loved him. The words simply escaped, creeping against his skin. When he's playful and carefree, the spontaneity of him gets to me—in a good way—but I took the rush of back seat sunset sex one step too far. I went for it with my feelings, expressing more than I should have said, which is out of character for me. I typically take things too seriously and I can be uptight. I'm responsible, I tell myself. The situation pushed me to be irresponsible with my emotions.

But the truth is I'm choking. Suffocating from commitments. I want a little room to breathe, be free, be silly, and Hank personifies those things for me at times. Now, another trait of mine takes over—I'm worried.

When he picks me up on Sunday, I'm a bundle of nerves. As we drive through the hills north of Los Angeles, Hank takes my hand and holds it on his thigh, but he's quiet. It's early evening, and I have no idea

184

where we are going. I open my mouth to speak, but I don't know what to say. Hank seems lost to me, deep in thought, as we wind through the streets.

Eventually, we arrive at a large, gated home. I've never visited this area as I don't mix with the rich and famous. The iron gate opens, and we creep up the circular drive. The house appears to sit sideways on the lot, shielding the front entrance from the road. A large ramp zigzags next to the front steps.

"Where are we?" I question, a touch of wonder in my voice.

Hank parks and brings my hand to his mouth. His eyes close as he kisses my knuckles.

"This is Kit Carrigan's home." He pauses, and my stomach twists as I glance back at the house—a sprawling 1970s ranch which looks a little outdated. The bright white brick reflects the late afternoon sunlight, and the house makes me think of a hospital for some reason. Large wooden double doors dominate the top of the front steps. The dark wood is a sharp contrast to the white stucco surrounding it. With pressure in my chest, I wait for Hank to explain.

"I know it seems strange to bring you here, but this is where I'd like you to meet someone. Tommy and Edie will be here as well. He moved pasta night to this place tonight."

My brow pinches. I've heard of the Sunday night pasta ritual, something practiced when the boys were on the road. Tommy wants Collision, the band he manages, to have a homecooked meal and hang out like a family. The practice is more sporadic when they are home as Tommy and Gage have their own families to spend time with on weekends. I'm not certain if I should be honored or concerned by the tension in Hank's voice.

"Who are we meeting?" If I ever believed people could rise from the dead, this moment is one of them. For the briefest minute, I fear Kit Carrigan is actually alive and living in this house, and for some sick reason, Hank wants me to meet her. What he says next floors me almost as much as my original thoughts.

"We're meeting my son."

+ + +

As Hank leads me toward the house, he remains quiet. My insides roil at his lack of explanation, the omission of him having a son, who—from what I surmise—is a child with Kit Carrigan. The oddity is Hank seems just as tense as I do, squeezing my hand enough to cut off circulation.

"What is it?" I ask as we wait at the front door.

His mouth opens, but he closes it once the door opens. Edie welcomes us inside, kissing Hank on the cheek and hugging me.

"Deep breaths," Edie whispers in my ear while she hugs me. "It will be okay."

I'm not certain what to think until we enter the living room. Tommy greets me next, kissing my cheek and shaking hands with Hank whose eyes can't leave the young man sitting in the center of the room.

Tommy waves us forward. "Lawson, this is Hank. Remember me telling you about him."

A mechanical device creates the answer from Lawson. "Yes."

"Hank, this is Lawson Carrigan."

Lawson Carrigan sits in a wheelchair. His hand curls over what looks like a laptop. Hank stares, unblinking, as if he's never seen his son before. Dawning comes slowly as I realize Hank *hasn't* met his son before.

Stepping forward, I crouch in front of the chair. "Hi, Lawson. I'm Midge," I say quietly, trying not to stare at any one feature other than his eyes, which don't focus on me. They match Hank's steely gray.

A computerized voice replies with a greeting. I turn back to look at Hank and see him wiping his eyes. He takes a seat on an extra-large white leather couch. It's circular, ancient, and sterile like the rest of the room. A large white brick fireplace centers the space with uncovered windows on either side. No personal touches decorate this space. No pictures. No plants. No knick-knacks. The massive room is lacking warmth.

"Hello, Lawson. I'm Hank." He pinches at his eyes. "I'm sorry it's taken so long to meet you." Lawson isn't looking at Hank, but his head shakes. Without responding by his machine, Hank looks over his shoulder at Tommy. "Does he know who I am?"

Tommy shakes his head. "We should talk later. Lawson isn't deaf," Tommy explains. "He can hear everything."

Hank's head swings back to Lawson. "I'm sorry," he whispers, his eyes roving over his son. "I'm so sorry."

After twenty minutes of awkward, stilted conversation, an aide appears to take Lawson to his rooms. In that time, we learned Lawson has cerebral palsy. Unseen to us, he has an entire wing with support staff. With round-the-clock care, he lives in a functioning home instead of an institution. However, I wonder if he's lonely. Hank follows the aide to learn more about Lawson's set-up, and Tommy goes with them. I collapse on the couch and dissolve into tears.

"It's a lot," Edie says. Sitting next to me, she wraps an arm around me.

"I have so many questions, but the first thing I'm thinking is how grateful I am for my boys and how sad I feel for Lawson."

"I'll tell you what Tommy tells me. Don't feel sorry for him. He's amazing, and he's had no worries. He's taken care of. His aides are wonderful. And he's loved."

"Doesn't he feel alone, though? He's so secluded."

"He goes to a day school for therapy and returns home every night, just like people who work or go to school. He has a good life." Edie pauses.

"But he lost his mother, and he's never known his father." I stare at Edie. "How did Hank not know?"

Edie shakes her head. "I don't understand it all, either. I assume they all had their reasons. I'm not saying I agree with any of them, but I wasn't a part of this world when those decisions were made. I have to remember that and respect it." Edie's glare hints at deeper meaning. I need to accept things as they are because I cannot change the past.

My hands cover my head as if holding in my thoughts. Tommy and Hank return, and awkward silence reigns in the space.

"I'll start the pasta. Darlin', join me." Tommy's directness doesn't surprise me. Hank and I need a moment. From the stunned expression on Hank's face, he needs more than a minute. After leaving us alone, Hank remains standing, his hands slipped into his pockets. We stare at one another before he looks away.

"I don't know what to say," I say to fill the quiet.

"I don't either. My head is spinning with so many questions."

"Hank, did you know?" The question comes out harsher than I intend, but I can't grasp not knowing he was a father.

"I had my suspicions but never the answers."

"How could she keep this from you?" I demand, my irritation at a dead woman growing.

"She had her reasons." It hits me. Hank was an enabler; Kit played off his weakness—her.

That's a terrible excuse. I bite back my retort. Then I think of all the times he said he asked her to marry him. How could she say no? How could she keep having sex with him, knowing he was the father of her child, and never tell him? I want to understand, but I just can't. Something in my face shifts Hank's expression. Suddenly, he's on his knees before me. Cupping both my hands in his, he leans forward and kisses them.

"Please don't leave me," he begs softly, lowering his head to my lap. My forehead rests against the back of his head. My heart breaks for him.

No, it's already broken. It shatters and crashes like shrapnel, exploding with confusion and disappointment in someone dead.

"I want to understand, but there are so many gaps." Hank needs to explain a few things. Unfortunately, explanations will have to wait. Edie enters the living room with a glass of wine for me and an invitation for us to join them in the kitchen.

In an effort to pretend we've all known this secret and nothing unusual has transpired, Tommy entertains us while he cooks by telling stories about shared experiences with Hank. It's like a game of Remember When.

"I left home to start a band," Tommy begins. "Denton, my cousin, a guy we hooked up with named Tucker Ashe, and me. We had a few small hits on our own—"

"Ever hear of "Wait For You"?" Edie interjects, attempting to add me in the reminiscing.

"I loved that song," I say, smiling despite the other emotions rumbling inside me.

"That was before Chrome Teardrops, darlin'," Tommy corrects her. "We fell apart after that hit. And then my sister joined us."

The room grows silent, their memories filling with a woman I've never met. Edie eyes me. She didn't know her either.

"My sister could sing like a church bell, which is where our musical career began. Our father was a pastor. We sang in the choir. Rock 'n' roll was for sinners. Guess Kit and I wanted to sin." Tommy winks at Hank. "She left home a year after me, catching up with her own attempts at fame."

"Kit toughened up her sound, and after Bruce—" Tommy glances up at Hank, and I rack my brain as to who Bruce was. "She needed a new band. She wanted to start fresh. Girl rockers were popular. She needed a drummer to up her beat. We met Hank in a bar, taking out his anger at his old man with sticks on his kit." Tommy chuckles. "Kit says it was fate."

My heart drops, and I raise my wine to my lips, swallowing the bitter alcohol so I don't have to look at anyone. There's a pun there—her name and his equipment to produce music. The irony isn't lost on me. Fate indeed.

"Anyway, Hank was the addition we needed. Kit became Kit Carrigan and Chrome Teardrops. Denton stuck it out with us until Kit got sick."

Silence creeps in again, ghosts roaming the kitchen.

"How is Denton?" Hank asks, changing the subject in a minor direction.

"Haven't spoken to him in a while. Heard he might be in photography or something. Hitched up with modeling. He always was a pretty boy. Last time I saw him might have been . . ." Tommy thinks for a second, swiping his fingers through his hair like I've witnessed Hank do. "Might have been the funeral, so eight or nine years?" The comment lingers.

"Been a long time," Hank says softly.

"Too long," Tommy replies, shaking his head at his old friend. "You look so much better, man."

Hank and I sit on a set of stools at a large kitchen island. His thick hand comes to my lower back, rubbing gently. "I feel so much better than I have in a long, long time."

Tommy's lips crook, the corner curling, and I can see him as a rock star. Girls swooning at the pebbly voice with a hint of Southern drawl.

"Love has a way of doing that," he says.

A million retorts swirl in my head, but I stay silent. Tommy steps toward his wife, kissing her open mouthed for a moment. I look away. I can't watch. I see where Gage Everly learned to be passionate about his wife. Then I remember Edie came after Gage and Ivy married. My heart drops again. I've never known such passion. I turn to see Hank watching me, and I fight the tears. I thought he was it—the spark of something—but I don't know how to feel at the moment. His hand continues to rub my back, but his touch feels so distant.

After we eat, Edie and I do the dishes while Tommy and Hank discuss Lawson.

"What's next?" Hank asks.

"What do you mean *what's next*?" Tommy replies.

"I mean, I want to see him, get to know him. Take him out of here."

"Wait a minute," Tommy snaps. "Lawson isn't going anywhere. This is his home."

"This is a prison, haunted with memories."

"For who?" Tommy barks. "This is the only place Lawson has known for twenty-six years. He stays here."

I startle at the age. Hank's involvement with Kit goes longer than a few rolls in the hay and a couple of nights here and there. Twenty-six plus years to be exact. Again, I consider Hank and Kit's relationship. He loved her for a long time, nearly as long as I've known Paul.

"What about me? I'm his father." The sharpness to Hank's tone makes me flinch.

"He doesn't know that. You can come around and hang with him, but for how long? Fatherhood isn't a fleeting thing. And he doesn't even understand what having a father means. The only male figure in his life has been me."

"Well, whose fault is that?" Hank growls.

"I did what she asked," Tommy defends.

"We were friends."

"She was my family."

Edie's sharp intake of air seems to punctuate the moment, and again, I feel like I'm missing something. She hisses Tommy's name under her breath.

"We stopped being a band family long before we broke up, Edie," Tommy adds, his tone still harsh.

"Family is forever," Edie states as if reminding him of something. Tommy's head falls before he shakes it back and forth.

"Dammit, woman," he mutters. His hands come to the island as if bracing himself. Hank remains standing, arms crossed over his large chest. We aren't getting anything resolved tonight between these men. In fact, it might take many nights to mend them. It took years to separate them.

"I think..." I swallow before I continue. "I think we've done a lot.. .learned a lot..." I hesitate. "For one night. Maybe let this sit and start again tomorrow." I sound like the leader of my marketing team when we stumble on a concept. Fragile hearts fill this storyboard, and we need to step back.

"I agree with Midge," Edie adds, her voice pitching a little stronger than necessary. "Hank met his son. There's a lot to accept." Edie narrows her eyes at Tommy. "Baby steps."

"Twelve of them," Hank mutters, and I recall the path to recovery for addiction. He has a long way to travel once again. Edie smiles at Hank's comment. Tommy's focus remains on the granite countertop.

"We'll talk tomorrow." Tommy decides, and Hank tips his chin in agreement. Then, looking at me, he needs an escape.

"Thank you for dinner. Pasta night must be a hit." I step forward to Tommy who envelopes me in a tight hug.

"Don't let him go," he mutters into my hair before pulling back. A thin line forms on my lips because I can't pull off another fake smile. I reach for Edie next.

"Call me as soon as you can." I appreciate the sisterhood and her sense that I'm breaking inside. I need to spend more time with my new friend.

chapter 26

I'm Fine Is Another Lie

[Hank]

My thoughts spiral like the curves we follow down the hill. Despite sitting so close to me, Midge is slipping away. Tonight was too much, even for me. I don't know what to think, how to feel, what to do. I'm numb inside. Absolutely cold.

"Where are we?" Her small voice fills the SUV. I drove to Brut's without thinking. I should take her home, return her to her normal life with her beautiful boys, but I can't let her go.

"Brut's place." My voice sounds defeated, which is how I feel at the moment. Whipped. Beaten. Done. "Can you come in for a bit?"

The house looks sad under the dim headlights. Larger inside than it appears on the outside, it's a solid place but run down by lack of care. Most days, it's even more pathetic looking in broad daylight.

"Stay." There's more in this command than waiting for me to open her car door. I need her to stay with me.

Midge nods and I exit the truck, circle the front to help her out of the SUV and escort her to the house. Keeping my hand wrapped around hers, I hold onto her like she might float away, a giant red balloon drifting upward. I lead her directly up the stairs and into my room. My big bed with a wooden headboard fills the space and rests between two windows. A tall dresser stands against another wall.

"I need a shower," I say, pointing over my shoulder at the open door to my bathroom.

Midge sits heavily on the edge of my bed. Her silence disturbs me. I'm bone tired and want nothing more than to lie down next to her, but

I'm chilled, shaking inside. I need to relax. I need to explain myself. I just need a minute.

Once I enter the shower, all I allow myself to focus on is the hot water. Baby steps. One step at a time. One day at a time. I'm back where I started six years ago.

Lord, grant me the serenity to accept the things I cannot change.
Courage to change the things I can.
And the wisdom to know the difference.

I cannot change what Kit kept from me, and I cannot change Lawson's condition even though I will beat myself up for both things. Lawson's diagnosis could be a result of choices I made. Choices Kit made. In either case, I could have been more involved in Lawson's upbringing.

More. I could have done more.

The warm water hits me in the face, and I keep my eyes shut to the spray. One hand rests on the pipe above the showerhead and the other presses against the tile wall. Two smaller hands surround my waist. I should be surprised she followed me, but instead, I'm grateful for her touch. A kiss falls between my shoulder blades before her chest rests against my back. I rub her arm and then slip my fingers between hers. We remain silent for too long. I don't want to lose this moment with her—holding me, comforting me with her gentle quiet. Moisture covers my face, and it's more than the heated water. I shudder, and she kisses my shoulder blade.

"I'm fine. I just need a minute," I croak.

"You need to talk," she tells me softly, but in a strong tone.

"I don't know where to start."

"The beginning is always best." She kisses me one more time, then turns her head, embracing me from behind.

"I was just a kid myself when I met Kit, and I was so enthralled with her. She was a few years older than me, on the edge of something, and I just wanted to be a part of it. I didn't know her husband, but he sounded like a loser, and when Kit found herself alone after his death, with her

194

sweet baby, Ivy, I wanted to take care of her even though I was still young myself." My hand fists against the steam-coated tile before me.

"She wouldn't have me at first. I thought it was a game of cat and mouse. Kit loved to flirt, and she fought the attraction. When she finally gave in, she didn't want me permanently. Not in a long-haul kind of way. But she didn't have a problem fucking me," I snap bitterly. "Keeping me? Committing to me? Nope."

I shudder again.

"We were a band on the rise. Kit was instantly successful. We fucked around with each other, but she had flings on the side. I did, too. It was a vicious circle. We always came back together, and I thought one day I'd just wear her down like I did the first time. Then she had another baby.

"I wasn't supposed to know. She took six months off. Disappearing to find inspiration, she claimed. Restore the muse, she told us. But I needed to know she was okay. I followed her one day, went to her home, and saw her getting out of a car with an infant carrier."

Thoughts race as I recall my concern for Kit. Tommy wouldn't give me any information.

I squeeze Midge's fingers, grateful she's behind me and not witnessing the wetness dripping down my face. I tip my face under the spray to wash away tears I shouldn't shed for Kit. Grateful to have Midge, I lean forward, propping my forehead against my outstretched arm and continue.

"I questioned Kit, and we fought. She told me she wasn't discussing him with me. Ever. She was adamant. Didn't want to hear me ask if I was the father. Didn't want to hear my accusations of her sleeping around. Doc couldn't tell me anything. Tommy said it was a roadie's kid. All the non-disclosure agreements we had on one another prevented us from speaking to anyone else. The dirt was so deep on each of us, no one would talk, no one would tell."

My fist taps several times on the tile. The water is turning cold, but I don't feel anything with my recollections. I'm numb as I've grown over the years with unanswered questions and unrequited love.

"Fuck, I hated her at the time. I wanted to quit the band, but I couldn't. What would I do? Work for my dad? I didn't finish college. I didn't want to work his trade. I wanted my dream...and the drink...and the drugs...and the girl." Fuck, did I want her, no matter how good or bad we were together. No matter how good or bad we were to one another. I slap my hand on the wet tile, startling Midge behind but my other hand still holds hers and I squeeze even tighter, afraid to let her go as I reveal more.

"I still loved her, and eventually, she came around. One night, she'd need me, and that's all it took to start the cycle again. Around and around and around, we went. Nearly fifteen fucking years. Then she got diagnosed with cancer. She cleaned up. She went for chemo, but there wasn't much hope. It metastasized quickly. I sank deeper because I couldn't help her out of a killer disease." I blow out a breath remembering when Tommy told me about Kit. Tommy, not Kit herself.

"I never questioned Kit again about the kid, like she asked. Ivy once hinted something. Suggested Lawson might belong to me, but I was too blitzed to think I heard her correctly or follow up."

Recalling the situation, I pause and lower my head in shame. I was too afraid to lose her, lose the band, so I honored her threat and never asked again—until it was too late for answers.

"What did Ivy say?" Midge prompts, her lips pressing to my skin while she speaks.

"She said, "She loves you, Uncle Hank. In her own way. She always loved only you"." I exhale again at the reminder. "We never said I love you. It was *I love when you fuck me*. Never used the phrase in any other manner or under any other condition." Kit never loved me. What we had couldn't have been love.

"Then one night near Kit's end, Ivy told me there was never a roadie, always me. Ivy thought Kit needed me despite always saying she didn't want to rely on any man, and Ivy believed I needed the truth in order to let her mother go."

Midge's forehead hits my back, her arms still wrapped around my middle. Despite the now cool shower and the sadness of my memories, my dick grows harder with the proximity of Midge's fingers. I want to lower her hands, make her take me in them, and force me to forget for a few minutes. I want to be selfish when I shouldn't.

"I'll give you a second," Midge says, shivering at my back.

The release of her naked body from mine chills me even more, but I hold out before I step out of the stall and wrap a towel around my waist. I find Midge sitting on my bed against the headboard in my t-shirt.

"Little lady, are you naked under that tee?"

"Maybe," she teases, her lip curling genuinely for the first time all evening. I crawl up the bed toward her, and she slips down to her back, scooting under me. Balancing on my elbows, I brush back her hair, looking into her gold-speckled eyes.

"I want to get lost in you tonight." The admission is raw and real. I just want to lose myself, bury myself inside her, and think only of us.

No more Kit.

No more past.

No more hurt.

Midge lifts her head, kissing me tenderly while holding my face in her hands. Already sporting a half wood, a couple of hungry kisses skyrockets me to full mast. I tug at the towel to remove the barrier from around my waist, in order to feel the heat of Midge's thighs under my damp skin.

"Fuck, I want you, little lady. I want to disappear inside you." Her mouth opens, her tongue finding mine. She hasn't kissed me like this before—so desperate and frantic. She's unraveling, which is how I feel.

"Midge," I warn.

Taking control, I rub against her, letting the wetness of her entrance coat my tip. I push my shirt up her middle and devour one breast, latching on and sucking hard. I'll mark her with the suction. I want to leave her wearing more than my shirt on her skin. Tugging the shirt over her head, I flip her over.

"Let me take you like this," I groan, my dick heavy against her ass.

"I've never . . ." Her voice fades and I sense the panic.

"Not up the ass, baby. Just from behind." I need inside her, and the reverse position will draw me deep.

"Kneel up," I command, pressing back for her to hitch her ass in the air. My hand smooths over the perfect curve of her backside. Damn, I like her like this, but I want even more of her. "Sit up. Hold the headboard." I reach for a condom in the nightstand while she scrambles upward. Once sheathed, I position my knees under her, my dick poised at her entrance.

"You okay with this?" I mutter, anticipating the moment I'll disappear into her. She sits on my lap with her back to me.

"Yes," she breathes.

Nibbling at the juncture of her shoulder and neck is my only warning. She grunts at the invasion. Swift but cautious, my dick fills her as I tug her down in one thrust. We still for a moment, allowing her to adjust to the angle. Deep in this position, she swallows me whole, her ass hitting my abs. I snake one arm around her stomach, pressing her to me. Moving her at my will, I lift and lower her, building a slow repetitive rhythm while she clutches the wooden headboard.

"Fuck, I love being inside you. Warm. Wet." *Wonderful*, I exhale. Hammering at her, I hear her breath hitch. I own her at this moment, and I'm right where I want to be—lost in her—or, rather, found by her. I'm going to blow too quickly as she lets me take her, move her, love her.

I love you, my head screams, but I can't say it. Not like this, not for the first time with Midge.

"Middy." I breathe.

"Fill me," she says.

And I implode, stars dotting my vision as I press upward, shooting off inside her. She stills, engulfing me. My fingers leave imprints on her hips. I'm holding her to keep from floating away. Leaning forward, I rest my forehead on her shoulder.

"You didn't," I mutter, disappointed in not getting her there first.

"I'm fine," she whispers, but I recognize in her tone, she's not.

I'm not certain I am either.

chapter 27

Ghosts In the Bedroom

[Midge]

Spent, Hank pulls out of me, using his disposed towel to wipe us off. Then he flips to his back, tugging me to his chest. I'm draped over him until he shifts, rolling me onto my back and lowering himself so his head rests on my breasts. His arms lay along my sides. My fingers comb through his hair, stroking over his head, scratching lightly. The tension releases from him, and his weight grows heavier.

My thoughts, however, weigh the heaviest. I can't possibly sleep although I'm drained from the evening and slightly edgy from the lack of an orgasm.

How would it be to find out you are a father to an adult child with special needs? It's hard enough to prepare yourself for an infant when you are young, but then to layer on all the additions in Hank's case. I can't imagine what he thinks or what he feels. The lies Kit told him. The truth he should have fought to seek. This is beyond my comprehension. It's another reminder I'm not part of Hank's world. The rock star lifestyle is a mystery to me. One I never pondered or sought. I like music well enough, but I don't think about it further than my interpretation of a song. There's a person behind the lyrics—a human with a life, who lives with his own demons and dreams. Just like anybody else. Though, Hank's story seems extreme.

Almost fifteen years in an emotionally abusive relationship—that's what he's lived. One where his heart ruled his dick. He couldn't see how unhealthy Kit was for him, though his other addictions might have also clouded his decisions. I could dismiss his problems as a result of fame, but I can't be so cavalier about his life. It's unfair to Hank who has such generous heart. He's been taken advantage of because of it.

I continue to stroke his head, letting his solid form melt over me. I could love this man completely, but he has a difficult journey ahead of him. He doesn't need me in his way.

He shifts, and I twist in search of a clock. I need to get home. Gently removing him from my belly, I roll opposite him and reach for my clothes. Something pinches inside me. He didn't hurt me. I hate to admit I liked the roughness, but I pause. I wish the intensity of our moment was for me.

"Where you going, little lady?" he mutters, his voice groggy with sleep. I stand and slip my dress over my head. The T-shirt material is casual as I didn't know where my mystery date was going to lead.

"I need to get home. It's a school night for the boys." I straighten my dress and search for my shoes.

Laying on his back, Hank wipes a hand down his face. "Don't leave," he whispers. His eyes plead with mine, but he's not seeing me, not really.

"Hank." I exhale as I take a seat on the edge of his bed. Reaching for his hand, I wrap my fingers over his. "I like having sex with you. Like it a lot," I tease without humor.

"I like having sex with you, too, little lady." His smile grows, but the sparkle in his steel-colored eyes remains missing.

"But it's turning into more for me."

"Midge—"

"And Lawson needs to be the *more* in your life. You need to be all in with him. A child. A son. Wow, Hank, he should be your number one priority."

"He will be."

"That's how it should be for a parent. You'll do everything for him. I know you will." Hank stares at me, his forehead furrowing in question. "It will take time, but he'll understand who you are. Who you were meant to be."

"Midge?"

"I know it's late…all these years. It must be a shock to find out he really is yours, but you'll be great for him. You'll be just what he needs." A tear slips from my eye, and I'm not certain if I'm trying to convince him or me. Hank needs to step up to this discovery.

Perching up on an elbow, he grips my fingers tighter within his and says, "I plan to do everything I can. I have a lot to learn, but I'll get there. I have to."

"I know you will," I repeat. "You're a good man, Hank Paige."

"What are you not saying, little lady?" His voice deepens as he swallows.

"I can't compete."

"You aren't competing with my son."

"No, I'm competing with a ghost." His eyes widen, and I continue before he can speak. "I understand loving someone else first. I was married for fifteen years. I thought Paul was my everything, but divorcing is different. It's a choice; whether both parties agree or not, it ends with a choice."

"Midge." There's a warning in his voice, but I continue.

"Death isn't a choice. As much as you might have prepared for it in this case, someone important was taken from you before their time, before your time. You loved her, Hank, and I understand that. I do. But I can't fight her memory."

"You aren't," he says, his voice suddenly weak.

"I am. Lawson will be a constant reminder of her. God forgive me for speaking ill of the dead, but she lied to you. She wasn't good to you, honey, and you deserve someone who will be. You deserve to be somebody's someone." I take a deep breath, swallowing as I blink back the tears. "But so do I. With this new discovery, you aren't ready for me. Lawson is another notch in the struggle of your love for Kit. Beautiful, famous, lying Kit. And I'm not her." My voice squeaks with bitterness I feel toward a woman I've never met, who destroyed the heart of this man, and continues to do so from the grave. "Your life is a love song, only I'm singing the wrong lyrics."

I draw his fingers up to my lips, kissing his warm skin. His scent lingers. Manly. Woodsy. I stand before more tears fall. A crying woman is the last thing this man needs.

"I don't want you to go," he admits, and it almost breaks me.

I want to crawl back into his bed and hold him, but I have my own heart to think about. I can't take anymore tonight. And I have responsibilities—three of them—waiting for me at home.

"I don't want to leave, but I already called an Uber," I lie.

He sits up and reaches for me, calling out, "Kit."

And that's my cue to go.

"Fuck!" The word follows me out the bedroom door. "Midge!"

I skip down the stairs to find Chopper sitting in the living room.

"Midge?" His eyes widen in surprise.

"Could you give me a ride?" My voice shakes as I ask, tears running down my cheeks. "I want to go home."

chapter 28

Advice From All Over

[Hank]

Fuck, fuck, *fuck*. I slap a palm on the mattress as I hear Chopper's car roar to life. Sitting up and reaching for my boxers, I race to the first floor to see headlights swing out of the driveway.

"Was that Midge I heard?" Brut says behind me.

"Fuck!" I yell, hands fisting my short hair. I can't believe I called her Kit. It just slipped out.

"What happened?"

"I'm an idiot," I huff, spinning to face my brother standing in the doorway to the kitchen. He's eating a cupcake, but I don't have time to question where he got it.

"Whatcha do now?"

"I…" I step around the couch and fall onto the cushions. "I called her Kit."

"You what?" Brut bellows, then points the partially eaten cupcake at me. His voice rises an octave. "During sex?"

"How do you know I had sex with her?" Brut's eyes roam to my boxers. Sitting forward, I cover my face, swearing into my hands.

"What happened?" my brother repeats, taking a seat on the chair opposite me.

"I took her to meet Lawson. It didn't go like I thought." I scrub both hands down my face before brushing over my head, holding my neck.

"Told you to tell her," Brut mocks with a mouthful of cake, icing sticking to his lips.

"She had the interview. It was more important for her." My thought process was all her, despite finding out a few days ago about Lawson. Brut shakes his head, wiping at his lip.

"She broke up with me." The thought startles me. *Did she break up with me?*

"What is it with you and women?" Brut snorts. *As if he's some expert.*

"She's different."

Like a teenager, Brut rolls his eyes and takes another bite of his dessert before he singsongs, "She has a nice personality."

"Fine. She smells nice, and her skin is so soft. She's like that cupcake, melting on my tongue, and yes, she is nice. She's sweet, caring. I know I'm her first for a few things. The passion she's willing to display with me." I pause, inhaling, recalling upstairs. "And you should have seen her with Lawson. I'm standing there, trying to take it all in, and she gets down in front of him to greet him. And her boys. Her boys are her world. They're good kids, and she's making sure they'll be good men despite her cheating ex-husband. And she likes me. I know she does. She isn't Kit—"

"Then why did you call her Kit?"

"We were disagreeing about Kit. It just came out."

"Sounds like it should have stayed in," Brut points out.

"She says she's fighting a ghost." Brut raises his brow in question. My voice falters. "She's not." My heart knows there is no comparison, but my head got in the fucking way again. *Calling her Kit.* I smack my forehead. What a fucking idiot!

"I warned you about this shit," Brut admonishes. He sighs, falling back in his seat, then adds, "Quite a pair, aren't we? We both have our heads up our asses."

"Admitting something about Lily?" I watch Brut crumple the cupcake wrapper in his fist.

"Lily and I are a dead issue. Twenty-one years dead."

"Yeah, well, it took me twenty years to feel alive, Brut. I'm forty-three. I'd say there is still time for you, too."

I stand, leaving Brut with his empty wrapper, and head to my room for pants. Minutes later, I find myself outside, staring at the cloth in the back of the garage. The tarp covers every inch, but the outline gives away the instrument. My fingers twitch inside my pockets. *It's been a long time, my old friend.* The cement floor is cold under my bare feet. I'm numb again, staring at the set that gave me a dream for a little while.

"Don't do it," Chopper says from behind me. I don't flinch although I didn't hear him return.

"Don't do what?" My voice chokes.

"Instead of thinking about crushing it, why don't you play it?"

I stare at the covered kit. At one time, sticks were a part of me, an extension of my arms. Then the music died, and I stopped.

"What do you know?" I snark, turning to look at my nephew. He's the spitting image of Brut at that age.

"I know I just drove home a lady who silently cried in the seat next to me the entire way. Whatever you did, she wasn't angry. That woman is *sad*." He emphasizes the emotion.

"Angry?" I snap. "Why would she be angry? She just broke up with *me*."

"The woman I drove home was not a woman who broke up with someone, Uncle Hank. Midge is heartbroken." Chopper stares at me with the only part not matching my brother—the eyes of his mother.

"What do you know about heartbreak?" My chuckle lacks any real humor.

Chopper scoffs back. "I'm twenty-one. I know plenty."

"Yeah, so worldly." I snort.

"You need a grand gesture." He shrugs, stuffing his hands into his jacket pockets.

"What the hell is that?"

"Something big. Something that shows you're serious about her, about you two together."

I blink at my nephew.

"Like asking her to marry me?" I exhale. In a drunken stupor, she said she'd say yes, but I recall too well the poor decisions made under the influence of alcohol.

"If that's what it takes to win her back. But from her tears, I'd say she needs something more than a proposal. Midge doesn't need a husband. She needs a man."

"How do you know these things?" I huff, rubbing a hand over my bare chest where I've developed a sharp ache.

He taps his heart. "Told you, I know plenty."

chapter 29

A Grand Gesture That Isn't Big Enough

[Midge]

"I don't know what to do," I say into the phone, cupping my forehead in my hand. It's Monday morning, and I sit at the reception desk. I don't want to be here, but I don't have a choice after not landing Pendelton. After five text messages and three missed calls, I decide to respond to Edie.

"Since I quit my job and hoped to get a new one before my last paycheck ran out, I'm not certain what to do next." I breathe heavily. "Sweet cheese, I never should have quit. Maybe I should call Katrina and beg her to take me back." I cover my eyes, swollen and dry, the tears finally at rest. My heart literally aches, my chest is burning. I didn't bother with make-up to hide my pain. I wear my glasses instead.

"You can't go back." Edie's tone holds firm. "You won't go back. This is a sign. Brut said you could stay for as long as you need, right?"

"But I don't want to take advantage of him, and the pay isn't enough. I already weaseled my way into this position in order to get the Pendelton pitch." Brut has been very kind, saying he feels responsible for Pendelton dicking me over even though it wasn't his fault. After speaking with him first thing this morning, I called my ex.

"I also had the pleasure of telling Paul I might need help from him to make my cut of the tuition payments." Sarcasm drips from my voice. Cowering to my ex-husband and asking him to step up was the last thing I needed after last night, but it was time to tear off all the Band-Aids. Paul needed to know my new financial position.

"How did that go?"

"Not well. After all we'd been through, I thought he could give me this time to figure myself out, considering he used time during our marriage to do the same for himself. He didn't quite agree, especially with his upcoming wedding."

"Fuck exes," Edie huffs. "Well, you have a job at Restored Dreams for now while you look for something else. Just take one day at a time."

"I know, but I shouldn't stay here. Things are. . .complicated." Hank and I have been a whirlwind from the moment we met in Edie's bathroom, like high winds circling around one another, getting caught up in a storm of great sex. That's all we were, right? I choke on the thought. Tears prickle my eyes again, but I will them back. I don't want to shed another tear for a man who doesn't want me. *Kit.* Her name echoes through my ears on repeat. My nose burns and I worry unwanted tears will follow. *I'm so stupid.*

"Is it Lawson?"

"No." I sigh. "No, it's not his son." It's the woman he produced said son with. A female rock star phenomenon with a big secret and a cold heart.

"When I first learned of Lawson, it was a bit of a shock. I mean, who keeps such a secret? The place is like a morgue—a sterile memorial to Kit. But it's what Tommy thinks is best for his nephew," Edie reiterates, and I'm reminded Hank hadn't prepped me in any way for the surprise of learning he had a child with the love of his life.

"What does Ivy say? He's her brother."

"Tommy's his legal guardian. However, Ivy has become more vocal. She's found a new passion with the birth of the therapy school. She doesn't think Lawson should be a secret, but Tommy disagrees. He doesn't want Kit's name dragged through the mud from the grave. He wants people to keep their fond memories of her and not criticize her in memoriam."

"Does that even make sense? What about those closest to her? Forget fans. What about family? Why didn't they all know, and why can't they share in Lawson's life with him?" My concern momentarily returns to a secluded man with special needs, closed off from society, but more importantly, shut away from other human beings related to him.

"Honestly, I know what you're saying. It's the one area where Tommy and I disagree. He's stubborn when he wants to be." She snorts. "Lawson *is* Ivy's brother. She does the best she can to include him in her family, but I know she wants more. And I'm not certain the best place for Lawson is locked in his mother's house. Thank goodness for the day school with therapy and the round-the-clock aides."

We pause, each with our own thoughts.

"How is Hank doing with all of this?" Edie hesitates, and the question stops my heart. I shouldn't have left like I did. I'm guilty—like Kit, in some ways—of running away from him. Then again, he called me *her name.* I've moved from tears to anger. I *was* there for him, willing to give him whatever he needed and even give him up so he can concentrate on this new discovery. Calling me his ex-lover's name proves our hearts are not in the same place.

"Hank has a lot on his mind right now," I surprisingly defend. "But that's the way it should be, right? Lawson will be a big responsibility." I scrub at my forehead, wanting to believe what I suggest.

"Midge, honey, Lawson is Tommy's responsibility. Hank can't just step in." She stops. "Unless he's planning something extreme. Some kind of custody battle or—"

"No, no, I don't think he'll do that. He just wants to get to know his son and learn what he can to be a part of his life, but he wouldn't take those measures." At least, I don't think he will. I feel as if I no longer know him.

"Tommy's so happy to see someone like you in Hank's life. You're so good for him."

I don't respond. Instead, I close my eyes again, choking back the lump in my throat. I walked away from him. How is that good for him? But I had to protect *me.* My heart cannot take another crack. Hank means more to me than hot sex. *I thought we—* I shut down the thought. It doesn't seem to matter what I thought. We are moving in separate circles—one where I believed we were intersecting—but I'm clearly outside the ring.

I look over at the wilting flowers on the corner of my desk. I assume he bought them, thinking I would get the job with Pendelton. The champagne-themed cupcake sits in the refrigerator with a congratulations ribbon wrapped over the cellophane packaging. I blink a few times at the thoughtfulness. He's sweet, just not enough on *me*.

"Midge?" The concern in Edie's tone breaks through my thoughts.

"I should probably let you go. I have work to do here, and I need to find somewhere else to work." The statement tastes bitter. I have nothing against being in this garage. In fact, I'm less stressed here than my previous employment, and the change has been rather nice. I go home at a set time and no work follows me. However, I need more income than Brut pays me.

"Maybe I could ask Ivy if there is a place for you in the therapy school."

Cripes, I can't take more handouts. "No, Edie. That's sweet, but I'll figure things out," I add with weak confidence. "I always do."

"What about starting your own business?" Edie offers, and I snort in disbelief.

"Please. I can't start a business right now. I need to feed my children first." The exaggeration is a bit extreme, but I can almost picture Edie nodding. She knows what I mean. She told me she worked for years in a job she was good at but didn't fulfill her like her position as manager of the therapy school. *Gotta put food on the table somehow*, she joked.

"Is everything okay between you and Hank? This is a lot to take in." Edie softly adds.

"I've gotta go," I practically whisper, slamming my eyes shut once again.

"Okay. Call me if you need anything. Let's get together this week."

"Sure," I say, my voice lowering. We hang up, and I pinch my forehead with my fingers. It's going to be a long day.

"Why didn't you say you needed more money?" The gruff voice startles me, and I spin to face Hank, arms crossed and leaning against the waiting room door. I'm ready to accuse him of eavesdropping, but the concerned expression on his face matches the pit in my gut. I can't look at him. I refuse to feel sorry for him. It's my turn to wallow in sorrow. My heart aches and I turn back for my computer although I'm blankly staring at the screen.

"And why can't you start your own business?" The question brings to mind the night I told him of my dream. I'm blinded by the sweet memory of us dancing.

"I can't." It's the only explanation I can give him. I see the reflection of him in my screen, but I don't want to talk about this. I don't want to talk at all. I need to find a new job and quickly.

"What about Pendelton?" Hank was pretty adamant I shouldn't work for such a man, especially with his son's advances. I tried to explain it was more about proving myself than getting the job. I wanted to feel I could acquire the account on my own.

I shrug, hoping to dismiss Hank, but I feel him step closer to my chair. I hear the rustle of his hand in a pocket and sense him lifting an empty coffee mug from the desk. Something metallic rattles against the ceramic and I turn with curiosity.

"If you still want to work for him, he'll see you. I guarantee it." His eyes weigh on the side of my face, but I don't look up. Instead, I focus on the mug and the two metal cylinder pieces inside it.

"What's this?"

"Spark plugs. His precious Bentley won't start without them. I expect he'll be calling soon. Better be ready for interview number two."

I can't help but look up, questioning what he's done. His only response is a wink before he turns toward the garage.

chapter 30

A Grand Gesture, Take Two

[Hank]

Pendelton's low-rise building was sleek and modern with an exterior black glass. Dishware posters decorated the interior. The antiquated products were at odds with the contemporary lines. And with Midge's designs. Being here sent something cold creeping over my skin. I don't really want Midge working here, but I knew she wanted to prove herself to the ass, proving something to herself, and I wanted to help her see she could do anything. This was my grand gesture.

"Can I help you?" A pretty little blonde asked from behind a high-counter desk. I didn't have an appointment, but Pendelton would see me. We'd been working on his pricey toys for a decade.

"Hank Paige. Pendelton is expecting me." When Midge didn't get the job, I made him a counteroffer, either see Midge as he promised, or his vehicle wouldn't run. He didn't believe my proposition, so I was here unannounced to make good on my threat. Instead of the old, white-haired man with a mousy looking mustache, I was greeted by a man in his late thirties, clean-cut, sharp suit, tugging on his cufflinks.

"May I help you?" he offered, sneering at my hand and thinking twice about shaking mine. Grease sat under my fingernails. I left it there on purpose. "I'm Julian Pendelton."

"I'm here to see the old man." This guy was definitely the one who interviewed Midge, and my fingers twitched to punch him. We stood facing off like one of those this or that comparisons. He was prim, trim, and refined, like some of the dishes portrayed in the pictures on the wall. I was the chrome edge and leather straps on Midge's designs.

"My father is busy. What can I do for you?"

"I'm thinking you remember Midge Everette. She interviewed here last week. She and your father had a deal."

Julian smiled slowly. "Of course, I remember her." The implication was clear. Midge made an impression, and this man hoped to collect on his offer.

"She's my girl," I clarified for him. "And your old man made her a promise. I'm here to see he holds true to that."

"Why do I sense there's a threat in your statement?"

"No threat. I keep my promises." My eyes narrowed.

"I'll pass on to my father that you visited." He straightened his already stiff cuffs and excused himself.

As I exited the building, I couldn't miss the Bentley, parked front and center before the building. A quick unlatch of the hood, and I found what I needed, proving I was loyal to a fault.

I straightened the cuffs of my coverall as I strutted away.

+ + +

Although it's nearly midnight, I chance a call to Midge. I let the day pass in silence after dropping my gift in a mug on her desk.

"Did I wake you?" I hear her rustle under the sheets, and I wish I was there. I'd smother her with my apology, kiss away her fears, and draw her against me.

"You okay?" Her voice remains steady, distant, and cautious. I don't like the separation I feel from her, but I know I'm responsible for the space between us. Her silent treatment earlier in the day nearly killed me. I don't want the distance to be a reminder of another time, another person, although it is. However, the separation also gives me a moment to reflect—I did this to myself. Midge was willing and wanting to give me an out for my son, when I didn't want to lose her. Then, I pushed her over the edge. And still, she asks how I'm doing, as if she's worried about me, when I'm concerned about her. It's a strange to consider she really cares about me.

"I'm good," I say for lack of something else. I swipe a hand over my hair. *Shit, this is difficult.* "So, Pendelton finally called." It isn't a question. She sent me a text earlier in the day to tell me he got my message. I've been at the crisis center since three and it's been a hectic evening.

"What did you do?"

"I just made him hold up his end of the deal." Silence fills the line, and I imagine her twisting her lips with thought.

"Why?" It isn't a question I can answer, knowing she's upset with me. *Because I love you.* That's the truth I'm seeking to prove.

"It's my grand gesture," I awkwardly explain. "I want to please you. I want you to be happy. If working for Pendelton means you get what you want, then I want that for you."

"You didn't have to do that," she says, not addressing what I've just admitted.

"I wanted to." I want to do everything for her. "Let me drive you there tomorrow. It's insurance," I tag on the end, sensing she'll object.

"Insurance for what?"

"He'll actually see you. He's not getting his engine running until he does." She huffs softly. I miss her laughter, and my heart pinches knowing the sadness in her is my fault.

"You nervous, little lady?" I cough to cover the slip. I'm trying not to pressure her, but I can't help myself. She's my little lady.

"No." She pauses. "I think it's lost its luster, but I guess I should thank you for looking out for me. I know you must have done more than take those plugs."

More. I owe her so much more. I want to give her everything. I dismiss her probing statement. I don't want to explain the altercation with Julian Pendelton.

"No thank you is necessary, baby." I wince at the use of another endearment, but I can't help myself. I want to wrap her up and hold her, and I'm tempted to U-turn to her house. I'm on my way home, and my bed wouldn't be the same since I had her there last night. Her scent fills the sheets. Her actions fill my thoughts. Her warmth fills my heart.

"Let me drive you tomorrow," I repeat.

"You don't have to do that." Her voice softens.

"Please. I want to."

"Okay," she hesitates. "The meeting's at ten."

"I'll be ready." Tomorrow won't come soon enough.

+ + +

Leaning against the hood of Brut's SUV, I wait. Midge seemed anxious during the ride to Pendelton's, fidgeting with her skirt, then rubbing at her forehead. She remained quiet. Hopefully, it was nerves for the interview and not me.

She returns forty minutes later. Crossing the parking lot, she takes my breath away in her tight red skirt and high heels. She's a vision of businesswoman on a mission, and the determination on her face goes straight to my pants. I'm hardening as she strides toward me, and I itch to wrap her in my arms and kiss the crap out of her when she gets close to me.

I hold the thought. Her lips curl slowly, and I step forward. "Well?"

"At least, he saw me this time." She shrugs, a touch of the confident woman fading a little. Her forehead pinches, and she reaches for it. "He said he'll get back to me."

I open the SUV door for her, telling her I need a moment. I step up to the Bentley, return the plugs, and then turn toward the building. There's a sense of being watched, so I salute the glass. *Asshole.* He better give my girl a chance.

Climbing into the SUV, I find Midge with her head against the window, stroking her forehead again.

"You okay, baby?" Her eyes close at the endearment, but I don't care. I'm concerned.

"I've worked myself into a headache. It will pass." She continues to rub, massaging her temples. We drive a few minutes in silence, and I wait on edge for her to explain what happened.

215

"It was good, though, right? He loved it." I can't stand the quiet between us.

"I think I did well. He was attentive, unlike his son, and took notes."

Suit guy comes to mind, and I cringe. He's the type of guy she should be with, dressed the way she is. She's smart and talented in a business sort of way. They would fit one another, and I grip the steering wheel harder. I don't want her to fit with the uptight suit. I want her with me. She goes silent again, her head resting against the glass. I reach out for her leg, and when she doesn't brush me off, I squeeze.

"I just need some acetaminophen or something," she groans.

A half-hour we're back to the shop, and she squeezes her temples again as she sits at her desk.

"Why don't you go home?" I offer.

"I don't want to upset Brut. I already took time this morning. It'll pass in a little bit." She sits up, but the strain on her face hints at the pain.

Sometime after noon, I demand she take a break. The computer must be adding to the ache.

"Lie down for a bit in the office. I promise no one will disturb you."

"Maybe I should just go home?" Even her voice sounds stressed.

"Can you drive?" I don't trust her nod. She doesn't look well. Stepping forward, I lead her to the office.

"Just an hour. I'll feel better in a bit."

I don't know why she's trying to quantify the time. If she hurts, she hurts. I spread a blanket over the couch and help her to her side. She curls into herself, clenching at her head. It pains me to watch her, so I kiss her hair and head to the shower. I'll have work to make up, but right now, I need to be close to my lady.

chapter 31

It's Just Science

[Midge]

I drift but don't sleep. Drills zoom in the background. I think I hear water running. I will myself to melt into the couch. Not certain how much time passes, eventually, I sense someone near me. Fingers brush over my hair, and I recognize Hank's touch.

The cushions at my back are removed, but I don't question anything. My head is killing me, like a vise wanting to squeeze my brains out. The pain above my left eye is severe enough I can't open it even though the lights are off in the office and the blinds on the windows have been pulled. Gentle hands shift me, and Hank lies beside me. I can't even muster the energy to ask what he's doing.

"Lift," he commands softly, and I pick up my head, my eyes opening in a fog. He presses my head back down against his bent arm. His other hand comes to my head, massaging light circles on my temple with a tender thumb.

"That feels nice," I mutter although I'm not certain I speak. A light kiss on my forehead rewards me, and I realize the words left my mouth.

"I hate seeing you like this, little lady." His typically rough voice sounds deeper, the concern like a warm bath enveloping me. We stay quiet a moment as he works his magic with his fingers on my head.

"Were you like this with her?" The question isn't angry or sharp or sarcastic. I'm curious as I recall him brushing and braiding my hair. I'd like to think I'm *not* a jealous woman, but I realize I am in regard to Kit Carrigan.

He stiffens beside me. "Like what?"

"Intimate."

His body relaxes.

"Isn't that a fancy word for sex?" he chuckles softly.

"I didn't think so. It means tender, close, connected."

"Then no. She didn't suffer like this, but she would get stressed out. Sometimes, I needed to talk her down from the proverbial ledge. She was confident on stage but unsure off it." There's more he isn't saying, and with the pain in my head, my heart can't handle any more. He kisses me again, lingering at my hairline.

"Please, don't think about her right now." His voice cracks, and I shift against him. I nod but the movement is jarring; however, his body heat seeps into me. He smells freshly showered and spicy. He cleaned up for me. My leg slips between his.

"Did you see Lawson?"

He chuckles in response. "Lady, quit worrying about everything. I'm going to see him tonight. I found a transition counselor, and she's helping me figure out how best to enter Lawson's life." It must be so difficult. It's not like someone said, *surprise, I'm pregnant,* and he has to learn to be a father from scratch. He's starting at the top, when the child is an adult and has special needs in addition.

"That sounds like a good plan."

Another kiss meets my forehead while his thumb moves over my skin. We grow quiet a second.

"Intimate," he repeats as if he's been thinking about the word. "I like the sound of that." I smile in response, because I don't really want to talk anymore. Sensing this, he adds, "Rest, little lady. Let me hold you. Let me be here for you."

The words remind me of our first meeting. Hank is here for me, and I walked away from him. I'm so confused, and it all adds to the pain in my head. Settling into the rhythm of his massage, I allow my body to relax, drifting deeper against him. It's a weird state of consciousness, not being able to move, and right now, I don't want to.

+ + +

There's really no rest for a mother, so hours later, when I'm finally home, Liam springs on me. "I need to make a volcano."

For the love of all that's holy, what?

"When is it due?" I'm holding my breath, but I know the answer.

"Thursday." Thankful for small miracles, this gives us two nights to work on this thing. I don't even want to ask how long he's known about it or complain that he has baseball practice in an hour, and we don't have a single supply. After two hours and a hundred dollars at the local hobby store, I have the ingredients for a kickass volcano. Of course, it's almost nine o'clock when Liam gets home from practice, and he wants to start the project. We're mixing up *papier mâché* batter because I can't have the kid who wants to use a simple soda bottle and a mint candy.

"We need to make it look as real as possible." He uses hand motions to emphasize the boom he thinks this project should express. He's been working on research behind the scenes, and I'm proud of him for not asking me for every detail. I'm more worried about his paper than the physical volcano, but tonight I don't have time for proofreading. As he's stirring up the mush for the *mâché*, the doorbell rings, and I can't imagine who is soliciting at this hour. Assuming it's a marketer of some type, I peek through the window first and find Hank standing on my stoop.

"Hank." As I open the door, I breathe out his name like I need to intake him for air. He looks so good standing under the front light, his hands in his pockets like a nervous teenager. My heart skips a beat. "What are you doing here?"

He looks down at his feet for a second and then up at me, eyes silvery. "You broke up with me." My mouth opens, ready to protest. I didn't. I just wanted to give him the space he'll need for his son. He speaks before I can explain. "I'm not letting you."

He steps into the living room, forcing me against the door, and kisses me tenderly in his Hank way. Soft pulls and full exploration like he wants to touch every corner, every crevice, before he'll release me. I'm stunned into submission, and my eyes remain closed even after he pulls away.

"Mom!" My name brings me back to reality. I hear the scrape of a kitchen stool on the wood floor.

"Hank, tonight probably isn't a good time to—"

"Hank," Liam calls, standing between the kitchen and the living room. "Come see my volcano."

Hank peers down at me, a smile slowly forming. He leans in to kiss me quick, and I brace myself for the too-short connection. Only he stops, lingering. After three short pulls at my lips, he steps back. I'm stunned again. He's changed it up. Still holding the doorknob, my back against the wood, I watch his backside as he heads for my kitchen and Liam's science experiment.

+ + +

Around ten, the *papier mâché* needs to set. Hank has helped Liam practice the volcano over the sink as a test.

"All experiments need a run-through before the real explosion," Liam tells me although I'm certain this is something Hank said. "Results can be inconclusive without thorough investigation."

I snort at the scientific jargon before telling Liam he needs a shower and bed. Staring at the mess he made, I shake my head while Hank gathers up the supplies and forms a neat arrangement on my island counter.

"Thank you for this." I nod at the organization and a hearty looking mound that might resemble a volcano once it's painted.

"Glad to see you feel better." He winks.

"Thank you for that as well."

"Anything you need, little lady." He busies himself with the cleanup, but I sense he's doing it to distract himself.

"How was Lawson?"

He stills, pressing down on the island. His head hangs. "I'm in over my head. I wanted this so badly." His head shoots up. "No, I wanted the truth so badly. Yet now that I have it, it isn't helping. I'm angrier with her than I was before. And I hate myself for all the things I did, thinking it's my fault Lawson is the way he is."

Stepping toward him, I grip his wrist. "You know that's not true. It's genetics and mutations and all kinds of things I don't understand, but it wasn't something you, or even Kit for that matter, did. Lawson just is who he is."

Hank nods, taking my hand in his and raising it to his lips.

"I can't do this alone." The implication lies underneath. He wants me to be there for him.

"I'm so sorry for the other night. I shouldn't have walked out like I did." His hand cups my jaw.

"Please forgive me for what I said." He swallows, unable to repeat what he did. "It just slipped out, and it will never, ever happen again." His head lowers to rest against mine. I prepare to tell him he can't know such a thing when he explains. "I had this moment when she was in my head because you were speaking about her, and then you had the look like you were ready to bolt. And I pushed you through the door by calling out her name. I'm so sorry."

"It was a lot to take in at once. You hadn't exactly told me the truth about Lawson." We haven't covered this omission yet, and I need to know. "Why didn't you say anything?"

"You had the interview, and I wanted you to focus on the job. I knew it was important to you, and I didn't want to be any cause for distraction. You're a worrier, little lady. You would have deviated." He's right in some ways. His revelation would have consumed me as it has the past few days. "You needed to do you."

"I thought we could do us," I whisper, and to my surprise, his mouth crooks.

"That's why I'm here. For us." He kisses me sweetly a moment before pulling back. "I want us together, Middy. Let's experiment."

I grin at his teasing pun, but his face sobers.

"I never knew I wanted a family until I thought I had a child. Then, I thought it would be like this." He nods at the counter. "Father-son time, but I'll never have it, not in the way I envisioned. No baseball games. No science homework. No band concerts. Nothing." His hands slip to my shoulders. "I'll never have what you have, Midge, with your boys. I didn't get a child. I got a twenty-six-year-old. I missed out on everything."

He tugs me to him, pressing me into his chest with one hand on my head and one on my back. "Don't ever be jealous of me, baby. You've had so much more. A beautiful house. A marriage. Great kids. You've had it all while I had the fame and nothing to show for it but a bedroom at my brother's, a kid I didn't know about, and a job as a mechanic instead of a musician."

I don't like how he makes it sound—degrading himself. He kisses my head and eases me back. "I know I said I want to make all your dreams come true, but I don't know how. I have nothing to offer you. I'm being selfish because I want you to make all mine come true instead."

I leap for him. Forgiveness and sorrow mix with kisses against the island. If it weren't for the damn volcano, I'd ask him to spread me on the counter and take those words to a new level. I also have Liam upstairs, and the click of the back door lets me know Ronin is home from a study session. Hank and I break away like guilty teenagers.

"Hey, honey. Get all your homework done?" Ronin scoffs as he passes Hank and me. Standing opposite each other, we each hold a counter as if we need the anchor, so we don't attack.

"Yeah. I'm headed to bed." He looks at Hank. "Ever consider shaving a bit? Might not leave all the evidence on her neck." He continues to the living room as my mouth falls open.

Hank chuckles, and our gazes meet. His eyes twinkle with mischief, and he reaches for me. We come together again, making out like kids desperate to remove clothing and knowing we can't. Slowing eventually, I walk Hank to the front door.

"I'll see you tomorrow," he assures me. "I'm so glad you feel better."

I feel so much better, and it's all because of him. Three little words linger in my head, but I won't use them again. Can I keep my feelings in check? I'll make things between us experimental instead of emotional and I'll let this first round fizzle a bit.

Results inconclusive. More data needed.

chapter 32

Sleepovers . . .With Children

[Hank]

Friday evening, I have another intake meeting with the counselor and Lawson. Things do not go well. Lawson is agitated and acting out, and I worry I'm the problem. He has no idea who I am. I have no idea if he remembers his mother, and I'll never know if she mentioned me to him. It's nearly ten o'clock when I find myself outside Midge's door. She hasn't been answering her phone, and it makes me nervous. Her boys are with their dad for the weekend, and she told me she didn't have any plans, so when I knock, I'm a bit surprised.

"Elston?" I question. "Is your mom home?"

"She's already in bed." He lingers at the door, holding his arm up high on the wood, showing off his thin muscular frame. He's built for seventeen but not like my forty-three.

"It's early. She okay?" He's not inviting me in, but I'm not leaving until I have an answer. Not to mention, I really want to see her. I need to talk.

"I think so." He twists to glance at the staircase.

"Aren't you supposed to be at your dad's?" It's none of my business, but Midge mentioned that trouble continues with his father.

"Yeah, but Mom said I could stay home this weekend." He looks down at his feet and shrugs. "I got a date tomorrow night anyway."

My brows raise, and silence grows between us. My leg twitches. I'm a little itchy to see his mom.

"Elston, may I speak to you like a man?" His head pops up, bright eyes looking right at me. "Ever love a girl, kid?"

Elston tilts his head. "If you want to speak to me like a man, how about you not call me kid?"

"Fair enough." My lips twist, holding back a chuckle. Kid has balls, I'll give him that. "Ever lay with a girl? I don't mean sex. I mean sleep next to one. Just hold her."

He tips up his chin, hesitating a second before answering. "Yes." Rubbing a hand over his head, he looks away. "It seems even more intimate than sex."

My eyes widen. There's that word again. "But you cared about the girl, right?"

He swings his eyes back to mine. "Of course."

"Then I hope you'll understand. I'd like to step upstairs and check on your mom."

His eyes narrow. "You do realize she's my mom." He shudders. "Just...*ew*..."

"*Man,* don't ever *ew* over your mom. She's still a woman even if you don't want to think about her like that. Believe it or not, she can be more than a mother. She's a person. And one I care about."

He nods, and I'm hoping we understand each other, though having no practice with teenagers, boys, and their mothers, or anything else related to kids, I have no idea. He surprises me by stepping back.

I take the steps two at a time, slowing my pace as I near the top. Slipping into her room, I find the space dark with moonlight streaming through the large window. I kick off my boots.

"Midge," I say softly, not wanting to scare her yet feeling guilty for waking her. She faces away from me, so she rolls, looking over her shoulder.

"Hank? What are you doing here?"

"I tried to call, but you didn't answer. Wanted to make sure you were okay." I sit on the edge of the bed. She's tucked in, and I don't want to take more advantage than I have, especially if Elston decides he wants to check on us. Suddenly, I feel like the teenager in the house, but I don't care. I need to be close to her. Shifting to my side, I curl up behind her. I force her to roll back to the position she held so her back is to my chest.

Wrapping an arm over her waist, I tug her closer to me although the blankets are in the way.

"Where's Elston?" she asks.

"He let me in." I pause. "I want to be intimate with you."

She quietly laughs as she shifts to look at me over her shoulder.

"Is that code for sex because I can't with Elston in the house, and besides, I have my period."

What? *Shit.* I release her and press up on my elbow. "Are you okay? Do you need something?" I act as if she's sick instead of dealing with something natural.

"No." She chuckles at my overconcern.

"Then can I be intimate with you? Close like you said the other day." I'm holding my breath, because I really want this with her.

"Of course, honey." She rolls back to face the window, and I wrap over her again. Breathing into her hair, I nuzzle my head into the back of her neck.

"Rough night?" she prompts, knowing I saw Lawson.

"I'm worried I won't connect with him. There's so much to learn, and I'm so behind. So much time has passed."

"You'll be fine," she says softly. "Parenting doesn't come with a manual even if you knew him as a baby. Every day is one day at a time."

"I've heard that saying before. Every day in rehab." I don't really want to talk about that experience right now, though. "Why does life have so many steps?"

"Sometimes, I think life is just one step at a time. Addiction or not. Can't change yesterday. Can't do anything about tomorrow. Just gotta deal with today."

"Lady, I love you," I blurt into her neck. We both freeze a moment, and I need her to look at me. I perch up on my elbow again and gently press her shoulder twisting her to face me. "I mean it, Midge. I didn't just say it to say it. I love you, intimately."

"I love you too, honey." Her lips curve slowly, and I lean forward to kiss her. Her mouth is sweet on mine, icing on my cupcake of happiness at the moment. I pull back too soon for both our liking but with her monthly predicament and Elston in the house somewhere, I don't want to push anything. I just want to hold her, something I can't say I've done often in my life. I cuddle up behind her again, tugging her as close as the blanket barrier will allow. Wrapping my arm over her, I hold tight, almost afraid she'll slip away. Her arm loosens from the covers, and she slips it over mine. Holding my wrist, she leans forward and kisses my knuckles. It's *intimate*, and for the first time in my life, I feel like I'm in a good place.

L.B. DUNBAR

chapter 33
Offerings

[Hank]

On Monday, I find Midge staring at the computer screen. She was on her cell phone only moments ago, taking a call outside and pacing back and forth. Seeing her appear and then disappear through the view of the front glass door made me nervous. When she stepped back inside, she covered her face for a moment and then straightened, walking stiffly back to her desk. *Her desk*, I repeat because I like seeing her here, finding her close, and catching her smiling at me. As I near her, I hear an exaggerated sigh.

"What's wrong, little lady?" I've startled her, and she spins, the chair creaking with the speed. She blinks up at me as if she's trying to focus.

"Ever want something so much, only to discover later it isn't what you thought it would be?"

Strangely, I do know the sensation. Kit had been that for me, but then another thought strikes. Does she mean me? I rub my chest, pain radiating inside the cavity. Am I disappointing her? I'm not who I used to be, and although I'm confident in myself, I know being a musician seems more glamorous than a mechanic. Midge is all polished chrome while I'm dented steel— scratched and rusty. Did she change her mind?

With hesitation, I ask, "What happened?"

"Pendelton offered me the job." Her shoulders hunch before she shrugs.

My eyes widen with excitement. I'm so proud of her, and I'm ready to tell her as much when I note her body language suggests she doesn't feel the same way.

"That's terrific?" I hesitate, uncertain why she appears so *blasé* about the offer. This is what she wanted.

"It is great. I presented a darn good campaign and the possibility of growth in his dinosaur company. But now, I'm not so certain I want to work there. Not if this is how he treats me, or any other employee for that matter. He only saw me so he could drive his car. I don't want to turn tricks every time I have an idea for the man. Not to mention, his son gives me the heebie-jeebies. I can't start a job where I might be harassed before I get my way."

I have to agree with her on this matter. I'd be on daily alert, prepping to punch Pendelton's dick-wad son if he neared her.

"But you deserve the job. You might have had to jump through a hoop to get his attention, but once you had it, you must have wowed him."

"That's the thing. I already played these games at Bigle, and it sucked." She shrugs again. "I'll just have to find something else."

"So what? You're going to keep working here?" The question snaps sharper than I intend, but Midge is too smart to order parts and take calls from some of our asshole customers. She can do the job, no question, but should she? No. *No way.* "What about going out on your own? Starting your own company?"

She shrugs again, her expression one of defeat. "It takes a lot of money, and I'm not in a place for that right now."

She told me about her ex-husband and how he wasn't pleased to pick up the tab on his own kids' tuition for their fancy high school. There's nothing wrong with public schools, but I understand where her kids go offers more opportunity; besides, they are used to where they attend. No need to change things. Be a man, I say. Pay for your kids.

"Brut says I can stay here." Her soulful eyes look up at me. "Is that *not* okay with you?"

My chest tightens at the thought she's gone to Brut already. She must have talked to him before she declined Pendelton's offer. It's Brut's business, and I don't have a say one way or another. If he offered to have her to stay, it's fine. I can't say no. I mean *no*—because I want more for her—but seeing her every day brings me selfish pleasure.

"Of course, it's okay. I just want you to be happy, and this place isn't it."

"What's wrong with this place?" She looks around, and I follow her gaze, taking note of the improvements she's made to the outer space. It's free of oil and grease, smells like vanilla, and looks relatively clean. Still, it's a place that means I settled. I caved because I had nothing else once the band collapsed.

"Even I don't want to be here, so how can I suggest you stay?"

Her head tilts. "Why don't you want to be here? This is your father's legacy to you and Brut. Besides, your brother is here, and you get along well enough. You can do your thing here."

"Do my thing?" I scoff, my fingers twitching with the old feeling of holding drumsticks. "I'm far from doing my thing."

"What else is there?" She pauses a beat. "Are you referring to your band?" She gives me a look, narrow-eyed and unreadable. "If a band is your thing, why didn't you start a new one?"

Kit died, rests on the tip of my tongue, but that really isn't the truth of it. We could have carried on, I suppose. Could have gotten a new female lead singer, but it would never have been the same. Kit *was* Kit Carrigan and Chrome Teardrops. We were just background noise, and I have not a ratty-tat-tat to show for that time in my life. I couldn't move on because no one wanted me. I was a risk in my condition, a has-been in my prime because of my reputation.

"It's not so simple."

She stares at me, waiting for additional explanation, but I don't wish to share. I'm tired of rehashing Kit and calling up my failures. I look around the cleaned-up waiting room and rap my knuckles on the counter. "I need to get to work."

+ + +

It's late when I collapse on the couch opposite Brut's desk. I've been staying after hours to work on my own baby. The Mustang has been neglected too much these past weeks.

Brut's working on something with reader glasses on his nose.

"Getting old, man?" I tease.

"You wait. Your time is coming." He continues looking between some report and the computer screen. I fiddle with the torn leather on the back of the couch, staring at my thick fingers tugging at the loose piece.

"What's on your mind?" I look over at my brother. He's pulled his glasses down to the tip of his nose, and he peers at me over the frame.

"How do you know something's on my mind?".

Brut crosses his arms on the desk and stares at me. "Because I know you, unfortunately." He's teasing. He's also right.

My big brother knows too much about me, and in some ways, I've taken advantage of him. I thought about what Midge said earlier. Brut took me in, welcomed me home after I fucked up, and he never blinked. He gave me a job, knowing I could do the work even if I was a bit rusty, and he never complained. He never griped although this wasn't his dream any more than it was mine.

This is your father's legacy to you and Brut.

We might not have wanted the place, but it's offered financial stability, and if we wanted anything else, why didn't we go for it?

"What did you want to be, Brut, when you were a kid?" He stares at me with uncertainty on his face, like if he admits his dream, I'll laugh.

"Doesn't really matter anymore. I am what I am."

"And what are you, Brut? In the grand scheme of things, what are you?"

"You hitting the bottle again? These are kind of deep thoughts for a Monday evening." He chuckles, knowing I'm not drinking. He squeezes his forehead with his finger and thumb, like he's holding in long-lost opportunities. Like Lily perhaps.

"You know I always wanted to bang my drums with a band, tour the world and shit. I got to do all that. I blew it, but I did it. But what about you?"

"First, you didn't blow it. You guys were on top of the world while it lasted. Cancer is a shit thing, and Kit getting it so young was a heartache. But never say you were a failure, Hank. You had it all. Sometimes, losing is beyond your control."

I watch my brother, his worldly comments sinking in slowly.

"But I blew all the money. I lost my home. I lost the girl—"

"You never had the girl. Not the way you should have had her," he interjects before sighing, removing his glasses, and looking down at his desk. He knows what he's talking about. Kit and I were reckless—a mistake I can't make myself admit. Brut had a girl once, and she was into him the way you want a girl to be. Caring. Committed. Intimate. Only, he blew it.

"Anyway, I might have been famous, but I have nothing to show for it."

"You have Grammys," Brut scoffs.

"I don't even know where they are."

"What's brought all this on?" Tipping back in his chair, Brut places a finger against his temple.

"Midge." Brut stares, waiting for clarification. I sigh. "She didn't take the job with Pendelton, and I applaud her decision because he's an asshat. But she deserved that job, Brut. It isn't fair that she feels she failed, and it also isn't fair I can't help her. I *want* to help her. She needs money to go out on her own and start her own business, which I know she can do. She has damn good ideas even if I don't understand all of them. Look how she straightened out things here."

Brut nods, rocking in his chair. "You should see the ad campaign she came up with. New logo. New tagline. It's really gonna give the place some life and make it mine. Ours," he corrects.

"Is it ours, man? I feel like it's always been yours. I don't deserve the second chance you gave me." I look at my brother, really look at him. His hair might be snow white, but the scruff on his face is only salt-and-pepper. He typically keeps his face clean-shaven, though, so I'm surprised at the change in him. He isn't as edgy as me, thinner, softer but still strong. In fact, I appear the older of the two of us from living life too much. When did Brut live?

"Don't even go there. You're my brother. When you have nowhere else to go, home is where you go. What's really happening inside that big head?"

I swipe over my skull with both hands at the mention of my large cranium. "I'm just frustrated. I want to give Midge things, and I can't."

"Midge loves you. Returning that love might be all she needs."

"I *do* love her," I snap.

"I know." Brut winks.

"But I want to help her do *more*. I so fucked up." I sigh, and Brut lowers his head, pressing at his temple again. It isn't all about money. I want to show her I support her. From my side of the fence, she's had a good life. She hasn't had a pampered life, though, and I want to pamper her.

"You have the money."

"What?" I balk, my elbows coming to my knees, hands clasping together. He just called this place ours. Is he thinking. . .? "I can't ask you to put up money from this place, if that's where you're going."

"Nope. You have your own money. You can do as you please with it." We continue to eye one another, and I'm completely lost as to his meaning. He leans forward, crossing his arms on his desk again. "When things were going down for you, I made you sign a Power of Attorney, signing everything over to me."

"You what?" My eyes widen as I sit upright, and then I glare. "I don't remember this."

"I'm certain you wouldn't."

We both take a moment to reflect on some of my low times. Blackouts. Unexplained bruises. Missing pieces in time.

"Why would you do that?"

"You were drowning in self-misery, and I couldn't watch you piss away everything you worked for, so I had to do something to save you from yourself, at least in the aspect of your finances. I had you sign the papers, allowing me to take over."

"How?"

"Got you drunk." He laughs bitterly, and I grin weakly at the strong possibility.

"So much for sound body and mind," I mock. "I lost my house. Foreclosure. Bankruptcy." Brut looks away as I speak.

"I sold it."

"Out from under me?"

"You were so far down, there wasn't an *under* for you."

We glare at one another before Brut looks away, a vexed expression on his face. I'm too stunned to speak, struggling between the lies, manipulation, and gratitude.

"How could you keep this from me?" I snap.

"I figured I'd tell you when the time was right."

"And when would that be? According to you."

"Now." His lips curl, but I don't find the humor in knowing all my assets are still available to me, at least in some capacity. Thinking of those lost Grammys, I ask. "Where are my things?"

"In the attic."

"And the money?" I swallow at the possibility I still have some.

"In an account, earning interest. Some is in small investment funds."

I blink. My brother took care of me, but he lied. Anger settles into me swiftly.

"Is there anyone who hasn't kept a secret from me? First, Kit with Lawson. Now, you with this." I'm pissed.

"Midge." He pauses. "You said she told you she loves you. I believe she was telling the truth when she said that," Brut adds, softening his tone. I want to kick his ass for throwing her in my face, and then kick my own for not noticing Midge is the only honest thing in my life. Trustworthy. Innocent. Everything.

"Can I have access to the money?" I ask sheepishly as if it isn't already mine. "How much do I have?"

"I'd say you have a few million."

I fall back on the couch. *What the fuck?*

"Then why am I living in a bedroom in your house and working here?" I bark, the insult hitting my brother like a punch to the gut.

"Whenever you're ready, I guess you can go." His voice lowers to a tone reminding me of our pop. However, there is no venom behind his suggestion, only the sting of hurt.

"I don't mean it like that." I exhale. Brut doesn't question me although I can see he wants to know just what I do mean. My chest aches with the lie, but somehow, my head recognizes he did this to save me from myself. Losing my house and thinking the money vanished, along with a few other things, cemented my decision to get clean. It was either that or be homeless; although my brother wouldn't have let me live on the streets. *When you don't know where to go, you go home.* He welcomed me into his house when I left rehab, and I just stabbed him for it.

"A history teacher," he says quietly.

"Pardon me?"

"I wanted to be a history teacher. I did well in the subject and thought I'd be okay as a teacher." One second from laughing, I stare at my brother until I see he's serious. He would have been good with kids. He's great with his son. He's intelligent. And has the patience of a saint—just look at him with me. He shouldn't be here anymore than Midge. I'm a selfish bastard.

"Do you need money for this place? Want to go back to college?"

Brut's head pops up. "I'm too old to go to school."

"You're never too old for change. Just look at me." I wave a hand before me.

"Nah, I'm good here, and we don't need the money for this place."

"So can I have some for Midge?"

"That's up to you. It's your money." He presses back in his seat, his expression puzzled. "But you can't fix things for her. I see you playing white knight again, and I don't think money is what that woman needs most."

"You just let me worry about my girl. This will solve everything for her."

+ + +

Midge is blinking up at me across her kitchen island. Her expression blank as her mouth hangs open.

"What?"

"I'd like to front the money for you to start your own marketing business."

Her head shakes, a smile curling her lips momentarily. She looks cute in her plaid pajama shorts and a red tank top. Once she accepts my offer, I'm gonna lay her out on this island and nibble her pert breasts, the nipples peaking under the thin material like an invitation.

"I can't." Her lips flatten.

"Why not?" I snap. Staring back at her, I'm shocked at her abrupt answer.

"Because I don't even know the first thing about running my own business. I wouldn't know how much money I need, and I certainly can't take money from you."

"What's wrong with *my* money?" I huff, gripping the counter, mirroring her position opposite me.

"Nothing. But it's yours." She waves outward from her body toward me.

"That's the point. It's mine, and I'm giving it to you."

Her entire body sags, her hands coming to rest on the counter again. We face off a second before she looks away.

"I can't accept it. It's sweet of you to offer and super generous, but I can't accept your gift."

"Why not?" I practically whine like a petulant child not understanding.

"Just no, Hank."

My arms are crossed, biceps bulging with tension, and I glower at her. She shivers.

"Don't be afraid of me," I say, softening my tone and lowering my arms. I circle the island, reaching out to cup her jaw. I don't like the momentary fear on her face.

Her eyes dash back and forth between mine. "I'm not frightened, but I can't accept this."

I search her face, wanting to comprehend. "This could help you. It can fix things."

"What things?" she questions. "I'm not broken, and I'm not broke. Not yet, at least. I have applications out there, and I've investigated other avenues."

Her fingers typically hold my wrists when I cup her face, but only her eyes reach mine.

"Like what? What things?"

Shrugging, she says, "I've reached out to other former clients I know from Bigle Marketing and a few on the list of who we wanted to impress. Some of them are willing to listen to me as an independent contractor."

"That's-that's great, right?"

She shrugs again. "It's a step forward."

Ugh, damn steps again.

"I still wish you'd just take the money. Look at it as a gift."

"It's very generous, but I don't want to owe you." Her voice softens although the words sting.

"You won't owe me anything. I'm the one who already owes you," I tease, stroking her cheeks.

"For what?" Her lips twist, and her brows furrow.

"For doing *more* with me." I lower my head and take her lips. She's so delicious, and within seconds, I'm crushing her against me, lapping at her lips and hoping she can taste how I feel. I want to give her everything. What's mine is hers.

She pulls back a bit when the kiss slows. "What's *more* mean?"

"You said you wanted more a few weeks ago, and I want more with you." She stares at me, eyes uncertain, and I realize I'm not explaining myself well. I repeat her sentiments. "More kisses, more than being okay. More of everything."

"I more you, too." She grins. "But I'm not taking the money. It's not like we're married. We're dating. It's too much."

I pull back at the comment, looking directly into her eyes. "If we were married, would you take the money?" It's an honest question, but her answer surprises me.

"Hank, I'm not having this conversation with you." Her tone grates over me as she tugs her face from my hands. Didn't she say she wanted *more*? What the hell?

"Why not?" *I could marry her*. I would do this in order for her to accept my gift. She stares at me, her head tilting as if she can read my thoughts.

"You aren't going to marry me so you can give me the money. Money you didn't know you still had. You should enjoy it yourself. Use it for Lawson. Or. . .or. . .go on a vacation or something." She waves out a hand again, before slapping her thigh in frustration and the stinging sound echoes in her kitchen.

"I don't want to take a damn vacation," I bark

"No."

My mouth pops open. "You told me you would say yes if I asked."

"I was drunk."

Rattled as if she struck me, my head shakes. Her hands lift for my biceps, but I step back.

"Fine. You're right. I would say yes, but not like this, not because you only want to help me." Her eyes search my face, but she can't see the pain behind my rusty armor chest, where I realize I'm nobody's shining knight.

Never will be.

chapter 34

Seduction Junction, What's Your Function

[Midge]

Hank looks crushed after I reject his gift. The offer was a generous, but not one I could take in good conscience. He earned that money, and as he just discovered he still has it, I don't need him sharing it with me. I meant what I said—if we were married, it would be different—but we aren't married, and I certainly am not marrying him for money. Dollar bills are not the reason I'm with him. In fact, Hank is aware I had no idea who he was or how he was famous. I don't care about that—what he once was. I only want him in the present.

With this thought in mind, I decide I want to show him how I feel about him. I have a Mom's Night function at the high school where I only need to make an appearance before I can escape. Hank has been working late at the garage the past few nights. We've fallen into a routine of him sneaking over to my house whenever he can and staying as long as he thought respectable, but I feel us separating.

The actual garage is a place I rarely visit. I don't understand the parts, the terminology, or the mechanics of the automobiles. I just want four wheels and an engine to make my car go where I desire. However, Hank has a special project. After he isn't answering his phone, I call Brut who tells me Hank is most likely still at Restored Dreams.

It's late April in California, and this means rain. I'm happy with the weather this evening as I need my old dress-length raincoat to pull off my plan as well as a stiff dose of liquid courage and a shot of confidence. I pass on the alcohol and take a deep breath instead. I have keys to the outer office and find Hank right where Brut suggests—bent over his black Mustang, the hood open and his head buried inside. Heavy music thunders inside the garage. The beat—something velvety, loud and pulsing—matches the rush in my heart and the thump at my core. I fidget with the belt of my coat. Because of the music, Hank doesn't hear my heels as I cross the cement floor.

I touch his shoulder and step back in anticipation. I knew I'd startle him.

"Holy fuck." One hand covers his chest while the other holds up some kind of wrench, primed and ready to fight off his attacker. His eyes rapidly run from one to the other of mine, then he drops the metal item and tugs me to him. "You scared the ever-loving shit out of me."

I chuckle into his chest, inhaling his scent. Man. Oil. Hank. I've missed him the past few days, and I melt a little into his hold, relieved to be in his arms again. Then he presses me away from him, and the heat between us is gone too quickly.

"What the hell are you doing here? I thought you had some lady thing tonight." He steps back, taking in my appearance. The plum-colored trench coat covers me to the top of my knees. My legs are bare, and I wear my favorite black heels. His eyes narrow, and he takes a deep breath. Afraid he'll retreat too far away; I reach out for him. My hands make contact with his forearm.

"I figured since you were avoiding me, I'd have to get your attention somehow." My body trembles, and I feel like a psycho ex-lover, like Glenn Close in the movie where she has an affair and then boils the bunny rabbit. *I won't be ignored.* Cripes, I'm losing my shit over this man.

"I'm not avoiding you."

I dismiss the sharpness in his tone. "I want to apologize for the other day."

His lips twist, and he crosses his arms. His biceps bulge under the black t-shirt. My hand follows the fold, refusing to let go of him until he listens to me, and I get what I want because right now, my body hums for him, aching for something only he can give me. I want to *give* to him as well.

"I know I hurt your feelings by not accepting your gift—"

"I'm not hurt," he interjects, the roughness of his tone not disguising the truth.

I hold up a hand to halt him from speaking. "I understand why you did it. Why you offered. You're a generous man. Offering something like that. . ." I squeeze his forearm and cover my chest with my free hand. "You have no idea how much it touched me that you wanted to give me something like that. Such a gift. Your show of faith. It means a lot that you believe in me so much you are willing to part with something you didn't know you had."

"I'd do anything for you," Hank says, his voice smoky. His Adam's apple bobs as he swallows.

"I know. It's why I feel the way I do about you." With that, I release his arm, taking a deep breath. I need to reroute. Focus, I tell myself. You got this. "This is your baby, right? Is it safe to look inside?" I muster courage I'm suddenly not certain I possess, but I'm not backing down. I want this too much.

Hank's brow pinches. He showed me his black beauty once, explaining to me all about it in jargon I didn't understand, but this large piece of machinery is important to him. And powerful looking, like him. I open the driver's door, flip the seat forward, and climb in the back.

The music in the garage dulls only a little inside the car, which smells of old leather and forgotten years. I smooth my hands over the black interior, feeling the soft, worn material before I slide to one side of the seat and turn to face the open door. Hank leans in with one arm on the doorframe, the other on the roof.

"Why don't you join me a second?" I peer up at him, spreading my arm along the back seat. "It feels cozy back here."

Leaning forward, I slip off my heels while Hank watches me. His eyes follow every movement of my hand sliding off one shoe and then the other. Taking another deep breath, I lift one leg, positioning my heel on the back seat. I shiver as my foot hits the cool leather and at the heat in Hank's eyes. His quiet ruffles my nerves, but I won't give up. My coat slips open over my thigh just the right amount to reveal what I'm wearing underneath.

"What the fuck you doing, little lady?" His voice teases, and a growl rolls through his tone. He's still watching me, not making any attempt to move from the position where he stands.

"It's a little warm in here." My eyes don't leave his as I unloop the belt and undo one button at a time. One. Two. Three. Four. I slip the material to the side and notice Hank run a hand over his face. Two fingers swipe around his mouth and stroke down his neck.

"Middy," he groans.

"Join me," I purr, the sound low but pleading.

He hasn't moved and I'm on the verge of thinking he isn't interested in what I'm offering. My coat slips farther open, exposing the thigh length slip of material hardly containing my breasts and hitched up enough to reveal the lace covering my lower region.

"Why are you doing this?"

The question stops me, and my eyes sting. Lowering my leg, I press my thighs together. I tug the fallen side of my coat over my shoulder. It's obvious he isn't going to act on what I'm offering despite the steely glaze in his eyes. If he has to ask me why, I probably shouldn't be doing this.

"I guess...I thought...maybe I should just go." Who knew money would be a breaking point in our relationship? I'm sitting upright when he climbs into the back seat. His presence fills the space.

"Midge, what are you really doing here?"

I'm a total failure if I have to spell it out for him. "I thought I was seducing you, but obviously, it isn't working. If you don't want to see me anymore because of the money, just tell me." I guess I need direct instruction. I don't want to play games with him.

"I don't want to."

My head shoots up as I'm scrambling to get my feet back in my heels. I twist to look at my foot, no glass slipper here. My prince crushes me. A finger comes to my chin, turning my face back to his, but I close my eyes. The tears well at my embarrassment.

"I mean, I don't want to *not* see you. I want to keep seeing you…" His voice drifts, and I'm visibly quaking. I can't open my eyes, or the tears will leak.

"Are you afraid of me?" My lids crack slowly, and he demands, "Talk to me."

I don't know why he keeps asking me these things, begging me not to be frightened of him. I'm petrified of him—how I feel about him, that is. The level of my emotion for him consumes me most days, but especially today for some reason when I've missed him more than I should admit.

"I'm not afraid of you," I snap. "I'm-I'm…I'm horny."

The word hangs between us. Mortification fills me as I admit how badly my body wants to get off and get off by him.

"You want me to fuck you, little lady?" His voice lowers to a whisper, and the sinister hint rushes over my skin.

I remember questioning once if a voice could make you orgasm, and I'm certain he just did. My knees come together, but in the next instant, I'm being dragged forward, my back hitting the seat under me. He tugs open my coat, examining the silky material slipping down enough to almost expose one breast and hitching up enough to reveal the thin lace covering my privates.

"You wear this for me?"

I nod. The plum-colored ensemble matches my jacket. I don't own lingerie, but I thought I'd treat myself to treat him. Rough fingers tug the thin lace edge of the top down, releasing two swollen globes to greet his heavy fingers. He squeezes them both, and I gasp. He's rough, his fingers callused but firm. He pinches both nipples simultaneously, and my back arches.

He's kneeling, and he spreads my legs so one graces either side of him. He reaches behind his neck and tugs his t-shirt forward in that sexy male way. My hands find his hard abs and climb upward, exploring the sculpted hills and valley of him. Thick. Solid. Big.

He grips each wrist, clutching them both in one hand and positioning them over my head. With his free hand, he wiggles his pants down his hips a bit. Instantly, his hard length springs free. Holding the base of himself, he swipes over my wet heat, the lace saturated with my longing.

"So fucking wet," he mutters, shoving the lace aside and spreading my slick folds by dragging back and forth torturously through a place ripe, ready, and waiting to swallow him. I love how he loves to watch us join together.

"I'll fuck you, little lady," he says a little harshly, a mixture of passion and frustration.

I look up at him as he watches how he's coating his length. My thighs clench, and my clit pulses. Tears fill my eyes again at my intense desire for him to enter me. *More.*

"Condom," I whisper, and something in his eyes shifts when his head flips up to face me. He pulls back, fumbling with his back pocket. A wallet falls to the floor. I watch as he rips the foil with his teeth and then sheaths himself. Sweet cheese, why is that so sexy? I don't have time to ponder the thought because his firm hand returns to holding mine hostage above my head. He impales me in one swift thrust. I grunt at the welcome intrusion and wrap both my legs around him. My heels remain on and lock over his ass.

"Touch yourself," he commands, watching himself enter me.

"Let go of my hand."

He's hammering into me, his hand holding my wrists captive, the other balancing under my backside to move me in rhythm with what he needs. He loosens his hold enough so I can free one hand which drifts to the sensitive spot. I lightly stroke. I gasp. Then I rub, applying more pressure over the place I know will get me where I need most.

"Holy hell, lady. You are so goddamn hot."

He thrusts hard enough to rock the car. I'm spiraling as he jackhammers into me, and I touch myself. Then I implode. I bite my lip to hold back the explosive sound in my throat.

"Scream," he demands, and I open, his name a prayer echoing through the classic car and out into the garage. The thumping music drowns out my call. He stills his body, only one part of him pulsing, releasing, jetting off inside me. I feel relief but still wired—weird, actually. It wasn't enough of him. I could go again. *More.*

"Feel better?" Hank asks as he pulls out of me a little too quickly. I nod, unable to answer.

"Do you know how hot you are like this?"

"Do you know how much I love you?" I counter, the words catch in my throat. Hank kneels between my open thighs. His head shoots up, and he stills. I take a deep breath. "I love you, and I'm sorry."

"I thought you just wanted to—"

My mouth falls open before he finishes, and my heart crashes. This is an off-the-cliff, shattered windshield, flipping vehicle kind of accident. I'm crushed as I scramble to sit upright. Hank envelopes me, his lower body between my spread legs. Peppering my sternum with tender kisses and soft suction.

His head pops up, frightened silver eyes begging me for something I can't read. "I was too rough, baby."

I have no idea what he means. I'm numb inside. The moment of lust is lost, and we remain naked. Raw. Ripped apart. I lift a shaky hand to his cheek as I suddenly recognize what this is and *isn't.* This wasn't me seducing him but triggering his fears.

"You're never rough with me," I say, swiping a palm around his head. My heart still races, caught between running away and the sprint of what we just completed. "You're a gentle giant with a good soul and a generous heart."

"I don't deserve you," he mutters against my skin, his forehead buried above my breasts. My nose burns, my eyes heating, but I dismiss the potential tears.

"You deserve every inch of me, and I want to give it all to you."

But there's a ghost in this back seat, and I don't know how much *more* of her I can take.

L.B. DUNBAR

chapter 35

Reckless Affairs

[Midge]

The next night, I need another girls' night out. Hank has an early shift at the crisis center, and it's just as well. I can't face him. I decide to call Edie, as she's the only person who might understand my predicament. She's the closest friend I have as most of my prior friends were work colleagues.

"Hey, Midge." Her chipper voice heats my nose, and my eyes sting. I will not cry again, I warn.

"Hey."

"You okay, honey?"

"I don't think so." A tear slips as I recall how I wanted to climb Hank like a tree, nearly begging him for sex, and then he pigeonholes me in the same category as his former lover because I want him.

"Want to meet for a drink?"

"Yeah, but I need to take Liam to baseball first." It's my turn for carpool. I drive there, and another mom drives back. For one teeny-tiny moment, I curse my lack of freedom. I can't do as I please because I'm a mother. Then recalling I *am* a mother, I curse my wanton behavior.

"I'll come to you bearing gifts of wine," Edie suggests. "We'll make it a girls' night in."

An hour later, Edie arrives with Ivy. "Hey," they say in unison, holding up wine bottles as I open the front door. For a moment, I sense a *Bad Moms* scene happening in my living room, but then I realize this isn't a PTA meeting.

This also isn't exactly what I had in mind as the conflict in my heart involves the young woman's mother. I'm not *un*happy to see Ivy, but I can't speak as freely in front of her about her mom. I mean no disrespect to the dead, but I can't keep fighting Kit's memory.

Following me to the kitchen, the ladies each take a seat on the island stools, and I stand opposite them to pour our glasses.

"To friendship," Ivy says.

"To love." Edie winks.

We clink glasses, and while they sip, I gulp. The whole glass goes down before I take a breath.

"Oh, boy," Ivy whispers, covering her mouth with loose fingers and staring at me.

Edie exhales, watching me with knowing eyes. "What happened? It's Hank, isn't it? What did he do?"

Ivy's gaze weighs on my cheek, almost as if she recognizes in me her mother's distant agitation with the same man. I don't know that I can speak what's on my mind, and I remain silent a beat.

"It's my mother, isn't it?" Ivy drums her delicate fingers on the counter. Her lids close a second, and I glance over at Edie.

Immediately, Edie's hand rubs her niece's back. "No, honey. No." When she looks up at me, she realizes she's lying. *I'm sorry*, Edie mouths, understanding I needed just her and not Ivy tonight.

I open my mouth to speak but stop myself. Then try again. "It isn't your mother directly," I begin. "It's more Hank and his inability to let her go. I feel like I'm constantly being measured against her." That isn't exactly true either. Kit was fabulous and famous. I don't want to be those things, and her fortune isn't where the comparison lies. What I can't combat is their relationship. I seem to set off a trigger within Hank. He somehow interprets sex as that's all I want and misses out on my feelings for him.

"Don't. Please don't feel that way," Ivy begs with water-filled eyes.

"I can't help it. I don't want to be jealous of them." Second-guessing my statement, again, I retract it. "Actually, I'm not envious. Their volatile relationship sounded unhealthy."

"It was." Ivy nods. "My mother…she used him, abused him. She even wrote a song about it. She'd call him to get what she wanted…sex with him or to get high…and then she'd toss him to the side when she was done."

My mouth hangs open at the harshness of her words. Ivy continues, "And Hank always gave into her. He's a decent man, but he was so stupid when it came to my mom. Their reckless affair wasn't secret, either. My mom didn't have to tell me things for me to know what she was doing and how she treated men. I'm tough on Gage for these reasons and refused to go out with him at first. I didn't want that kind of relationship…one that fulfilled lust instead of love."

"Don't you think your mother loved Hank, though?" I ask. Kit had to have feelings for Hank. I don't want to believe she was so heartless. Why else would she have relied on him for almost two decades?

"I think she did in some way, but she was so bitter about my dad's overdose and leaving her behind with a toddler that she refused to attach herself to anyone else permanently after that. She always said being single and keeping secrets was for the protection of Lawson and me, but how did it help us?" Ivy looks at Edie.

"If she told Hank the truth, he might have been supportive, helpful even." Ivy's faith in Hank endears me to her. She isn't speaking ill of her mother; she's just confused by her mother's decisions.

"So what happened?" Edie asks me hesitantly.

I chuckle humorlessly, because what else can I do. I don't think I have any tears left. "I thought I was apologizing for hurting his feelings by seducing him." I pause, closing my eyes. "That is so embarrassing to admit. Instead, I only confused the issue. He says he loves me, and I love him, but there is definitely something *between* us."

The comfort of Edie's hand covers mine, and my lids flip open. Sympathy fills her eyes.

"I'm sorry," Ivy offers, and instantly, I'm asking why. "My mother messed him up. He wasn't innocent in the games they played, but if she had committed to him, he wouldn't have reacted as he often did with her. He wouldn't have trust issues, I guess."

Hank told me of the affair they had. The back and forth between them. The one-night stands to spite the other. The late-night booty calls. The distance between them afterward. A thought comes to me, and I'm hesitant to ask. I'm afraid of the answer.

"Hank's always asking me not to be afraid of him. Do you know…did something happen?" I swallow, feeling the roughness of his fingers on my wrists but knowing in my heart he would never hurt me.

"My mother defined diva behind the scenes. It was one way to protect her heart and keep the band on track to the top of the charts. She'd yell at him, throw things at him. He'd throw things in response but never at her. There were rumors he hit her once. Uncle Tommy lost his shit about that. My mother admitted it was all gossip, but the speculation broke Hank.

"Honestly, he's just too soft for violence. The media, Mom said. They only want a story, not the truth. She was diagnosed with cancer shortly after that rumor, and a new focus began." Ivy chewed her lip. "She refused to let Hank near her, propagating the story. I like to think she just wanted her immediate family close, but the band was her family just as much as blood was. She pulled into herself, holed up at her house, and only let Tommy and me take care of her needs. I never wanted to believe spite or jealousy held Hank back. Knowing the truth of Lawson proves what lengths my mother went to keep Hank at a distance."

"You knew?" I question. Edie looks surprised as well.

"Like I said, Mom and I didn't have many secrets between us. I loved my mother. She was all I had for years. Her and the band, but that doesn't mean I agreed with everything she did."

"Why didn't you tell Hank sooner?" The question seems irrelevant and also none of my business. I'm holding up a hand to apologize for the inquiry when she continues.

"I tried once, but in my grief over my mother, and with my own issues at twenty, I didn't pursue what I knew. Hank disappeared after my mother's funeral. I heard he was pretty bad off, and I figured he didn't need this new revelation to push him over the edge. Life got in the way after that, and it never occurred to me to speak up until recently."

I couldn't fault Ivy. The responsibility to share her mother's secrets didn't belong to her. My heart softens to Hank's portion of Kit and his history. Life was rough for Hank and his heart was fragile toward his lead singer. I can't imagine loving someone so intensely, but I imagine the chase was another addiction.

"Did Hank ever get to say goodbye to your mother? Or tell his side of the story to anyone?"

"He talked to Tommy and Denton Chance, their other band member, but Uncle Tommy was too wrapped up in Mom, and Denton was over Kit and Hank's tirades. Denton was finished with the band's shenanigans before they even officially split. As for saying goodbye, I don't think Mom ever let Hank close enough. She didn't even want *me* there most days."

"That's not true," Edie interjects, her hand shifting to Ivy's back again, where she rubs gently. A silent moment passes between them.

My heart breaks in more ways than one for Hank. Unrequited love. Unfounded speculations. Lacking closure. No wonder he's broken. Their whole relationship was an emotionally abusive clusterfuck.

"Let's not talk about them anymore." I offer a weak smile. "Tell me about Tommy, and what's going on with Gage?"

I swore I wouldn't be jealous as Edie fills me in on the sweetness of her husband. The wine flows, and my mood lifts a little to hear of the goodness of one man toward his wife. I'd like to keep the faith of love in our forties. Edie's interrupted in her storytelling by a text from said husband, and I turn to Ivy.

"Time to spill," I tease, hoping for more good vibe romance. I've seen how Gage kisses his wife. It's criminal but endearing. They make a beautiful couple, but I'm aware good looks can hide ugly secrets.

"There's nothing more to report. I still think he's having an affair. They go on the road again in a month, and it's the perfect opportunity for his groupies to follow him." Bitterness rings in her voice, and I don't blame her.

"Why do you think he's having an affair?" I question, and why is she so resigned to accept his infidelity?

"I still don't believe it," Edie adds, looking up from her phone and flipping it over.

"The phone calls. The sudden hang-ups. The mystery appointments. He's doing something," Ivy explains.

I'm so sad for this young woman, sadder for her than myself. I don't wish even one half of what I went through in my marriage on any other woman. It's painful to watch someone you love slip away from you, and it hits me. Hank went through what I did. He suffered as I had. He watched the woman he loved reject him repeatedly. Then she died, leaving unanswered questions and years of self-hate. I understand him a little better, but I still hurt for me. If he can't let Kit go, then there is no room for me in his heart.

I don't really know how else to impress upon Hank that he could be it for me. I could take a second chance on love, if only he'd accept one as well. If he wants *more* with me, he's going to have to *give* more to me, and I don't mean his damn money.

"I guess I always thought it was inevitable. I mean, Gage Everly is a rock star. I know how these things play out." Ivy sighs, and my thoughts return to her.

We've come full circle in the sadness department, and the night has literally turned into a pity party. The wine has gone down too easily, and I'd like to say I'm buzzed, but I'm not. The heat inside my blood boils out the alcohol.

"I don't think it has to be inevitable. You're young, beautiful, and caring. From what I've seen, you're a good mother, a concerned sister, and an excellent director for a school catering to those with special needs. There is no reason to cheat on you. You're perfect and, rock star or not, he can still be a fucking moron if he doesn't see all that in you," I defend.

Ivy bursts into tears, and I worry I've overstepped my bounds. Edie instantly stands to embrace her younger counterpart, and I'm immediately apologizing.

"Cripes, I'm so sorry. Don't let a bitter old lady dampen your sunshine. I'm sure it's nothing."

Ivy shakes her head against her new aunt. "No, you're right. I don't deserve this. I expected Gage to understand. We promised if one or the other felt the desire to stray, we just needed to speak up. Be honest and let the other go."

I don't know if I could have been so accepting of such conditions, but she seems confident in the vow they made to one another. She straightens, her shoulders stiffening. She sniffs. She's a beautiful woman as I said, but we all get ugly when we cry, and why not? Heartache hurts. It's not pretty, so why should sobbing be?

A knock on the door startles me, and I assume it's Liam without a key. Heading for the front door, I hear soft laughter on the other side of the wood—deep, rumbling, and all male. When I open the door, I face three breathtaking men on my stoop.

"Hello, beautiful." Tommy greets me in his sweet Southern drawl. He steps forward to kiss my cheek without waiting for an invitation to come inside. Gage follows, looking over my shoulder for his wife. He nods as he passes me.

Hank remains last, hands in his pockets as he watches me. He hesitates, and I want to pull him to me, wrap him in my arms and tell him I'll never be like her. My heart reminds me that wrapping around him will only force me to fall. I'm already falling, and I'm holding my breath, waiting for the broken body. He steps forward after I don't speak. He doesn't lean in for any kisses, and a thought strikes me. He never kissed me last night either.

I gesture toward my kitchen and find Tommy with his arm around his wife's shoulder. Gage stands before his wife, but the tension between them is threefold the stress between Hank and me.

"What the fuck is going on here? Why is she crying?" Gage doesn't look at anyone but speaks directly to his wife, who has silent tears dripping down her cheeks again. He swipes at them with thick thumbs.

"Why are you cheating on me?" Ivy blurts, and I quietly gasp. *Sweet cheese*, this could get bad quickly.

Tommy removes his arm from Edie, and Hank's presence behind me stiffens my back.

"What the fuck?" Gage barks. "I'm not cheating on you. Are you insane?"

"I don't know. Am I?" Ivy snaps back at him.

"I—" Gage spins to find an audience. His eyes leap to Edie.

Tommy nearly growls in warning. "Don't even go there."

"I'm not. Just… Edie, help me understand." He's thirty years old or so, but he looks like a child. Caught between anger and bewilderment, his deep dark eyes flare with rage.

"I think you and your wife need to talk," Edie offers softly.

With that, Gage spins back to his wife. "Gorgeous, no. Just no." He swipes more tears. With his hands on her flushed cheeks, he's primed for the kill of his signature kiss and leans forward. Ivy pulls back, and Gage freezes. None of us can miss the slight she's given him. Her cold response throws Gage off. "What the fuck?"

He steps to the side, slips an arm around her back, and scoops her off the stool. "Hank, take us home."

I'm confused why the men are even here. I thought Hank had a shift at the crisis center this evening. At least, that's what he told me, and my mind races. As if suspicion is contagious, I suddenly question Hank's honesty.

Gage exits with Ivy in his arms, and Tommy speaks to Edie. "I guess I'll be riding with you, darlin'. Or better yet, you need to let me drive."

Somehow, I find a double entendre in the statement, and my heart shatters like a wine glass on the floor. I recall Hank driving into me last night, in the back seat of his Mustang, and the sudden car-crash feeling returns.

A thick hand comes to my shoulder, but I tense.

"We should talk, too." He leans close to my ear. "But I need to get Gage and Ivy home first."

I nod, overwrought by all that's transpired in the past hour. Suddenly, the front door opens, and Liam walks in, cheerful and energetic despite a two-hour practice.

"Hey Hank, want to see my new mitt? Wanna play the new MLB game I got? Wanna have ice cream with me?"

My heart breaks at the fire of eager questions. Hank has infiltrated into more than my life, and I curse at the pain our separation could bring to my boys, especially Liam.

"Gotta get Gage and Ivy home tonight, pal. But I'll see you Saturday. How about pizza after your game?"

Liam has another doubleheader, and I like how Hank has his schedule memorized, but it adds to the growing fissure inside me. Hank Paige will break me, and I never expected my life to be so complicated at forty.

chapter 36
What She Didn't Know

[Hank]

We never got the chance to talk the other night, and I am a goddamn idiot, I decide as I doodle on the calendar at the hotline help desk. Thoughts of Midge consume me. Her body underneath mine, moaning, moving, taking me in. Her heart, open and raw as she apologizes, as she says she loves me. Her emotions overwhelm me.

My emotions overwhelm me. Have I not had my eyes open? She wasn't fucking me; she was seducing me. In true dumbass form, I misinterpreted her intentions. She wanted to apologize for hurting my feelings and thought getting close would soothe the sting, and she was fucking right. But I fucking blew it. The instant we finished, and she blurted, *I love you*, I knew, I just knew I had it all wrong in my head. Why hadn't I believed her? Why didn't I accept it?

Because fucking Kit messed with my heart, but no more. From this day forward, I will not let Kit interfere. I'm telling Midge everything tonight, clearing the air and then making her promises I intend to keep forever.

I'm supposed to meet Midge after Liam's game because I work the day shift at the center. We actually meet people face to face on this shift, and these are the moments I feel my best because I'm truly helping someone. The teens passing through here are a mess, and I can only hope to reach them before it's too late. I instantly think of Midge. I don't want it to be too late for me either. I'm slow on the uptake, but I'll be loyal on the downswing.

I stand to hold open the door for a few of our young regulars when a woman with greasy, long hair slips inside. Instantly, I sense she's older despite her small frame. Not intending to touch her, I stretch out an arm to stop her just inside the hall. Her head snaps up, and her glazed eyes try to focus.

"Hanky? I've been looking for you." She swipes at her nose with the back of her hand, sniffling deeply before lowering her fist. She sways on her feet, and I reach for her shoulders.

"Steph, what are you doing?" I should be angry she found me again. In fact, I'm downright pissed off, but I'm also a bit shaken. Everything about her looks familiar to my past, and I don't want a trip down memory lane. Memory is a fickle bitch, though, and the images flip through my head. Drugs. Alcohol. Women. The stench coming off Stephie isn't good.

Her hands shake as she reaches for my wrists, but she misses. Her head rolls to the side. She's so fucking high.

"Got some place private we could go? I could give you something." A cracked fingernail attempts to slide down my chest, but I suck in my breath, not wanting her touch. I want nothing to do with her or her proposition, but I can't turn my back. This is the crisis center. We're here to help people like her.

"Let me get you some coffee. We can talk," I offer. I guide her to a seat in a small sitting room with a couch and two chairs. Not wanting to be alone with her, I avoid the confining space of an empty office. I'm pushing her gently backward by her shoulders, keeping an arm's length distance between us. To my surprise, she lets me lead her. Her knees hit the back of the sofa, and her surprise brings up her hands. She grips my t-shirt with two tiny fists.

High Stephie is a strong Stephie, and as I press her downward, she tugs on my shirt, forcing me down with her. I fumble, faltering over her. My hand catches the back of the couch before I tumble completely. My knee comes between both of hers, pinning me to the cushions. She giggles as she hits the soft, shaggy fabric.

"Steph, whatcha doing?" I growl as a throat clears behind me.

I spin and find a teenager looking at me, wide-eyed and questioning. My position over Stephie looks precarious. The angle of my body. My knee between her thighs. The shortness of her skirt. It's compromising, but fuck, it's anything *but* what it appears.

"Ronin?" I choke.

"I wanted to talk to you, but I can see you're busy."

What the fuck is Midge's kid doing down here? This isn't a good part of the city, and I can't even begin to wonder what's on his mind.

"Scram, little dumpling," Stephie slurs. "Hanky and I have business."

I press up off the couch and spin to face Ronin. His eyes pinned on Steph. Her legs spread, revealing what I can only assume is something that should be covered. Ronin cringes.

"We do not," I say, keeping my eyes on Ronin, pleading with him to back away and not misunderstand this situation.

"I'm just...I'll just..." Ronin points over his shoulder to the hall, twists a little at the waist, and then bolts.

"Dammit," I mutter, stepping forward to follow him when I hear a thump against the couch. I turn to find Steph has slipped to her side. Her eyes closed. Her mouth open. Her nose bleeding. Stepping back toward her, I instantly feel for a pulse. A memory so vivid, so alive it nearly strikes me blind. Goddammit. Her skin feels cold, her pulse weakly beating.

"Reggie," I shout, seeking the supervisor. The second call I practically scream. Reaching for my phone, I dial 911 as Reg enters the sitting room. "Overdose." I swallow, keeping my fingers on Stephie's neck, my own body shivering at all the possibilities this could mean.

+ + +

Stephie's been pumped, prepped, and set on an IV drip to clean her system. The road to recovery is going to be a lot longer than one night in the hospital, and I only hope she'll get where she needs to go. The road went untraveled by me too many times before I had my wake-up call.

Losing everything I physically owned. Losing the one thing I could never own. Nearly destroying a life.

"Kit was right. You're a good man," Stephie moans, her voice groggy as her head rolls on the pillow. She looks old—used and abused—and probably not even forty. The professional groupie life is a difficult path. Her hair lays limp and scraggly around her bony, thin face. Did I ever find her attractive? I shudder at the thought and think of Midge. I'm ignoring what Stephie says, disappearing in images of Midge. Her beautiful, thick brown hair, not a hint of gray but filled with highlights. I want to watch it change. I want to see her grow old. Her smaller size but ample curves, which she isn't afraid to show off, at least in private with me. I think of the plum-colored lingerie she wore the other night under her raincoat. My girl has some gumption. The thought of her as mine reminds me I'm hoping I'm not too late.

"She really loved you," Stephie adds, and my attention leaps back to her.

"Who?" I ask. The sick feeling in my gut tells me I should know the answer.

"Kit, silly. She always talked about you. She said she could rely on you."

I snort in response. "That's not love."

"We all knew you were fucking each other more exclusively than most of the boys."

I cringe again at the reference to the open sexuality of all of us back then. How meaningless it all was.

Stephie continues. "She was stupid not to marry you, always bragging that you asked, but playing it cool that she didn't want marriage." My stomach roils at the thought of Kit belittling my proposals. "But she loved you, and she should have just said yes." Stephie's eyes close. I should let her rest, but she's riled me up and I need to speak.

"She never said she loved me," I scoff, trying to blow off the suggestion like Kit so coldly dismissed my proposals.

"Sometimes you don't need to say the words to have emotion be heard, Hanky. It's right there before your eyes if you really want to listen." I'm ready to scoff again, thinking this makes no sense, but the more I consider it, I wonder. Am I still not listening? Do I not hear the sweet sound in Midge? I want to hear her love. I want to be somebody's someone.

More, whispers through my head.

At every turn, Midge has been telling me and showing me she's willing to give me everything. I'm missing it with the shit deafening my head instead of fully opening my heart.

"It doesn't matter now," Stephie says, swallowing hard, her lips cracked and chapped. Her eyes still closed. Her head rolls away from me, as she falls back into the blissful abyss the hospital offers until her system cleans itself enough to move on.

"The hell it doesn't," I mutter, speaking to myself. I've been alone for too long, especially within the relationship with Kit. Love isn't a one-sided album. There always has to be a B-side to the A-side. Any drummer knows the rhythm works best with two sticks not one. I'm tired of being alone, so tired, and I have a willing person before me to share my life with me. What the fuck have I been waiting for?

chapter 37

Eavesdropping Never Pays

[Midge]

Hank doesn't show after Liam's game, and eventually, we leave the ballpark. The plan was to meet us at the field, but it's getting dark, and Liam hasn't eaten. Myself, I have no appetite suddenly. Hank promised we'd talk tonight after dinner. Yesterday at work had been difficult at best anticipating what would be said and knowing it might be the last time Hank and I are together as a couple. I'm prepared to end things if we can't come to terms about Kit. I have to be open and honest about my feelings, but that means he does too. He needs to find closure, or he'll never be able to move on—with me or any other woman.

As we sit at the pizza parlor, I check my phone. Nothing from Hank. He must be tied up at the crisis center. I applaud his dedication to helping others. He has the good soul and generous heart as I mentioned the other night.

Reflecting deeper, I realize wanting another person as part of your life could be a one-way street. Hank of all people knows this, and I do, too. He loved Kit, and when she didn't return the emotion, it crushed him, crumpling him up and throwing him out like the trash. I am far from feeling like garbage, but I'm also not feeling treasured by Hank.

Maybe it was too much, too fast. I'd had a fifteen-year marriage which was pleasant and supportive until the final years. Even at that, I see the lie I told myself as we moved our family to California for my husband's lover six years ago. Hank had a long, destructive and debilitating relationship and never reached closure. I could forgive him his wavering feelings, but it doesn't mean I could reach him on the level

I needed. That something *more*. That somebody's someone. Dammit, I deserve it. Hank or not, I tell myself, but I recognize the lie.

I want it to be Hank.

I focus my attention on Liam as best I can. Talking to preteens can be like plucking eyebrows, difficult to find the fine hairs while struggling to tug out the gray ones. *Do you have homework? What do you think of the call at first base? How do you think you did today?* Liam answers my numerous questions in monosyllabic replies.

"What's wrong?" I finally ask. His shrug says more than his words.

"Why does Dad have to say so much? Why can't he just watch?" The abrupt question startles me. "What do you mean?"

"He's so critical of everything. Telling me to relax in one breath and then winding me up in the next. Why can't he be like Hank?"

I blink. Hank has attended quite a few games, and the comment drops my heart. Between the science project and nights helping Liam with the new math, which I absolutely do not understand, Liam has formed a special bond with Hank. One, I admit, I hadn't been paying enough attention to if he is comparing Hank to his father.

"Daddy's just trying to be supportive." This shoots Liam's head upward.

"How is he supportive? He only comes to a few games. He didn't help me pass the math test or finish the volcano. He didn't even come to the science fair." Liam's right. Hank came instead.

"Liam." I falter. I don't know what to say. I work hard at holding back my negative sentiments about their father. What Paul did wrong, he did to me, *to us*. It hurt our children, but it wasn't directed at them. I refuse to defend him, though.

"Forget it," he says, taking a deep sip of his soda.

I'm actually relieved. I don't have the energy to justify my ex-husband's actions.

"You like Hank?" I ask instead, knowing the gentle prompt might be a huge mistake. I like Hank. I *love* Hank, but I'd never keep Hank if I thought he couldn't handle my sons. Although I know the answer from Liam, I still want him to explain to me the depth of his feelings.

"He's cool." Liam shrugs again, fiddling with the straw in his glass.

Those might be the deepest sentiments I'll get from him. I'd like to think he's cool, too, but an hour into his absence with no phone call, I'm no longer thinking: *It's cool.*

+ + +

When we return home, the older boys are in the kitchen, and I stop when I hear Ronin and Elston with raised voices. I don't want to intrude if they're sharing a brotherly moment. It's rare for Elston and Ronin to get along.

"You need to tell her," Elston says, his voice concerned, his tone strained.

"Elston," Ronin warns. "This will really hurt her." *Oh, girl talk.* If they can't be friends, I still want them to respect one another and be confident in their brotherhood, brother-ship, or whatever, to speak to each other about things like girls.

"Better to tell her than let him keep pretending." Elston sounds exasperated, and I linger, knowing there's trouble in eavesdropping, so I tell myself, *I'm just curious.*

"You should have seen him. Draped all over her. Her skirt hiked up. I could see her cooter."

I cover my mouth, holding in the snort. Cripes, who teaches my boys these things?

"Don't call it a cooter. That's just-just not..." I picture Elston shaking his blond head.

"It was disgusting, and I can't believe he'd choose someone like her over Mom."

My heart stops. Wait. *What?*

"What a fucking asshole, and after his whole *let's talk like a man* speech. And telling me how he cares about her. Just *ew*," Elston rattles.

What? Just wait a minute! What is he talking about? What are they saying?

"Hank doesn't deserve Mom." Ronin's voice cracks. My sensitive boy sounds on the verge of tears. "He seemed so cool, but I know his past. He might have played those drums like a master, but he womanized like one as well. He drank, too."

Much to my satisfaction, Ronin isn't a fan of drinking. Disappointment rings in my middle son's tone as I flip through emotions.

My heart races in two patterns. One bursting with pride at my children's devotion and one breaking at what they aren't explicitly saying.

"Think he fucked her after you caught him?"

Oh, my God. Two hands cover my open mouth, holding back the urge to vomit.

"Who knows?" Elston snaps. "But good riddance, drummer boy."

chapter 38

Don't Give Up on Me

[Hank]

I'm eager to get to Midge's house the next morning. I tried to call during the night, but all my calls went to voicemail. Even my text messages remain unanswered. I tell her there was an emergency. Then I panic and promise I can explain everything, worried Ronin told his mom what he saw, what he *thought* he saw.

"Don't give up on me, little lady." It's the last message I leave with hope she will listen to me. My ears are open, as are my eyes and my heart, but my steps are heavy as I move up her front walk.

After ringing the bell, I hear shuffling behind the door. Muffled voices, and a slight bang occurs, before the door opens.

"What do you want?" Elston snaps, his brother Ronin behind him.

"I'd like to talk to your mother." My arms cross, a defensive stature kicking in, but this punk ass gives it right back to me. He's going to protect his mom, I can see it in his eyes, and I can't fault him.

Still, I need to see her.

"She isn't here," Ronin says behind his brother, arms crossed to match my stance. Not nearly as robust as his sibling, he still refuses to let me over the threshold like his brother.

"I'll wait," I demand, stepping forward when Elston holds up a hand.

"My mother doesn't allow strangers in the house when she isn't home." His voice drips saccharine sweet and sarcastic.

"Good thing I'm not a *fu*...a stranger." My eyes catch Liam in the background, and I curb my cursing.

I don't quite believe Elston's statement, nor do I like the implication I'm an outsider. For a second, I wonder if they're covering for Midge, who hides inside the house, but then again, she would never send her sons for her. If there's one thing I've learned, she'll face me and want answers. I think back to the first time she confronted me when I perched her on my brother's desk and ate her like the delicacy she is.

"You are now," Ronin interjects with a snarl.

"Ronin, what you saw…it wasn't what you thought."

"Save it for the judge, mister," he blurts, and I don't even know what that means.

"What were you doing at the crisis center anyway?" I ask.

Elston's head twists to his younger brother as if this question hasn't been asked.

"I was dropping off a friend." His voice squeaks as his head lowers.

My need to help crashes over me. "What happened?" My concern is returned with a glare.

"None of your business." It would have been my business had I stayed at the center. Instead, I traveled with Stephie to the hospital and waited until she was out of immediate danger. I couldn't help her more than that. She needs a sponsor, but I can't be it for her. I'm too close to her past, as our histories wind together, but I offered recommendations of places to call and people to meet if she is ready to keep herself clean. Only Stephie can make those decisions, no one else.

Liam peeks around his second brother's arm. "Why can't we let him in again?"

"He cheated on Mom," Elston snaps, and I feel like I've been sucker punched.

"Ronin," I groan, swiping a hand down my face before I can look at Midge's middle child. "That is *not* what happened. It's a crisis center, and she was having a crisis."

"Oh, I bet she was having a crisis," Elston retorts, and I see his hand twitch. If he wasn't a kid, only seventeen, he'd be on the floor in a second.

Instead, I take a deep breath and clasp my itchy fists. "You watch yourself, kid. And don't disrespect women like that."

"Because you respect them so much?" He's back to sharp eyes and an even sharper tongue. Sarcasm isn't pretty on a teenager, and I almost laugh at his balls.

He reminds me of myself.

"I respect women plenty, especially your mother. I'd never cheat on her. And I'm not having this conversation with you until I speak to her first."

Elston shakes his head, and it's Ronin who speaks. "Well, she isn't home. She said she had errands, but I think she just wanted to be alone. We don't know when she'll be back."

"Why don't we like him anymore?" Liam asks all innocent, his head whipping back and forth between his brothers like a tennis match.

"He wasn't good to Mom," Elston adds. "He treated her like Dad did." I could hate this kid for the comparison to a man I know treated Midge poorly.

"Elston," Ronin cautions, his eyes shifting from his big brother to his little brother, issuing a warning.

"What did Dad do?" Liam asks all innocent, and I swipe a hand down my face again, before imploring Elston to shut up before he digs himself too deep.

Liam looks up at me. "You can't divorce her. You aren't married." He pauses a second. "Are you breaking up?"

The horror on his face nearly breaks me. I want to reach forward and pull him to my chest, but with the glare Elston levels at me, I don't move.

"We are not breaking up. Absolutely not. We are just getting started." I meet Elston's stare head-on before I see the hesitation in his eyes. His brows pinch slightly before he looks away.

"Either way, she isn't here," Ronin reminds me.

"Like I said, I'll wait." I've been waiting so long for someone like their mother, what's a few more minutes, hours, days? I spin on the stoop and take a seat, briefly glancing over my shoulder to smirk at a seventeen-year-old. Elston steps back, forcing Ronin farther into the house, but Liam curves around his brothers.

"I'll wait with you." He walks to the front stoop and takes a seat on the bricks next to me.

This kid. I look down at the brick step, and a chuckle hits me. Literally, I'm pausing on another step in my life.

How is that for irony?

+ + +

I'm pretty certain *waiting* isn't one of the twelve steps of recovery, and as the time ticks by, I grow more restless. Midge doesn't really think I cheated on her, right? This is all a misunderstanding. I just need to tell her what happened.

A light touch comes to my wrist, and I flinch at the contact. I turn toward Liam, forgetting for a moment I had company. He's been playing on his phone the whole time he sits next to me, but I've given up looking at mine. Midge isn't answering any type of message.

"What are these for again?" Liam points at the two bands around my wrist, hesitating that I might reject his touch.

"You startled me when you touched me," I reassure him. "My thoughts are kind of deep at the moment."

"Mom gets like that too sometimes. Sort of in her head and she doesn't hear us call her name or enter a room. I thought it was just a girl thing."

I chuckle. "Yeah, what do you know about girls?" He's only ten, but then again, when I was ten, I'd already felt up the thirteen-year-old babysitter. I don't want to think of Liam doing those things yet. *Stick to baseball, kid.*

"Not much. I'm not all gooey for them like Elston and Ronin. Dad says my time will come. Mom says don't rush it. I have girls who are friends, though. That's cool." He nods like this is an accomplishment.

"That is cool. Friends are really important." I think about my friends—the ones I used to have and the ones who never were true friends.

Tommy comes to mind as the true kind. He's trying to pick up with me as if we never left off. There's a lot of water still drowning the bridge, but I can see him working to repair the damage. Even Gage, who I didn't pay much attention to when they were punks and just getting their band started, has included me wholeheartedly into their fold. I miss the band. Then I reflect a moment—honestly, I don't. I'm in a better place where I am, who I am, and with who I plan to spend my time in the future. "Girlfriends can be awesome, too. When you're ready, though."

"Mom is your girlfriend, right? I mean, I see you kiss her, and she's always watching you when you walk around a room. She smiles more, and she has those gooey eyes." He rolls his eyes. "She wasn't like that with my dad."

My heart clenches. I don't want him to think poorly of his father, and it's none of my business how Midge's previous relationship went. I mean, they're divorced, so it's over. Yet I'm a twinge happy I draw her eyes like he says and make her smile.

"She is my girlfriend, and I plan to keep her, despite what your brothers are saying. They're misinformed. Do you know what that means?"

"I'm eleven, not stupid." He raises an eyebrow at me.

"Got it. Well, your mom and I had a misunderstanding, thanks to Ronin's misunderstanding." I pause. That isn't exactly true. I saw her shut down after the other night in the back of my car. As I sit next to her son, I shouldn't think of such things as her naked body underneath mine, christening the leather of my car with the scent of her. But I need to recall her expression—the confusion, the sadness, the miscommunication— between us. I interpreted one thing while she clearly meant another. There's more than just one misunderstanding at the moment. "I just need to talk to her."

I'm hoping that's all I need to do to convince her, but as the time passes, I'm beginning to wonder.

"What do those mean again?" He nods at my wrist.

"The leather symbolizes 'weaving' people together, like my old band, and the brown beads remind me it takes a team." His brown-haired head nods slowly. "A team for support. For love."

"You might need a team to win back Mom. Elston, Ronin and I have to do that sometimes. When she's upset with one of us, we stick together to get each other out of trouble." His head continues rocking, and to my surprise, an idea comes to me from this ten-year-old, who is not stupid at all. Not one bit.

chapter 39

Worth The Wait

[Hank]

After two hours, I decide to quit looking like a stalker on their front stoop. I'm up to thirty-seven text messages and endless calls going unanswered. Liam looks bored sitting with me, and we've run out of shit to talk about. We covered baseball, girls some more, the bracelets a third time, and his brothers. Not his mom. Not his dad. I'm thankful for the company, but my ass numbs from sitting on the brick. I need to regroup, so I drive home, and to my surprise, a welcomed package sits on my front porch.

"Thank fuck," I mutter as I exit the truck and rush up the walk. "Lady, I've been waiting for you at your house. Where you been?"

Her eyes hide behind large, round sunglasses. Her hand shakes as she adjusts the frame on her nose.

"I've been sitting here, waiting for you."

I chuckle in relief although the presence of humor remains missing between us. I settle on the wooden steps to sit next to her, and she moves over.

The movement makes a statement. She doesn't want to be close to me. Her lip trembles as her eyes remain forward. Under the side frame, I see a tear forming, and I want to reach over and take it from her. *No more tears because of me, Midge*, my heart screams.

"I guess we're quite a pair," I say softly, bumping her shoulder with my bicep. "If we've been waiting for each other at our respective houses, that says something positive about us, right? There's still an us, right?"

I rub my chest when she shifts away from me.

Her eyes still forward, she speaks. "I just want to hear it from you. Just tell it to me honestly." Her fingers spread on her jeans and then ball into fists as if she needs to hold something. I reach for her hand and force her fingers between mine. Her head hangs, her eyes burning into our joined palms. I squeeze, warning her I'm not letting go.

"Ronin came to the crisis center. It was teen day, and we intake new kids. It's one of my favorite days, like I once told you." She keeps still, but she's listening. Step one complete. "Stephie snuck into the center. Remember her? She was at the party, when we met, and once again at the garage."

Her head swivels to mine, and I want her to remember our first meeting, the one in the bathroom, when she looked into my eyes, and I wanted to take all her worries. Instead, I've given her more concern. *That changes now.*

"Anyway, Stephie overdosed."

"Cripes." Her body shifts, and she squeezes my hand. I'm grateful for her knees leaning against my thigh suddenly. One more part of us connecting.

"When she came to Restored Dreams, she wanted drugs from me, but I swear on a stack of Bibles dripping in holy water, I do not do those things anymore." My gaze focus on the lenses shielding hers, but it's not enough. I need to see her pretty eyes even if they're brimming with tears. I push the frame upward to rest on the top of her head. She's so fucking beautiful even though she's been crying for too long.

"Ronin came into a meeting room when Stephie tugged at me. Being on drugs can increase the adrenaline, increase your strength. She grabbed me, and I stumbled. When Ronin walked in, it looked bad. I admit it was easy to misinterpret. He rushed out before I could explain, and when I went to follow him, Steph passed out. We had to call an ambulance. I was at the hospital most of the night."

"Is she okay?" Midge swallows as she asks.

"She will be." I pause for a moment, my hand growing sweaty as my heart races. I need to come clean. "She told me things about Kit. Whether true or not, they were nice to hear. Kit didn't have many girlfriends. Other women were either jealous of her or wanted to take advantage of her. The groupies following the band weren't really a threat, though. They didn't want Kit's fame; they only wanted the band." Midge tugs at my hand, but I draw it to my thigh and place my other hand on hers. "My point is…I let Kit go a long time ago, but bits and pieces still haunted me. I haven't really been with someone exclusively since Kit, so my ideas about relationships might be a little skewed. While I want to be loved, I have to give it fully in return. I understand that, and I want to give it all to you, little lady, because I feel you give so much to me. I'm an ass." I chuckle, my forehead furrowing as I beg her to understand. "I see you looking at me, and I talk myself out of it meaning anything. I hold my breath, waiting for you to walk away."

"But—"

"But you haven't yet. Each time there's an issue, you actually come to me, and it's refreshing. You don't run away, you run forward, and I want to be your finish line." My lip curls. Fuck, I want so much more. This rat race ends here, with me, with us. I want to hold her forever.

"I can't compete with a dead woman, Hank. I'm sorry. I want to be respectful, and I want to understand. I knew I wouldn't be someone's first, not at this age, not after already being married, but I can't keep feeling like she's between us."

"I understand. I put her there, but you also have to know you are *my* first. I've never felt this way before. Never." Midge's brow squeezes so tight, her skin crinkles. I lean forward and kiss her there. "You're my first, because I love you and you love me back. Not in a selfish way. Not because you need something from me. You're just here, and I want to be here with you. I want more, too, little lady."

Tears flow freely, her shoulders slumping forward.

"No more tears, though, baby." Her body continues to lean, and I wrap my arms around her, dragging her up into my lap.

She sniffles, squirming on my thighs. "I'm too heavy for you."

"You're a weight I want to carry. And no, you are not too heavy for me." I kiss her temple before pitching forward. Her arms wrap around my neck, and she lets out a little squeak as I stand, cradling her to my chest.

"Hank, what are you doing?"

I spin toward the front door, taking the few steps toward it. "I'm carrying you over the threshold." I press the door open with my shoulder, then kick it shut and head for the stairs. She nestles into me as we climb to my room. Gently, I lay her on my bed and then sit to unlace my boots. She watches me, unmoving as I tug them both off.

"Midge, let me make love to you, intimately." The request is so direct, she blinks.

She remains on her back, and I realize it might be too fast. I'll hold her, just feel her heart beating with mine. Instead, she sits up and removes her light jacket. I lie next to her, cupping her cheek with one hand.

"I love you," I say, and then I kiss her.

Every kiss has been a discovery. The first kiss. The slow kiss. The quick kiss. The lingering. The hot as fuck. But *this* kiss, it's new once again as we take our time to work over one another, sucking, sipping, licking. I don't know how long we've been at it, but eventually, it grows more urgent. Clothing gets removed between more kisses. My shirt is discarded, so her delicate fingers can trace over my abs. *Fuck, I like when she touches me.* Her sweater goes, so I can cover each breast, latching on until her nipples peak and a red mark blossoms.

I stand and peer down at her. Her hair sprawls over my pillows, her limbs spread, ready for me. Her jeans come off next. Removing my own jeans, I watch her watch me. The intensity in her eyes says everything. She wants me. She wants *more* from me.

I grip her ankles and slowly drag her toward me. I want to take my time, but I'm also so hard. My dick dances before me, stiff and eager to enter her. My palms climb her shins, wrap over her knees, and lift her by the back of her thighs. My knees bend, pinning me to the edge of the mattress. Holding her body like this, so open, so pliable, I can't wait to connect with her. My dick springs forward, aching to make us one. I hold her where the curve of her ass meets her legs and drag her along the length of me. She's slick and ready, and I want inside. I want *more.*

"I don't want any more barriers between us." I mean condoms, ex-lovers, miscommunication, and anything else that keeps us separate. "I want to own every crevice, every crack of you, little lady. Fill you and seal you to me." My voice scratches, rough and raspy as I slide through her tender folds. She's coating me, and the sensation is unreal.

I watch my undulating and then look up to find her watching us.

"But I don't want to just fill you, I want to fill you *up*, your heart, your soul. All of me for all of you." Her eyes jump to mine. She clenches her thighs, and I sense she's getting close, waiting for me, but I want her to hear me—her love to hear mine.

"Do you get it? Do you understand me?" I'm practically growling, but I'm not fierce. I'm intense. I need her to know. "I love you."

"I love you, too."

With that, I slip into her—slow, purposeful—until my dick disappears completely. I love this connection, this feeling, this sensation. I'm bare in there, raw and exposed, because that's how I feel with her. That's how I want to be, with only her.

As I drag back, her thighs fight me. She wants me to stay within her depths.

"We'll get there, baby. I promise." After a few slow thrusts, I can't take the lazy pace. She's frantic on the bed, and I love how she wants to race—not rush for a finish line—but sprint nonetheless. My speed increases, choppy at first until we find the dance, our bodies moving as one. With my hands under her knees, she opens so wide for me, drawing me into her heat.

"I love you like this." I stammer, the force of me entering her shifts the bed. The headboard taps against the wall. The frame scratches on the wood floor. I don't care. I want every sound to be from her, from us together. "But I love you...more."

Finally, she gives me the sound I seek most—my name on her lips as she screams with pleasure.

+ + +

Hours later, we linger in bed. It was a rough start to a Sunday but pure pleasure to forget everything and spend the day between the sheets. Midge called her sons to say she'd be out all day. She told me she'd explain everything to them later. As she lay spent from round two, her thighs wrapped around my hips while my head rests on her chest, she strokes my hair. Her short, blunt fingernails cause me to shiver, but at the same time, I relish the touch.

"What do you think will happen to Stephie?"

I perch up on my elbows, suddenly concerned Midge hasn't gotten the message. I love her, only her. "I hope she gets help, but she can't be my problem. I don't mean that coldly, but she's too close to me in some ways, and she needs someone outside her past."

Midge nods, her eyes drifting off to the left.

"Seeing her like that, it was an eye-opener for me."

Her gaze returns to mine. "How?"

"All that I'd done. All that I could have been. The spiral went deep for me. Looking back, I can see I didn't really want that life."

"Is it that easy to say?" She's still brushing over my head, and my body feels so replete. I don't want to talk about old things anymore, but I want her to have all the answers.

"Maybe. Hindsight is twenty-twenty and all that. I think one reason I corkscrewed so far down was because I just wanted someone to love me for me. I wanted to be somebody's someone." I lean forward and kiss her. When I pull back, I kiss her sternum. Her heart, slow and steady under my lips, just like things should be.

She cups my head, and she forces me up to look at her. Her bright brown eyes glint with gold. "You are." She pauses as her lips curl. "To me."

chapter 40

Family Always Says They're Sorry

[Midge]

A few weeks pass, and Hank and I are in a much better place. He spends a lot of his free time at my house—what free time we have. Between baseball games and a spring concert, along with Hank's crisis center hours and my search for jobs, we're swarmed by life. We talk again about the money, and I tell Hank how I am happy to work as a marketing consultant for a while I learn more about the possibility of going on my own. Thankfully, he lets the subject drop.

Mother's Day weekend we have plans. Gage invites Hank and me, plus Edie and Tommy to join him on Saturday for something special as Sunday is the official day for mothers. We receive no other instructions—just join him at their home.

When we arrive at their oceanside home, I'm dumbstruck. It's gorgeous with a first-floor wall of glass overlooking the water. It's breathtaking in grays and whites, and comfortable in a way I wouldn't expect from the rich and famous, especially in comparison to my rare visits to Kit's sterile home. I check my emotions at the door when I visit Lawson with Hank. He needs me, and he reminds me often.

After a quick tour of the house, Gage ushers us to their family SUV. The kids aren't coming with us today, he explains, as six adults climb into the large passenger vehicle. We travel east, curving through the hills, and at first, I think we might be heading to Kit's home. Dread fills me. The house is a mausoleum to the dead, and the stark whiteness remains cold and unfeeling. Yet after a few more twists in the road, we pull up to a gated home. Gage presses in a code, and we coast down the drive to eventually park before a sprawling house.

At first glance, it appears as if two homes have been attached, but the streamlined architecture enhances the overall beauty of the structure. One side is single level. The main entrance, marked by a set of double doors, is surrounded by glass panels on either side. This foyer connects the other side of the house, which stands two stories tall. The Spanish terra cotta roof tiles gleam in the spring sunshine and the white stucco house reminds me of a vacation villa.

As we sit in the SUV a moment, I notice Gage watching Ivy instead of admiring the house.

"What do you think?" he asks.

"It's lovely," she sighs, expressing my thoughts exactly.

The landscaping softens the brick with a variety of greens and something fuchsia blooming on a vine along the front wall. Gage smiles and presses open his door. He touches Ivy's arm, suggesting she wait, and the rest of us climb out of the SUV. Standing in a semi-circle on the drive, Gage helps his wife from the vehicle and then puts his arm around her.

"Welcome home, gorgeous."

Edie's breath hitches, and my mouth falls open. Ivy blinks up at her husband.

"Happy Mother's Day, little mama." He reaches for her stunned cheeks and drags her to him for a powerful kiss.

He bought his wife a freaking house for Mother's Day! I look away from the private moment. It's too intimate to witness.

I peek up at Hank, whose smile beams. "You know something about this?"

He nods sheepishly, his grin growing. Tommy chuckles, and I turn to him. His arm wraps around Edie from the back. He kisses her neck before glancing up at the house.

"What do you think, baby girl?" Tommy addresses Ivy who stands still in shock.

"You bought me a house?" she says softly, but we stand close enough to hear. We should probably give them some privacy, but Gage's slow curling lips tell me he's pulled off something big.

"The house is yours, yes, but it's for all of us. Ava, Emaline, Granger." He pauses, slipping his hands to her wrists. "And Lawson."

Tears spring to my eyes. Edie's already dabbing at hers.

"What?" Ivy whispers, still too stunned to move.

"Tommy and I agreed your mom's house is too cold and needs too many improvements to make it a home for us. Plus, I don't think it would be good for us to move in there. I wanted something for us. *Ours*. It was fucking hard to find a place big enough with all the specifications and handicap accessibility we need, but I did it." He waves a hand at the house. He turns back to his wife, whose eyes haven't left his face. "All those phone calls. Appointments. They were about this."

"You weren't having an affair?"

My heart breaks at the hesitation in her voice, yet a hint of relief fills her expression.

"Baby, we already talked about this. No. Definitely not." Gage's voice softens as he tries to reassure his wife.

Tears fill her eyes and slowly leak down her cheeks. Tommy's soft chuckle next to me adds to the tender moment.

"Princess, he can give you phone records and calendar appointment sheets if you wish, but I can confirm his story. I went on too many of these damn home showings to say he had time for anything else."

"I'm so sorry," Ivy says to her husband, tears falling harder as she covers her face in shame.

"Ivy, gorgeous, I wouldn't want anyone else," Gage murmurs, cupping his wife's face again. "I love you. I love us. I'd be fucking out of my mind to cheat. I'm sorry I made you worry. I just wanted to surprise you." He kisses her forehead.

"You bought me a house?" Ivy repeats, robotically, looking up at him. A weak smile graces her beautiful face.

"You wanted Lawson out of that house. You wanted to spend more time with him, include him in the family, so I found this. He can have his own wing where we can join him but still have our space. There's a pool and a therapy tub for him. It's amazing." Gage's excitement grows as the color returns to his wife's face.

She launches into his arms, and they kiss like a porn movie is being filmed in their new driveway. Her legs wrap around Gage's hips, and his hands bury in her hair.

As witnesses to this borderline pornographic scene, the rest of us laugh nervously until Tommy snaps, "Gage."

"Care," Gage retorts, but his tone is all tease as he holds his wife on his hips.

"*Sooo*," Ivy drags out the syllable. "Show me everything."

Gage doesn't release his wife until we reach the door. Inside, I try to keep my jaw up as I take in the lavish space and open concept. The kitchen is something from a home décor magazine, and as we admire appliances, Gage pulls his wife toward the grand staircase for this half of the house. Tommy continues the tour to the other side of the home, guiding us through a private living space, smaller kitchen, and Lawson's new bedroom. Two more rooms finish the hallway.

"This is for the on-duty nurses." Tommy points at an open door, displaying a light-yellow room with a double bed covered by a daisy print duvet. He stops at the end of the hall and waves us forward. I step into a masculine looking room of light gray with dark brown furniture. A king-size bed takes up most of the space, but it's a comfortable room with sunlight streaming through the double-pane window. "And this last one is for you." Tommy nods at Hank, and I look up at my flabbergasted boyfriend.

"What?" Hank chokes, swallowing what I can only assume is a lump in his throat.

I have one as well. This is an amazing gesture.

"You never had a home with your child, and we both know he can't live with you in his condition. The liaison suggested that Gage treat him like any other adult living on his own by having a guest room. Only you aren't a guest, Hank. You're his father. Gage wanted you to have a space in case you wanted to stay the night."

Sweet cheese, I'm fighting tears as I watch Hank's face. He blows out a breath. Ever see a large man crumple with emotion? Me either, and my heart rips from my chest at the fight in Hank to keep the tears at bay. He pinches the bridge of his nose, holding the corners of his eyes a moment before blinking rapidly.

"We'll give you a few minutes," Edie says softly, her hand on her husband's chest.

"Maybe twenty." Tommy winks. "Don't come to the pool house."

Hank chuckles, and I'm sensing the two men share a moment of history. Edie leads the way, and Hank and I are left alone in his new room in his son's home.

+ + +

The stunned look in Hank's eyes is all I can focus on.

"Holy fuck," he mutters. He hasn't moved, and I worry he'll tumble over. Touching his wrist, I watch as he blinks down at me, then eases onto the edge of the bed.

"You okay?"

"I think I'm numb. In a good way." He twists slowly, taking in the space.

With a deep exhale, he reaches for me, tugging me to him. I fall over his lap, straddling him as he wraps both arms around my back and holds tight. I curl my arms around his head, pressing his cheek to my chest. A shudder rattles his body.

"No, Hank," I mutter, bending forward to kiss the top of his head and linger. "Hank, honey, don't cry." I pull back, but he squeezes me tighter, not releasing me.

"Why did it take so long to find you?" He pinches his eyes again, his face avoiding mine a moment. I press him back and remove the trace of his tears with peppering kisses. My heart aches.

Without opening his eyes he whispers, "I wish I'd met you sooner."

The sentiment is sweet but not realistic. A man like Hank Paige would have never been interested in me. I believe everything happens for a reason, but I can't think of one reason Kit Carrigan emotionally abused this man or why he thought he had to drink so much.

"I think we met when we were supposed to meet. When we were ready, or maybe when we needed each other most."

"I needed you so much earlier in my life, little lady."

I continue to cup his face. My lips brush lightly against his.

"I need you *now*, honey," I say with another quick kiss. "There are some things I can never wish changing. My kids are those things for me."

"I don't want you to wish them away, baby. If anything, I want a little more of everything with them, too."

Hank has been wonderful with the boys, considering our misunderstanding weeks ago. He accepted Ronin's apology and opened up to them about his history. He handles Elston's surliness. Of course, Liam already adores Hank and finds no reason to dislike him even for a second. I could remind Hank he has Lawson, but I already understand his feelings. Finding out he has an adult child isn't the same as discovering he has an infant. He's missed out on so many things. The squishy toddler. The whiny teen. He wants experiences.

"You're an amazing mother, Middy. I would have loved to have babies with you."

He's not dismissing his own child. He's simply admitting he wanted more. More children. More time with the child he has.

"Sweetheart," I say softly. I'm forty-one, and while I'd love to give Hank a child, that ship has sailed. To be safe, we agreed I'd go on the pill. "I would have loved to give you a baby."

"Maybe you could just let me share the ones you already have." He leans forward to kiss my chest, avoiding eye contact once again.

My heart contracts. *This man.*

His hands rub up my sides, his lips kissing my chest, nuzzling the deep vee of my shirt to get to the swell of my breast. I'm balancing on his thighs, not wishing to crush him or imply anything, but the more he sucks at my skin, and the closer he gets to my nipple, a pulse beats under my skirt. Hank's hands slip under my shirt, massaging firmly along my sides.

"I love your skin," he mutters, sucking me once again. Nimble fingers begin to unbutton my shirt.

"We probably shouldn't be doing this here." I laugh until he bites my nipple over the cotton material of my exposed bra.

"If this is my room, I want to christen it properly."

Laughing nervously, I like the thought. I want to be with him, but I don't want the other couples to know what we're doing.

"Maybe we should get back out there and see what everyone else is up to."

"Sex. That's what they're doing. Each other." He hesitates between lolling his tongue over the swell of my breast. "Shirt. Off." He growls, and the vibration of his chest ripples against me. Leaning back, I do as he says and slowly remove my top. Hank's hands squeeze harder at my sides, working his way just under my breasts but not touching me.

"You're like a personal lap dance."

"Cripes." I choke, not wanting to consider him ever receiving one, or three.

"As I'm all about equality, I'll match you." He balances me on his legs while he tugs off his shirt in that guy way.

Maybe I'm the one who wants the lap dance. That is, him dancing while I sit on his lap. Our skin makes contact as his arms span my back. He tugs my hair, and I tilt back. This gives him more access to my neck, and he nibbles, teasing me once again by getting close to that spot—the one along my collarbone where he knows I like to be nipped.

"Little lady," he whispers, and I know what he wants. He tugs down my bra and lifts one achy globe upward. The nipple peaks in his direction, hard and ripe from his attention. "You know I love your tits, baby." Hank sucks firmly, latching on to worship me. He'll leave a mark from the suction as well as his scruffy jaw. He releases me with a popping sound.

"Middy." He presses back against my hips, forcing me to slip off his lap. He stands, nearly knocking me back, and lowers his pants, including his boxers. Sitting back down, we gaze at one another a moment before I lower to my knees. "Little lady, what are you doing?"

"I'm christening the room." My fingers crawl up his thick thighs and circle the silky shaft—erect, solid, and waiting for me.

"This isn't what I had in mind." He teases as he massages my shoulders, and I kiss the tip of him, licking a circle around the crown. "Fuck, baby."

His hands come to the back of my head, fingers delving into my hair. I open and take him in as far as I can, twirling my tongue around him. Flicking over the pulsing vein and lapping at him like he's my favorite treat, I recall the first time I did this to him. Frosting on a cupcake.

Hands come under my arms and lift me. He tells me to remove my panties and pats his thigh after the request. Without fully exposing myself, I reach under my skirt and remove my underwear. Hank watches me, and I'd feel self-conscious if I didn't like the way he looks at me.

Possessive. Passionate. All his.

I climb back over his legs as he holds himself upright. It's a sexy sight.

"Like what you see, little lady?"

"I love it," I purr, lifting my eyes to his. "I love you, honey."

His mouth finds mine, devouring me, forgetting about other intentions for a few minutes. He tugs at my lip as he pulls back.

"I love you, too, baby. I *more* you."

My lips curl as he positions himself under my skirt. I rise on my knees a bit, using his neck as leverage. One hand guides his length, the other wraps around my backside, and he slips in.

Deep. Penetrating. Fulfilling.

Suddenly, I feel risqué knowing people might be waiting for us. My skirt covers what we're doing if someone walks in, but neither of us is wearing a shirt. Then again, Hank's pants are at his ankles. The moment feels scandalous, but I feel sensual. I roll my hips, building a rhythm against Hank. The pace gives new meaning to lap dancing. Hank holds me by my ass under my skirt, squeezing and encouraging me as I increase the beat. He feels so good like this, so deep, and I'm finding friction in a new way in this upright position. I clench harder than I think I ever have.

I'm fighting forces, feeling like I'll slip off his lap, and holding on tight in an effort to remain connected to him.

"Don't drop me," I mutter, my movements exaggerated, luscious and languid. My head falls back, and I clasp his neck.

"Never let you fall, baby. I'll always hold on to you."

I'm forcing myself down on him in a pattern of clench and pulse. My head comes to his shoulder. I want this to be for him, but I'm finding it's definitely about me at the moment.

"Lie back," I whisper into his skin before licking up to the shell of his ear. He brings his shoulder to his chin as he tilts his head.

"That tickles." I cover his mouth, but I can't keep the pace and concentrate, so I draw back and push against his shoulders. I don't follow him down but stay upright. His eyes never leave me.

"Tug down the other side," he says, watching as I follow his command to release my other breast. I cup both and squeeze them together. "Fuck," he mutters, biting his lip like he has more to say, but now isn't the moment.

I'm still rolling over him, the position filling me as the nub that triggers pleasure finds friction against his pubic bone. Hank and I have made love in several positions. I find it unbelievable we can experience something new, but we always do. Each time, it feels different. Each time, it feels like something I haven't done before because it's always a first time for me with him.

"So close, lady."

I don't know if he means me or him, but I'm almost there when he pins me to his hips. His fingertips squeeze, and the jolt inside sets me over the edge. Sweet cheese, I like the sensation of him jetting off in me.

Hank pulls me down to his chest, holding me once again like he did with his tears. Both arms wrap around me, pressing me into him. He's still inside me.

"I'm sorry I can't give you babies, honey."

"Don't you worry about that, little lady. You're all I need." He kisses my forehead. "But I'd like to have something else with you one day. Maybe a home like this. A permanent place for me with you."

"I'd like that," I say. I'd love to just see Hank in my home, joining me in my bedroom.

"Middy, I don't want to just have sex with you once in a while and only sleep with you here and there. I want you every night."

My breath hitches as he stole my thoughts, but I try to make light of our shared emotions.

"Sex every night?" I laugh, teasing him. "I'd be too tired for that."

"I'll let you rest. In between times." He forces my chin up and draws me down for another toe-curling kiss. He slips out of me, but I don't move. I don't think I've ever been so happy.

His expression grows serious, and my smile slips a little until he says, "I meant what I said. I want more of you, little lady, and then some."

chapter 41

A Band of Brothers

[Hank]

I'm nervous although I know what I want, which drives me forward as I enter Midge's home a week after Gage gifts his wife a house. I'd been thinking about things long before the extravagant present, but this week, I'm determined to carry out my plan.

I meant what I said—I want us to blend. I've been spending lots of time at Midge's home and reconsidering my situation at Brut's. It might be time to move out on my own because it might be too soon to move in with Midge. However, I want to assure her I want the *more* we talked about. I want us to be together someday sooner rather than later.

Midge is out tonight with the girls. Ivy's already shopping for things for the new house. I carry three pizzas because these boys can eat. Setting them on the island counter, I stand around with the guys, chatting about baseball and their summer plans. Their dad is getting married soon, and Elston can't stand his future stepmother. It worries me he might feel the same about me if I become his stepfather. The idea of being part of this family makes me smile. Elston and I will figure it out.

We made amends the same evening Midge and I spent the day in bed. I took her on one of our casual dates and then came home with her. I explained a few things about myself, my past, and my connection with the woman Ronin saw. Ronin opened up to explain how a girl from his band was threatening to kill herself, and Ronin didn't know what to do. He told the girl he wanted to hang out with her, and then drove to the crisis center where he thought I could help him.

It broke my heart a little that he came to me, and I wasn't able to help at the moment, but I told him how proud I was of him to try to take care of his friend. I also thanked him for trusting me to be there and apologized that I wasn't. He understood after I explained, tears filling his eyes at my story of Stephie compared to his accusation.

"I was just looking out for Mom," he said, and I respect that in these boys.

"Of course, and that makes you a good man. Your heart belongs to your mama first."

As soda cans empty and the pizza boxes clear, I realize I only have so much time before Midge gets home.

"I wanted to talk to you guys about something. Man to man," I say, looking up at Elston. We've come to a silent agreement. He's the man of the house. I don't plan to encroach on that, at least not exactly. "You guys know I care about your mom."

"Oh no, please don't talk about Mom." Elston refrains from using *ew*, knowing I don't like it.

"But he's got that gooey eye thing going," Liam adds.

"What's the gooey eye thing?" Elston questions, peering down at his younger brother.

"Where he goes all gooey eyed talking about Mom, like you do when you talk about Eliza," Liam explains.

I laugh. Elston reaches out to cuff his little brother. Eliza is Elston's new girlfriend. Having her gives him a little perspective on his mom and me.

"Okay, well, I more than like your mom. I love her," I admit, holding my breath as I wait for that to sink in. "And I'd like to ask her a really important question, but I want your permission first. All three of you."

"Oh, my God," Ronin squeaks, covering his lips. A smile breaks out on his face, his bright blue bangs falling into his eyes.

"What?" Liam asks, looking at his older brother.

"Hank wants to ask Mom to marry him." The oldest's eyes focus on mine. His lips twist. He's thinking.

287

"Typically, a guy goes to a girl's pop for this, but as your grandparents are in Chicago, and you guys are a touch more important, I'd like your blessing."

"What are we blessing you for?" Liam makes the sign of the cross at me like a priest. Elston grabs his hand and shoves it down.

"He means he wants us to give him our permission to marry Mom."

"That's cool," Liam says, shrugging his shoulder. "Can we still live here?"

"Of course." I pause. "Well, we need to talk to your mom about that, but I'd like for us to stay here. I'd like to move in here when the time is right." I figure being honest is the best policy. "But let's do one thing at a time."

"I'm okay with it," Ronin adds.

Elston stands with his arms crossed, his head hanging. "What does this mean for us?"

"Nothing changes. You're still the man of the house."

Liam snorts. "Mom's the man of the house." He makes a funny expression, and the boys laugh in agreement.

"I mean nothing should change for you. Respect your mom at all times, and we'll have no problem." I direct my gaze at Elston.

Elston nods slowly. His voice remains quiet as he says, "Okay."

A weight I didn't realize I was holding lifts off my shoulders, and I open the small brown bag on the counter.

"I have something for each of you to show I'm committed to you as much as your mother." Reaching in, I pull out six bracelets. Three of them are woven leather with a silver clasp. The other three are bright blue beads with three brown ones. Liam's eyes open wide as he stares at the loops. I pass one of each to each of them.

"When I was in the band, we received a silver band because we were named Chrome Teardrops, and silver is a strong metal, binding us together." I point at another bracelet I found buried in my drawer and added to the collection on my wrist. "I'm giving you leather ones, like this"—I point at the original band I wear, the one symbolizing friendship between Tommy, Denton, and me—"because, well, you're younger, and

I thought leather would be easier to wear." I slip a new woven leather from my pocket, matching the ones I've given them, and wrap it around my wrist as a symbol of my connection with them. "This has four leather straps as we are four men." I pause.

"The second bracelet I wear, the one with brown beads, symbolizes how a team needs more than one person and no one person is more important than another in a circle. I'm giving you each a similar one with blue beads to match Elston's eyes." His head whips up. I continue, "And I want you to remember no one will look out for you more than an older brother." I think of Brut before adding, "There are three brown beads for Ronin, Liam, and your mom. You're the family first, but I'd really like to be a part of it."

I wait as the boys slip the bands on their wrists, then I add another one to mine. I can't help the smile on my face as I look around at our matching accessories. My heart gallops. I don't know if I've ever been so happy, but then Midge comes in the back door.

"Howdy, boys," she teases, her eyes sweeping over the empty pizza boxes and cans of soda. I might have let Liam have one too many.

He's the first to speak, hopping off his stool and heading for his mom. "Look what Hank gave us." He takes a moment to explain the meaning, and Midge rubs his back while he speaks. Her head comes up after a quick kiss to his forehead.

"That's beautiful, Hank. Thank you." The room grows quiet, and I'm center stage again. This isn't the big moment, but...

"I have something for you as well." I walk around the island, not certain her kitchen is the best place to handle this, but I want the boys as witnesses. "You already know how I feel about you. I love you. Tonight, I told the boys the same thing. I'd like to be part of your family. I'm not pressuring you. There's no rush, I just want you to know I'm all in. You're my someone." I reach into my pocket and pull out a band of tiny cut diamonds.

"Hank," she gasps, covering her lips with her fingers.

"This is a promise ring. A promise that you're the only one for me, and I want to be the only one for you. I want more. And I promise, one day, I'll ask."

Her head pops up.

"One day, I'll ask," I repeat softly.

"Yes," Midge blurts, her eyes filling with tears, but her face is anything but sad.

"I don't want to rush things." The idea of moving in with her, it's a big step...*another step*...in the right direction, but I understand she has the boys, and if I move in, there needs to be a solid commitment.

"Yes." Midge giggles.

"I didn't ask anything." I snort, chuckling at her enthusiasm.

"Yes. To the promise of one day then." She holds out her left hand, and I slip the ring on her third finger. My own eyes might water a bit at the sight. One day might be too long to wait.

chapter 42

He Popped

[Midge]

The boys have gone to Paul's wedding. I respectfully declined the invitation, and Hank wants to take me out to celebrate. A real date, he says, although I don't want to see him all stuffy in a suit. We agree on a drive out to the beach and a casual seafood shack. He has a key to my house, and I hear him let himself in. I'm still in the bathroom, fixing my makeup. I don't wear much, but I want to look nice, maybe freshen the look a little. I'm wearing another surprise under this dress as he told me how much he really did like the purple number I wore to seduce him. A simple wraparound dress covers me for now.

As I hear him climb the stairs, I look at the ring on my finger. With little diamonds, it sparkles in the light. It's not pretentious or flashy, but petite and pretty, like me, Hank says.

"Middy?"

"I'm in the bathroom." It's still bright enough in the early summer evening I don't need a light in the room. I have a candle burning from the bath I took, taking a few minutes to relax before our night together. The boys will be staying at the hotel with my former in-laws after Paul's reception, so Hank and I have the house to ourselves.

He enters the bathroom and stops the second his eyes meet mine in the mirror.

"You are so beautiful." He exhales on the compliment, and I blush as he steps up behind me. His cheek presses to mine as he wraps his arms around me from behind. He stares at us a moment.

"We look good together," he says to the reflection.

291

We do.

"We look happy."

His smile grows. "I am." He kisses my neck before looking up at me again. "I'm happy to be your someone."

I chuckle at his sweetness. "I'm honored to be your someone." This earns me another kiss, and he lingers at my neck.

"You know I want more with you." It's a question, but it doesn't need an answer. He wants everything with me, and I'm pleased to give him whatever he needs. His hand slips to mine, and he flattens my palm to force my fingers wide. He peers over my shoulder and down at the ring.

"Is this the day you promised?" I tease. It's become an occasional joke.

"Today?" I'd question.

He'd respond with a kiss and say, "Not yet." He understands I'm teasing. There's no rush, as he said, although I miss him at night when he can't stay in my bed.

"I can't ask you in the bathroom." He chuckles against my skin, and I shiver.

"Yes, you can. Besides, the bathroom is where we met." His eyes leap up to mine, his arm tightening on my waist, and I grin.

"Midge," he groans, staring back at me in the mirror. My smile falls, but it doesn't disappear. My body melts into his. He looks at me now the same way he did the first night we met, like he wants to give me something and take something. How strange it is to find it's love. Both sides. Two sticks for drumming as he once told me. Give and take. It's a rhythm, and the beat matches our hearts.

"Just ask me already," I tease, sounding desperate and decide to stop the game.

He'll ask me when he's ready. He lowers his head to place another kiss on my neck, lingering another moment before standing to his full height. His hands come to my hips, and I lean forward to fix my lipstick. Bending at the waist, I stroke my backside against him. I'm opening the cap and leaning forward, reveling in the feel of him behind me as I do the mundane and apply lipstick. I pause to ask, "Where are we—"

"Will you marry me?" His eyes shift from silver to steel as he watches my reaction in the mirror. I'm still leaning forward, lipstick in one hand, as I stare back at him in the reflection.

Is he serious? Is he teasing?

"Yes," I whisper to his image, and I straighten, wanting to turn and look at him. *He's kidding, right?* Still watching me, he slips one hand in his pocket and pulls out another ring. He wraps an arm around me from behind, and I no longer make eye contact in the reflective glass. Instead, I glance down at the three-carat stone he's holding before me. Simple. Stunning. Solitaire.

"Hank," I whisper, his name lingering in the air.

"This isn't exactly how I wanted it to happen, but you're right. This is how it started, and I knew the moment you caught my eye in that mirror that you would be mine one day. Those eyes whispered to mine for more, and I'll never look away from you."

I watch our reflection as he slips the ring on my finger to join the other one. The promise of one day is here.

"*I love you,*" he mouths.

"I love you, too. And more." He spins me, taking my cheeks in his hands and staring directly into my eyes.

"More," he says, before kissing me, and I know every day with Hank will be a discovery...and more.

epilogue

Forty-One Years Old

Three months later

[Midge]

I wake alone in the bed, but not alone in my heart. I hear the noise of a new school year beginning downstairs. Today will be a day of several fresh starts. I look down at my left hand as I often do and marvel at how lucky I am. A beautiful single diamond stands above the tiny-cut diamond band and a solid silver one. Stacking rings signify my marriage to Hank.

"How long you two been together?" Lily once asked.

"Not long enough," Hank told her. "And I've been waiting too long for her."

Once Hank asked me to marry him—the official question—he decided he had waited long enough for me. We married a week later at the local courthouse. We didn't want to keep playing games of hide-and-seek—meaning hide in the bathroom for sex or have Hank sneak out during the night. It might seem fast to some, but my boys and I were ready for Hank to officially be part of our family.

I slip from the bed, tug on my robe, and head down the staircase. My stomach flutters with all this day will bring.

"Big day for your mom today," I hear Hank say from the kitchen.

"She's gonna be great," Liam says.

I've paused on the stairs, listening to the general morning chatter between my boys and the man I love. He's making lunches and checking schedules. I smile with a shake of my head. Who knew how great forty-one would turn out to be?

"I love her office," Ronin adds.

My office. I like the sound of that. I decided to work from home in a space above my garage. The boys helped me clean out the clutter over the summer and Hank fixed up the walls. Today, I'm pitching Starlight Farms, in Montana of all places. It's a video-chat conference. After all my designs for Pendelton, I want this account to take my suggestions and make them come to fruition. Not to mention, I think it will add to their company...and mine. I'm taking the risk to go out on my own.

"Ronin, seven o'clock. Practice."

Ronin groans but I hear the smile in his voice. He's thrilled Hank is his new drum instructor. Hank broke out his old kit and moved it into our garage. He makes Ronin practice under his tutelage each night and then takes a turn himself. He admits he doesn't want to go back to his old rock 'n' roll lifestyle, but drumming seems to be a part of him. I like to watch as he bangs away, getting lost in his head and worked up. I worry at times he's projected back to some memory, some image of him and her on stage, but then he looks up at me. He always catches me watching him as if he knows I'm there.

"It's your eyes," he says. "I'll never look away."

"I have a date tonight," Elston announces. His girlfriend is cute, although a little shy around the noise of men. She'll learn, if she sticks. Then again, Elston is too young to be so seriously involved. He's only a senior in high school.

"Not tonight," Hank warns. "Bring Eliza here."

I chuckle. With summer over, Elston can no longer date on a weeknight as we return to school days and he knows it, but he's always pushing just a little. Thank goodness Hank is made of strong stuff. He rolls with the punches from my oldest. It's been a summer of learning and loving with a few lessons in parenthood in between.

"What's tonight?" Elston asks.

"We celebrate." This man. Such confidence in me.

"What are we celebrating?" Ronin asks.

"Let's not step ahead of ourselves," I say, descending the final steps into the kitchen. There is one thing I'm confident Hank will celebrate, although I'm nervous to tell him.

"Life is one step at a time." Hank winks at me. "I'm ready to climb."

I smile and he bites his lip. We try to keep the PDA on the down-low in front of the boys but sometimes I just want to tackle him despite them. Lately, I seem out of control with sexual need, but I now know the reason in addition to my insatiable attraction to him.

"What are we having for dinner to celebrate?" Liam asks.

"Hot dogs," Hank says, completely serious. "In a hallway."

I sputter my orange juice, choking a bit as I mock-glare at Hank. Memories of the night before flip through my mind. Elston's eyes narrow before he groans, adding an *ew* with an eye roll. He gets the joke. He's seen *We're the Millers*.

"I like hot dogs," Liam says and Hank chuckles.

"I don't know what we're having yet, but time for school, young men." Hank's taken to calling my boys this and Liam loves it. Elston likes to pretend he doesn't, but I think he secretly does. The boys shuffle out the door with wishes for a good school year.

"What time is the call again?" Hank asks.

"Ten."

He glances at the clock on the stove. He goes to Restored Dreams around nine. It's only seven. Suddenly, he looks over at me. I recognize the expression in those silvery eyes.

"How you feeling about the call?"

"Good," I lie. I'm nervous, but it's a good nervous—exciting even.

He rounds the island slowly and my stomach flutters. I like how he looks at me, like he could devour me. He had his way with me last night, but I seem to be ready to be his again. He reaches out to brush my hair behind my ear.

"You got this." He's been saying this for weeks. I have to admit, he's a confidence booster. My eyes drift to the array of items littering the island for lunchmaking. He let me sleep in. I've been extra tired lately.

"You're kind of good to me," I tease, slipping my arms around his waist.

"You're good *for* me," he retorts before his mouth finds mine.

I love his kisses, long and languid, and within moments, his tongue slips past the seam of my lips. Without missing a beat, I'm lifted to the counter and hear the clank of jars and crinkle of a bread package shoved aside to make way for me. I'm all for making love on this counter but there's something I need to tell him, and today seems like the perfect day.

I pull back slowly, and Hank moves his mouth to my jaw.

"Honey," I begin, telling myself not to get lost in his lips on my skin. "I need to tell you something."

"Sure, little lady." His mouth continues a trail to my chest and my robe is drawn aside to reveal swollen globes longing for his attention. He mutters against my breast. "I love your tits."

"They love you." I softly laugh, but gently wrap my hands on the sides of his head and force him to look up at me. "Hank, I have to be serious a second."

With this his head shoots up. Sitting on the counter, I'm more equal with his height and his eyes are level with mine.

"Talk to me." I love the intensity in his tone. He wants to listen to me although I'm hoping what I say isn't really an issue of concern.

"Remember how I said I wanted to be somebody's someone?"

Hank's head twists and his eyes narrow. The silver dulls to gray. "Yeah."

I cup his cheeks to squash the concern I see in those eyes.

"How would you feel about being somebody important to someone else?"

Hank gasps. His brows shoot up to his hairline. "I don't want to be with anybody else."

I chuckle though his fear is not funny. "No, honey. I mean a different kind of someone. Maybe a little someone." I'm willing him to understand although I can see he doesn't. "Maybe a little girl someone."

His forehead furrows. A deep crease forms between his brows.

"A little girl someone?" he continues to question me with troubled eyes.

"Say, arriving next winter, around Valentine's Day maybe." I'm suddenly holding my breath as he appears so puzzled. Then he tilts his head.

"What are you saying, little lady?" He swallows. His eyes closing as he exhales. I can almost feel the hope coming off him.

"I'm saying there's the possibility of another little lady loving you, Hank. As her daddy." His eyes jump to my belly, and he rips open my robe. The swollen breasts he's enjoyed and the bulge of my stomach he's ignored finally make sense. I took a pregnancy test a few days ago. I thought it was just the pill messing with my body. I hadn't been on it for over twenty years. Instead, it turns out...

"I'm pregnant, Hank."

I've only seen this solid man crumble one other time—when he was given a room in Lawson's home. Now, he falls to his knees, his mouth seeking my belly before his arms wrap around my lower body. He buries his face in my stomach and his shoulders tremble.

"Hank?" He simply shakes his head against my lower abdomen, refusing to speak to me. He tugs me tighter to his cheek but then quickly releases me.

"Am I hurting her?" He stares at my skin below my belly button.

"No, sweetheart." My hands return to his face, and he peers up at me. "I can't guarantee a girl, but just maybe." I bite my lip.

"You're okay, right?" I know what he means. We've discussed how I thought I was too old for a baby, but apparently my body disagrees. "How did this happen?"

I chuckle as we both know the logistics, but also, I've been on the pill a few months. "Sometimes these things just do." I'm thinking it was Father's Day weekend. Paul got married around then, and Hank and I had days, and nights, to ourselves. Our alone time gave Hank all that he ever wanted...inside me.

"Just when I couldn't think of more to make me happy..." He kisses my stomach and then slowly stands. His hands come to my cheeks. "You make me *more* happy than I ever thought I'd be."

"I more you," I whisper.

"Thank you," he says followed by kisses to my eyes, my cheeks and finally my lips. "Thank you for loving me and more."

epilogue 2

Life Break

[Brut]

As I drive south on Highway 5, the coast comes into view on my right, and the weight of Los Angeles, the shop, and Chopper slowly drifts away like the waves on the shore. Then again, the Pacific Ocean is a mild tempest and thoughts of those waves set my heart pattering in a way I hardly recognize. I'm excited and still a little surprised at how all this happened...

"You're sending me on vacation?" I stare at my younger brother and co-owner of Restored Dreams. The auto repair and body shop has been my business for nearly twenty years, and I don't think I've ever had an official vacation.

"Yep. Give yourself some time off, Brut. I got this." With Midge, his new wife, standing behind him, her light brown eyes beaming at me, I know my brother means it. He can handle the shop alone for a week.

"I wouldn't know where to go. What to do." I don't know why I'm trying to talk myself out of this. I could use some time off. I'm tired. Plain and simple. I need a life break.

"Don't worry about it. I've taken care of *everything*." The emphasis on the last word has me worried for the first time in this conversation. Midge steps forward, her excitement hardly contained as she hands me a padded manila envelope.

"We rented you a house at Ocean Beach. You can surf. Sleep. Anything. Just relax."

My head snaps up at the mention of surfing. It's been a rare treat over the years. The coast is so close but just far enough away from

Pasadena that I couldn't overindulge. Not to mention, as a single father, I hardly had the freedom to head to the beach each day.

"I pulled your old board out of the garage. Sent it off to a shop to be cleaned and waxed." Hank really has thought of everything, and my heart skips at the possibility.

A vacation. I blink at Hank. He's always been a good brother—a bit wayward and reckless but good with me and my son. I know part of his attentiveness comes from guilt. He hasn't had an easy life, and I stood by him when the pieces crumbled. He thinks he owes me, but he doesn't. He's my kid brother, even at forty-three, and I love him. It's that simple.

I turn the envelope over in my hand. Inside is a lease agreement for a week and a set of keys.

"I don't know what to say." I swallow the lump in my throat. This is too generous, and I'm still a bit shocked at the idea of getting away from this place. The garage was never my ideal employment, but with my son, Chopper, and then the death of Pop, it fell into my lap. Restoring cars was something I could do but wasn't who I wanted to be.

"Just go. Have fun. Do you remember what that is?" Midge teases me.

I like my brother's woman. I might have joked I'd steal her from him if he didn't quit being an ass, but I knew from the moment I met her, she would only be Hank's. She looked at him the way I wanted someone to look at me. I had that once. I wish it had turned into something more, but it was so long ago it's a distant memory.

"Thanks, guys," I say, letting the memory fade and pulling my head back to reality. My weak gratitude seems insufficient. "And yes, smartass, I think I remember what fun is." I laugh to cover the hesitancy.

Do I? I wonder. Do I really remember what fun used to be?

It's been three days since Hank and Midge announced this gift, and a whirlwind of double-checking Hank's understanding of the schedule until Midge finally says, "I'm here. Don't worry."

Knowing that Midge was our former office manager sets me at ease. She was a quick study and went above and beyond what we needed to organize and clean up the shop. She set up things in an efficient and easy way for me to maintain if I dedicate an hour a day to the admin things. Thinking of Midge makes me smile. Again, she's been good for my brother, and I like her in a sister-in-law way. We'd been a clan of men for too long. Midge joining the family brought three more boys—her sons. We need some sisters.

The thought reminds me of a pair of sisters I once knew. My lip curls at the memory of the blonde hair, blue eyes of the younger one. She had the sweetest smile and amazing lips, especially when they were on me. My smile fades, remembering why I lost her. I don't know why I did what I did to her.

Really? my heart chastises.

It was because of me, my dick recalls. The snicker from the evil appendage gets choked off when my heart remembers it wasn't even a good lay that fucked my life. My stomach turns with the thought.

Exiting the highway, I let the memories go. The roar of water crashing to the shore pulls me back to the present where I'm safer to live. I park in the drive and stare at the narrow two-story house. My heart sprints. On the other side of this structure is the ocean, and I can already feel the excitement that something amazing is about to happen to me. Grabbing my bag, I head around the house, and my breath catches. The view is beautiful. Rolling waves, bright sunshine, and surfers on the sea. I can't wait.

I enter the house. The living area faces large glass doors that open to a partially covered porch. A cozy open-concept kitchen falls directly behind the seating area. The stairs to the upper level are at the back, tucked behind the kitchen, and I climb the steps two at a time. I want my swimsuit and a beer. Then the surf.

As I reach the top step, I think I hear water running. I pause at the sound and decide it must be the ocean playing tricks on me. The house has air conditioning, but I want the windows open and the rhythmic crashing of the water to fill my ears. I turn into the first bedroom, set my stuff down near a dresser, and hear the running water again. It sounds like a shower.

Taking a step toward the bathroom, I hear singing.

Words of loving someone later, being better when she's older, being the greatest love of her life filter through the air as I open the door to a steam-filled space and a female voice belting out the off-key song.

Did Hank do this? Did he hire a girl for the night for me? For the week? He jokes I need to get laid. When he mentioned he thought of everything, is this what he meant? I pause a second, taking in the silhouette of a feminine body, twisting and turning behind the glass enclosure. The heat of the room is sweltering, and I whip off my shirt to wipe my face. A spattering sound hits the tile floor of the shower, possibly shampoo rinsing out of her hair. Her voice continues to squeak out lyrics. Strangely, the appendage that gets me in trouble begins to rise. I really do need to get laid, but can I do this? Can I fuck a hired female?

Another off-key lyric and I decide I can't. I step forward, preparing to tell the woman she'll need to leave. She doesn't hear me call out, "Hey," so I'm left with no choice but to open the stall door to get her attention. The first thing I notice is a large cupcake tattoo in hues of purple and pink on a smooth hip, and then she screams.

Continue reading Brut and Lily's story in **_Restored Dreams_**.

bonus scene

Later

[Hank]

I didn't realize how full my heart could be.

I had Midge as my wife. What a concept at this stage of my life.

I had her boys coming to me for advice and treating me like a father. Elston, Ronin, and Liam were amazing.

And then there was Lyra.

My little girl is my pride and joy . . . and a total stinker. We should have named her Trouble.

"Hank," Liam drones from the room behind the stairs. His private domain for video games and hiding out from his little sister who is a terror.

As I near the entryway, I pause a second taking in the sight. Liam has grown since reaching high school. His limbs are long and lanky. Not exactly the stature for a baseball star but he's still playing.

Currently, he has a knee bend up toward his chest and his arms tucked inward, shielding the game controller from Lyra who loves to push the buttons. With Elston and Ronin both off to college, Liam is the only sibling Lyra has left to torture.

"Hank," Liam moans again as I watch my toddler try to stick her hands underneath her brother's bent knee, through his legs, and upward for the controller he lifts over his head so she can't reach it.

Oh, doesn't he know anything by now.

Lyra only takes the challenge as an initiative to climb. A foot on the edge of the couch, hands on her brother's kneecap, she leverages herself upward like she's scaling a mountain.

"Lyra." Liam laughs. "You little minion. Get off me." Despite himself, Liam can't fight his sister's attention or the fact he loves it. As the youngest of three brothers, now he's the big brother to this munchkin. And regardless of her wanting to be wherever he is, he kind of loves her wanting to be near him.

Unless he's playing video games.

"Come here, sweetheart." I step into the room, reaching for the little love of my life. Her mother is the big love. Midge is just everything. Her patience. Her kindness. Her ability to endure raising four kids at varying ages while running her own business out of our home.

Our home.

It never gets old to call this house *ours*.

We thought we might need more space when Midge announced Lyra was coming, but Elston and Ronin agreed to share a room for a while before Elston went to college. True to his word, he went to Illinois which is a little too far for Mama Bear.

"Let's go find Mama for lunch." I tug Lyra upward while she struggles and kicks out her legs, still reaching for her brother.

"We-uhm." Lyra's little arms stretch outward, but Liam only shakes his head without missing a beat of his game.

Tucking an arm around her toddler belly, I press my face into her neck, inhaling the sticky scent of apple juice and a hint of baby wash. Her skin is rolled like rubber bands around her wrist and ringed at her neck with baby fat, but I nestle in, peppering her with kisses there.

Quickly, she forgets Liam and giggles. "Dada."

I have a short list of words that are tops for me. Hearing my child call me Dad is one of them.

When Midge and I married, the boys and I agreed that they didn't have to call me Dad. They had a man who held that label even if he wasn't always the best father.

I hadn't been the best father either. Then again, I hadn't known I was one until nearly thirty years later.

Calling me Dad is something Lawson won't ever be able to say. I missed out on all the years where I could have picked him up, nuzzled into his skin and peppered him with kisses. My adult son is a stranger to me, but I still see him once a week. Sometimes more.

Our families—the Carrigans, the Everlys, and the Paiges—have merged.

"Wunch," Lyra reminds me as I carry her out of the room. Shifting her over my shoulder, her head dangles at my back while I tip her feet upward. She loves this position.

As we enter the kitchen, Midge comes in the side door. Her office is out back. My wife is a powerhouse, and she rocks a hip hugging skin and silky blouse plus heels I'd like to feel digging into my backside later.

"What do we have here?" She approaches with a brow arched, taking in how I'm carrying Lyra.

"I don't know what you're talking about." With Lyra's pudgy ankles clasped in one hand, I lean for Midge, pressing a too-quick kiss to her lips. Pulling back, I decide I need a better taste of her and lean in for a longer pull. Her mouth eagerly meets mine. She steps closer to me, placing her hands on my chest, and smiling against my lips.

"Why do you have Lyra upside down?"

"Lyra?" I question, pulling back and spinning around. "I haven't seen Lyra. Do you see Lyra?"

A squeal of delight comes from my baby girl as I whirl round, giving her a view of her mama. The tension in her toddler body tells me she trying to reach for Midge, but I quickly spin again.

"Where's Lyra?"

"Dada." She giggles, gently smacking at my back to get my attention.

I nip at her ankles over my shoulder. "Now where did that little minion go."

"I not a win-min." Her small palms pat at my back, and I tug her forward, knowing too much time upside down and her face turns bright red. Sliding her over my shoulder, I pull back my head and stare at her. Her hair is wild from being over me.

My expression is one of surprise. "Oh. There you are."

Two little hands clap my cheeks, brushing over the bristle on my jaw. "Dada."

Lyra's little eyes narrow, forcing me to look directly at her eyes which match mine. *She's* all mine. Her pudgy shape. Her extra round face. Her curly hair. She's my spitting image as me as with a devilish streak that mirrors me as a kid.

"I was looking for you." Leaning forward again, I rub my nose against hers.

"Iz here." She presses at my face, forcing me back so I can see her. She's right here. In my arms. Giving me a look that will one day grow into eye rolls and strong sighs and puzzled expressions. I've seen that look on Elston and Ronin as teens. Liam is perfecting it as well. I'm not ready for Lyra to grow up.

Thank goodness she's only three.

"What are we having for lunch today?" Midge asks, coming closer to Lyra and me, and rubbing a hand up Lyra's back. The touch draws Lyra's attention and I'm forgotten. My daughter lunges for Midge who easily catches her and pulls her from me.

The loss is only momentary before I wrap my arms around Midge, holding our little girl.

"Wyra hug," Lyra whines, circling her mother's neck and hiding her face.

"Daddy wants a hug, too." I wiggle a brow at Midge.

Her soft smile tells me I'll get my hugs in later.

With kids, it's always later. But I'm thankful that I'm not too late. Late to love. Late to a family.

Midge taught me these things, although I like to think I taught her the same. She might have thought her life was over at forty-one. But at forty-five, I'd say she's in her prime. My wife is hot.

And when she looks at me like she's looking at me, I want to beg Liam to watch Lyra and whisk Midge up to our bedroom.

Later.

I'm grateful for *laters*. Those moments when Midge is mine alone. We share a bed. We share our bodies. But most of all, we share our love. With each other. With the boys. With Lyra.

More. We give everything more.

"You okay?" Midge asks me, watching me as I'm lost in my head a second.

"Just wondering what to do for lunch. How about hot dogs?" I arch a brow, hinting at an old joke.

"No wot wogs." Lyra pulls back from hugging Midge, pouting her lips at me.

Midge laughs. "How about later?"

"Later," I whisper, although my deep voice can't go low enough. Midge gnaws at the corner of her mouth, fighting a smile.

Yeah, later.

"Dada. Muggets."

"Muggets?" I laugh. Chicken nuggets it will be, then. I'll be having lunch with my two best girls.

Who could have imagined life could be so good . . . later.

Thank you for taking the time to read MIDLIFE CRISIS.
Please consider writing a review on major sales channels where ebooks and paperbacks are sold and discussed.

more by L.B. Dunbar

Sterling Falls
Seven small-town siblings muddle their way through love over 40.
Sterling Heat
Sterling Brick
Sterling Streak
Sterling Clay
Sterling Fight
Sterling Touch
Sterling Stone

Chicago Anchors
When your eyes are on the silver fox coach, more than the ball.
Elevator Pitch
Catch the Kiss

Parentmoon
When the mother of the groom goes head-to-head with the single father of the bride.

Holiday Hotties (Christmas novellas)
Holiday novellas certain to heat the season.
Scrooge-ish
Naughty-ish
Grouch-ish

Road Trips & Romance
Three sisters. Three destinations. All second chances at love over 40.
Hauling Ashe
Merging Wright
Rhode Trip

Lakeside Cottage
Four friends. Four summers. Shenanigans and love happen at the lake.

L.B. DUNBAR

Living at 40
Loving at 40
Learning at 40
Letting Go at 40

The Silver Foxes of Blue Ridge
Small mountain town, silver foxes. Brothers seeking love over 40.
Silver Brewer
Silver Player
Silver Mayor
Silver Biker

Sexy Silver Foxes
When sexy silver foxes meet the feisty vixens of their dreams.
After Care
Midlife Crisis
Restored Dreams
Second Chance
Wine&Dine

Collision novellas
A spin-off from After Care – the younger set/rock stars
Collide
Caught

The Sex Education of M.E.
The original sexy silver fox.
When a widowed professor decides she'd like to date again, and a local
fireman volunteers to give her lessons.

The Heart Collection
Small town, big hearts - stories of family and love.
Speak from the Heart
Read with your Heart
Look with your Heart
Fight from the Heart
View with your Heart

A Heart Collection Spin-off

MIDLIFE CRISIS

The Heart Remembers

BOOKS IN OTHER AUTHOR WORLDS
Smartypants Romance (an imprint of Penny Reid)
Tales of the Winters sisters set in Green Valley.
Love in Due Time
Love in Deed
Love in a Pickle

The World of True North (an imprint of Sarina Bowen)
Welcome to Vermont! And the Busy Bean Café.
Cowboy
Studfinder

THE EARLY YEARS
The Legendary Rock Star Series
A classic tale with a modern twist of rockstar romance and suspense.

Paradise Stories
MMA romance. Two brothers. One fight.

The Island Duet
Intrigue and suspense. The island knows what you've done.

Modern Descendants – writing as elda lore
Magical realism. Modern myths of Greek gods.

about the author

www.lbdunbar.com

L.B. Dunbar loves sexy silver foxes, second chances, and small towns. If you enjoy older characters in your romance reads, including a hero with a little silver in his scruff and a heroine rediscovering her worth, then welcome to romance for those over 40. L.B. Dunbar's signature works include women and men in their prime taking another turn at love and happily ever. Along with her #sexysilverfox collection, she's made Amazon Top 10 in Later in Life Romance with her Lakeside Cottage and Road Trips & Romance series. She is also a *USA Today Bestseller*. L.B. lives in Chicago with her own sexy silver fox.

To get all the scoop about the self-proclaimed queen of silver fox romance, join her on Facebook at Loving L.B. or receive her monthly newsletter, Love Notes.

+ + +

connect with L.B. Dunbar